ORPHANS OF
CANLAND

ORPHANS OF CANLAND

A NOVEL

DANIEL VITALE

STRÏJ PUBLISHING • LOS ANGELES • 2022

ORPHANS OF
CANLAND

"There is no ontological difference
between a set and the elements of a set."

— MICHAEL WEEKES

PART ONE

1

Sept 30, 2088

Hello, nascent journal.

This morning, after my breakfast of salted beans, I was left alone, and I wandered into the garden. I spotted an Opilione with each of its eight legs perched on a different leaf, frond, or stem—floating. I cupped my hands around it, careful not to press too hard, and brought it inside to show Helena. When I held it up to her, she took my wrist, pinched the arachnid's leg, and threw it out the door.

You went into the garden without supervision? she said.

It's OK, I said, Opiliones aren't venomous.

What's not? The spider? How can you say that?

Opiliones aren't spiders, I said.

I wanted to refer her to *Fearsome Allies: A Guide to Learning and Loving Arachnids*, but it would have been pointless. She hates that book. Plus, as Helena said, the point was that the fact of the Opilione in my hand meant I'd been digging in the garden, where she has told me not to go. If I can stay away from the stove and knives and candles and even my own fingernails, and not drink clear liquid without asking what it is beforehand, and not go running at top speed or so much as try to pedal a bike, why couldn't I have stopped myself from going into the garden? And don't blame my executive functioning—I have excellent impulse control for a twelve-year-old. Opiliones, aka harvestmen, may be harmless, but many other things in the garden are not. Fanged invertebrates, thorny stems, invisible traces of disease left by reptiles, birds, and arboreal and subterranean mammals. How would I like to contract some virus left behind in the feces of a bat? How about getting bitten by a vole, a rat, or some eyeless Spalax? I don't think so.

Helena sighed and said, There is a responsibility that comes with living here.

In Canland, I replied, smiling up at her to show I understood.

Helena squinted at me and asked if I was joking. Sybil says my comedic timing is improving (and if anyone would know, it's Sybil). In this case, though, I was not joking.

Helena said, No, our home, Tristan. You're part of a little eco-system here. When you try to save every last little creature, you put yourself in danger, and then we have to take you to the Safe Haven. Do you understand? I can't tell if you're with me when you look at me like that.

Yes, I said, we're like a Part within the Part.

Helena said nothing.

She's so pretty, except for the lines by the sides of her mouth, which deepen when she frowns and make her look old. She has a perfectly straight nose, some freckles across the middle of her face, and good eyes—she only needs glasses when she's reading and writing. And she has a thick, healthy body that's both soft and strong.

I did some rational thinking, then said, But if I can feel myself getting bitten and I can see a snake is doing the biting—

If there was a snake, you'd try to pet it, she said. One of her eyebrows went up, and I laughed at her joke.

It's not funny, she said, kneeling. I know you're curious, but you can't put yourself in danger over and over and over . . .

She kept talking. I was expecting her to condition me when she stopped, but she didn't.

Finally she sighed and said, You're with me, Tristan? and I said, Yes, and she asked, What's another unsafe thing like going in the garden?

I said, Sneaking off with futures into the field for a Practice of Agriculture lesson—

Why? she said.

The answer was ripe for the plucking. But I left it on the vine too long, examining it to make sure it was perfect for Helena, and it rotted off, fell away, splat.

Deep frown lines formed on Helena's face. She doesn't like it when I stare at her, but I can't help it. Then she explained that today was hard enough for her as it was, because of a demonstration in the Part Center against her for a law she proposed, a law that will keep Canland's population from getting out of control, and which Tobias (Sybil's dad) is going to announce his support of too, which will surely make people even more upset, seeing as he contributes at the Canland mortuary, and we haven't had a natural death in Canland in five years.

It's very complicated, she said. So can you try to remember the things we talk about? Can you be sagacious? I know you like that word.

I nodded, smiled, and said, Yes.

She stood up and went down the hall to her room, mumbling back to me that we were leaving soon, and to just stay inside for now. Even play a bit of piano if you like, she said.

But I didn't want to play piano. I used to enjoy it more when Michael lived here and I could play whatever I wanted, but now I can only play what Helena says. Instead, I went down the hall to Dylan's door and banged on it with the sides of my hands so I wouldn't break my knuckle skin. After about two minutes of knocking, he opened his door and threw his fist forward, stopping a millimeter from my nose. Then he stepped aside and let me in.

It was all red and humid. Grow lights hummed and misters

sprayed the walls of plants. Bees and ants were at work in the terrarium. Meanwhile, monitors displayed coded languages like some technophilic cuneiform. The Sensorium rested on the desk, the same desk as where Michael taught me how to use the English language to convey Sensible Feelings, and where he taught Dylan how to use a Sensorium since even before Dylan was expelled from school for fighting. We're the only home in Canland with its own Sensorium, so Helena told us not to tell anyone about it. I don't think our school even has a computer. Dylan sat at the desk and pressed his eye to the microscope, removed the slide, and squirted a tincture of whatever was on the slide into the tank on the floor, which pumped water up through a tube and into the soil.

His bedsheets were ruffled with sleeplessness. I sat at the edge of the bed with my feet just above the floor and asked if he was coming to the Canland mortuary. He replied by saying, Wanna see something cool?, and then showed me how to look through the microscope to see two algae cells undergoing fission. I watched through the eyepiece for at least several minutes as translucent blue-green fans slowly sprouted more fans, and all the cells that comprised the organism swam and contorted their membranes, like people milling about Canland. The life sure didn't seem microscopic.

Dylan told me he was going to pollute the terrarium's oasis and see how long it would take for all the animals in there to die. Why? Well, because, as Dylan put it, You know the methane bomb in Lake Superior? Remember, Beautiful? Well, it's going to displace millions of people. WORLD says they're developing a reagent to suffocate the algae and stop the bloom, but one of the waste reallocation guys recovered something improperly disposed of in the Canland College waste tank, so I'm going to try it with what little was left in the tincture he found—not that I expect any illuminating results, or that it's even the same stuff they're planning to use in Lake Superior. Don't get me wrong—this is just to alleviate my extreme boredom while some satellite feeds upload.

Dylan hadn't seen the sun in a week or maybe more and was looking pale. He had a colony of pimples on his chin and smelled salty and sour, like cheese, which didn't bother me, since no smells bother me, whether manure or pungent breath or dairy that's turned. In fact, I love Dylan's smell. He sat still, but his head moved like a reptile's from the terrarium to the Sensorium to me. He said, You and Helena leaving for the mortuary soon?

How did you know we were going to the mortuary?

Other than that you just asked me if I was going?

Sybil will be there.

He said, Yeah, Beautiful, I figured as much, given she and her dad live in the back.

Dylan is in love with Sybil, but she's not in love with Dylan, though she does love Dylan. I don't really understand, but that's how she once explained it to me.

Dylan sighed and said, My ego wonders if Helena's proposing a teenage vasectomy bill just to prevent me from having a child.

I laughed because I thought he was joking, but when he didn't laugh, I said, Why would she do that?

Dylan seemed to ignore my question. He went over to his dresser and mused aloud, Tobias Chariots is like a caterpillar who spun his cocoon and thought it better not to become a butterfly, but I didn't expect him to openly endorse Purism. Then he sniffed hard to clear his nostrils and said, And Viceroy Hugo's obviously not gonna say anything, since the more Purists we have, the lower our ecological detriment report stays.

I told Dylan that Sybil said on our walk home yesterday that it doesn't matter if you're a Purist or Practicalist because, so long as you live in Canland, you accept it.

He laughed in a quiet way that turned into a throat-clear and said, Anyway, Helena asked me the other night to accompany you, which I'm happy to do, just in case things get violent, like when the crowd of protestors threw stones through the mortuary windows on the day Viceroy Hugo ratified Helena's Mandatory Teenage Abortion Bill. You remember?

He took off his black T-shirt, smelled it, and threw it in the corner of the room, then extracted a fresh and identical one from his dresser, put it on, and rubbed a sprig of mint clipped from our garden on his neck and armpits. Every night after dark, he bikes twenty miles out of Canland with a waste tank hitched to his chrome bicycle, then twenty miles back with a fresh, cleaned, emptied tank, and yet, he is still fat. His nipples are like pink moons. He used to practice martial arts with Michael and might still use tai chi as a meditative practice. I can't be sure since whenever I see him, he's either at his desk or eating cheese. I'd like to take up a physical practice, though I certainly won't ask Helena for permission anytime soon—I think martial arts falls into the garden category, or even a more extreme one.

Dylan said, Point is, despite all the time with you I miss out on because of the work I'm doing on satellites and in the Sensorium, Helena's usually awake when I leave for my waste runs, and she filled me in, and I thought I should keep you safe, but that it would also be a good chance for you and me to spend some time together.

You just said Helena asked you to take me, I said.

And Dylan said, Good ideas are had by many. Helena's bad ideas come from her alone.

Dylan then took out a tube from under the pile of clothes in his dresser, stuck it in his nose, inhaled, returned it to its hiding place, then sat back at his desk and started scrolling down the monitor and typing on the keyboard.

Have you made any progress in finding Michael? I asked.

I'll know when I find him, said Dylan.

What are you going to do when you find him? I asked.

I don't know, he said. I'll decide when I see him. Kill him, maybe.

I said nothing. Dylan turned around in his chair and said, I'm just kidding, Beautiful.

I laughed and said, I know.

What is there to do? Dylan wondered aloud. WORLD sent him somewhere he knew no one could find him, so why not try to find him? I guess it's just to know where he is. You don't want to know where he is or what he's doing?

Whether I want to know where Michael is seems to me beside the point. It would be like wanting to know where a famous painting was—it's out there, in an Arts Part where it can serve its special purpose, regardless of my proximity to it. When Michael left, he didn't say when he would be back, and while, yes, I would like to see him again, I didn't see him much before he left for this current expedition. I barely have memories of the two of us, although it could be said that he's taught me more than anyone, even if Helena now criticizes his methods. The way I see it, the electrotherapy couldn't have hurt me, so if it was going to create new neural pathways and improve my verbal, sensory, and memory processing, plus whatever else might have developed too slowly or not at all because of my analgesia, then I was glad to have him do it, and if he were still here, I would still have no objection to him guiding me through lush Sensorium Actualizations, reading me the English translation of an old book called *One Hundred Years of Solitude*, which is my favorite of all the ones he's read me, and listening to old composers, which most or all other people in Canland don't have access to, administering me shots of cortisol, adrenaline, oxytocin, neuropeptides, opioid receptors, and asking me how I feel, happy or sad, or how about angry or offended or nervous or paranoid. But Helena has said repeatedly not to hold our breaths for Michael's return, to proceed as if he matters to us only insofar as knowing our WORLD benefits and our blood types matters. Which is good advice, seeing as, ever since Michael's departure over a year ago, Dylan's shut himself in his room for days and weeks at a time to infiltrate networks and commandeer satellites, leaving only at night for his contribution, and yet is still no closer to finding our dad.

Michael could be anywhere from:

the Amazon Rainforest Restoration Project, to

a Disaster-Exposed Metropolis Deconstruction Site, to

the Danakil Depression, harvesting heat-tolerant superorganisms, to

a Waste Rake in the Great Pacific Gyre alongside thousands of other contributors, to a WORLD Research Center with Arturo Eagles himself, to

maybe just the other side of the mountains west of the California Inland Valley Desert-Greening Project, assessing slopes for terrace farming, only a few hours' bicycle ride away.

I said to Dylan, I hope you find him. The Sensorium made a noise and the monitors stopped displaying new text. Dylan unplugged the Sensorium, then he entered coordinates for a WORLD Satellite Unloading Station in Iowa, then switched off the monitor. He turned to me, edged his face toward mine and in a low voice said, We were never here. Then he winked and kissed my forehead. He dimmed the grow lights and touched as many leaves and stalks of plants as possible, as fast as possible, whispering to them.

In the kitchen, Helena was filling her vial with a ribbon of grappa. Helena's conditioned me not to drink clear liquids unless I see them being poured, because of the time I couldn't stop giggling. WORLD—Worldwide Objective: Restoration, Longevity, and Dominion—doesn't ship alcohol, other than for the Founding Celebration. But Viceroy Hugo still gets Helena bottles of grappa. They've been friends since before the founding.

Helena strung the crystalline vial around her neck, hidden under her cotton button-shirt. She stored a few insulated jars of vegetable stock in our trapdoor storage cellar where we keep our produce and said, You know, Dylan, at least when your father locked himself away, he wouldn't come out smelling like a caged animal.

Dylan did a little jig and said, Oh the monkey apes his daddy, even smells the same. You're hilarious, Helena. What did you do today?

Helena stepped close to Dylan. He only recently became taller than her. She whispered something in his ear before passing down the hall toward her bedroom. Dylan stood there, staring at a vague spot on the floor. I put on my sun goggles and my pollution mask. When I faced Dylan again, he was chewing his lip and pulling back his lank black hair with both hands on top of his head.

Helena came out of her room, pinning up her hair, the ends

shining gold and white like the ends of pins in the light fanning through the window, the way my hair does. She always looks like she's just been pressed fresh by the sun, her long linen skirt without a single wrinkle.

I rode pillion on Dylan's chrome bicycle toward the Part Center. As we pulled up the road, I glanced back at our neat and boxy single-story adobe home, the tent-covered garden of carrots, celery, parsnips, and fennel, the fronds so light they swayed without a breeze, remembering my time in there this morning when I found a harvestman stepping along between stems, hidden from the sun, and I lifted it out in the cup of my hand. It was so delicate yet capable. I'd felt as though I was holding a precious artifact of Earthly intelligence, evidence of the value of our Restoration Part.

The haze blowing in on the summer winds made the sky a sheet of hot silver. It was 105 °F today, maybe a bit hotter than usual for this time of year, but not prohibitive. Dust is still coming off the topped mountain. It's a good thing WORLD exists. Hopefully Canland's tenacious WORLD ecological defense agents found the bandit miners who dynamited the mountaintop and sent them to a Long Term Rehabilitation Part.

Dylan's cycling made a cooling breeze, a convenient foil for my inability to sweat, aka anhidrosis. He pulled the bike around a leaning copse of blue gum trees, trailing Helena by a few yards. Past the greened border of Canland I squinted at a blur of pale desert, trying to gauge the distance between here and the mountains. I know it's seven miles, but they look so much closer.

When we crested the slight grade, we saw, surrounded by chanting Canland College students in the Part Center, Helena's head, the size of a large wagon, carved from wood. And instead of chopping up the effigy, which at least could've been turned to mulch and not sent a carcinogenic behemoth into the air, one torch-wielding student held the flame under Helena's chin, and when it caught fire, the protestors cheered. They were apprehended by neither COHO (the Canland overseers of human order) nor any WORLD ecological defense agents. I wondered where they got the wood.

Perhaps a WEDA supported their protests and turned a blind eye as they hacked down some of the young pines Canland's been trying to grow in the foothills. The fire crackled and a cloud of smoke floated low through the sky like sediment in a river and we were all the fish below watching it drift toward us, thickening. Helena turned to me from the seat of her own red bicycle and said, Don't take your mask off, then biked down market to the mortuary.

That was when the trouble began.

As Helena pedaled forth, Dylan spun his bike around and rode us back the way we came. He pulled off onto a communal housing street in the shade of a copse of eucalyptus trees, and vomited in the middle of the road. He wiped the tears from his bloodshot eyes and said, Sorry, Beautiful, I think the heat got to me. I'm a bit dehydrated, plus the tube—agh—you mind if I have a sip of water? He took my bottle out of my knapsack and then went to squat in the shade.

I looked at the communal housing stack, flat-topped and three stories high, like a miniature ziggurat, or a giant sandcastle, each unit set with one thick glass window. From its hay-dry lawn, there grew a tree. But the tree was skeletal, fruitless, colorless. It was a warning for what happens when your attention turns away from the goal of Restoration.

I stepped to it, and peeled away a chip of its bark. The flesh beneath was gray with rot, and not a single invertebrate was sucking at the heartwood.

A voice shouted from the adobe stacks, Hey! Oh! What do you think you're doing? Get away from there!

Sometimes what people have is not abundance. What is a dying, fruitless overlong root to me may be a source of great joy to someone else. What is a squashable bug to someone else is to me evidence of an Earth at continuous work for 400 million years, according to *Fearsome Allies*. When I turned twelve this year, Dylan gave me that book for my birthday. The last time I saw Dylan before today, last week maybe, I once again asked him where he'd found it. Waste, he said. I thanked him again and he said, Beautiful,

I gave it to you like a year ago, you don't have to keep thanking me. But it's my favorite possession, so I did, again and again.

A man came storming across the lawn and boomed at me to back off, or he was going to ask for our registration numbers and report us to COHO.

Dylan retched in the street.

I told the man I didn't know my registration number.

He shouted again to get the hell off his property.

I did not realize this was a question of property. To me the issue was the deadness of the tree. There seemed to be a fundamental discrepancy in perception between me and the stentorian man towering over me.

Yeah, my property! My tree! I planted it! Get off my property! Get away from my tree!

What kind of tree is it? I asked.

Pomegranate, he said.

There are no pomegranates on it, I said.

The man looked over my head and harangued Dylan for vomiting in the middle of the road, specifically his road. They debated whose duty it was to clean up such a thing—Dylan's or the man's or WEDA's—and further discussed the nature of public versus private property, especially in a Restoration Part like Canland, where the immediate well-being of us all depends on the well-being of the land.

I didn't know it just yet, but I'd soon learn the man was Asher, the adoptive father of Malakai, a boy at my school, who others make fun of, and who often says equally insulting things in retaliation.

We planted this tree! Asher yelled.

In Canland's soil, Dylan said.

I'm sure you'd be singing the same tune if I'd vandalized your street, said Asher.

I registered Asher's sarcasm and felt proud of myself.

It's the Earth, said Dylan. It's neither yours nor mine.

Asher stepped to the edge of the lawn and said to Dylan, You didn't almost die to become registered in this Part. Your mom was wiping your ass when I was out there fighting for Purism so that Parts like Canland could exist today.

Please accept my apology for not being born thirty years earlier, Dylan said.

Watch how you talk. I earned my place here. Before they registered me, they had me humping water twenty miles a day and digging canals just so I could bring a bit of food back home.

And I bike human waste twenty miles outside Canland every night, Dylan said.

So you think the whole Part belongs to you? Because you've got a contribution? Because you don't share your house with fifty other people? I know who you are, Dylan Weekes.

And you. Asher pointed at me. He probably identified me by my pollution mask and sun goggles.

Then you know my parents founded this Part, said Dylan.

Don't you get it? Asher shouted even louder than before and slapped his chest a bunch of times. I do! Every day I do. I adopted Malakai, I brought him here because I wanted him to have a life, I fed your parents' land in exchange for a promise that they wouldn't throw me out. And yet, I still have to defend myself against people like you. I fought the same war as your parents, just like Malakai's parents did, only they died defending the planet from Traditionalists.

I'm not a Traditionalist, Dylan said. Don't align me with those zealots.

You're no better than whoever planted salt around my tree, clipped its branches, and pissed on it. And why? Because we weren't here during the founding, we weren't born here, we take up space and resources? You think this is all yours, you think you can puke wherever you want and you don't have to clean it up. We carried this tree in a pot while we searched for a home, we kept it alive, and we planted it when we came here two years ago. But still, we had to prove our worth before they registered us, gave us a home, food for three meals, water for baths. The Diaspora of the Environmental Collapse needs somewhere to live. And now that there's more DOTEC here, waiting like Malakai and I waited, people destroyed our tree as a signal to us! Practicalists claim it was a DOTEC militia that dropped a methane bomb in Lake Superior, and Purists say that the Earth was trying to tell us something by coming so close to killing us all. No one wants us! What do we have to offer? Well, I want to know what you have to give! Because now I need resources that I don't have to revive this tree! So unless you plan on helping, or cleaning up your stomach contents in the street, step away!

I'm trying to convey Asher's voice here. Sometimes I forget emotionally loaded information because without feeling attached to an event (especially one that would activate someone else's fear and stress centers), my brain sees no reason to remember it. In this way, my memory is a bit like a pond, with heavy things sunken on the bottom, and fun little words and factoids kissing the surface like dragonflies. But hopefully by keeping a journal, I can become more emotionally aware.

Then Asher placed his hand on my chest and started walking me into the street.

Dylan stepped to Asher. Warned him that if he ever touched me again—

Then Asher pushed Dylan in the chest.

So Dylan shoved Asher aside, and delivered one of his practiced roundhouse kicks to the midsection of the weakened pomegranate tree. Asher screamed and rushed to the felled trunk.

We got on the bike. Dylan rounded a tall eucalyptus wall, bark peeling and curling healthily from the trunks, showing ivory underneath. As I looked back, I saw Asher kneeling in front of his communal house with the tree's severed top half held horizontal in his lap, crying.

I'll take a short break now—I don't want my hand seizing up twice in one day. Reminder to write: Sybil and me—Feeding DOTEC—DOTEC attacks Sybil—back home with Dylan—Piano, claws—Conditioning—Journal.

Back.

I'd like to say before I begin again that I do wish Michael were here. Even though he wasn't around often, the times when he was were good. Helena says that writers think their fear of death is more profound than everyone else's, and they have tried to make a profession of cheating death, but that is not possible, and that is not a job, according to her. Similarly, of Michael, she has said, He claims he's saving the world for you and Dylan, but he's just afraid of being forgotten, like all men, but I don't care if I'm forgotten, the world would likely be better off without me, without all of us, but here you are, so while we both decide to keep on living, it is my duty to care for you, Tristan.

Under Helena's supervision, I've never once been in life-threatening danger. But one day, when I was six, Michael forgot to change my diaper for so long, being so preoccupied with his work, that feces got into my blood through my lymphangioma scars that were fissured by diaper rash, and because I was not exhibiting any pain, signs of fever, etc., for such a long time, I eventually went into shock. Michael had to rush me to the Safe Haven where Cole treated my infection and operated for a fifth time on my lymphangioma (Cole's saved my life countless times, from the day I was born, but I'm lucky not to have had to see him in a long while because it means I haven't needed medical attention).

But Michael has done so much good for me too. My first memory is of when he hiked up the Notch with me strapped to his back. I remember feeling like I was above the Earth, looking down on the tops of the eastern Canland mountains, the ridges like grooves in a brain, peaks like the serrated vertebrae of a sleeping Earth-titan, soaked in rosy dawn. Canland to the west was a green-gold stretch of silence, the grazing animals littler than ants, and roads thin as a Pholcidae's asymmetrical web. Michael's whiskered cheek was like sandpaper on mine as he looked back at me over his shoulder to ask what I thought, and I saw his face very large and close compared to the entire world that rolled out before us. We watched the morning light erase the shadows, but not even in the brightest day could a single person going about their contribution be individualized from that great height.

This was before people started jumping.

When Dylan spun us back up to the crest of the hill, Helena's head was blackened and skeletal and pulsing an orange glow, still feeding a fire that once in a while caught a breeze like a fleck of dust in your nostril, and the flares sneezed with a whoosh. He paused for a second and I got a good look at Canland beyond the smoke—the high eucalyptus walls protecting the fields from big gusts, the vine tents strung up over the thirsty arroyo, the western single-story adobe homes like ours, the northeast adobe stacks where I never have reason to go, and at the northernmost edge, the white dome of the Sensatarium (perhaps a handful of people are in there now, using their earned benefits, in a communal Sensorium Actualization) and the lone satellite tower beside it—communicating the Actualization to the Sensatarium—stretching skyward, higher than the trees. We flew down past the Part Center where people in short lines at the canvas-roofed kiosks craned their necks to the effigy burning on its six-legged round iron pedestal in the pale Earth that constitutes the baseball field's outfield. The empty semicircle of bleachers faced the empty stage. Hardly anyone was biking on the roads, and a maintenance contributor was taking the chance to smooth the bike and carriage grooves out of the native gray-orange dirt. We pulled up outside the mortuary. The smoke was dense and near.

Dylan skidded the bike sideways to a stop. Sybil took a step toward us and Tobias cawed at her to not wander off, even though she's fifteen. Dylan nodded his head to her, then looked at his feet. Sybil's curls were shiny, despite the daytime dark. She faced me and moved her arm in one big arcing wave, like I was faraway, even though I was right in front of her.

Where were you? Helena said to Dylan.

Defending your honor, he said.

Am I going to get a letter from the viceroy? Helena said.

No, he said.

Sybil widened her eyes and looked back and forth between them with just her irises. Sybil and I laugh at nothing on our walks home from school. Sometimes she'll make up stories using different voices, and sometimes she'll do impeccable impressions of the people in our lives. The audiences at the Part's occasional theater productions always enjoy her performances. She's very funny. At her mother's funeral, I remember everyone was crying except the two of us. Tobias was melted against the side of his dead wife's coffin, sobbing and heaving on the floor, and Sybil leaned over and whispered to me, Jeez, Dad, get over it. Sometimes she gets sad and angry, and when she does, she says things like, No I don't want to talk about it. Sometimes, when it's really bad, she'll go silent. But she still walks me from school to the top of my street, and then is usually fine and talkative again the next day. Even though she's a present, and has other present friends, she's never ignored me on the grounds that I'm a future. In fact, she stands up to anyone who says nasty things about me, futures or presents. She's always been there for me, even while mourning her mother's death this year.

All of which is why I felt so sorry when I did not protect her today.

Helena called my name to get my attention. She pointed to me, then to herself, and said, You're looking at me?

I nodded and also gave a thumbs-up. With my pollution mask and sun goggles on, no one could see my face.

She pointed to the burning effigy. That's your mother's head, she said.

I waited.

Don't forget that, she added. Then she turned to watch it burn.

On a table outside the mortuary was a petition for Helena's new teenage vasectomy proposal. The page was half full with signatures.

Two Canland College students stepped up to the table and started to castigate Helena, Your indifference to human life is a devolution of the violence that brought the world down!

She responded calmly, Friends, you are fighting for something you never had, something that was never real.

But they persisted in attacking her, You hypocrite, easy for you to say, your husband's contribution to WORLD protects you as you write laws to control the population, but you didn't abort your second pregnancy—which is when Sybil grabbed my hand and started walking me away—and how much energy Canland has spent to keep him alive!

Helena held up one finger to quiet the students, then turned to Sybil and me, and said, Be safe.

Sybil replied, Yes, of course. Thank you, Helena.

Talk about real? one student shouted. Our children will never be real, because of you!

No DOTEC, Tobias told Sybil, leaning in and shaking his head, which made his cheeks wiggle. He stutters a lot and cares about his daughter. He's stubby and has a comb-over.

OK, Dad, Sybil said.

I mean it, he said. They're dangerous and desperate, and I don't like you getting close to them.

I heard you the first time, Sybil replied. With our fingers interlocked and strides synchronized, we made our way across the road to market.

Meanwhile, Helena turned back to the two students. Please, she said to them, continue.

Dylan wasn't around anymore. I asked Sybil where he'd gone, and she said, You didn't see him go?

No, I said.

He announced he was leaving, she said.

Did he say where?

No. Sybil raised her eyebrows at me and then said, Dude, you have to pay attention.

Sorry, I said.

No sorry, just, for your own safety, be on the lookout. What were you thinking about in the meantime?

Well, I was thinking about suicide, I said.

All right, she said. What about suicide?

I paused to think and thought about the rise in people jumping off the Notch and wanted to know what it would be like to feel even a fraction of the pain it would require to do that, but couldn't begin to because I never have. But I thought, if I wanted to do that, to jump, I might require someone to tell me, It's OK if you do this. But then that approval might give me a reason to live, abate my loneliness, so to speak. So maybe the answer to the question of paralyzing sadness and loving encouragement is to conduct a frank examination of what you mean to the Earth. That's what Helena does—she helps people arrive at the conclusion that they are a bane to the planet and the innumerable accidents of nature, and that the self-interest that keeps the human individual pining for more than existence tautologically grants us is going to kill us all. That's what she's written in some of her speeches, which she gives at Canland College and in the Part Center, and sometimes practices aloud at her writing table while I listen from down the hall.

Are you sad about the people jumping off the Notch? Sybil asked.

I might have said yes to someone else, but I don't need to lie to Sybil.

I didn't know any of them, I said. So, not sad.

Are you OK with it?

They can do it if they want.

But should they? she said.

If it's best for Canland.

And is it?

Helena says it is, I said.

And does that make it true?

I thought, if not true then at least defensible, and I said so.

She said, Well, I guess we're all just trying to justify our existence, one way or another.

Sybil has always believed in spirits, ghosts, incorporeal entities, maybe even god. But I don't.

The line at the rations kiosk was short. Sybil traded a voucher for one bag of jerky and one bag of dried fruit. I took a long swig of water under my pollution mask and checked my pulse and blood pressure on my bracelet, and they were both normal in the

lingering midyear heat. The summer—despite highs of 121° F—
passed without any heat-related deaths. The shaded lean-tos were
always occupied, people congregated under the vine tents, and
all agriculture contributions were fulfilled at dawn and dusk. Our
Part's ecological detriment was higher than usual, but Viceroy
Hugo insisted it was worth it to keep the fields irrigated, the harvested food refrigerated, and the Part's registered safe, even if it
would cost the Part WORLD benefits in case of a natural disaster.
Yet we still managed to plant another thousand trees in what used
to be scree and talus slopes, and we installed another half-acre
of solar panels to keep the water coming in and the Sensatarium
working and the food storage centers safe. And at the end of each
day, everyone was comfortable in their adobe homes.

We stood outside the perimeter of the protesters, where there
were Purists protesting the protest. Purists shouted, Stop polluting
our air! and, You're killing birds! Which was countered by the
Practicalist protesters yelling, You're killing humans! and, Evolution is natural law!

I expected to eat the provisions in the Part Center with Sybil, but
she took my hand again and walked us out among the nodding
cows in the pasture at the base of the hillock, atop which the hu-
mongous coast live oak grows, the only life here older than the Part.
No one knows where it came from or who planted it, but it's so old
that its crown reaches all the way down to the grass and spreads
in a circumference of fifty people holding hands. And now, in
hindsight, I wish I had suggested we turn around, said that Helena
wouldn't like us going all the way out here, it's not safe for me, it's
WORLD's job and the Part's job to take care of DOTEC, not ours. But
the truth is, it didn't even occur to me. I was just following Sybil.

She let go of my hand. She was wearing all her stone rings. They
belonged to her mom, whose name was Polly, who was an apiarist. She died outside of Canland on a research assignment. I don't
remember the specifics.

I followed Sybil past the grazing cattle through thin ankle-high
grass. She explained then that she had given her rations away to

DOTEC a few times before, for which Tobias had reproached her. Just because we had a little less to eat, she said, shaking her head.

Forty or more DOTEC were on the hillock, most of them lounging in the shade of the tree, a few sunbathing, chatting and laughing, savoring morsels of food. Leaning against the trunk, I saw through a gap in the branches two people playing a game. One person was wearing a headscarf, in keeping with the fashion of Canland to keep women's long hair from blowing all about in the wind (though I prefer to keep mine in a ponytail, and Helena uses pins for hers) and had a hand resting on her globular belly. The other person was younger, had a wild head of curly black hair, and was laughing with their head tipped back and mouth wide open. For aesthetic reasons, this second person was so captivating to me that I didn't want to look away, which has never happened to me with a human before, only nature.

While Sybil searched for DOTEC most in need of rations, I stood back and watched the captivating person and the pregnant woman play a game with arrangements of sticks and stones in the grass between them, high-fiving and pumping their fists, giving the impression they were working together, or at least rooting for each other. Competition seems like a great source of joy for people. I think baseball would be fun, if I were allowed to play it. But I'm not really competitive anyway.

An older man with a wiry beard and no shirt to cover his sun-orange torso approached and started jawing at the two DOTEC, very animated. The captivating person said something back to him, and the pregnant woman hid her face in her shoulder. The man knelt and placed his hand on the captivating person's shoulder, which was thin like mine and exposed by their tank top. They swatted the man's hand away, then turned their shoulders to face the man squarely and stared right into his eyes. Then the man backed away and moved along. The sticks and stones game appeared to have ended. The captivating person lodged their hands in their hair and shook it out. Then they nestled themself against the pregnant woman, and the two of them looked out from under the tree, toward me, beyond me, at the Part, the mountains, and the smoke.

Meanwhile, arguments sprang up all around Sybil, who was offering the rations to a mother and her future-aged children, a boy and a girl. These arguments centered around the question of who deserves aid most: the people who suffered most before they got here, or the people most likely to become registered contributors, or the people most in need of help right at this moment, say, a mother and two children, or is it the mother's fault for making irresponsible choices regarding her family life to have two kids on her own? That last comment incited some pushing and shoving among a gaggle of young men while young women crossed their arms and shook their heads.

I went up beside Sybil and introduced myself to the family of three, briefly removing my mask and goggles to let them see my face. The young daughter hid her eyes in her mother's armpit and the son gazed blankly at me, and the mother said, Hi, thank you for your generosity, but we can't take what's yours. Sybil insisted and laid the bags at their feet and said, You need this more than I do, I can't imagine what you've been through.

Then, while I was putting my mask and goggles back on, the old bearded shirtless man started running toward us with down-hill momentum. His eyes and mouth were wide open. He thrust himself at Sybil, landing on top of her, mounting her and moving his hands all about her stomach, making animal sounds. His body blocked her face from my view. After only a few seconds, a COHO pursued the scene and raised his whistler, and with a sound like a needle piercing glass, perforated the man in the side of the head, and he fell to the ground motionless.

After Sybil gave a statement to the COHO, we headed back to the mortuary, which is also the Chariotses' home. I turned around to see the captivating person, but they were no longer there. Sybil didn't speak on the walk back. I asked her a couple times if she was OK, but she said nothing. I hope she's fast asleep right now, and has forgotten about today.

I can't imagine it's easy to sleep in a house full of coffins after burying your mother in one, although maybe Polly was cremated and her coffin was ornamental. I can't remember. I bet Tobias wishes he could move them out, but that's their situation and it's his contribution (although, with so few deaths in Canland, he's often assigned supplemental contributions), so what else can they do?

I've been through bad things. No one as close to me as a mother has ever died, but I've been through things. I didn't come home for the first three years of my life. My survival was uncertain, and I was kept in Research Centers, not developing a bond with my parents. I bit off the tip of my tongue while I was teething and now have a lisp. I picked my nose so vigorously that one nostril is nearly shut and the bridge looks like it's had the cartilage removed. I've had sixteen corneal abrasions, an even eight in each eye. The pigment of my lips doesn't know quite how to navigate all the bitten, scratched, licked, chapped scar tissue. Then there are the scars on my chest where the doctors inserted a VAD to help my heart beat steady and strong, on my abdomen from my precautionary appendectomy, the dotted maps of IVs on my arms (my veins like to hide), and the archipelagos of scars and felty scabs on my tush from my all the lymphangioma surgeries, which need to be checked at least once daily to make sure they're not swollen or open or infected—that's why I've got dentures I remove and caps I stick on my fingernails before I sleep, why I wear goggles indoors and out, why Michael spent so much time developing my vocabulary and the mechanisms by which I can communicate the things I should be feeling and to understand that when someone else, for instance, loses their home and has to walk across the hot continent to our Part and beg for food and wait for housing to develop, it's best to try to help them.

But because we tried to help, a DOTEC attacked a registered. Now people probably hate DOTEC even more. So maybe it's best just to play your part. Sybil wouldn't go and say another actor's lines, would she? Besides, she hasn't done a play since her mom died.

Back at the mortuary, Helena was orating to a small gathering. I don't know who among them were Purists or Practicalists or volunteers or students, but she was saying, Mother Nature's been battered, nearly destroyed, over mere hundreds of years—a split second on the watch of Father Time. We did swift damage to the pastoral ideal. Millions of people wander across the plains, through mountains, along roads that once ensured security, now in search of new homes. Civilizations once poised for prosperity at the edge of the sea have left ruins to be discovered in a thousand years, with any luck. We did what we said we never would: we went to war against ourselves. Raise your hand if you fought. Now, keep it up if you fought for Earth.

The young ones in the crowd never raised their hands. They looked around at the older people, who all had their hands up.

Remember what we fought for, Helena said. And look what we've done here, in just twenty-three years, adhering to WORLD's policies of austerity. Five square miles of green, surrounded by bare desert all the way out to the mountains. The Practicalists say they want what's in their name, but what about the human desire for wealth and bounty and permanence is practical, when the same fate awaits every living thing? Tobias should know! Helena said, and everyone laughed. She went on, We're the only species that gets to contemplate death, and we fight over the meaning of it, and yet we sense it everywhere in the Earth we walk. Death is what sustains life. I only know as much as you all that we're here to delay death for as long as possible. But there are those brave persons of our Part who have confronted death, and for a split second, know more than any living thing. They reconciled themselves to the truth of what our world needs, and bravely departed from this poisoned air.

She pointed out to the smoldering effigy of her head.

Tobias appeared beside me and pointed to Dylan, sitting in the street on his bike with his arms crossed and one foot serving as a kickstand, watching Helena.

I looked at Sybil. She was staring at a point of sky far past the rising smoke-serpent.

I said, Bye, Sybil.

She didn't answer me.

I got on the back of Dylan's bike. He pedaled away from the mortuary and asked how my day had been. I said it was good. I didn't tell him what had happened, and I didn't ask him where he'd been. I didn't want him to get angry again.

Dusk set in as we rode down our street and arrived home. Dylan poured me a bowl of veggie soup, lit me a candle, and went to his room. I ate alone, perusing the dictionary to retain and sharpen the verbal tools with which Michael equipped me. Then I sat at the piano and started with the pieces Helena has permitted me to learn—Chopin nocturnes, Beethoven's *Moonlight Sonata*, and some Mozart variations on "Twinkle, Twinkle, Little Star"—but then I grew bored and lazy, so I started making melodies up. I played freer and faster than I ever had before. I don't know where the music came from, outside of me, from the instrument, or from within myself, but I was certain that if only Helena could hear me play this well, she would allow me to play whatever I wanted, for audiences to enjoy, and to connect all our natural loves for music, the most innate and scientific form of art. She might even send me to an Arts Part. I feel a tiny thrill just thinking about it.

But I played for too long. My hands seized up. I didn't know how long had passed since I'd sat down to play, but the candle had gone out and it was pitch black inside the house. Not wanting to injure myself, I stayed seated on the bench, calling out Dylan's name. He didn't hear me—he was probably in the Sensorium—so I waited for Helena to come home.

Hours passed before the door finally opened. Helena lit a candle on the shelf in the mudroom, and then slowly and methodically several more candles overlapped to illuminate the house. Helena's eyes were red and slow as they passed over me and my paralyzed claws. She went down the hall and returned with a muscle relaxant in one hand and a needle and syringe of Botox in the other. The shadows running from her nose to the corners of her mouth were deep. She put the pill between my lips and said, Hold it. Then she drove the needle into the flesh between the thumb and forefinger of both my hands. She produced a glass of water. I swallowed the pill and she took the glass back.

This is why you play only when I tell you, she said.

Then she had me explain to her what I'd done wrong, and while I did, she conditioned me as usual. My left cheek and ear tingled for a little while, but it obviously didn't hurt. I was just sorry I had made her do that to me. I know how much she hates to. She's said to me that I'm the greatest tragedy of her life, and she has endured many tragedies.

From now on, I will not make Helena's life any harder.

She helped me get ready for bed. Took out my teeth and washed them, stuck caps to my fingertips, checked my scars. I had a clean pair of pajamas tonight. She kissed me where my face had tingled, and sent me to my room to tuck myself in.

I lay awake for some time, making up songs in my head, before my door opened. I couldn't see her in the darkness, but I knew it was Helena by the sharp floral smell of grappa. She sat in my desk chair. I don't know if Dylan was still in the house; I hadn't heard him leave for his waste run.

There was a stampede today, Tristan, she said to me. I know you and Sybil went up to the tree and talked to the people there. She's lost my trust completely. I don't blame you. But there was a stampede in the pasture after you left. Two wolves came down from the mountain and attacked the cattle. Before the wolves were perforated, a young boy who was playing in the grass was trampled. Eight years old. Sol Diaz, one of your fellow futures. All I could think was how easily that could've been you.

I blinked to let her know I was listening, but I don't know if she was even looking at me. She was a blur in the darkness.

Remember when you used to wear that helmet? she said. That padded cloth, with the chin tie? To protect your brilliant, beautiful brain. You always asked why you had to wear it, said you didn't like it, because you couldn't see your hair. It's the only thing I've ever heard you express discomfort about. So I took it off for you. And now I'm waiting for the day you split your head open.

I wonder if Helena knows what it's like to play piano and feel like you are entering another world, and once you are in that world, how difficult it can be to leave.

After Helena left my room, I listened for her bedroom door to shut. Then I took some paper out of my desk and started this journal.

I should try to get a bit of sleep now. It's late. Or early. But I didn't want to forget today.

2

THE FUTURES ARE outside for Practice of Agriculture. I'd rather attend Economic Austerity with the presents than fill my exemption period with independent reading, but there are stringent policies regarding futures advancement. I wish I had my journal here with me, or that I could put a date stamp on my days and remember everything exactly as it happens. But it's not so bad—there are books here at my disposal to keep my mind moving, presently a large volume titled *Regrettable: American Apologies for Obscene and Clandestine Acts of Imperialism*, and a chapter about America's 1961 deposition and assassination of Patrice Lumumba, the first freely elected leader of the Congo, and the installation of a dictator in his place. Michael never read me much nonfiction. I'm probably the only future who actually reads during their independent reading period, but then again, I'm also the only one who has independent reading alone. Not even the librarian is here. I read a sentence about competition over mineral mines in a province called Katanga. Then I close the book, stand up on my chair, and drop the book onto the table. The echo ricochets off the metal ceiling beams. I sit back down.

I look to the wall across from me, at the woodblock print of Arturo Eagles. His square jaw and bulging eyes are of the sort that I imagine populates Idealist Parts. He is depicted signing the word *sunrise*; it's the sign with which everyone together begins the school day, and I do it again now. The woodblock's header reads, *Worldwide Objective: Restoration Longevity Dominion*, and the footer says, *Canland: Doing Our Part*. I love living in Canland, and would love to have a meaningful contribution one day.

Another slam echoes through the library, as if time were a corkscrew. Helm Roctern has his big boxy fists resting on a table, his bouldery shoulders rounded forward, and his great big teeth grinning at me from inside his beard. When the echo stops, he laughs, puts his hands in his pockets, stands straight and tall, and strides toward me.

"Hi, Helm," I say.

"What's up, T-Bird?"

"Reading," I say. "Everyone else is outside."

"Well." He sits diagonal to me. "Loneliness breeds genius."

Helm proffers me one of his fists, bigger than a child's head. I punch it lightly, and he winces and shakes it out like I've hurt him. People sometimes use me to amuse themselves, but Helm tries to amuse me. He once even had Helena come to the school to discuss my progress in his Creative Thought and Expression class. The three of us sat in his classroom, Helm silent and wearing a very grave face for a long time, but then his mouth broke open in a smile, and he said how wonderfully I was doing. I missed Helena's initial reaction, but I didn't hear her laugh. I laughed, though. Then I felt her hand on the back of my head, and she was smiling at me with just the corners of her eyes.

Helm leans back and crosses his arms over his continental chest.

"That's my personal experience, anyway," he says. "To finish my story collection, I had to become a recluse." He loosens a finger from his bicep to wiggle it at the bookshelves. "Have you read my book?"

Helm wrote a book of short stories called *This Blood Is Not My Own*. There are three twine-bound copies in Canland, all punctiliously handwritten. The Board of Advancement did not deem it impressive enough to propose that Helm transfer to an Arts Part. I read the first story. I don't remember if I liked it, and can only recall a few details, that it was about a soldier who doesn't want to fight anymore, and when he comes home from the war, he wants to become a father, but something stops him. It is of course possible that this is not the story, and I'm super-imposing Helm's life onto the story instead—Helm fought in the war, and he isn't a father, even though he's older than Helena and Michael.

He leans forward in his chair. With his fists on the table, he rubs his knuckles together.

"You're probably too young to understand it anyway," he says before I can respond, since I sort of forgot to because I couldn't decide how. "To say nothing of your precociousness, Mr. Weekes! But it's not for everyone, and that's all right too." Helm scratches his beard so thoroughly that it makes a noise, like wind through leaves. "Your mother's review wasn't too kind," he chuckles, as if his throat's all full of gravel. "But she is rarely kind when it comes to matters of the heart, which creativity is, as you know, with your piano. Your pianizing. How's that going?"

"Good."

"Good," Helm says. "Find the necessity in your art. If you can find the necessity, you'll never stop doing it, which is of course the only point of art, that it transcends the humdrum." He looks me straight in the eyes. "Art is the least inadequate solution to answering our infinite questions with our finite means."

Helm says things like this to us in class, which I enjoy, but not everyone does. One of my fellow futures, Leo Laughton, thinks Helm should go off to an Arts Part if he loves to navel-gaze so much, because Canland only has room for real contributors. Also, last year there was some drama surrounding Helm when he assigned the presents to read *A Modest Proposal* by Thomas Swift, which suggested that poor Irish families in the eighteenth century sell their babies to rich families as food in order to solve

Ireland's economic problems. Viceroy Hugo, in his annual address to Canland, condemned and dismissed Helm's tacit implication that he, Viceroy Hugo, could be swayed to write a policy in any way influenced by Swift's essay, and even took it so literally as to assure his audience that there would be no cannibalism in Canland. Helm defended himself, saying the essay was obviously a joke, written and promulgated in preindustrial Ireland to illustrate a point about class and economic structure, and what Helm was trying to teach his students was the effectiveness of satire as a creative tactic. A few days later, Helm issued a public apology and was allowed to continue teaching, just not that essay. The question was where he got the essay.

I know he got it from Helena—she told me once when she was talking loud and nonstop.

But where did she get it?

"Necessity in what you do," Helm mutters, nodding and staring at the table, his mouth pinched into a bunch of tiny wrinkles.

Helm's basically entirely pockmarked or haired, and is always sweating, and his sweat carries dirt, which, plus all his years in the sun, makes it difficult to tell if his ancestors came from the east or north of the Mediterranean. His eyes are dark brown.

"You thought about contributions? Specializations?" he says.

"Oh, I'd love to specialize in entomology, if I can."

Only, I'm not supposed to go in the garden, so I think the study of insects is a long shot.

"Or something in Part planning," I amend.

"Part planning," he says. "That's a good one. Keep the roads working. Get the water from the reservoir to the people. Get the waste out. You kind of need to come up with practical answers to impractical questions. It's an art in a way. It requires conviction!"

His voice gets loud and for some reason it makes me laugh. Then he starts coughing and slaps his chest.

"You know what I mean?" he says.

"No."

"We're in a transitional state, is all," he says. "So it's important you pick something you're going to love. Now, not everyone gets to do what they love, but they learn to love what they do."

Helm turns around in his chair, like he's looking for someone, but then he shifts back toward me. He looks at the cover of the book I was reading. He doesn't react, but I bet he's already read it. Helm's pretty smart.

"Do you love what you do?" I ask.

"Oh, sure," he says. "What's not to love? I get to help mold the minds of the next generation." He moans and then, with both hands, presses the center of his forehead and drags his fingers outward. He does this repeatedly, like a self-massage. When he stops, he looks into his hands and then laces his fingers together. "Well, it's better than it used to be. Life is a gift."

"Do you only think that because you almost died?" I ask.

"Lots of us almost died. I just think the people who are most at peace are the ones who knew what they'd be dying for."

"And you knew."

"Well, when you join the military, you pick a side, not a cause. They tell you freedom is the cause and America's the side. But when the Evanescence happened, yes, we all had to choose."

"How did you choose?"

"It wasn't much of a choice. My brother was in a tank blown up by Traditionalists."

If Dylan was blown up, I'd choose the side that opposed whoever killed him. "So you fought against Traditionalists," I infer.

"Simply put, yes. Only, it wasn't simple. Traditionalists recast themselves as Practicalists when it became clear that their cause was a bit like going line dancing on a sinking cruise ship."

"What's a cruise ship?"

"It's a big boat where people used to go on vacation. Only, you never really get off the boat because there's so many activities on the boat. But you're in the middle of the ocean the whole time, so there's no escape. It takes a gallon of gas to move it four inches, and it goes for hundreds of miles."

"I see."

"The fracking was sort of when—sorry, remind me, what do they tell you in your History of Canland class?"

"That Arturo Eagles accepted us into the WORLD Parts System when he saw all the good work we were doing."

"OK. Well, that was about twenty years ago. Do they go into what happened before that?"

My underdeveloped amygdala hampers my formation of some memories, which is why Michael tried to improve my memory processing via electrotherapy, and my sensory processing via Sensorium Actualizations. It accelerated my verbal skills and made me love music. But as far as my attention span in my History of Canland class goes, there is room for improvement.

"Maybe," I say.

"Yes. Right. Well, listen, don't tell your mother I'm telling you this."

"Helena says that if someone says that, then I have to tell her."

"Oh. Well, then go ahead. I don't know why I said that, since she did write the curriculum, and it seems to be working well enough for our young people." Helm coughs into his elbow. "I don't know what your parents did with you, but they should do it for everyone."

I'm not sure if that was a compliment, though I can't imagine Helm would insult me. He's always been complimentary of the work I do in his class, even though I lack, as Helena says, the emotional gamut to touch human hearts with the figurative, which is why she limits my piano-playing to certain rudimentary tunes. If I tell that to Helm, he might think of less Helena as a mother, or less of me as a pianist, and that would be misguided, since Helena only ever protects me, and I'm an adept musician.

"Michael is on a research mission," I say, sort of forgetting what we're talking about.

"Your dad's as smart as they make 'em, don't get me wrong. But people get bored here, and when they feel like they're not making a difference, they leave. We have to realize we're at the beginning of everything again. I remember the earthquakes in Los Angeles, the sinking of New York, the wildfires from Oregon to West Virginia–before the war, even. People thought that was the end. They started calling it an Environmental Evanescence. Slow fade. And then–" Helm sighs at me and crosses his arms again. "OK, T. I'm just gonna tell it, OK?"

"Sure."

"So, about 2050, the American president, Gerard Blackstone–brown-haired, blue-collar guy, never went to high school, followed in his father's footsteps as a maintenance man on oil wells, better with a hammer than a pen, but his ambition knew no end, and he might actually have been the first president with a beard in a century-and-a-half. Blackstone had a sort of Icarus complex, or inferiority complex, one of those, because of all the people who thought he was too stupid to ever amount to anything, and still believed it after he became our nation's president. He was basically looking for a way to save the world, so he traveled to Israel a whole lot because Israel was making massive strides in desert greening and sustainability."

"We're a desert greening project."

"Yes. So, while he was over there, Blackstone was also making alliances with Saudi Arabia to gain access to their oil deposits. But people didn't like that, because of all the natural disasters occurring in North America and around the world. And Israel really didn't like it, and they renounced their alliance with the U.S. Now, President Blackstone, once a hero of the people–maybe it was a messiah complex, I don't know–he couldn't believe he basically singlehandedly fucked, er, sorry, *ruined* what might've been America's most important alliance. So he went off the rails–drinking, having affairs with politicians, even closing American borders. He passed an executive order that big corporations distribute their wealth to all the poor people. And to help stimulate the economy, he figured it was best to just frack for the oil already in our continent. He opened up a fracking well along the New Madrid Fault, which led to contaminated drinking water, methane emissions, all this nasty stuff destroying towns and small cities in the south and the Midwest. And then, the fault slipped. Basically half the people in Indiana, Missouri, Tennessee, and beyond, were left without homes, water, or even roads. Whether or not that earthquake was a coincidence, people blamed Blackstone. So now, you had millions of people from the heartland of America, plus the people from the coasts who'd already been displaced by floods and earthquakes, homeless and wandering. WORLD called them all the Diaspora of the Environmental Collapse. Only, within DOTEC, there were all these different groups who believed the Evanescence happened for different reasons. Some people chalked it up to centuries of sustained environmental abuse. Others blamed the impulsivity of one crappy president. But everyone thought everyone else was ignoring the truth, and that made them feel angry and unprotected, which is a scary feeling, especially when felt simultaneously by a whole continent, basically, of grieving and desperate people watching nature die. You're with me so far?"

"I knew fracking was bad."

"Great. So, we have a bunch of people, pissed at the government, with no homes and a bunch of guns. We have a military, made up of personnel with opinions of their own, who are being deployed on American soil to keep Americans in check. Not good at all. Militias started popping up. And these militias ranged from Purist to Survivalist to Traditionalist, with a sprinkling of the religious. Under the umbrella of Traditionalists, a militia of many factions formed, called Matthews, named for the Bible verse Matthew 5:29, which says something like, if your eye causes you to sin, throw away your eye, or something to that effect. It doesn't make a ton of sense to me, but I guess a lot of people connected with it, because Matthews made it their mission to abduct President Blackstone and remove his eyeball—which they did. They took him into the desert and spooned out—sorry. Is it hard for you to hear about violence?"

"I don't really care. But actually, I'm curious, are people still religious?"

"Well, in Canland, we have the Secular Observation House. People here don't reference god so much. Maybe it's because a collapse of most of Earth's visible ecosystems was literal enough for everybody. Although, it's nobody else's business who people talk to in their free time, if you ask me. That said, Jewish shops and synagogues were frequent targets of the Matthews. Actually, a lot of churches were blown up too. And mosques, now that I think of it. Well, so anyway, when Traditionalism broke apart, a lot of them became Practicalists, and so less, you know, dated in their thinking. But the Traditionalists who remained, whether Matthews or not, carried on the war. It was a losing effort, but they still did damage, hoarding fuel and land, attacking u.s. military outposts. I always felt my job was to keep the peace, but one day I was in a tank following another tank that my brother was in. A military helicopter commandeered by Traditionalists flew over us and blew up my brother's tank in front of me. I shot the helicopter out of the sky."

Helm's looking at the table as if he's watching a scene play out on it, like he's in a Sensorium. It's difficult for me to tell what he's feeling—difficult to interpret his tone and also keep my attention on everything he's saying. Helena sometimes tells me, usually when I've said something rude, that it's not what you say, but how you say it. The pitch of Helm's voice isn't changing much as he talks. But if I listen only to his tone, his words fall apart like random sounds without meaning.

"It was chaos. There was no one in charge. People were freeing animals from zoos, monkey-wrenching factories, spiking trees— that's when you drive a metal spike into a tree so the bark grows over it and when the loggers come, their chainsaws hit the spike and bounce back at them. But when the nukes started going off and turning forests into ash—it's hard to talk about, to be honest, the trail of nothingness that all the fighting left. Everyone lost people they loved. Nothing was maintained. Not even the fucking internet. Sorry for swearing."

"It's OK."

Helm wipes the sweat from his widow's peak hairline and sort of grumbles.

"Well, so what it all culminated to was WORLD coming to power. See, the whole time, there was this young rich genius named Arturo Eagles, who kept his trillions of dollars of personal wealth in the WORLD Research Centers, and kept his people employed and developing solutions and new technologies for the Evanescence. The whistler, actually, was one of his inventions. It was a construction tool, originally. You could punch through steel with the compressed air inside, but now the COHO use them. From a distance, it puts a shallow depression in a person's flesh, like a vaccination scar, but very painful. But up close, it can—well, it's not good."

"I saw a COHO perforate a DOTEC on the hillock last week."

"Oh, right. Yeah, he had internal damage, I heard. They put him on a carriage and took him out of Canland." He pauses. He breathes loudly through his nose. "Anyway, Arturo Eagles was responsible for bigger inventions too—you know, food storage units, solar energy, environmental cleanup technology, and, of course, the Sensorium."

"Of course."

"That's kind of where we are. Arturo Eagles established the Parts System to divide people based on their vocation, their status, and their role in the future of Earth, so to speak. Limited travel, limited power, no global economy. Parts adhere to the WORLD regulations and they get the benefits of WORLD—Sensatariums, solar panels, emergency resources."

"Green Line access," I say.

"Well, you only get on the Green Line if the viceroy gives you a ticket, and that adds to the Part ecological detriment report." Helm frees a web from inside his chest. "It's no wonder people get bored and leave. They have families out there that they miss." He nods. "But we're doing good." He looks at me and the smile lines around his eyes fold up momentarily. "WORLD is a Practicalist organization, but it needs Purists to function. Equilibrium. Like

Canland. The California Inland Valley Desert-Greening Project. Somehow, it's worked."

"Were you a founder?"

"No, no. But I got here near the beginning. They had me fetch the scrap metal to build the college." Helm slaps his bicep three times. Then he starts coughing again, like a chorus of bears. When he's done, his eyes are teary. He slaps his chest and swallows.

"Sorry. I was saying, this place is set up nicely for you. I remember when I first got here, it wasn't much more than an old abandoned military compound. Before all the pines and blue gums and the vine tents, the wind sometimes got crazy. We'd get sand blowing into our homes. Plus all the debris out there, fighting the war—" Helm pats his chest and takes a deep, wheezing breath. "We were all so afraid at the new beginning, but we had each other."

Tears pool on his lower eyelids, more than from the coughing. He turns his head away for a second and wipes a lachrymal splotch on his sleeve.

"Sorry about that, T. Some changes in my personal life. You never know the ways heartache can sneak up on you. You see, I met my wife here. We've been together fifteen years. I'm fifty-eight years old, and just now we're separating. It's one of those things you never see coming."

He takes a long pause. I nod with a face I've practiced, like I am understanding and condoling. I think people feel they can tell me upsetting personal details about their lives because they see that I'm not exactly the most invulnerable guy, and so they don't feel like they have to impress me. Helm scratches his beard again. I try to think of a question to help distract him, the way Sybil does when she sees me drifting off.

"Are there still militias?" I ask.

"Oh, I'll bet. I think that's why people are wary of registering DOTEC into Canland. They don't want to put the work they feel they've poured into Canland in jeopardy. They don't want violence. Which is why I'm wondering if what the college students did with the effigy of your mother's head—sorry—wasn't a move toward Traditionalism. Now we've got all this suicide-as-politics, population concerns, DOTEC living under the tree. I just want everyone to get along."

"Me too."

"People do terrible things when they're afraid. Look no further than that book you're reading."

"Ha. Yeah."

"Don't act out of fear—act out of bravery. But you can't be brave unless you're afraid."

"You can't be brave unless you're afraid," I repeat.

"Although, I guess you don't really get afraid," he says.

"No."

"Well, then you've got nothing to worry about." Helm stands up and pats my shoulder with a hand that could crush me. "Thanks for the talk, T-Bird. I gotta grab a book and get to my classroom. Nice to see you here."

"You too. Thank you for the history lesson."

Helm gives me his fist again and I bump it and he shakes it out in fake pain. He smiles from inside his beard and then goes to the shelves. Without searching for very long, he pulls a copy of his own book from the shelf, holds it up to me and winks. Helm seems very proud of his book. I'd like to be proud of something I create one day, or even just teach someone about history through my eyes. If there's anything I've learned from Helm's history, it's that people have something in them that makes them violent and capable of enormous destruction. Perhaps that's why Tobias and Helena didn't like Sybil and me going to see the DOTEC on the hillock a week ago—because sure enough, one of the DOTEC was violent toward Sybil.

As Helm leaves the library, the bell rings, like an enormous iron hummingbird, once used to wrangle up the prisoners who occupied these halls when it was a small correctional facility near the military base, before the catwalks were removed (which explains the high ceilings) and the cells were turned into classrooms, and it became our school. Helm covers his ears with his hands as he walks out; when the bell dies, I realize I should have done the same. I remember to cover my ears about half the time. I put the history book back on the shelf and head to Meteorology: Predicting Patterns in Climate Cycles.

.

"Dylan came over last night with his Sensorium."

I remember beaches without a human in sight. Thousands of tiny turtles raced from sand to sea. Gulls dived for their newly hatched food. Fish lanced. Pelicans swooped over waves with open beaks. Crabs latched onto rocks. Foam crashed and left a sheen on their shells. Dolphins breached in threes. A humpback defied gravity. Sunlight turned the water gold. Some turtles made it home.

"Tristan, you in there?" Sybil says.

"Yes, now."

"Dylan brought his Sensorium to my house last night to impress me, or frighten me, I don't know, but he put me in an Actualization of a Restoration Part that had been ravaged by fires. It looked like a pencil drawing. You understand? There was nothing. People were hacking down these trees and feeding wood through chippers and bleaching it and treating it because what else were they going to do with it since it was all burnt to a crisp. A lightning strike, and no rain to put it out. Some people were leaving, carrying whatever they could on their backs. Others were hiking up a mountain, a march of at least a couple hundred people, and one by one they launched themselves into the gorge."

Roshana's up at the front of the line and on her tippy-toes trying to reach the guava she's been talking to herself about the whole time we've been in line, but she can't reach it. A present behind her says something that makes Roshana pluck a lower guava. When she turns around, she's holding the guava up and frowning at it, then she shuts one eye and bites into it with a crunch. Every day at school for the past three years, the students have been hoping the fruit's ready, and today it is. We step up in line.

"Questions so far?" Sybil asks, her way of making sure I'm listening.

"No."

Sybil bites her bottom lip. It leaves two small red marks. "There was this girl about my age in the line of people. She looked straight up at the satellite. I know it wasn't real-time, and I know she doesn't know me, but she knew someone might've been watching, and I was. She looked like she didn't know what to do. Like she was asking for help. All the people she knew were going to kill themselves, and she didn't want to."

"Did she?"

"No one turned around." Sybil bows her head. I can see her vertebrae stick up in back of her long neck. "She had no one left."

"Why did Dylan put you in that?"

"I asked him what it was like out there. I wanted to know."

"Canland is better than everywhere else."

She looks at me with her round brown eyes. "No, it's not. It's the same."

I smile. "That's crazy, Sybil. You're a nut."

She looks away from me, out over the top of the school's fence, toward the mountains. She's been quiet all week, since the incident on the hillock. Yesterday, even though she walked me home, she didn't reply to anything I said, so I stopped talking.

"I've been thinking," she says. "This place doesn't work. It's the desert. You can't just make it something else."

"But they did. WORLD can save the Earth because we saved this place."

"This place is awful, Tristan."

"I think it's beautiful."

"That's not what I'm talking about," she says.

The rest of the line steps up, but Sybil doesn't, so I wait with her.

Roshana is standing in a shaft of sparkling light, squinting up at the unending sky, eating her pink-fleshed guava.

"What I mean," her voice a whisper now, "is that the people here are miserable. They're all going to march up that mountain and—" She moves her eyes back and forth between mine. I picture someone having thrown a handful of freckles onto her pale face. She sighs. "There's so much I want that isn't and never will be here. I asked Dylan to show me how things were. He could have shown me something like a utopian Canland, an actually self-sustaining desert greening project where people aren't so bored and skeptical, to convince me that there's a future here, to get me to stay. He could access any satellite he wants, to show me any place that might be perfect. Of all people, don't you think Dylan would want me to stay? Why would he try to scare me?"

"Maybe to keep you here?" I say.

Sybil looks at all of my face, the way she sometimes does. As far as I can tell, she isn't feeling anything, though I know that's not true—Sybil's always feeling something, she just doesn't always show it. That's how she's explained people to me: they're always feeling something.

There's some shouting by the tree. Leo and Lilly Laughton, the towheaded twins whose parents are accountants in Canland's Treasury Department, are arguing with our bespectacled Practical Math teacher, Gwen Horn, over their choice of guavas, and she tells them to just pick a fruit and get on with it. Leo pulls one down and bites into it but spits it out before chewing and starts complaining to Gwen, "I told you, it's not ripe, why the hell were we told these were ripe? The presents probably took all the good ones. I can't take this preferential treatment." Leo's only my age, but he's a really swift talker.

"Leo, you don't speak to your elders that way, and certainly not your teachers," says Gwen. Gwen's Black and has short hair and wears a necklace with big ceramic charms.

"Gwen," Leo says. "If I were sold a bicycle whose chains all unraveled the moment I started pedaling, I'd be right to ask for a refund at the very least, if not a brand-new bicycle, and that's assuming I'm not even injured or traumatized."

"Leo."

"This guava," he says, holding it up, "is not a guava. A guava is a food. It provides nourishment. It is supposed to be fleshy and sweet. This is a green rock, not a guava. It's only fair that I get another. Which would really only be my first."

Leo's sister Lilly says, "Shut up and chew harder."

Gwen has turned away and occupied herself with the next student in line.

"Gwen!" Leo shouts.

"Quit being a turd," Lilly says to her brother.

Leo shoves Lilly. Lilly punches Leo in the face, and Leo drops his guava. Leo slaps Lilly's wrist and her half-eaten guava falls in the dirt. Roshana, skipping through the courtyard past them, squashes Lilly's guava. She lifts her foot to examine the underside.

"Roshana!" Lilly's voice is the highest I've ever heard a human's go. "What are you, spectral?" Then she shrieks, expressing her anger nonverbally.

Then Gwen Horn comes over because children are her real specialty—math is sort of her second love—and she gathers the three of them together in a huddle. Meanwhile, the line keeps moving since we don't need supervision because we're just picking fruit.

As soon as Gwen leaves the three of them—Roshana still holding her fruit and Lilly and Leo without theirs—Lilly pulls Roshana's hair and then takes Roshana's guava for herself. That seems to be the end of it for Roshana, but Leo and Lilly are still fighting over the half-eaten guava. Roshana bends to wipe her shoe clean. She looks around, and then slowly brings her hand to her lips and licks the juice off it.

"I want to live in a place where people love their lives," Sybil says. "Where people can do and be whatever they imagine. I have an imagination. I want to use my heart. I want to act."

"Well, you are amazing at it," I say.

"I get nothing from those dated, uninspired productions in the Part Center. I want to do new plays with real actors who care about making something the best it can be."

"That's what Arts Parts are for," I say.

"It's what the human heart is for."

"You sound like you've been talking to Helm," I say, with a tint of humor.

"Helm doesn't understand. If he did, he wouldn't be here. I have no reason to stay here."

"You have lots of reasons," I say, but I won't list them out loud. I don't want her to explain why these reasons aren't good enough to keep her in Canland. "You should talk to Helm about pre-Canland history. I think it will put things in perspective."

"Maybe, Tristan, but it also won't change the way things are. If I stay here, I'll contribute as, what, a mortician? And I'll live my whole life pretending I don't want anything more. My dad isn't even there. He's always gone, out of his mind, vacant. He's like cold air, passing between rooms. At least my mom died doing what she loved. This was a miserable year, and why won't next year be just as bad? I asked Dylan to show me what it was like out there, and he showed me people jumping off a mountain, and he said, 'This isn't how it is everywhere, but it's how it might get here. I don't want to see this place go that way.' I don't want to be here when more people I love get swallowed up by the boredom, or become so scared and desperate that they buy into this net-positive crap, Tristan—purity, becoming one with the Earth, all that. You don't understand. You don't get anxious. But so often it feels like I can't breathe."

She's smiling, but her lips tremble. I wish she had said something earlier. I think I would have been able to help.

"I used to pray to my mom," she says. "I used to ask her to come to me. I used to ask to hear her voice, her laugh. I want to see her in a dream. I want to be able to imagine her here again, but she keeps slipping out of my mind. I haven't heard her voice or seen her face once, in a dream, in a flash, even mistaking someone else for her. I need to find a place where I can hear her."

I don't remember Polly too well, just that she brought me some honey once. I can't taste it in my memory, but I bet I liked it. Helena had said, after Michael left on his most recent mission, fourteen months ago, that Polly, a devoted apiarist, makes a real contribution to the environment, instead of investigating theoretical matrices like Michael and a certain son of Michael's (aka Dylan), which is the highest praise I think one can get from Helena. But then, of course, Polly died on an excursion for her contribution, so it makes sense that Helena wouldn't want me to specialize in entomology.

We walk all the way up from the back of the line to the guava tree. Sybil's taller than most of the boys. She reaches up and picks two fruits and gives them both to me.

"Do you understand what I'm telling you?" Sybil says.

"Yes."

"You've made this past year livable. Do you hear me?" she says. "You have made my life better."

"Thank you," I say.

"Remember my first day back at school after my mom's funeral? The birds were all acting funny, and at the end of the day, when everyone was walking out of the school, all those crows flew across the path, and everyone ducked, and you just stood there, and a crow landed on you and just perched right on your head? That was the hardest I've ever laughed in my life." She laughs a little now. "When I got home that day, I finally, for the first time, cried about my mom, for hours. I wanted so badly to tell her about the connection you had with nature, like the birds knew something about you, that they could sense you weren't afraid, and you wouldn't harm them."

I remember, but I didn't think much of it at the time. The memories near the surface for me are: stifling our laughter during Polly's funeral; and the time Sybil heard Leo call me *the stuff of nightmares*, and she said to Leo, "The person who shared a womb with you doesn't even like you, what does that say?" and then Lilly corroborated that fact—"It's true, Leo, I don't like you"—and then Sybil gave me a tight hug and we walked home holding hands; and there was the time that Dylan climbed on the roof of our house to impress Sybil and she just watched from the street and curled her hair around her finger while Helena screamed at Dylan to get down, but then he did a headstand on the roof and Helena went inside and said, "Let him fall for all I care, he deserves to die," and Sybil just kept curling her hair around her finger. Then Dylan did a front flip on the eave and wobbled but kept his balance, and Sybil turned to me and said, "Why's he doing that?" and I replied, "I think he's trying to impress you." "Will you tell him I think he's being impressively stupid?" she said, and then we both laughed. But that was before she and Dylan stopped being close. Now I guess Sybil isn't close enough with anyone to keep her here.

She's been watching me, waiting for me to finish thinking.

"Please don't go," I say.

"I can't live here," Sybil says.

"Do you know where you're going?"

"Yes. I can't tell you, though. If anyone found out, they could come find me."

"What if someone wanted to find you?"

"If they really wanted to, they could. You could one day—but not yet. Stay here a bit longer. Take care of your health. Learn everything you can. Then come find me."

"Dylan's in love with you, you know."

"I know. He'll be fine."

"Well, when are you leaving?"

"I don't know."

"Maybe never?"

She sighs and smiles, but it's not her humorous smile. "Maybe."

I look down at the two guavas in my hands, then up at her again. "What about our walks? Who's going to walk me home from school?"

"You can walk yourself home. I think you've been able to do that on your own for a long time."

"I don't know," I say. Sybil's always believed in me. She's helped me grow. I wouldn't even know how to joke without her. If this is what she wants, then I can't get in the way of it. The least I could do is believe in her.

We pace the perimeter of the square courtyard, staying close to the school's cement walls that enclose the dirt on which present boys fake-punch each other, future girls eavesdrop from just outside the huddles of present girls, a future boy sneaks up behind a present girl and pinches her bottom, and Gwen Horn leads him out of the courtyard and into the school by the ear. Malakai, Asher's adopted son, sits against the wall in the shade with his knees pulled up to his chest, looking at the unbitten guava in his hand.

I take a bite of one of my two guavas. It's perfectly ripe. The seeds snap between my dentures. After I'm finished with it, and I'm holding the second guava in my hand, Sybil takes my empty hand in hers. She's wearing all her rings—rose quartz with a pink striated luster, the love stone; obsidian, blacker than putting your head inside your shirt indoors at night and shutting your eyes; and Lemurian quartz, containing lost and magical lands. Each stone set in a gold band.

She hugs me and kisses me on the forehead, and some present boys whoop and holler, but Sybil just smiles at me and ignores them.

"Thank you for everything," she says.

"You're welcome. Thank you."

Sybil lets go of my hand and turns and passes through the sandy courtyard for the indoors, for the last time, maybe, but I hope not. Perhaps she'll have some change of heart later tonight as she is gathering her things and readying to set out, thinking of everyone she's leaving behind, remembering all the wonderful things about Canland. No, not for the last time, I am choosing to believe. But she doesn't look back or stutter a step or graze a hand along the side of the building. Nor does she glance at Malakai, seated beside the doorway, who doesn't look up at her or even seem to notice that she's passed him either, as if by her own declaration of intent she is invisible, as he too seems to be, sitting in the shade of a guard tower. Today and every day this week the towers have been garrisoned because of the violence on the day of the effigy burning. The mood at school was somber on the day we mourned Sol Diaz.

I step up to Malakai, proffering to him my second guava. He waves his hand to signal a *no, thanks*. He probably knows it was Dylan who split his tree in half.

"Sorry," I say.

"For what?" he says.

I'm not stupid. I can tell when people think I'm stupid by how they look at me and by their inflection. I remember when Sybil helped me interpret inflections. She would say *What* am I doing, What *am* I doing, What am *I* doing, What am I *doing*? Then we argued by going back and forth saying, *I* love you, I love *you*, I *love* you! Michael said deciphering people is enough of an art to sustain humanity, and he's a researcher. But even his research carried him out of Canland. Helm's an artist, and he lives here. But is he happy here? Would he be more of an artist if he left? Is he fighting the urge to leave too?

I abandon the train of thought, the way Helena wants me to when I get obsessive, and turn my focus to Malakai. I know he knows that I know he knows about Dylan. What I don't know is what it's like to have your parents die, and to be a DOTEC, and to have people hate you for it and kill the tree you and your adoptive father carried across the continent to Canland, looking for a home for yourselves and your pomegranates.

"What?" he says, loudly. He holds up his guava. "I have one." It is still unbitten.

"Do you not want another?"

"Please leave me alone."

Malakai's about Dylan's age, but while Dylan's got sort of an axolotl-like youth to his features, Malakai's brow is like a geological formation, his eyes hiding in caves. I leave him alone.

I'd like to give the guava to Roshana, but she's under the tree, jumping and swiping at the branches, sweating down her temple.

Gwen Horn appears outside again and shouts for Roshana to stop. "You've already gotten yours! Take it from Leo. If you'd crashed your bike, you wouldn't get another, would you?"

"But I didn't crash my guava; it was stolen," Roshana says.

"Unfortunately, stolen items are usually not replaced in full by the seller," says Gwen.

Then a present boy whose name I don't know calls over, "That sounds like some Traditionalist crap to me."

And Leo says, "Tell me, I'd like to know, what's so awful about Traditionalism? Sounds great to me, in fact, since, if this was a Traditionalist society, I'd bet you on my life that my parents would make a better living than Helena Damon-Weekes. Admit it, Tristan."

"Admit what?" I ask, now involved.

"Jeez, look at you—you got a second guava. My parents are accountants. Without them, Canland would fall apart. Your mom's a seamstress. You only get everything because of your dad, and he doesn't even live in Canland anymore. You shouldn't have even been born!"

"Enough!" Gwen Horn marches into the middle of the courtyard. Everyone is looking at her. "We don't speak to or about each other like that. The health of Canland begins here, in school, at that tree, with that piece of fruit in your hand." She is yelling, pointing at my hand, but she's looking at everyone at once. "It's not about a guava—it's about how one person can ruin it for everyone. If you want more than what's granted simply because you want it, and you think that because you want it means you deserve it, then we will repeat all our past mistakes! We have to learn, or there will be no more guava tree to pick from. Does everyone understand?"

In the silence, I think about how the Laughtons are probably withheld certain benefits because of Leo and Lilly's being twins, which is a circumvention of the Part's population control laws, while I, however, am technically a violation. But because Helena and Michael are founders and Michael's a researcher, we aren't withheld anything—we have our own house, and priority at the Safe Haven, and Leo doesn't know it, but we have a computer and a Sensorium. I think it's reasonable that Leo might not be so fond of me.

The hammering bell kills the silence, and Gwen waves her hand, and everyone shuffles back inside.

But I linger, then go back to the tree and place the second guava at its base. I notice as I stretch out my hand that Sybil's pink ring is on my left ring finger.

.

There are few things that are truly fast, like birds, solar-powered vehicles, and baseballs. People walk pretty slowly, vegetables take time to boil, and even fires are slow; they just give the illusion of speed because they're constant. Maybe it's because fast things usually end fast. Like the valley gusts, which sometimes get up to fifty or eighty miles per hour, but only for a moment, and then the air is still, as the eucalypti, aka blue gums, rattle with the remnants of the speed they've sliced up for our safety. Gravity, on the other hand, makes the Earth spin so fast we don't even feel it— so fast that nature had to build opposing forces like feathers and roots and even the moon. Gravity makes things fall so fast that I don't register the moment before the Earth swings up to meet my chin, and so there's no resistance to absorb the impact that's resulted in my chin being covered in dirt and blood. Fortunately, I didn't bite my tongue—if I hadn't already bitten the tip off, this might have been the end of it! It's not like I had very far to go, only about four feet, so it's probably good that I didn't lock my arms in front of me or I might have two broken wrists.

My parasol has slid out of reach. I push up to my hands and knees. Leo's straight ahead of me, clutching his gonads through his shorts and moving the whole fistful in a circular motion, waggling his tongue. He picks up my parasol and comes toward me, slapping it in his open palm, and with his practiced baseball bat swing, he thwaps me in the upper arm. He's a very good baseball player and often complains about there being no serious competition, but brags that he'll still one day make it to an Athletics Part. I get to my feet and ask, "Did you just push me?"

He repeats what I've said, only with a lisp to make fun of me, and then says, "Where's your girlfriend? Did she realize you're spectral and then run away?" He thwaps me again, but in the side of the thigh. I just feel quick pressure and a tingle. Leo laughs and says, "Jeez, you really are an experiment, huh?" and raises the parasol over his head like a hatchet, but then Lilly tugs the parasol downward from behind him and tries to wrest it from his grasp. Then Roshana joins the cause of yanking my parasol away from Leo. I set my knapsack down and start to clean and bandage up my chin. I hear Leo shouting obscenities at Lilly, and when I look up, she's flailing her foot, trying to kick him between the legs, but Leo grabs his sister's leg and twists it. They both fall to the ground—Leo trying to push Lilly's face in the dirt, Lilly still trying to strike Leo in the lower abdomen. All the four hundred other students are up ahead on the path, walking home and not seeing this, except for Roshana, who's standing beside me, watching with me. She sighs loudly and puts her hair in a ponytail, smoothing the loose strands off her face. My parasol's next to her foot like a dead snake, unaware of its insentience. Roshana hands it to me.

"Thank you," I say.

"You're welcome." Roshana's very pretty, I think. She's shorter than me, has skin darker than Gwen's, and usually eats three dried apple slices at a time, like a sandwich. She also asks the DOTEC presents lots of questions, but they ignore her, and yet she keeps asking more questions like, *So, you really never lived in a Part before?* and, *What was the deadliest animal you saw out there?* The DOTEC tend to sit together at lunch, and the Canlanders voice some concern that the DOTEC are plotting to steal their food, and I actually even once saw the Canlander presents all at once cover their plates when Malakai walked by. There are a lot more

Canlanders than DOTEC, who actually aren't even DOTEC anymore since they're registered now, with the most recent batch having been registered about a year ago. I overheard last week after the crazed bearded man on the hillock attacked Sybil, a Canlander present say to Malakai, *Wait, so you're a* DOTEC *orphan—that means you should jump off the Notch and free up some resources, right?* Helm overheard that one too, and punished the kid with shifts in energy manufacturing, which people say is a horrible place to have to go because of all that pedaling with hot energy units buzzing around you just to create, like, a hundred calories. But other than that, the kids are mostly friendly toward one another—it's important we all get along, so conflict gets resolved quickly.

Lilly bites Leo's wrist and Leo punches her in the side of the head and she bites down harder and Leo screams and pulls his wrist away so fast he starts bleeding. He's crying, and Lilly's crying too, as he goes running off, and she chases after him, yelling, "I'm sorry, Leo! You started it!" and he yells back at her, "Leave me alone! I hate you!"

"You OK?" Roshana says to me.

"Yes."

"Sorry Leo sucks."

"I don't think that's your fault."

Roshana laughs with her mouth open like she's waiting for another guava to magically appear between her teeth.

"My dad never wanted me to go to school," I say. "He thought it was too dangerous."

"That's weird."

"He thought he could teach me better, and he was right, but my mom said I had to go or I wouldn't learn how to interact with people."

"Your chin is bleeding."

As I'm redoing my gauze and bandage, Roshana says, "I have to go."

"Oh." I finish patching up my wound. "Do you want to walk home together?"

"I think we live on different streets."

She starts walking ahead.

"Want to be friends?" I say, several paces behind.

Roshana turns around and shrugs. "I don't know. Sometimes you say smart things in class. And I guess you're nice. So we can be friends. But don't tell anyone, OK?"

"OK," I say.

"See you tomorrow."

"Bye."

She starts skipping forward, but then settles into a normal walk.

The day's burning bright. I stop and take a sip of water. Pollution mask and sun goggles on. Parasol up. Heart rate: 78—perfectly normal, no beta blocker required.

I turn around to glimpse the school again because sometimes the facade shines vibrant yellow in the afternoon sun. I see a COHO opening up the gates and Malakai reentering the grounds. Helm greets him and places an arm around his shoulders, taking him back into the building. The school is the color of egg yolk. The barbed wire atop the cement wall glints. I start my walk home, without Sybil.

Canland's not a prison. In the WORLD Rehabilitation Parts, unscrupulous people live in tiny cells with others like them, and they perform the most unpleasant tasks, like wading through landfills and spraying the thousand-year half-life garbage with organic matter so that insects will feast on it and accelerate the decomposition process, or harvesting crops to be sent to WORLD xenodochia—for all the wandering DOTEC in need of assistance—only to find themselves sitting down to a meal of necrotic vegetables. And there is no autonomous expulsion from a Rehabilitation Part; you are killed if you try to escape. That's not Canland. We don't have people here who are guilty of espionage or murder (Long Term Rehabilitation), nor of energy theft or planting invasive species (Short Term). I don't know what Sybil is looking for. There are Introduction Parts (for controlled invasive species) and Idealist Parts (where everyone is healthy and there is never a shortage of rations or entertainment) and Athletics Parts and Arts Parts and Spectral Parts (where people with abnormal neurological conditions receive coveted benefits for being research subjects) and Technological Parts (where things are always invented) and Post-Industrial Parts (where nothing is invented) and Cosmopolitan Parts and Metropolitan Parts and Defense Parts and a range of Research Parts and, of course, Rehabilitation Parts, plus some other Parts I can't remember (there's even something called a Rogue Part, which is a horrible thing where DOTEC steal and hide from WORLD), but none of them is better than a Restoration Part, where life is always springing up around us and we contribute extensively to the health of the Earth.

I hope Sybil's happy, wherever she goes. But what I really hope is that she shows up at my door tomorrow morning, saying, *Hey, Tristan, ready for school?*

Helena will want to know why Sybil isn't at the top of the street as I come home, like always. And she will want to know why I have a fresh bandage on my chin. I will say that Sybil had to pick up hygiene products from market and was given grief about her registration status by a Practicalist kiosk attendant on account of some shoddy administrative work as the month turned over and she was apparently unaccounted for in the most recent census. She was feeling woozy because of something to do with the reason for which she needed the hygiene product, and trying to be conscientious, I insisted she go straight to her home to take care of herself, assuring her that I am capable of walking a half-mile home alone without incurring an injury. And everything was going very smoothly up until I fell on the way down our street, if you can believe it, right up there on that rock, and I chose to bandage it up right there on the spot as low-stakes practice for caring for myself. One could even say I became less helpless today. Isn't that excellent, Helena?

I will definitely not tell her what really happened.

I repeat the story to myself as I round the Part Center, nearing the pasture by the hillock.

I hear two DOTEC laughing and see them double-high-five beneath the coast live oak. One of them leans back against the tree with her hand on her curving stomach. The other stands and stretches their arms up high, and the light pouring through the leaves and branches of the oak, as if glass were separating us from the sun, makes the person appear not quite real, or once real, but now phantasmic, from some other time, visiting. This is the person I wrote about in my journal. They are waving in my direction.

I turn around and face the Part Center. There's a dark starlike pattern in the Earth where the effigy burned atop the iron pedestal with a penumbra of windswept char surrounding it. Some of my fellow futures are running through the outfield, screaming and smiling, leaving footprints in the blackness.

I look back at the pale green hillock and see the wild-haired person coming toward me.

3

Oct 10–11, 2088

I thought it was strange they recognized me—since they'd only
seen my face for the brief moment I'd taken off my mask and goggles while Sybil was giving away her rations—until they pointed
out that I was the only one in Canland they'd seen wearing a
pollution mask and sun goggles in the couple weeks since they'd
arrived. I explained to them, Everyone else stopped wearing theirs
a couple months after the bandit miners topped the mountain, but
the dynamited peak still sometimes burps hazardous particulates
into the air, plus the sun goggles are more of a reminder not to
stare into the sun than protection against it, even though I now
and then forget anyway.

Then they let out a little giggle. Their voice was sort of high and
tremolo like hummingbird wings. I like the way you talk, they
said with a giant smile of overlapping teeth. And then they said,
I'm AB, what's your name? Tristan, I told them. Then AB said that
even without my face gear, they'd still recognize me as the one
whose mom's head they burned, with the brother who goes on the
nightly bike rides, and the tall girlfriend who always walks him

home. You always seem to have a space carved out next to you, they said. Sybil's not my girlfriend, I said. AB made a complicated face and said, OK sure, but also, even besides all that, your hair, I always notice your hair. My hair? I asked. Yeah, your hair, your hair, they said. I like your hair, should I say it again? No, that's OK, I said.

The way AB spoke to me, so easily and without interrupting themself, the way they were always moving, adding in words like their mouth moved faster than their brain, and especially the way they laughed, throwing their head back with a clenched grin, was like a person who'd gotten so good at being a person and having a body, they didn't have to think about it. Now and then, AB would reach up, their elbows high like pterodactyl wings, and shake out their oily, curly black hair falling like vine around their face, and their eyes, which were so light a blue, they were translucent and reflective, like water, and barely had any pupils at all, blinked and then got wide, while their jaw looked like it chewed the back of their tongue, laughing and talking at the same time. I could never move that freely.

AB said they remembered my face was remarkable, but couldn't remember what it looked like, and asked if they could see it again. When I took my mask off and exchanged my tinted sun goggles for my normal ones, they said, So what's the story? And I said, Analgesia, and AB smiled and made many simultaneous movements with their face and limbs and said, No way. I said, Yes way. AB laughed and shook their hair out, and then they pulled the skin of their tricep and it stretched for inches and inches, then returned to its form when they let go, and then AB said, I have EDS. I asked, What's that? And they said, Ehlers-Danlos Syndrome, a connective tissue disorder—it's like I'm mostly made of air, you could say. And I said, You are mostly made of air. Then AB made a face I guess like a snarl and said, Ha-ha. Does that hurt? I asked. AB said, Everything sorta always hurts, if you can't tell. They indicated all their blooming bruises like purple and yellow galaxies, permanent ones like the darkened pith at the center of a tree, and fresh ones like ink stains.

I said, What's it like to always be in pain? AB said, I got my ways of coping with it, but usually it's like I wanna crawl out of my body and see what's left of it. The realest wound, though, is how I'm fifteen and I already know how I'm gonna die, which is a feeling that comes and goes like a stray animal looking for food, but at least the pain's constant, almost like a pet. And, you know, life's not going to be kind or fair to me, and that's fine, not every person gets a kind, fair life, that's just the way it is, there's no real reason for it, and I can cope with that, but I also do think the one thing—because everyone should have one thing of their own they know to be true—is that every person should have the time when they're young and feel like they can live forever. But my heart's gonna fail one day, a valve's gonna tear, and unless a surgeon's standing over me when it happens, well, I just hope I get a moment of painlessness to say, Oh man, what a beautiful life, or at least the wherewithal to decide for myself that that's not true, that life was shit, but to get to not be afraid at the end of it, you know? Just to be able to say a few words, put my stamp on my own life, and maybe someone will remember I was here.

I said, Well I'm the opposite, in a way. I have to diagnose every little thing that happens to me, or else a paper cut could be my demise.

Your lisp is cute, AB said, then laughed, shaking out their hair and looking all around. I supposed that, being DOTEC, they probably weren't used to the natural beauty of Canland.

Do you like living here? I said.

AB said nothing as their eyes memorized my face—not in the furtive, disguised way that Sybil's explained to me, when people see me and then look quickly away, self-conscious of their awareness of my facial abnormalities, feeling bad for feeling bad, even though they don't realize that I have no feelings of self-consciousness of my own about my face, but in a way that made me believe that AB's also gotten used to other people looking at them in unusual ways. This rare emotional recognition I displayed had made me feel like I knew AB better than I realistically could have after only a few minutes. AB finally said in response to my question, The tree's nice.

They were wearing baggy pants and no shirt, and the way their torso looked in combination with their cheeks, jaw, and throat made me ask, Are you a girl? and AB said, No, I'm not a girl, and I'm not a boy either. I got a lot of ways of categorizing myself, but boy or girl's not one of them.

Which made sense to me. I don't think that my behavior is all that informed by my chromosomal makeup, but maybe I'd think differently if I had some other combination.

(To note: I hope I am doing AB's voice justice; I've never heard anyone talk like them before. This is a difficult exercise, placing myself in someone else's shoes, but perhaps, as Michael might think, a necessary one, the culmination of all the fiction he read me. I also probably have Helm to thank for his Creative Thought and Expression class.)

AB said, The differences between boy and girl are wider than I've got the stuff to span.

I wasn't sure what they meant, but they winked and poked the tip of their tongue out, and kept on talking.

They said, What I'm worried about is that Sasha's six months along, and I'm thinking it's not super likely that Canland's gonna lavish acceptance upon the DOTEC popping out of another DOTEC—not in this political climate. Hopefully, she can get registered before that, but even if she does, I've had better days out there than I'd've had here if I was registered is the truth. It's boring here, don't you think, and the people are nasty, sullen, violent, like they're expecting it to all go away any second.

I like it, I wasn't shy to say.

Yeah. Well, what's a Restoration Part gonna want with a DOTEC like me, always a heartbeat away from death, all the contributing day . . . I'm more of an idea person anyway, if you know what I mean.

Yeah, I said, I like ideas. It runs in my family. My mom writes laws and speeches and my dad is a WORLD researcher who goes on classified missions.

Wouldn't go around shouting that through cupped hands, you know, if I were you. I saw a lot of DOTEC out there plotting to take down WORLD researchers and all the people who get the big benefits. Then AB grimaced and said, Sorry, Tristan. I didn't mean to freak you out. I'm sure your dad's fine.

I said, It's OK, my mom reminds us often of the possibility that he's never coming back. Although, if he does die on his mission, I'd prefer it be by natural causes, rather than a technological debacle, or a militia.

Or that he not die at all? AB said.

Well, then he'd be choosing not to return, I said.

AB narrowed their eyes and stepped so their face was right in front of mine, blocking out the bright metallic sky. That was the best look I got at their eyes. I noticed that in the blue surrounding their pinhole pupils was a corona of yellow, and their irises were enclosed by thin black circles. They're taller than me, so they had their head tilted down, and their wild curly hair fell in front of their face, and I felt a distinct certainty that our recent ancestors had come from very faraway parts of the Earth, and yet here we were in Canland, standing face to face in the pasture, an oak tree on the hillock behind AB that they're sleeping under tonight, in the middle of a greened desert valley between two mountain ranges as permanent as anything.

Just as I was starting to wonder where they'd come from, AB said to me, You know, I was in a militia. It was the most exciting and miserable year of my life. We camped, we traveled, we fought. Everyone in the company was starving to death. I'd never seen people so deranged; they barely looked human. When people starve, their hands and feet swell up, and their eyes go big and empty, and then the body starts eating itself. They go crazy. So anyway, a rover passed through, and I abandoned the company.

What's a rover? I asked.

AB grinned and curled their tongue against the back of their top teeth, and said, What a beautiful thing, to be able to ask that question. Rovers are just SPVs driven by WORLD overseers of order, in the Partless land, hunting for DOTEC. The rover that found me took me to a xenodochium, but it was overcrowded, so they gave me the option to either remain a DOTEC, or go to a Part for orphans. I chose the latter. It was terrible. The people were violent. There were barely any rules. It was easy to get tubes, though, and I need tubes to manage my pain. I started six years ago. I was only nine. Now I can't stop. Once, my pain was so bad that I thought of ending it. Then I got a fresh tube, but it was too dense, and I inhaled too much, and they had to resuscitate me. Then the Part expelled me. Sasha found me sleeping under a highway. She wasn't even two months pregnant then. We went to the coast, just to see it, like a final event, but we were still alive at the end of it, maybe because it didn't seem so amazing to us, it was just water and debris. So then we wanted to find a Part, and she followed the infrastructure leading from the water desalination plant all the way up to here.

I didn't know what to say, perhaps because I'd never experienced any life event of that scale, aside from my time with Michael in the Sensorium, and I'm not supposed to talk about that, so I said nothing.

AB licked their top teeth inside their lip. They said, I bet painlessness is like a form of blindness, like, not an absence of suffering, but a suffering from absence.

I replied, It's an interesting question. Then . . . well, I wish I'd referred AB to my favorite book *One Hundred Years of Solitude* and said that it's as if my parents are the Buendías, and I am Melquíades' Sanskrit prophecy, and they've spent a century trying to decipher me, all the while practicing their own alchemies and fighting an endless war against the banana republic.

Or I wish I'd said, The harvestman knows pain before it even feels it, but it is kind for that, and instead of attacking when attacked, it will detach its body from a leg to avoid death, and will cluster with thousands of others like a massive cloud of smoke, so when a predator approaches, the cloud will animate and disperse and send the predator running for easier targets, as if the harvestman's whole mode of survival is based on pretending to be scary, and while most other arachnids are sort of cannibalistic loners, Opiliones are gregarious pacifists.

But what I think I actually said was—and I'm sorry, journal, for the possibility of falsifying past events, it isn't my intention to alter reality, but only to understand it and how it takes shape in my individual perception, which is only one element in a set of a billions that, like Michael says, comprise the entire set, and when one element is altered, the set is altered (and we logically arrive at the necessary pursuit of perception and truth bending toward each other, oh, Michael would be so proud if he knew I remembered all this)—Well, you see, AB, my parents tried to give me the tools for answering emotional questions with logical means, so while I can, for instance, arrive at a conclusion that my mother will be angry at me if I put myself in danger, it isn't an impulse in me to avoid a situation just because it's dangerous.

AB's eyes opened wide. They shook their head at me. They showed their teeth and said, Oh god, what did they do to us? Then they laughed again and moved their hands all through their hair so it got even bigger and curlier, and it was like we were at the beginning of the conversation again. I didn't want to stop looking at them.

In books, when people are in love, sometimes they sweat. But I don't sweat, so I couldn't rely on that. Still, my feeling is that I would like to observe AB at all hours of the day and learn how they eat and sleep and maybe even go to the bathroom. And also that I want them to observe me eating, sleeping, etc.

I laughed and said, I don't know, and shrugged my shoulders to show it. I was holding my pollution mask in one hand, sun goggles in the other.

We can be friends, you know, AB said. I said, I would love that. Then AB touched my arm and said, Look, Tristan, I wouldn't ask you this if I wasn't desperate, but your brother, he's a waste contributor, right? Is there a shot in the world you'd be able to ask him for me if he'd be able to get me tubes? I'd ask him myself, but you know how it's hard for DOTEC—there's a certain perception of us, and people make up reasons for why we still don't have homes. But I trust you. I feel connected to you. I don't want you to think it's the only reason I want to be friends, but I'm just in a lot of pain. I have one left, and it's almost empty. I dread having to try to sleep tonight.

I can't even imagine, I said.

AB looked away with just their eyes, then back at me, and asked, How old are you?

Almost thirteen, I said.

Well, AB said, maybe I'll even give you a kiss.

You don't have to do that, I said. I'll help you because I like you.

Then AB laughed and kissed me on the cheek and ran back up the hillock. The grass seemed made of springs. If I looked only at the hillock, I was able to imagine that all of Canland was grass, and for a moment, it was all I saw.

I made a decision to keep my conversation with AB to myself. But that meant wanting to write it all down. So, as I was walking home, and reciting to myself the specifics of the conversation, the specifics of my day with Sybil were squeezed out of my memory, maybe my last day ever with Sybil. She told me she was leaving Canland, and that she's not happy here. She even gave me her ring, as if it were a screw to keep her secret safe inside me.

Without her, I will be OK. But it might be the first time I'm not OK. Who knows? Maybe Roshana and I will become best friends. Maybe AB will teach me everything Sybil wanted to know for herself. After Michael left home, Helm became a good friend of mine. Only recently have I learned that life is made of people passing in and out.

At the top of my street, I took off Sybil's ring and put it in my knapsack so Helena wouldn't see it. Helena was working in the garden when she spotted me. She stood up, holding a trowel. She said, Where's Sybil? And I said, She had to pick up hygiene products from market and then she felt sick and went home. I fell, but I bandaged up my chin because I thought it would be a good opportunity to practice caring for myself and being independent.

So why are you late? she said.

Because at market there was a census bungle and Sybil had to argue with a Practicalist kiosk attendant who was dubious of her registration status and refused at first to give her the required hygiene products.

All right, all right, Helena said. Go inside so I can check you.

She took a wicker basket full of vegetables from our garden inside, and stored them in our trapdoor. She gave me an antibiotic and had me take off my clothes so she could check if there were any other scrapes or bruises, which there weren't. Then I sat on the toilet and waited for a poop to happen. She said, Remember not to push; call for me if you need me. Which I didn't. Then we ate eggs and tomatoes for dinner. Helena cooks it different ways, sometimes as huevos rancheros and other times as shakshuka, and it is always delicious. She's a chef and everything else.

After dinner, I did some Economic Austerity homework while Helena did her own writing at the table with her evening grappa. Dylan came out to grab a brick of cheese, but then went right back to his room without saying anything. It was a nice evening. Helena tucked me into bed.

But for some reason, I couldn't fall asleep. When I heard the door to Helena's room finally close, I got out of bed and started to write. It's after 0100h now.

There goes Dylan's door, open and shut.

There goes the front door too.

I could have seen him, but I hesitated. He won't be back for hours.

I could have written more about Sybil, but I don't accept her decision to leave.

I'm going to try to sleep again. I'll play imaginary piano on the mattress by my sides; a new song for AB. When I close my eyes, their face is all I see.

.

October 11, 2088

Sybil came to pick me up for school today! There was a knock at the door, Helena opened it, and there she was, just as I imagined. On our walk to school, I asked if she'd changed her mind. She said, There are a lot of people who rely on me. I replied, Yes there are, and when an element is removed from the set, the set is different, and who knows how Canland would function without you? To which Sybil said, I don't think the absence of one person alone can change how a Part runs. Trying to be wry, I said back, That's very Purist of you.

Sybil tipped her head back to see up into the branches of a copse of eucalypti. When she brought her eyes back down to the path, she said, Is your mom OK these days?

Helena has known Sybil basically since birth. When Sybil used to come over to play with Dylan, and I would watch, Helena would call her Sweetie. Helena hasn't called her Sweetie in years, probably. After Polly died, Helena would have private conversations with Sybil at the edge of our lawn, and Sybil would be looking down and away at the pale grass like she wasn't listening. Sometimes, Helena would hug Sybil. And sometimes, Sybil would just walk away. I know Helena was helping her, but maybe she was also testing to see if Sybil was in a state of mind to safely walk me to and from school, or if she was made delusional by grief.

I said to Sybil, Helena's been writing a lot, so she doesn't have as much time to talk, but she still finds time to preempt ailments I didn't even know I'd have.

That's good.

She's the best mom ever, I added.

Sybil was quiet after that. I realize, now, as I grow this stack of papers I keep hidden under my mattress, it's probably because she was thinking of her own mother.

We passed the Part Center. I tried to see AB, but I couldn't find them among the many DOTEC huddled under the oak tree for shade. I asked Sybil, Have you ever been in love?

68

I don't know why she took so long to answer because, after we'd taken maybe thirty or forty more steps—and by which time, there were other presents and futures walking nearby on the same road to school—all she did was shake her head.

I might be, I said.

Oh, really? she said.

Yes, I said. But I can't tell you who it is.

I see, she said. Secret love.

Well, I haven't decided yet, I said.

If anyone could fall in love here, Tristan, it's you. Sybil usually doesn't talk much to other presents or futures, but she seemed today to be paying more attention to each of them as the walking crowd thickened.

Are there places where people can't fall in love? I asked.

Sybil laughed loudly in a way I've never heard her laugh, almost like a yell. Other kids turned their heads at her. Then she said, Remember, a lot of parents met during the Evanescence.

I smiled to myself because it seemed Sybil was coming around to the fact that Canland is not as bad as she was thinking yesterday. We were quiet on the rest of the walk to school.

I fell asleep in class a few times because I stayed up late journaling last night. I even dreamed about AB, but as soon as I was woken up by a teacher or fellow future tapping on my shoulder, I forgot the dream, and went back to drawing a web of mutual beneficence, with Arturo Eagles and WORLD at the center, out to rungs of Research Centers, then to ladders of Parts, spreading to each individual contributor, even as I wished to go back to dreaming of AB's face.

I saw Sybil again as we left school. I asked how her day was.

Boring, she said.

I did a chuckle and said, Me too.

We didn't talk the rest of the walk, which sometimes happens. When she dropped me off at home, I said to her, I'm really happy you decided to stay.

She waved to me with both hands, walking backward, then

turned fast and ran up the street and disappeared around the copse of trees.

What are you smiling about? Helena asked when I got in the door.

I had a great day, I said.

Then I sat at the table with an early dinner of red beans and chopped celery, and Helena put her writing aside for a moment to ask me questions about what I learned and who I sat with at lunch, and as I answered, she said she was very impressed that I remembered not to talk while I chew.

·

Oct 13, 2088

Yesterday morning Dylan came home from his waste run a little bit before I was expecting Sybil to arrive. Dylan said he saw Sybil outside the mortuary and she was about to bike here to apologize that she wouldn't be able to take me because she had to go to school early as she'd been assigned to sharpen the spades for Practice of Agriculture. So Dylan gave me a ride to school. He smelled like the breeze off a waste tank, his eyes were bloodshot, and his greasy hair was flattened to the sides of his head.

I didn't see Sybil at school or after. Helm walked me home. He talked about how baseball is a team sport made up of individual games, a metaphor for Canland. I asked him about hockey, skeptical that there had once been a sport played on a floor of ice. I've never seen ice, except in Actualizations. When Helm dropped me off, he gave me a fist bump and then shook out the fake pain and laughed, but I was too distracted to laugh.

Helena said, Don't worry about Sybil. She's not reliable; remember, she endangered you.

Once, Sybil was at our house shortly after Michael had left for his most recent mission, and Helena had shut herself in her bedroom, crying, which is the only time I can remember that happening, and Sybil and I played what she called the Dinner Party Game where we got to imagine all the guests we would like to have over and what they would talk like, and we got to act out the dinner party, and it is the most fun I can ever remember having. Then it was time for bed, but Helena still hadn't come out. So Sybil checked my scars, and one of them was fissured, so she applied an ointment and a bandage, and helped me with my finger caps too, before she went home in the dark. That's what I remembered.

Sybil didn't come this morning either. Helena was biting her thumbnail with one eyebrow higher than the other when she said, Come on, I'll take you. Then she also picked me up from school, and she rode us straight to the mortuary.

Tobias was crying, bent forward in his chair, holding a letter. His comb-over had fallen out of place. He was mumbling something that sounded like Sweet Pea when he saw us and looked up.

Where is she? He was looking at me.

I don't know, I said. I thought she was staying.

What do you mean you thought she was staying? Was there some other possibility?

Tobias stood up from his chair and there was a big bubble of silence between us before he popped it, shouting, Say something!

So I said that she wanted to be an actor. And she wanted to see her mom. And she was bored and miserable and wanted to go somewhere she could dream.

The bubble of silence returned as they stared at me like I was . . . well, here's what Tobias said, to pop the bubble again: What are you, an alien? Speak! Cry! Do something, you insensate insect!

Helena then placed a hand on my shoulder and held her other one up to Tobias. He stopped shouting and slumped down into his chair and curled his knees up, fetal, a hand over his face, saying in broken sentences, which I had to piece together, that when Polly died, even though he didn't have all the answers, he at least had the answer that silenced the other questions, that she lived her time, but that with Sybil now, he had no answers, and never would.

So I said, I'm sorry.

Helena said, For what?

I said, For lying.

If our feelings are just the secretion of hormones, then I am sometimes left to react as a plank of wood. Which Helena tells me is frustrating for my interlocutor. But if I fabricate an emotional reaction, my interlocutor would be reacting to my falseness, thereby eroding the integrity of their feelings, and their reaction to my reaction becomes too thin to hold the weight of either of our thoughts and feelings. Emotions are like transactions, and sometimes I have nothing to trade with.

I decided to wander around the mortuary while Helena stayed with Tobias. In Canland, coffins are relics—most people here are cremated or taken out of Canland altogether after they die, to the Waste Reallocation Center. If I had to choose a purpose for my body after it stopped working, I'd obviously want it to be made into energy, or the soil for a tree. But a cherry wood box lined with soft cotton would be nice too. I grabbed the corded handle of one I liked. Maybe Sybil couldn't take the coffins anymore. Maybe she couldn't take the thought of people jumping from the Notch when her mother did not decide to die. She kept a secret from me and left me without her, to do what she felt she needed to do. Does that mean we're no longer friends? I lied for her; I told no one she was wanting to leave. And now, the friend I believed I would always have, because I chose to believe it, is gone. She might as well be in a coffin.

When we got home, Helena banged on Dylan's door until he opened it. He ignored her.

Hey, Beautiful, he said to me.

Did you know? Helena said to him.

About what?

Sybil.

What about her?

If I find out you're lying, I'll throw you out of the house.

I don't know what you're talking about.

Tell him, Tristan.

Sybil left Canland, I said.

Dylan stared at me for a while. His face didn't change much. Are you OK? he said to me.

Yes, I said, wanting this to be over, wanting not to give him or Helena anything more to worry about.

Great, Dylan said. Then he went back into his room. I'll have to ask him for AB's tubes some other time. He must have known Sybil was going to leave, but if he's in love with her, then why did he let her go? Is it related to Michael's absence? I can't fathom an explanation.

Helena knelt in front of me. Her closed mouth was spread wide, the shadows deep along the sides. You're not getting the idea to run away, are you? she said. You have to tell me the truth.

I'm not, I said.

Promise me you'll never run away.

I promise.

You're the reason for everything, she said. You understand?

Yes, I said, even though I didn't completely understand. But it seemed important to Helena that I understood, and I think I understood enough. I'm the most important person in her life. She doesn't ever want me to feel hurt, even when it is necessary in order to understand something complicated and unpleasant, which might paradoxically require that I feel hurt, to a lesser degree, as a sort of practice, like when she conditions me, which obviously never hurts and just leaves my cheek or head or ear tingling sometimes, especially when Helena goes super hard or uses a fist—none of which she did tonight, for some reason. Maybe it was evident enough that I was sad about Sybil leaving.

But if Helena's not going to condition me, it has to be because I'm learning. From now on, the only secrets I'll hold are:

Michael's methods of teaching me through Actualizations, electrotherapy, hormones, novels, and music;

Dylan's interloping on satellites and his algae experiments;

all the hours I've played piano when Helena was out and Dylan was in his room (this one is different because it's a self-secret);

my friendship with AB, who I wish Sybil had met, because they are beautiful and know what beauty is, and they came to Canland because it's better here than out there.

Yes, I want to find Sybil, but it's not worth throwing away a life in Canland just for a chance to have better dreams.

4

AUTUMN'S HARVEST MAKES more work for Helena: darning gloves; repairing baskets, bags, and winnowing-fans; sewing thicker sleeves to mute the stingers of insects and the spurs of weeds, and keep the cuts clean; making hats and other gear that provide protection from the sun and ventilation in the heat; knee pad, shoe, and tool-belt repairs. When weight strains the stitches, Helena fixes them. She's a master; her ability to patch my wounds is only a glimpse into her expertise. She hand-sews all her clothes, and the pair of shoes I now have were a pair she made for some other child, years ago, which were passed down to me—after she made some repairs, obviously. (Dylan once asked me, *If you have a hammer, and it's the only hammer you've ever owned, and after years and years, you replace the handle one, two, ten times, and the head three, four, twenty times, but never the two pieces at the same time, have you still only had one hammer?* I said of course not. He said he wasn't so sure—*because of the essence,* he said, though he did not elaborate.) Since Michael left, Helena's had to spend a lot more time at her gear contribution, but she enjoys it. She likes the seamsters, the types of people who take on clearly defined and attainable tasks requiring sustained focus. Realistic people, she calls gear contributors, and all the people who contribute at the Crafts Contribution Compound.

Before she left for her contribution today, she nearly kicked in Dylan's door trying to get him to open up.

"Can you look after Tristan, and actually look after him?" she said to Dylan.

"I'd never let a bad thing happen to you, Beautiful," he said to me, ignoring her.

Helena said, "Not sitting in your room as you rot your brain, but really do something—teach him self-defense, read a book, go outside," she said. "You have my permission."

"I gotcha," Dylan said. "Set theory, Marxism, birds and bees; you are relieved, Helena."

Five minutes after she left, she came back in to find Dylan sitting on the floor with me, listening as I recited facts from *Fearsome Allies* and answered the quiz questions and hypotheticals he thought up to test my knowledge. Helena said she forgot something from her closet. For another five minutes after she left, Dylan and I continued our quiz game. Then he asked if I wanted to see the advancements that the algae had made in the tank in his room and the discoveries he'd made about the half-life of the reagent he acquired indirectly from the Canland College Research Center via his waste reallocation contribution.

As I peered into the tank full of spreading blue-green fuzz, Dylan calibrated the Sensorium. "To investigate the progress made on the Lake Superior cleanup via satellite commandeering," he said.

It's not recommended for anyone to guide themselves through a Sensorium, the risks being near-certain temporary and possibly permanent neurological damage, including vertigo and psychosis, which is one of the reasons why most people aren't allowed to possess their own Sensoriums, plus reasons pertaining to energy consumption and especially data access. Sensorium conductor at the Canland Sensatarium—which is made of a material that's very costly and difficult to obtain, but is well insulated, and where there is constant electricity in order to capture as many satellite feeds as possible—is a coveted and vital contribution. But Dylan has been doing this for years, and he learned from Michael, so there's no need to worry.

He's been in the Sensorium for the better part of an hour now.

"Where are you?" I ask, but uselessly. It's impossible to hear anything outside a Sensorium when your head's in it, which is why it takes so long for him to answer when we knock, if he even does answer.

The same could have been said for Michael, who came out of this room, which was once his office, unpredictably, and sometimes there wasn't any way of knowing if he was even in here, or if he'd gone off on a research assignment without telling anyone, and if we asked Helena where he was, she would say things to Dylan and me like, "Where do you go if you prioritize the pursuit of new axioms over the family you chose to have?" And Dylan replied with something to the effect of, "You do nothing, Helena—you sit and sew and drink and write, and then you stand up and proselytize with your loose logic and bad metaphors and false promises." Then Helena would threaten Dylan, "Watch your mouth, I'll send you to a Defense Part, where you'll learn to shoot a whistler and be a WORLD drone. How's that? You want to discover the Earth? You can drive a rover all over creation. Then you'll truly know what it means to be lost."

And after that, Dylan would leave the house on his chrome bicycle, and I would say to Helena, "If Michael devotes his existence to the pursuit of creating new axioms of existence, then is he himself anything other than a concept?" Sometimes Helena would condition me not to say things like that—things that would alienate me in social settings—or she'd just ignore me. But if I said something simple like, "If Michael cared, wouldn't he be here with us?" then Helena would hold me and kiss my head and tell me that, no matter what, she would always be here.

Dylan flinches like he does when he's falling in a dream. When I have that dream, I just keep falling. He turns his head left and taps the sensory pad with each finger on his right hand, then does the same on the opposite side.

Some aquatic insect I don't know the name of swims through a small pond of algae. The water tank burbles. A millipede is motionless in the clear side of the water. The tiny pond farts a bubble of methane. Extrapolate this to Lake Superior. It's like another Evanescence. Millions more DOTEC.

The other day, I was with Helena, and I saw AB walking through market. Our eyes met, they winked at me from between two busy kiosk lines, and I raised my hand to wave. But then their eyes went wide and they started shaking their head, so I touched my pollution mask and then my sun goggles as if I were innocuously making adjustments. Helena grabbed my hand. AB tousled their hair to cover their face, stuck their hands in their pockets, and wove their way through the crowd, pirouetting past an apple vendor, and then took off running into the Part Center as Leo Laughton cracked a baseball in a rainbow arc across the sky. AB took off in a sprint, shagged the fly ball down, caught it barehanded, wheeled and threw it back to home plate in one fluid motion. Other kids whooped and gaped, and Leo hammered his bat overhead into home plate. Then AB sat in the grass and ate the apple they'd stolen from the vendor, core and all, watching someone fly a kite.

After a minute, a COHO came down from the hillock, all the way across the pasture and into the Part Center, seized AB by the elbow, and marched them back up to the coast live oak tree. Once up there, AB stepped out of the shade and waved to me again with both their arms, jumping up and down so their hair bounced, and I think they understood what I was saying to them by not waving back.

I open the drawer of Dylan's dresser. There's a tube right there on his pile of shirts. I pick it up and roll it between my fingers, put my eye to it to see what's inside—nothing but some sticky opiate that looks like fat built up inside an artery. I put it back where I found it. So many powerful things seem unremarkable at a glance.

The monitor rolls lines of inscrutable code, abbreviations and representations Michael never taught me and that, no matter how long I stare at the screen, I will never understand—it looks to me the way sheet music might to someone with no instruction, no instrument, no reference but their own imperfect voice, groping for middle C.

At some point while I was thinking up that wonderful simile, the lines stopped rolling, leaving a visual silence behind (thanks to all of Michael's work with me, these linguistic flourishes are coming easy). Dylan eases his fingers off the sensory pads. When he takes the Sensorium off his head, he has a half-asleep look on his face that I've seen when he comes out of his room for the first time in many days, like he's nothing more than an armature coiled in nerves and covered in fat and skin.

"Where were you?" I ask.

"Lake Superior for a bit, then roaming." He pushes his fingers into his eyes and flexes his jaw and breathes deeply. He sniffs his armpits. "Christ." He gets up and changes his shirt. While it's out, he inhales sharply and quickly from the tube. "Cleanup's going well, at least. You want to go somewhere?"

"OK," I say right away.

"Pretty? Bleak?"

Michael used to Actualize lush places for me. So I say, "Bleak," wondering if he'll show me what he showed Sybil.

"Past or present?"

Michael took me to places as they once existed. "Present."

"Occupied or abandoned?"

And for some reason, Michael showed me places where there were no people. "Occupied."

Dylan lets me sit in his chair. He fits the Sensorium over my head—anechoic silence dominates—and affixes my fingers to the sensory pads. Instructions appear: Stand—Walk in place—Sit—Imagine your HANDS in front of you—Wiggle your FINGERS—Make FISTS—Touch your NOSE—Count to TEN in your most PRECISE approximation of time—Look LEFT—RIGHT—UP—DOWN—Turn your

HEAD AROUND—Now the OTHER WAY—Wait while the Sensorium
calibrates the space around you—What you experience may dis-
tort your proprioception, cause nausea, dizziness, or seizures in
sensitive users—Improper use may result in permanent neurological damage—DO NOT DISCONNECT.

. . .

    I'm lifted off my feet, spun head over heels—the sky materializ-
ing as firmamental and starry, then slowly turning opaque and
charcoal-colored and so low that I reach my hand up to it, thinking I can touch it, but I can't, and then my feet come down on
solid ground. I look left and right at blackened dogwoods rising
from the roadside behind broken fences in empty fields swarmed
with flying insects, gathered in shadowlike masses on cattails—
they make my arms and legs itch—there's a pinch on my neck—I
must try to keep my balance wading through the tall grass and
the sticky sucking ground beneath—leeches on my ankles now—a
smell like tar and rotten eggs—and only the sounds of buzzing insects like many untuned strings. I wonder where the people could
be—a crow alights on the naked branches of a nearby tree—knocks
a nest to the ground—did the nest stay up there in the storm? or
was it built in the aftermath?—and splinters it apart with its beak
in search of eggs, but there's nothing—the crow is joined by two
others and they all fly up into the blustery fog, and out at the far
end of the marsh, there's steam rising like from a hot pot, and a
house larger than any I've seen before, but it's all broken, collapsed
inward—not from decay, but from force. I approach it—there are
craters in the front lawn, trees uprooted, sideways, sod hanging from its lifelines like entrails—so different from the places
Michael used to take me—furniture split and spitting out cotton,
opened and upturned like unearthed coffins. I walk up to the
front door and feel a stiff warm wind ridden by sulfur smells—a
child steps out and starts to cry—her father follows her out and
puts a hand on her chest to bring her inside—*Why did you make us
come back here?—Let's gather our things and get to the xenodochium,*
father says—she stares out at the marsh—vine everywhere, partly

disentangled but still clinging to structures and trees—*Where's Kora and Hallie?* she says—*They left earlier, sweetheart, much earlier*—*Will they be at the Xeno, the Xeno, there?*—*I don't know.* And on their way, father holding daughter's hand and mother holding screaming toddler, up the road, past vultures pecking at carrion, a hand directs my head leftward—my trustworthy Sensorium conductor—and guides me back to neutral. There's a church with an intact steeple and a venerable cross before me—the sky no less heavy, no less dark—a field slowly undulating out beyond the church, kiosks arranged but unoccupied, and in the cemetery, two children sobbing, kneeling, hugging a headstone, and two teenagers coming up behind them to ease them away and take them back inside the church. In a triage tent, a doctor assesses a thigh impaled by a foot-long tree branch, the man unconscious—elsewhere, a nurse shuts a pair of eyes and draws a blanket over the body, and an assistant pushes a wheelbarrow out into the woods to a ditch half-filled with broken, bloated, emaciated corpses. Sick, coughing patients lie near one another on repurposed pews, removed from inside and arranged as beds in the tent. The father turns his daughter's face into his stomach as he greets a WORLD xenodochium official, who shakes his head. I go to the front door of the church and look up at the cross. The mother is talking up to the cross, toddler buried in her shoulder—the cross seems as if it was lowered from deep within the sky—think of how people have fought wars over this symbol in which they find comfort, and how Christ and however many other people brought to it looked upon it with fear of the slow death awaiting them—then everything goes black and anechoic again. A message appears—DO NOT make any sudden movements. My fingers are slowly lifted off the sensory pads—*hypnagogic*—a word Michael taught me in this room—unclear of what's subconscious, what's intentional, what's the difference.

I was not there, and they did not see me, and the presence of my body did not so much as alter the path of an air particle, and yet it's as if I were the elements themselves.

The Sensorium is lifted off my head.

"Touch your nose," Dylan says, so I touch my nose. "Stand up." I do. "Walk to the end of the room . . ." I take a few steps. "Walk back . . ." And a few more. "Spin around." I spin. "Jump." I jump. "Do a flip." I stare at him. "Come on, a backflip. Or a headstand. Fine, say *sesquipedalian* in Latin."

"Sesquipedalian in Latin."

"How was that?"

"It was like I thought things I didn't know."

"Different than what Michael used to do?"

"I think so."

"It's nice, what he'd do. But it's not real. This is real. Did you feel afraid or upset?"

"No."

"Easy to see how you could get lost in that, yeah?"

"How long do you usually do that for?"

"Hours—fourteen, sixteen. There are horror stories of guys who do a whole tube before they go in, pass out, and wake up thinking they're somebody else, or somewhere else, or even still in the Actualization, and they just stop interacting with people."

"Wow."

"No wonder people hoard their benefits for Sensatarium time, right?"

"Yes," I say, opening and closing my fists.

"Imagine if everyone had access to that, anytime."

"Nothing would get done."

"Nothing would need to." Dylan raises his eyebrows and tucks his chin into his neck.

"What do you mean?"

"Where else would you have to be?"

"Oh, I see. You could live in there."

"Only, not really."

"Because it isn't real," I say, hearing my lisp a bit sharper now. "Or is it?"

"Ha." I smile and slap my knee. "How long was I in there?"

"Twenty minutes."

"Felt like hours."

"That's one reason why people die in those things."

"I'd better go use the bathroom."

"Please get it all in the toilet."

"OK," I say, and give a thumbs-up.

I didn't see a toilet at the xenodochium. It's easy to forget that people outside Canland suffer, with Canland being so prosperous and stable. AB has suffered in ways I never will. I don't know what they've lost, if they had a Before, and if this After is any relief. AB sleeps out in the cold tonight—it gets to fifty or even forty—another night without a verdict from the viceroy on registration, with dozens of other DOTEC, who think of their old lives, who wish for them back, as I know I would. Sybil believed it was necessary to help others, that it's what makes us human. After the first time I told her about how harvestmen cluster, she stopped me whenever she sensed I was about to bring it up again. She'd say, *It's different— we have a choice; we know what we're doing.* So, should I invite AB to my home, give them this roof, our food, my bed, a bathroom? Would Helena allow it? She helps me every day, so it's possible she'd approve of me helping others. Everyone has a moral duty to rescue those they can, to return what they owe to the world—the dog who pulls the limp-winged duck from the overflowing riverbanks; the self-sacrificial trees that tie their roots to halt the spread of fungus through the forest; the free human who fetters himself to an orphan in need. See, Sybil? It's not just humans—it's an Earthly leaning.

I've dribbled on myself. These pants are supposed to last another week before a wash. I take them off and lay them on the step outside so they'll dry fast. It's bright, the daylight grainy. Nothing moves on the street. Tall eucalyptus trees across the road rise above my eye line, and farther out, shrink to the size of a fingernail. I enjoy staring out from our front door, but would I still enjoy it if I lived in communal housing and had to look out at another adobe stack, or had a view of the people crowding the kiosks, or of the supply sheds, and the hoeing, pulling, planting agriculture contributors in their wide-brimmed hats?

I think I probably would.

Back in Dylan's room, he crouches on his chair, rounding his shoulders, his nose wrinkled at the monitors. He glances at me.

"All right there, Beautiful?"

"Yes, just peed on myself a little."

"Is that the extent of the damage?"

"Yes. Dylan, can I ask you something?"

There's an abrupt sound like grinding metal from the computer. He inches toward the screen, and scrolls through new lines of rapidly reproducing text.

"Do you think Sybil's safe?"

"I have never been more sure of anything in my life than that she is entirely safe and happy. By no exaggeration is she the most guileful and capable soul on the planet. I can't even think of a close second."

"Do you miss her?" I ask.

"Do you miss her?" he says.

"Yes. Actually, I have another question—"

"Hey, Beautiful—something just came up, and I'm going to need to give it the focus of a heart surgeon, because if I don't, then I could lose the satellite, which would be bad, or I could get caught, which would be worse, so how about I meet you out in the kitchen as soon as I'm done with this and we can have some cheese together."

"OK."

Dylan opens the door for me and then pulls shirts out of his dresser, sniffing them all. I linger in the doorway. He sniffs the tube and changes his shirt again.

I sit at the dining table and wait—not playing piano, not even so much as observing the garden, not doing any of the things Helena doesn't want me to. I flip through *Fearsome Allies* a few times, then close it. I wonder what's more boring: sitting doing nothing, or doing the same thing over and over. Loneliness breeds genius, Helm told me. He doesn't seem lonely. But neither did Sybil.

Although, once, Dylan and Sybil were in bed together. For a long time—years—he'd asked her if she wanted to get in bed with him, and he would sometimes sneak his hand up under the back of her shirt when they hugged. Helena and Tobias told them both to cut it out, and Sybil would avoid Dylan for a few minutes until he started making her laugh again with his wit. Not long after Polly died, Sybil and Tobias came over to our house. Helena and Tobias had much to drink, and Tobias fell asleep on the couch. It was nighttime, so Helena arranged my bed for Sybil and told me to sleep in Dylan's bed. Then Helena went to her room. I stayed up with Dylan and Sybil awhile until I got tired, and Dylan told me it was all right if I slept in my own bed. As I left Dylan's room, he was putting his hand up the back of Sybil's shirt and she was looking at him. In the morning, Sybil was reading at the table by a candle that had melted all the way down. Tobias was still asleep on the couch, but when Helena came out, he started, and then hastened himself and Sybil out of our home before Dylan emerged from his room—which he did not do for several days, like a troglobite, and when he finally did, he was very snappy with Helena and she warned him not to act too much like his father. I remember the details of that night so well because, after that, Dylan and Sybil stopped being friends the way they used to be— Dylan no longer accompanied me and Helena to the mortuary; Sybil no longer came to our house; they stopped going on bike rides together. There are alternate explanations, sure, but I think it had something to do with what went on in the bed after I left Dylan's room, because when I finally did get around to asking Dylan if he and Sybil fornicated, it was the only time I can recall him looking at me with clear anger. "No," he said, and then once again shut himself away.

The front door opens and Helena, backlit by a red twilight, comes inside, her muslin dress powdered with light sand, her hair a mess, sweat speckling her face like warts. It must have been hot today. I can hear a wind lift and die. She holds up my pants.

"Oh."

"Forgot these?"

"I spilled a little water on them and put them out to dry." I don't want her thinking I'm incontinent. Some lies are OK.

"Please tell me you haven't been sitting there this entire time."

I laugh. "No, we did things–science and books and chatting."

"Is there any reason I'd need to check you?"

"No, I was very safe."

Helena hands me my pants. I put them on. They're warm from the sun.

"You made sure no harmful animals latched on to those, right?" she says.

"Oh. No."

"I did."

"Thank you. From now on, I'll check my clothes and shoes, and if necessary, take off my clothes before I enter the house and flap them out so red ants, for instance, are flung off."

"Just be more aware, Tristan. If you leave your pants outside, re-member to bring them back in, and maybe flap them out. I never thought I'd be having this conversation," she says in a lowered voice as she goes into the kitchen. A minute later, she presents me with a plate of lentils and chopped carrots.

"So, how long have you been sitting out here?" she says.

Sometimes I don't know when to tell Helena the truth because I don't want her to be mad at Dylan, but I also don't want her to be mad at me; so is it a utilitarian question? As in, if Helena being mad at me only causes anguish to one person (her), and Helena being mad at Dylan causes them both anguish, shouldn't I make her mad at me? But what about collective anguish? What if her anguish at my lie is greater than the combined anguish of her and Dylan quarreling?

"Hey." She reaches out and lightly taps the table twice. "You can say. Dylan's choices are his."

It's like she can read my mind. It makes me feel like she is always there to protect me.

"Well," I say, trying to remember, taking a bite of lentils.

"Remember to say thank you."

"Thank you, Helena."

"Don't talk while you chew."

"Right." My distraction is manifesting in harmful ways. "Well, I would say it's been a couple hours."

"And up until a couple hours ago, what did you and Dylan do?"

"Sensorium—he did one, then he put me in it."

Her frown lines deepen. She closes her eyes and takes a long breath. "Did everything go OK? Did you feel dizzy, or—I don't know what your reaction would be—unusual?"

"No, I was fine."

"When Michael put you in Actualizations you couldn't walk straight when you came out. It made me sick." She brushes some flyaway hairs behind her ears. "What did Dylan show you?"

"The aftermath of a hurricane in a marshland."

"Was there violence or anything morbid?"

"There were wounded people and dead bodies."

"Can you identify how that made you feel? Sad? Sick? Angry? Scared?"

The fact is, I was mostly in awe of the Actualization; it had been a couple years since I'd been in a Sensorium—not since Michael lived here. "I didn't like seeing so many people suffering," I say.

"OK." She peels a callus off her fingertip. "Well, it's my fault for leaving you with him, but maybe it's not the worst thing that you saw that. You understand that it's WORLD's fault for not helping those people move out of the hazard zone sooner, yes?"

"Dylan's a very trustworthy Sensorium technician," I say. "He could contribute at the Sensatarium."

"Hey. Listen—this is important. That suffering is WORLD's fault. WORLD's idea of population control is letting manmade, natural-seeming disasters expedite a culling process. That's what your father does, and it's the difference between Purists and Practicalists—Purists want to facilitate an active cooperation between humans and the Earth; Practicalists want to clear space to bolster a hyper-industrial technocracy similar to before the Environmental Evanescence. I want to be explicit about why the Practicalist model cannot exist within any sort of sustainable moral framework."

Helena's lit so many candles, the adobe walls of our home are pinkish-white, and the air itself is the color of the desert floor at sunset. I look at her again to show her I'm listening.

"Sensoriums manipulate our natural senses and dull our desire to interact with other people, the Earth, and our own bodies," she says. "Practicalism ignores the needs of the individual in favor of this illusion of a specialized experience; whereas, Purism emphasizes the needs of the individual as the only means toward creating a society of contributors. We have, on the one hand, needs of the few, Earth as conquerable and at our disposal, rapid technological progression. And on the other hand, we have needs of the many, Earth as a gift we accept as it chooses to give, slow and necessary technological progression. The reason for the Parts System should be to keep everything from moving too fast, to delay globalization as long as possible, and not to oppress those who disagree with WORLD. Much of the debate hinges on accepting or rejecting the limits imposed on us by the laws of space and time."

"Interesting," I say. "Do you mean like by shrinking the Earth?"

"Shrinking the Earth," she repeats, and scrunches up her nose and smiles for a split second. "Who told you that?"

"No one—I made it up."

"That's a lovely way to put it, Tristan." She blinks her good eyes at me, and I blink too, because I'm not sure what to do when I get a compliment. "Dylan doesn't understand the seriousness of his rejection of Earth's scale. Especially because he actually agrees with me, even though he would never admit it. He's always done whatever he can to avoid being put in a box. It's not romantic; it's just fickle. He wants to stand for something good, but doesn't know how to without feeling like he's giving up part of himself. I'm not sure you can understand, but compromise is very painful for some people—"

Helena shuts her eyes suddenly and massages her forehead.

Sometimes she gets headaches, and sometimes even tremors, and needs grappa to cure them. Once, when her supply of grappa ran out, and before Viceroy Hugo could get her more, she cut herself while chopping apples. Dylan accused her of having done it on purpose, for attention, which led to her saying, "You don't get to hide in your room and then pop out and make judgments without being judged yourself, and do you really want to go there?" That time, like most times, Dylan chose not to go there, perhaps because he thought Helena would point out that he was kicked out of school in his first year as a present, and was assigned the most unpleasant contribution there is, hauling human waste (and now, when necessary, human bodies from the bottom of the Notch) all the way out to the Waste Reallocation Center, and that he'd never made anything of his specialization, which was going to be botany. Dylan might secretly be afraid of Helena.

She opens one eye, then the other, rises, and ambles to the kitchen to pour herself some grappa. She finishes it quickly, pours another, and sits back down with me, bringing the bottle. She peels another callus off another finger—this time with her teeth—and blows it off her tongue to the floor, then sets me with an even expression, maybe waiting for me to speak, or calculating what to say, or trying to decipher what is evident on my face, or not evident; she has always called me her greatest frustration.

"What do you believe?" she says.

"Well," I say. "I think that part of individualism is making the decision to help people."

She nudges the lentils toward me and watches me eat while she slowly drinks her grappa. I finish the whole plate without speaking. I love talking to Helena about how I should be. Who would know better than her?

She says, "So you think people should help others. What does that look like?"

A gas bubble rises in my throat. I cover my mouth and burp wetly. "I think, if someone needs something, and you can give it to them, then you should."

"You're OK?" she says. "You're not choking?"

"No."

She touches a finger to the rim of her glass. "So, what if their needs contradict someone else's needs?"

"Well, then I think you have to decide whose needs are more important."

"Give me an example."

"Well." I place my hand on my chin, to pretend like I'm having to think about this. "We could help a DOTEC by letting them stay in our house."

"That's very nice of you, but to billet a DOTEC would invite a risk to your health and safety. Do you want to do that?"

"No."

Helena clears my plate from the table and dunks it in the wash-basin.

"I understand," I say. "But Purists want the DOTEC to have good lives, right? And that's why they kill themselves? To make space?"

Helena leans her arm against the counter and places her other hand on her hip. She breathes loudly and stares at me from across the room.

"You have a good life, Tristan—much better than most people—but I want you to realize, I take such care with you because more for you means less for someone else, and that's a big responsibility to place on your life." She pauses and touches her thumb knuckle to the outside of her eye, then straightens up and crosses her arms. "You can leave it to me to worry about things like suicide. I just want you to be aware that there are people out there, without a Part, who are suffering. But WORLD is responsible for those people, not you. OK?"

"OK."

She comes toward me. "Come on, let's run you a bath. It's been a week and you're starting to stink." She sniffs me, makes a high-pitched sound, and smiles.

"I have a question."

"Come on, up."

I stand and follow her down the hall.

"In the Sensorium," I say, "the DOTEC were in a church, but I've heard that Matthews are violent."

"Not everyone who kneels before the cross is a Matthew."

"I don't believe in god, you know," I say.

"Well, good. Extraordinary claims require extraordinary evidence." Helena pulls a towel from a cabinet and hands it to me. It's cool and scratchy. She pulls a lever above the tub and the spout funnels out a few inches of water, then stops.

"Michael used to say that," I say.

"Because he heard me say it. And he believes in an omnipotent god, which makes him a contradiction, not complex." Helena takes the towel back and lifts up the hem of my shirt. I take it off and throw it into the corner.

"I think I'm complex," I say.

"No, you're very simple," she replies.

"Helm says god is the thing that gives people great talents, same as the thing that gives children disease."

"Helm talks about god in school?" Helena snaps her fingers and rolls her hand through the air, meaning for me to hurry up. Her patience is short with me, sometimes, and understandably. "That isn't god; that's genetics and environment. Don't listen to Helm. He's got that thing in his brain, you know? Military veteran." She twists an invisible screw by her ear.

"But you fought in the war," I say.

"Tristan, please get in the bath."

I take off my pants and step in. The water's cold, but I don't mind. Sometimes my analgesia can be very beneficial to our environmental impact.

"I didn't choose to," Helena says, kneeling by the tub, soaping up my shoulders. "But Helm volunteered to defend the United States, and then he got deployed on American soil to fight other members of his own military."

I look up to the ceiling. It's dark despite the candlelight. If I traded places with a DOTEC, I probably wouldn't mind. But my health and safety ensure my life, and I bring joy to Helena, which is what makes me important.

"Was war scary?" I say.

"I'm not talking about this now, Tristan."

"I would defend Canland," I say.

"I'm sure they'd have you on the front lines." She pours a cup of water over my head.

I grab the soap from her. "I've got it," I say. Then I smile at her.

She stands. Her frown lines are deep again, like I've done something wrong, but then she kindly says, "I don't want you getting the idea that you can't make decisions on your own." Her eyes, glazed and supported by soft pouches, stare down at me in the dim light. She opens her mouth like she's about to speak again, but then closes it.

I nod.

"Call me if you need me," she says, and leaves the bathroom.

Once she's gone, I slide down in the tub so the water is halfway up my body. I close my eyes and pretend I'm floating atop the ocean. One day, I'll be able to do everything for myself that Helena does for me, and I'll be able to do those things for someone else who needs me too.

. . .

October 15, 2088

Roshana ignored me again at school today, like most days since we agreed to be friends. She and Lilly are always together, but Leo's stopped hanging out with them. I tried joining a conversation with them in the courtyard, but Lilly said, This is private, and I said, Oh, sorry, and stepped aside and waited for the private conversation to end. When it did, Lilly said, OK, you can join us now, but as soon as I stepped into the triangle, Roshana walked away, so it was just me and Lilly, and then Lilly left too, to stand on the perimeter of a group of whispering present girls. I tried to socialize with some future boys, but they were doing slow-motion fighting and I didn't think it was a good idea for me to engage in that, even though I wanted to, so I eavesdropped on the present boys who were saying things about the present girls, and I thought, If Helena knew I was listening to those things, she would condition me, so I just went inside and waited by our classroom for Practical Math to begin. Then Gwen Horn came up to me and asked if there was something I was waiting for, and I said, For class to begin, and she said, That's not for another thirty minutes, go back outside. She went into the classroom, but I didn't want to go back outside, so I walked farther down the hall. As I passed another classroom, I heard a voice coming from the other side of a mostly closed door. It was saying, Doing the best he can, I wish you'd met, you'd love him, he's given us a good life, and I'm not afraid of him anymore. When I think I'm going to beat up other kids here for saying certain things about me and Asher, I remind myself that I have a better life than you two did, and that that's what you fought for, and succeeded, so now it's my turn to fight for what I think is important, and that's the rights of all the DOTEC, their protection, and the return to peace. I miss you and I love you and I hope you are able to see what a good young man I've become. Bye. I'll talk to you tonight. I was just feeling lonely. OK, bye.

When the door opened, I was standing with my ear in the space between the door and jamb, and then Malakai was staring at me. I waited for him to say something. What he said was, What the fuck are you doing? I said, Listening. He kept staring at me; his nostrils were pulsing. I asked, Who were you talking to? And he cursed at me again. God? I asked. Eat shit, he said, brushing past me. Who was it? I said, wanting to know, since I'd never heard anyone talking to themselves like that before. He came back toward me. Bending down, in a very low voice he said, My parents. I asked, Do you think they can hear you? He ignored my question and walked past me again. I noticed he was holding a book, but I didn't see what it was. He went into Helm's classroom, and I went back outside.

Roshana was standing beneath the guava tree, staring up at its branches. A COHO presided over the courtyard in a sentry tower. A future was getting down on his hands and knees behind Leo, and another future approached Leo from the front, smiling and saying, Hey, Leo, how's it going, and then pushed Leo so he fell backward over the kid on hands and knees. Lots of people started laughing, even Lilly. Then Leo got up, also laughing, and approached the kid who knelt behind him and said, That was a good one, and stretched out his hand for the kid to high-five, and when the kid high-fived Leo, Leo slapped him on the cheek with his other hand, then started screaming things even I know are vicious, and the kid started crying. There was no teacher supervising us, so some present boys had to step in to stop the fighting. I got away from all the drama, went up beside Roshana, and looked up into the branches with her, where I saw an orb weaver spinning a web between branches. I said, Did you know that an orb weaver eats its own silk? It can survive on the protein it creates. But then Roshana said that wasn't what she was looking at, she was looking at the empty spaces and wondering when the fruits would come in again. Why would I care about some dumb spider? she said. Then she walked away from me. I was standing alone then, right when Sybil would have come up to me, and I even looked around for her, even though I knew . . .

I remembered my first day at school, three years ago, when Sybil was in her final year as a future, and I'd only known her for six years then, not having met her until I came home from my stint in Research Centers that began the first three years of my life, and Dylan had just been expelled from school when Helena and Michael decided it was time for me to go, and I didn't know any of the kids except for Sybil, who was not yet officially my best friend, but when I saw her in the courtyard after lunch, she was talking to a semicircle of people all at once, making them laugh. I went up to her and interrupted and said, Hi, Sybil, and she looked down at me and said, Hi, Tristan, and then went on telling the same hilarious story to all of us, including me, as if I were just another kid, and in that moment I felt like I was friends with everyone in the semicircle.

But today, as I stood alone beneath the guava tree, it occurred to me how complicated it is to leave someone alone and also make sure they're not lonely, because it's impossible to know all the private things someone is thinking, which make them do what they do. When the metal bell rang, I remembered to put my hands over my ears.

Every day I leave AB alone is a day they are without a friend, a day no one knows about them—except the pregnant woman—and a day that I don't get to see their face up close, or make new memories for the day that I don't get to see them again, like the memories that are all that keep Sybil alive to me. But that day is so far away that it feels like it won't ever happen, like it is even less than a warning, it is like a scene waiting to begin beneath a satellite that has not yet passed overhead.

It's nice to have a journal where I can write all my thoughts.

. . .

SINCE SYBIL LEFT, Dylan takes me to and picks me up from school. Sometimes, he'll accelerate into a dip in the skirt of the path and send us airborne. It makes my stomach flip, but we always land as if Dylan has softened our gravitational pull, like the moon's. Then, on the wide straightaways, he goes so fast the gears whistle. I stick my face out past his shoulder and pull down my pollution mask to feel the wind slide off my skin. This is the fastest I ever go, and I love it, although we hardly talk on these rides because we're both facing front, and Dylan hurries us home so he can get back to his satellites.

A couple times this week, since I met AB, I've broached the subject of tubes, very cleverly, asking Dylan things like, "How old do you have to be to do tubes?" and "Do you think Michael ever gave me a tube?" Once, I even went so far as to ask Dylan, "Can I try a tube?"

He stopped the bike when I asked him that, turned around and said, "Don't ever ask me that again." Then, when we pulled onto our street that day, he said to me, "If I ever have a suspicion that you've been in the vicinity of a tube . . ."

He didn't finish his thought, but I understood. I've been thinking nonstop of ways to get a tube to AB, but the only strategy I haven't tried is asking Dylan directly. So now I pat the meat of his back and ask, "Hey, Dylan, can we stop off at the hillock?"

Dylan stops the bike short as harvesters cross the road—four women, all burned and tanned, carrying baskets full of fresh crops, two with hair tied back in braids, two with their hair covered by headscarves so I can't tell if their hair's long or short, all their sweaty shimmering limbs lean and strong like horses. One of the women glances at us, but the others go on walking as if we're not there. Dylan's head turns to follow them as they pass.

I'm not sure if he heard me, so I pat his back again and say, "Can we stop off at the hillock, please?"

"Why?"

He returns his attention from the women to the road and starts pedaling again. A baseball cracks off a bat in the Part Center. I try to find it in the air, squinting through my sun goggles.

"Well," I say, "I became friends with a DOTEC. They were really nice. Their name is AB. They have a condition that's like the inverse of mine—only, they have no way to manage all their pain. So, being friends with me, they knew that I know you, and they asked if I could get them a tube."

Dylan swerves the bike into the bar ditch. We go airborne, then land in the cracked, rocky traces of desert with barely a jolt. He accelerates across the flatlands and into the pasture. A calf with a white face and black body standing beside two motionless black cows slides its head along the haunch of the smaller of the big ones, then lies in the grass under the bigger one's body. The wire fence has been moved to shrink the grazing area—I assume because of the stampede that killed Sol.

"Which one is it?" says Dylan.

AB's lying on their side at the very edge of the oak's crown, half in, half out of the shade, blowing air through their thumbs, making reedy sounds. I point to them. AB makes a tremolo sound, then gets up. Three blades of grass go flying from their hands. They roll halfway down the hillock like a log, then pop to their feet and come bouncing across the grass. Dylan gets off the bike. There are WEDA posted all around, plus the one COHO I usually see here, the same one who seized AB by the elbow in the Part Center.

"Three bodies this week," Dylan says, "and now I have to deal with this shit."

AB's wearing shorts and an oversized tank top so their ribs are visible through the armholes. They stick out their tongue, tilt their head and wink at me. I smile, but they can't see me inside my pollution mask. I don't like having my face hidden. I want the dynamited mountaintop to stop dispersing debris. The wind and the cold at that altitude keep us from growing anything up there, so it was useless destruction. At least when the coastal cities drowned, pollution stopped blowing hundreds of miles inland, and birds returned to their natural migratory patterns. I take my pollution mask off and smile again.

"Hey," AB says to Dylan. "I'm AB. Tristan and I became friends the other day. He's the sweetest—"

"Shut up. If you come near my brother again, I'll kill you."

AB bites their thumbnail off and spits it out. "You have no idea how many times I've heard that. You don't scare me."

"I don't need to scare you. I'll kill you. Or have you expelled." Dylan glances from AB to me and back.

"I'm just a kid with chronic pain. I'm not a danger," AB says in a casual tone.

"You asked him to get you drugs." Dylan turns around to look at me. "What else did he say to you, Tristan?"

"I'm not a he," says AB. Dylan ignores them. One hand at a time, AB bends their fingers back so they nearly touch their wrist, and they bite their lip and blink twice at me.

Dylan's just waiting for my answer with his usual heavy-lidded stare. Out of everyone, he's the only person I never want to lie to. I don't need to convince him I'm OK on my own; he's always believed in me. If he knows I'm in love, maybe he won't care that AB asked me for tubes. Maybe telling people about AB will make our love real.

So I lift my sun goggles to my forehead. Everything turns blurry, the hillock just a giant slope of green. Like all creatures of nature, we lie. The difference is that, sometimes, we choose not to.

"They said they would give me a kiss," I say, "if I got them tubes."

I put my sun goggles back on. Dylan smiles at me. AB takes a step backward, away from Dylan, and says, "That's not true."

"You're calling my brother a liar?" Dylan says, turning to AB.

"No." AB's blue, black-rimmed eyes land on me, and they take a big breath and look up into the sky. "It's not the only thing I said. I told him I need them. I'm in pain, and I like Tristan, and friends help each other."

"You like Tristan?"

"I need tubes to survive, OK, the one I have is empty, and if I can't manage my pain, then I don't want to live."

"It's OK, Dylan," I say. "I like AB. I picture their face all the time. We wave to each other. I want them to be healthy so we can be together for a long time."

"What do you mean, 'be together'?" Dylan says. He shakes his head and pushes his fingers into his eyes. "Never mind—this is fucking crazy. Tristan." He removes his hands from his eyes. "Sybil's gone. OK? You're gonna make other friends, but this is not one of them."

AB's head looks like it's hanging off their neck to the side, and all their teeth are showing in a grimace. Their face is easier for me to read than most others, and right now they are assessing Dylan negatively, feeling sorry for me.

"You don't need to be friends with a drug-addicted DOTEC," Dylan says. "Come on, Beautiful, you're smarter than that."

I put my pollution mask back on.

"That's it?" AB says to me.

I wish they could know that I want to decide for myself, but that I have to trust what other people assess as dangerous for me.

Dylan looks at them again and reaches into his pocket. He pulls out a tube. "There might be a little left in there."

AB reaches for it, and Dylan pulls it away. AB falls into Dylan, and Dylan pushes AB lightly so they can balance on their own.

"If you go near Tristan again, I will make sure you are expelled."

AB licks their lips and then nods. Dylan hands the tube over. AB takes it, turns, and walks up the hillock, shaking their head, their curls swinging side to side. Halfway up, they pause and look back at me and hold their hands up—surrendering, I think. AB has been helped.

Maybe Dylan is right—I need to make other friends, with people who don't want to use me. Maybe it's best to focus on my specialization, think of how I'd like to contribute, and work on becoming a self-reliant human, rather than obsessing over someone because they happen to be in my dreams. Dylan eventually gave up Sybil, and even let her go.

Dylan pedals the bike away. There's a COHO watching us. His hand is on his hip, clutching his whistler.

· · ·

Oct 18, 2088

It's been a difficult week, now with four suicides. A coterie of Practicalists showed up to the vigil for the dead at the Secular Observation House, protested against Purism, and then offered everyone to sign a petition that Viceroy Hugo have Helena arrested. Helena's been at her writing table until late every night, amassing pages. She switches her metal nib from hand to hand when she writes so she doesn't ever have to break. It's been a couple weeks since she's come into my room in the middle of the night, but she's conditioned me for things she hasn't conditioned me for in years, like holding in a pee for too long, or asking what she calls *invasive questions*.

The other night, she was at her writing table while I was reading *Fearsome Allies* at the dining table, and she looked up from her writing and said, What are the ways it could go? Now, I don't know if I'd said something to prompt the question, but I took time to consider some answers. And there seemed to be three possible conclusions: one, that humans will save the Earth, and they will destroy it again and then survive again, and this will go on until a solar flare burns everything up or the Arctic methane shoals burst and suffocate everything, and whether or not the Earth remains a lifeless rock, *Homo sapiens* will not return to it; two, humans fail to restore the environment and, exiled from Earth, they must finally attempt in earnest to colonize a foreign celestial body to postpone (or relocate) their extinction; three, humans all come to understand that the machine will never outsmart the creator, and so cease trying to, and relent to a state of deferential cooperation with the Earth. Sometime in the middle of me saying all that to her, she looked up from her writing and said, Tristan, honey, please, I'm working. It is possible that she had not been asking the question to me.

Another unpleasantness is the discord over what to do about the DOTEC on the hillock, after one had disguised himself as an agriculture contributor, and went undetected for a week, until he was discovered sleeping in an underground storage unit beneath a communal house after pilfering the food, and was expelled from the Part and sent to Short Term Rehabilitation. Also, there was some quarreling on the hillock as the DOTEC leftover rations were delivered, which led to one DOTEC striking another across the brow, which left a gash that had to go two days without treatment before Cole received permission from Viceroy Hugo to treat someone off the Safe Haven premises. Some of the registered sat on the hillock with the DOTEC in protest of Canland's general indifference. Then a day later, a proxy came with a message from Viceroy Hugo that rations would be withheld for one missed contribution, and punishments would increase for subsequent absences. Everyone returned to their contributions, and no new housing construction has been approved.

Another unpleasantness: the wind picked up this week, so people are sneezing and dabbing their eyes a lot, and some of our tall crops were uprooted, and the smaller animals have sought refuge underground. A hazardous infestations contributor came to our house to eradicate the field mice who invaded our food storage unit (where I am absolutely not allowed and have never been) and ruined most of our keep. As I write that, I can see the comparisons people make between DOTEC and vermin. Helena doesn't want me in the garden, and she doesn't want me talking to DOTEC. What does that say?

On the bike ride home today—after Dylan gave AB a tube and then scared them away from me—as we passed Asher and Malakai's street, I asked Dylan what had happened to Asher after the incident on the day of the effigy-burning. Dylan said, He's fine, don't worry about it. And I said, He was very distraught about what you did to his tree, remember? And he said, Yeah, well, I was distraught about how he put his hands on you. I asked where he'd disappeared to that day. He said, You mean while you were busy not defending Sybil from getting molested on the hillock? I went to report Asher to COHO for his aggressive behavior toward you, so now he's under review at his contribution, and apparently working very hard; that's what I mean by *he's fine.* I thought about that awhile and then asked, What does his contribution have to do with our confrontation? And Dylan said, Why do you care about what happened to him? I said nothing—I thought it was obvious why I'd care, but there must've been something I was missing, so I told myself then not to care.

Following some silence but for the welder's distant hammer and the wheels turning under me, I then asked Dylan, Remember how you got expelled from school for fighting?

And he said, You mean because I defended myself? I'm not in the business of picking random fights.

I said, What did he do to you?

He tried to kill me.

How?

Don't remember.

And what happened to him?

I broke his spine so he could become a painter, and then he and his mom left Canland, and now he's at an Arts Part, very happy. Imagine if he'd stayed here and become a basket-weaver or a teacher or some other sad alternative for creatives.

I said, Why didn't they arrest you? And Dylan said, Why do you think? Because our parents are founders, I said.

Dylan spun the bike around the curve before our street so that I teetered on the edge of the seat, but I was held down by the seat belt across my lap. He sped up past the three single-story adobe houses before ours. Rod and Rosemarie were out in front of their house—Rod pruning and replanting the jade between our homes, and Rosemarie sitting in her usual chair, sipping from a glass with an herb leaf in it. I don't know what their contributions are that they also get to live in a single-story, but they're pretty old, the oldest people I know. Rosemarie called hello to us, and I waved back. Dylan skidded the bike across our lawn and chained it to the house while still sitting on the front seat. The late afternoon light was turning our house purple, and the door and two small windows made it look like an unfeeling face.

Dylan turned his head halfway over his shoulder and said in a low voice, It's because of Michael. Because he's on a mission that is utterly classified. He could literally be discovering the thing that saves us all. He chose to do that instead of be here with us in Canland. And good for him. And thank him too. He's the reason we get everything we do, the reason you get your medications and ointments, and the reason our house has an electrical outlet and I can use a Sensorium. And when I find him, he'll realize I should be there with him.

I stared at Dylan's broad, sweaty, black-shirted back. I imagined him leaving. I saw myself walking alone two miles across the desert to school every morning, and then two miles back.

Dylan got off the bike and said, Do you think if Helena and Michael stopped existing, anyone would take care of us?

I suddenly wasn't very interested in this conversation anymore.

Do you know what the word *devotion* means? he said.

Yes, I said.

He shook his head and made a sound with his lips like he was spitting. You know why people sneer at religion? he said. Because the ones who believe are still out there, searching. But there's no end to the boredom of wondering. (Or maybe he said wandering.) Everyone had a simultaneous near-death experience, so now we're content with the boredom of doing. Do you think I enjoy my contribution? It's a weird day when I admit Helena's right, and I'd never advocate for suicide—never—but she's right that Earth is all there is. It's the last stop. There's no spiritual relief to this.

He slapped his arm and then spread his arms out wide and looked everywhere.

So what about Sybil? I said. She's out there.

So's Michael, in a way. It's because of devotion. I don't know if you'll ever understand that, Beautiful.

He swept his hand back through his hair and then went inside, and I followed without even taking in the rare purple color that our house was turning in the dusk.

Helena's knocking around out there. Bye, journal.

5

October 31, 2088

I'll have to learn to ride a bicycle to get myself from place to place when Helena and Dylan are too busy, to help them free up their own time, or just when I get to the age when riding on the back seat of your mom or brother's bike becomes inappropriate, like having your mom wipe your butt, or taking baths with your sibling. I don't think about the future often, and I know things won't always be like this, and I don't want them to be, but I don't really have a specific vision for the rest of my life. Michael used to warn against directionless action. He'd say, You wouldn't embark on a trip across the continent without knowing where you're going, would you? Conversely, Helena cautions against writing conclusions before beginning the experiment. She says, Goals are good, but foregone conclusions become self-fulfilling prophecies. That's why what your father did to you was so awful—he had an idea of what he wanted to make you, he never paid attention to your needs, and he thought your analgesia was a blessing, an invitation to experiment with the potential of a developing human brain. So he read nonstop to you, put you in Actualizations, flooded you with hormones, electrocuted you, and yet, you still can't remember not to stare at the sun. So, no, you cannot try to ride a bike on your own. And no, you cannot stay home from school like Dylan, who was not withheld from school because of preternatural talents, if you'll remember . . .

Is what Helena said to me this morning when I asked if I could ride Dylan's bicycle to her lecture at the college today. She looked well rested, but her hands were shaking a little, so she kept missing a lock of hair as she tried to pin it up. She growled and poured herself some grappa and took it to her bedroom. I went into my room to write some things down. She thinks I'm doing homework.

Who knows what the future holds. Nothing in real life is a foregone conclusion. Maybe I'll go to Canland College. Maybe Dylan will work for WORLD in Networks. Helena could be viceroy of Canland.

There was a man in Canland I once heard about—I can't recall from whom, it could've been a serious conversation with Helena, or just gossip from my schoolmates—who was a very promising researcher, an early advancement from future to present, and granted early access to Canland College labs. A couple weeks into his first official term at the college, he illicitly procured some alcohol, and with two friends drank and wandered around the Part, so deep into the night that not even a COHO spotted them. They wandered out past the greened tracts of land, out onto the desert floor that's so flat and barren that, during the hours when the sun is highest and brightest, there are no shadows at all, and everything appears two-dimensional, and the mountains slide closer to you, and it looks like a backdrop painted for the plays at the Part Center, and where, on nights without stars, the land becomes formless, so you can't tell what's moving and what's still. He was apparently too inebriated to hear or infer anything from the shake of a nearby rattlesnake tail, so he stepped on it, and the rattlesnake plunged its venom-dripping fangs into his flesh. By the time he and his friends ran to the Safe Haven, his increased movement and heart rate had hastened the circulation of the venom, and the hemotoxins

degenerated his blood cells, so he went into shock, and then had
a stroke. And even though his life was saved, he suffered permanent nerve and organ damage, including total loss of speech and
movement. He lived a dismal final few years, being spoon-fed soft
food by his mother, eliminating into colostomy bags, placed in
front of a window to view Canland's stretch of desert and eternal
mountains, watching the morning shadows disappear and waiting
for the evening ones to form, waiting for his mother to lift him
into bed, and then out again in the morning, waiting, waiting,
waiting. He's dead now, but it's rumored that he's the reason that
laws regarding future advancement were tightened—also, a good
reason to have an embargo on alcohol. Had his frontal lobe been
further along, and sober, he might still be alive.

I don't want my life to go that way—a preventable injury mutat-
ing, turning me into an invalid. I want to make jokes with friends,
eat solid food and ripe fruit, picked by me. I want to feel the wind
I make riding my own bicycle.

Helena's been in her room for the better part of an hour. I think
we have to leave soon. We're having a picnic in the Part Center
before we go to the college. I haven't been to Canland College in
maybe two years, not since Helena was an arbitrator over intellectual property rights. She'd decide, for example, which department was awarded claim to a compact disc found in an abandoned house outside the Part—music or anthropology. Hers was
a respected position at the college, where most departments share
offices, classrooms, and storage space in an effort to consolidate intellectual achievement and explore ideas more holistically. I think
there was probably some pact made between professors and departments to stop with the pettiness and take it upon themselves
to allocate—and share—intellectual properties, rendering Helena's
position at the college obsolete. But now she has more time for
her gear contribution, which, if you ask me, is more important
to the Part than, for another example, who gets to look at Dürer's
Rhinoceros for longer—art, zoology, or history. I consider myself
lucky to have two parents so smart and driven that they founded

the California Inland Valley Desert-Greening Project—a mother who is overflowing with life lessons, and a father whose position with WORLD is so essential that even its most general description is confidential. His standing has given me access to literature as old as *One Hundred Years of Solitude*, and a book called *Infinite Jest*, which Michael never finished reading to me, and which I didn't like too much, though it improved my verbal processing; and also to access art as influential as the *Rhinoceros*, and music as wonderful as Bach, Mozart, and Beethoven. No one else in Canland has that sort of access except for a few select people at the college who, if engaging with those subjects, are most likely to be sent to other Parts in their advancement.

Weighing on my mind is Helena's lament regarding Michael's continual attempts to turn me into something I would never be— her wish that I'd never read a work of fiction or seen a piece of art that changed the way people saw the world. (Does she know that the rhinoceros that served as Dürer's model was chained to a vessel's deck, and toured around the globe as a treat for the eyes of kings until the ship wrecked and the animal drowned, and for two centuries, Dürer's fanciful rendering was what the West thought a rhino actually looked like?) It makes me wonder what she wants me to be. If I'm not allowed in the garden, and I can't ride a bike, then what?

Helena just opened my door and asked me to get ready to go. Five minutes. She didn't see what I was writing—just that I was writing.

Dylan still takes me past the hillock when he picks me up from school. We always see AB huddled against the trunk of the oak, shivering in Sasha's arms (even though it's been in the upper nineties these days), and Sasha stroking their hair. I always keep my mask and goggles on and never look at them. Dylan's told me that there's nothing we can do to help. He takes us that way as if to expose me to AB's suffering, and to have me practice ignoring them. Dylan goes right into his room when we get home and doesn't come out until it's time for his next waste run. Sometimes I hear him tinkering with our street's septic tank. I lie awake, listening, not getting up to journal since Helena's been bumping around out there well into the night, and I don't want her to come in and give me a talking to or a conditioning, because I want her to know that I'm doing very well.

. . .

ON THE BLANKET we've laid out, we eat tomato sandwiches as we listen to three nearby musicians, on guitar, violin, and wood flute, play a major tune that lifts and lilts with strange cadences, like the spider in my mind, gluing up the rungs of its web with the pluck of a leg. Helena and I don't speak as we watch and listen to them play. I focus on my chewing, trying not to think of any specific person's face as this rare accompaniment delights a small audience with song. When it's time to go, she says, "Ready, Tristan?" We fold the blanket up together and I mount the back seat of her bicycle, which is painted red and chipped a little here and there, with tires twice as wide as Dylan's. She pedals half as fast as him and never swerves or rides the fringe or catches air. We pass the hillock, but I don't look.

"Did you notice the costumes?" Helena says.

"No."

"The band—they were dressed like elves."

"Oh, then yes."

"You thought they normally dressed like that?"

"I don't know."

Helena yelps with laughter, and she keeps on laughing, and that makes me happy. We ride west, under vine tents, through the black stone heat-absorption fields, past the succulent fields with millions of glowing cactus needles . . . past the Crafts Contribution Compound, where Helena contributes, with its smithy and kilns and the woodshop and the lens cutter, the roofed lean-tos in which the gear contributors sit while they stitch and thread and reinforce . . . take the straight wide road past the wildflowers and juniper, the migrating clouds of bees, the young saplings that will one day be a forest, home to chipmunks and foxes and birds and more trees . . . beside the riparian sagebrush lining the shallow arroyo that feeds a trickle of water to all of Canland . . . and finally arrive at the three largest buildings in the whole Part, each one austere, constructed or renovated with recycled materials, and aesthetically unique. One, small and plain, is devoted to housing and recreation; another, larger and seeming as if pulled together by a magnetic force that attracted all the nearest metals, is devoted to offices, classrooms, and supply storage; the third, devoted to energy manufacturing, scientific research, and greenhouses, is the largest and newest-looking, though it is actually the longest-standing—a refurbished warehouse that used to store goods for one of the largest capitalist organizations on Earth, before the Evanescence.

Helena chains her bike to a rack outside the wonky classroom building. Most of the students lingering around are not in costumes, but the ones who are observing Halloween this year are dressed in heavy black-and-white makeup that I would describe as skeletal. There is one boy with straight combed hair who is supposed to be Arturo Eagles. There's also a primly dressed woman with half of her face spattered with cosmetics to make it look as though her skull has been crushed, and protruding from her waist is a strapped-on wooden shelf that is decorated with miniature rocks and shrubbery so it looks like the base of a ravine. She is holding in one hand a pamphlet, and in the other, a pair of surgical scissors. Her outfit—not including all the festive accoutrements—bears a resemblance to the one Helena has on now. I wonder if the likeness is intentional. The young woman's hair is pinned up too. Several students, some costumed in black-and-white makeup and cloaks, and others in regular clothes, are standing near her and against the side of the building, holding up big signs. One reads: HEATHER HORVAT, 37. MY MOTHER'S GRIEF COUNSELOR. WROTE BIRTHDAY CARDS AND ALWAYS CARRIED THEM AROUND, JUST IN CASE.

I remember the birthday card lady. WEDA issued her a formal warning, citing an abundance of unnecessary waste after waste reallocation contributors found a pile of birthday cards in the compost. She made them by starching and baking squares of cloth in the sun, and painted them with ink made from huckleberry, firethorn, powdered daisies, mud, sawdust, and charcoal. She was inventive. She jumped from the Notch a week ago.

We approach the building. The sign holders all contort their faces—their eyes roll back, their mouths open crookedly, their heads hang limply on their necks—as if to appear dead.

"Are you OK?" Helena says, holding the door open, letting me pass through.

"Yes," I nod. "Are you?"

She doesn't answer, but might not have heard me. She leads us to the lecture hall, and when she opens the door, I recognize the empty room as the auditorium in which, years ago, a few music students set up a piano and sat in the audience while I performed a short concert for them while Helena was in a meeting somewhere else. The students all clapped for me at the end. Helena descends the aisle now, hitching her satchel higher on her shoulder. In the topmost row, I sit in an aisle seat, put my pollution mask in my knapsack, and switch my sun goggles out for my regular ones.

"Can you hear me back there?" Helena says from the stage.

The way I know that Helena's the most important person in my life is because I'll be hearing her voice in my head, and then she'll start talking in real life, and it's like nothing's changed.

I give a thumbs-up. Helena gives a thumbs-up back and then puts on her pince-nez and arranges her papers on the stone podium. People start to file in and take seats. I wonder if Helena will take my suggestion to use spiders as a metaphor to explain self-sacrifice for the sake of posterity—the spiders who are eaten by their mates, knowing they'll be eaten. But do they really know they'll be eaten? Can they tell each other? Do they have stories? Tradition? Religion? Probably not. It is still a great metaphor, I think.

Helena waves from the stage to some of the audience members.

They exchange greetings and kind words. If this is a Purist conference, it's my first. Hopefully Helena will discourage all the Notch-jumping, the DOTEC-hating, and the Purist-blaming. She has a stage and an audience. It's up to her to close this violent chapter in Canland's history. If only she could get through to Dylan. I still don't understand the root of their mutual hostility.

Here she comes, marching up the aisle, lifting her pince-nez off her nose, sitting in the chair in front of mine, twisting herself back to face me. "You OK?"

"Yes."

"I'm safe up there, you don't have to worry."

"I wasn't."

"There are COHO right offstage, just in case. You're going to sit here?"

"Yes."

"OK. I'll be starting soon. I just wanted to say, I brought you here because I think it's important that you know not only what I believe, but how I advocate for it. You're going to hear me say some things that might upset you and some things that might make it seem like I don't love being a mother. But I do. You're the reason I believe what I believe. I want to leave you a better world than the one you live in now."

"This is the best version of a world I can imagine."

As soon as I say it, I imagine one day living in a Canland in which the arroyo is a river, and there are no rations, but a surfeit of crops, and the young uncertain saplings are a thick established forest, and the DOTEC all live in homes, have contributions, get treatment at the Safe Haven, and Michael lives with us, and Dylan eats meals with us, and AB is never in pain, and together we run through the Part Center, where Sybil performs, so beautifully inspired, and we chase down fly balls hit by kids who are my friends—or even by me! A world in which I'm allowed to play baseball, and play whatever songs on the piano I want.

But even I am different in that world. So, maybe, the biggest problem with my world, as it is, is me.

Helena shushes me and my thoughts. She kisses my forehead many times, keeping her head against mine. She smooths down my hair, breathing, "*Shh . . .* Stop thinking. Remember to breathe."

I take a deep breath. "I need to pee."

She pulls her face away. With her mouth small, she says, "You can go by yourself?"

"Yes."

"Hurry back."

"I will be swift and safe."

Just outside the door are the costumed students holding signs. One of them is looking at me—the one with the cleverly made ravine protruding from her waist.

"What do you call your costume?" I ask.

"I call it *Helena Damon-Weekes Takes Her Own Advice*," she says with a straight face. She blinks at me.

"*The End of Our Problems*," says a boy in skeleton makeup.

"*Freedom*," adds a girl wearing no costume.

"Oh. Well, do you know where the toilet is?" I ask them all at once.

"Around the corner, on your right," says the one with the elaborate costume.

I look over her face. She has blue eyes and light freckles beneath her blood-makeup. Her hair is somewhere between tawny and brassy, pulled back into a bun with curls falling by her temples.

"I feel sorry for you," she says.

"Why?" I ask.

"Lydia," says the girl wearing no costume.

"Your mother is evil," Lydia says.

The longer I look at her, the less she looks like Helena.

"No, she's not," I tell her.

"She wants to decrease the human population."

"That's a good thing."

"Not if it's by killing people."

"She doesn't kill people."

"Lydia, leave him alone," says the boy.

"He's a child—he needs to understand," Lydia says.

"I do understand," I say. "It's very simple."

"Is that right?"

"There are too many people."

"I've heard about you," Lydia says. "A lot of us have."

"Lydia!" the girl shouts.

"It's OK," I say. "You can't hurt my feelings."

Lydia sighs. "Have you ever had ice cream?"

"No."

"Me neither. It sounds like the most delicious thing ever made. All I want to do in my life is eat ice cream."

"I'm having trouble drawing the connection to my mom," I say.

Lydia's face is doing something, and I don't know what it means. Her mouth is curled up into her nose and her forehead and chin are all furrowed. Her breath is loud. I shrug and walk to the bathroom.

Lydia and all the other the protestors don't understand how good our life in Canland is. Some Parts don't even have a college. Canland has one because of Helena. Canland has everything it has because of Helena. She was here from the beginning. She looked around at this abandoned, barren land, felt the heat trapped between the mountain ranges, and said, defiantly, *Here—this is where we'll live.* And she and Michael and Viceroy Hugo led dozens, then hundreds, then thousands to Canland, and one root, one bug, one person at a time, made it a place that required the help of no one and nowhere else. Every detail that makes this place run on its own like a perfect symphony—the eternally working worms of the vermicomposting system; the vine awnings that suck up carbon and lower the temperature, plus all the vine growing in shallow beds on the roofs of the adobe stacks and pruned to cover the south- and west-facing walls; all the support species planted to protect the fruit-bearing trees; the mountain pines and the eucalyptus walls to slow the wind and shade the adobes; the trenches and the wells she helped dig, the fields she helped sow, the clay homes she helped build until the land was green enough for Arturo Eagles to recognize Canland's good work and reward us with solar panels, a Sensatarium, the clean electricity that runs through it, and a medical facility that can treat a hundred people at a time, in one beautifully symbiotic home for thousands of contributors to call their own—are all because Helena said we need to make places like this livable because one day there might be no escape, so let's get used to it. And then she helped found an institution of higher learning so all the students here today could learn to live in a Part that once was nothing but now is more than most people have, and refine what they believe, and then express it, even if that means they get to oppose the woman who fought for the possibility of their thriving existence. But even Helena would tell you, this place is more important than any one of us because it makes us all possible.

I shake my penis and dab it dry, wash my hands, and go back to the auditorium. All the sign-holders are gone.

Not gone—inside.

Helena's at the podium and the auditorium is full, the students scattered among the audience of, by some quick practical math, two hundred. My seat is still vacant. I sit, holding my knapsack in my lap. The man who waved before winks at me. I ignore him again. I'm sure we don't know each other.

I appear to have reentered partway through her introduction.

"As long as we're here, the fact of the crisis remains. And the crisis is not extremism. The crisis is compromise. Canland was built on our surrender to the Earth. You live here, so you must believe this too. I see your anger, I understand it, and I see that it is directed at me. But I, too, once had a checklist of all the ways I'd change the world until I realized, after years of fighting and working to build a Part that would be a home to thousands, that my younger self's ambition was not so different from the pursuit of Dominion. Like the generations before us, I thought the answer was in shrinking the Earth."

Shrinking the Earth—I said that to her. Or had I only said that to her because she once said it to me? We're like each other's mirror and I sometimes forget which side I'm on.

"We cannot capture an ecosystem. We must facilitate its restoration, then step aside. If you proceed under the assumption that what we are doing is anything other than necessary, then you will walk a hell on Earth more terrible than the elders here among you did. You will carry on a cyclical war, and you will return to where you are now, only with less. And you will remember me, us, who told you what we knew. I promise."

Last night while she was reading her speech to herself, she looked up and said to me, "You know there is no hell, right? A soul needs a body to feel pain. When the body dies, there is no more suffering."

I should've written it down so the scene would stay clear in my memory, but I'm guessing I thought then about Michael, and how he believed in the influence of some incorporeal thing's will.

She touches the bridge of her pince-nez, looks down at her papers, then scans the room.

"I just had a conversation with my son. He's twelve, and he lives with a congenital condition that makes him unable to feel physical pain. Obviously, this creates psychological complications, many of which are, thankfully, surmountable. But the most concerning thing, and the thing that never will change, is that he's never afraid. It took motherhood to teach me that fear is an indispensable asset. It tells us when something is wrong. He doesn't possess that basic emotion that transcends species—maybe the only emotion that is universal. My son does, however, have one thing humans often lack, and that some animals possess so inherently that we can hardly name it. It's an assumption of goodness. You might call it trust, but for him, there's no choice in the matter, so call it purity. He is more gentle, more forgiving, more well-intentioned than any person I've ever known. Just a minute before I stood up here, he said to me, 'This is the best version of a world I can imagine.' For a second, I couldn't help but hope that he was right, that there was something I was missing, some detail of our position that I'd gravely misinterpreted." She pauses, then smiles from the corners of her mouth. "At the risk of calling attention to the fact that he's a second child, I find myself desperately needing his life to count for something. I often fail to meet my standard of perfection as a mother, but I try to make him understand that we live in an imperfect and dangerous world. He has a hard time seeing that, but from him, we can all learn the lesson that we must constantly remind ourselves of the danger we're in. It is necessary to protect that which cannot protect itself. And this must be how we justify our existence, in surrender to the Earth."

Last night I said to Helena, "So, for me, which is it?"

And she said, "What? Which is what?"

"Well," I said, "do I have no body, or no soul?"

"They're the same thing," she said. "You're just a living animal, having a sentient experience."

"Michael always wanted me to consider the possibility," I said.

"Of incorporeal suffering? Go right ahead," she replied, giggling.

I didn't get very far with the idea.

"The population's going up again," she says now. "People are consuming more and wasting more again. Five hundred pounds of food post-harvest went uneaten last year in Canland—unforgivable. Meanwhile, we can't pass a motion to build homes for the Diaspora of the Environmental Collapse, who are living under a tree. You protest against me instead of their mistreatment. What makes you think we don't need laws to contain the population? What makes you think we can sustain unmanageably large nuclear families, and what makes you think you deserve to have them? All across this continent, children die from starvation, disease, exhaustion, and suicide. Where are they going to go? All Parts within a five-hundred-mile radius of Lake Superior evacuated because of an algae bloom—not because of a methane bomb thrown in there by one extremist group or another, but because the water got too hot. The water got hot, methane got trapped under surface scum, and an algae bloom rendered the biggest source of freshwater on the continent not just useless, but also hazardous. We settled in Canland because the desert withstands the heat, and we've slowly brought it back to life. But tedium and toil have a tendency to erase history, so let me remind you that for generations, this land was lifeless, ever since the theft of water by politicians two hundred miles south of here, in what used to be solid ground, a city, the cultural hub of America, that old world: Hollywood. We all still know what that word means, but we forget how it came to be. People settled in those desert mountains atop the ocean, where the sun always shined and the ocean sparkled, but for drinking water, they stole from the farmlands we've now restored, pumped it into their homes, their studios, their countless buildings, faster than rain could compensate, all so they could make television shows to sell products that they produced in factories built in developing countries to feed the rich and starve the poor. It was simple math. People went inside to surround themselves with their products in front of their televisions, that great technology that spawned the epoch of the Entertainment Age. They didn't realize that, just by sitting inside, they were destroying the outside. They took everything they could, and it made no one happy. And then they left us with the inexplicable to explain to you, their grandchildren."

She takes a small sip of water from a half-filled glass resting on a small table next to the podium.

"So now, to limit what entertainment can become, WORLD isolates artists in Arts Parts and athletes in Athletics Parts. They transfer researchers, bred in institutions like this one, to exclusive Parts of their own, where they advance Arturo Eagles' acronym, the Worldwide Objective: Restoration, Longevity, Dominion. In Canland, we serve Restoration. We provide evidence while ecologists, botanists, zoologists, and taxonomists continue to argue whether an ecosystem needs to strive toward equilibrium, if the presence of a dominant species sustains an ecosystem, or whether organisms will survive no matter the ecosystem's location and condition. Our greatest plight here is that we are aware we are experiencing not just progress, but evolution. Many of us are terrified that a life of contributions and modest consumption is the only way forward. I'm telling you—on behalf everyone who lived before and lives now, regardless of faction—it is. We must all agree that what we're doing is not futile. It is difficult, and it is necessary, to ingratiate ourselves with nature, to work in co-operation with it, and to ensure that, for all our suffering, our fighting, our witness to the Evanescence of our world, at least we learned the lessons we were supposed to."

I follow her eyes from one costumed, made-up head to the next.

"Thank you for listening to me thus far," she says to them. "I know you're probably waiting for the right moment to let me know what you think of me. My guess is that moment is coming soon, but I already know how you feel, so I'll ask you to please just listen a little longer."

She clears her throat and looks back down at her papers, then up at everyone.

"In Canland's first five years we grew the population to five hundred, and the challenge was to feed everyone. The children fit in a single classroom, and everyone who lived and survived had wandered here as DOTEC. Over the next thirteen years, the population soared to twenty-seven hundred, as we became able to sustain new children. But in the last five years, the population has added another eight hundred people, four hundred of whom were born here. That is outrageous, the hubris of humanity on bold display. We need to welcome in DOTEC, not make more children here. You might've thought I just came here today to reiterate what you already know I believe, and to inculcate the doubting minds with Purism, but I'm here with a much more serious objective: to formally introduce the Purist proposal that we subsume the Diaspora of the Environmental Collapse into Canland. We will give them homes, rations, contributions, and award them each registration. Then we will cease growth within Canland for the next ten years, aiming for a net increase of no more than ten registered per year."

The signs start flipping up over heads, blocking my view of the stage.

"I see all of those names. They matter to me. Every one of us has lost someone. And we'll continue to lose people important to us. Death is a part of life, and so is grief. That pain feels worse now than ever because all we have are the people in Canland. If you have family or friends in some other Part, you're separated from them, possibly forever, unless you want to risk everything you have here. But as long as we're in Canland, and Canland is all we have, we must improve our understanding of death, and make it something not to fear. I know it's a rejection of our most natural impulse, but people have lived in a natural state of fear and hatred for so long—forever—that the need for comfort superseded everything else, and led to our near-demise. Some species thrive under stress. They even require it. Pine cones need a fire's heat to release their seeds. The fire melts the seal, the pine cone opens, the seeds germinate, and the forest lives on. But without fire, the forest becomes vulnerable to infection, invasive species, loggers, miners, and, most of all, to the very fact of time. Time is all we get, and the double-edged sword of our intelligence is knowing that our time will end. To fight that fear, we spend too much time acting as though it will never end. Our penance must now be to live in acceptance. Anyone willing to accept this in the purest sense, for the sake of the rest of us and for our singular Earth, deserves the same veneration that military states once gave their soldiers, which made young men want to fight and defend their homes and families and the principles that—"

"Boo!" A female student shoots up out of her seat. She extends her arm and a finger toward Helena. "Boo!"

Now there are other students standing and shouting, "Boo!" and "Savage!" and "Murderer!" and they're walking with their signs raised above their heads up the aisle and out of the auditorium. I would estimate fifty of them.

"I will not address your backs." Helena slips the words through an ebb in the cacophony.

Lydia flicks her eyes at me as she leaves the auditorium. I think she's the last of the students to leave until a skinny boy with burnt red skin and platinum hair stands up and shimmies out into the aisle. The doors to the auditorium slam. The boy stops in the aisle, staring up at Helena. She stares back, making not a single movement, saying not a word. Then the boy reaches into his pocket and pulls out an object I can't see, but everyone ducks beneath the seat backs in front of them, and Helena drops behind the podium, and the COHO offstage steps out, pointing his whistler, and shouts, "Drop it!"

I tuck my head between my knees, waiting for the whistler's compressed air–like an owl's screech, the sound from that day on the hillock, the sound that saved Sybil from being further assaulted by that crazed DOTEC–but when I don't hear it, I lift my head, and the COHO, in his face shield, steps to the edge of the stage, his whistler trained on the boy. The boy appears to be holding up a whistler of his own. From where I am, all I can see of Helena is her shoes, beige sneakers made from eucalyptus trees, and now also a flap of the back of her long navy-blue muslin skirt. She is huddled down, pressed close to the floor, her body guarded by the gray and glittering podium that someone must have brought down from the mountain to be chiseled into its present authoritative shape.

"Hypocrite! What do you have to fear? It's only death!" The boy's voice cracks as he yells. "Face what you're making others face."

"Drop it, now!" the COHO yells again.

"You're sick! And a coward! This isn't even a whistler, it's a pestle!" He throws the object forward and it falls fast to the floor and ricochets against the front side of the stage with a hollow boom.

The COHO keeps his arms straight ahead, the metal piece gleaming at the end. Helena stands up now. She steps to the side of the podium and touches her hairline.

"Shame on you," she says. Heads start raising up again. "You've just frightened everyone in this room for no reason–people here who fought in a war to preserve the Earth so you could have a life that wasn't full of violence and terrorism. Shame on you."

"No reason?" the boy says. He puts his long, thin arms on top of his head. His voice pinches. "How can you tell people that the Earth would be better off without them, and then fear for your life when you're faced with me?"

"We don't insist that others fear for their lives, my friend," says Helena.

"Tell that to my girlfriend's unborn baby. Fuck you and your fucking abortion bill." The boy coughs the words. He starts back-pedaling up the aisle. Everyone's head has risen up, all eyes on the boy. The COHO lowers his whistler.

Helena steps in front of the podium. "The lives at stake are the ones that already exist—"

"All of you!" the boy screams, louder and harder than I'm allowed to, for fear of a hernia I'd never detect. He turns around, tears streaming down his face, and runs up, past me, through the auditorium doors with a slam. Adjusting her pince-nez, Helena steps behind the podium again and looks down at her written speech.

As the doors drag shut, I slip between them out into in the lobby where daylight is blasting through the window, and the sky is a radiant blue. Maybe there's no wind today, no sand, no haze.

The costumed students have vanished, but the boy's quick footsteps are easy to follow. I'm determined to thwart any jus-tification for his vitriol against Helena—she has only Canland's prosperity in mind—and although, like Helena says, the tension caused by opposing forces is good because it creates motion, when the tension becomes too great, things move too fast, and the forces break with violence, and can, in a blink, become useless. There used to be ubiquitous things called rubber bands, she told me, more convenient but much worse than twine.

I thread my arms through my knapsack straps. I lift my feet carefully but tell myself to hurry, and when I round the next brick-wall corner I see the back of him, leaning his forehead against a metal door, his arms limp by his sides. The boy is mut-tering to himself, "Wake the fuck up, man, get it together, can't you be strong for her, for once . . ."

"Hey," I say.

He spins around. His cheeks are flushed and his eyes, wide and full of tears, slope downward at the outsides. He's much taller than me, it feels like twice as tall, and his hair is so blond it's almost green. He clears his throat. "You're Helena's kid," he says.

"Tristan."

"Hope I didn't scare you."

"You didn't."

He sniffs, knuckling his eyes. "Well, I'm sorry you had to hear me say all that. Even if it's true, it's not a pleasant thing to hear someone tear your mother apart."

Just for now, I forego all my usual self-assessment that ensures I properly empathize and express and retain. I tell him, "I don't care, because what you said isn't true. Didn't you listen to what she said in her speech?"

Now the boy's eyes land on my mouth, and then my clothes, my long sleeves and pants. He's wearing short sleeves and shorts. I make my eyebrows come down above my eyes to show him anger, feel my skin bunch up above my goggles.

"Listen, little man," he says, "I don't want to get into it, OK? It's not my responsibility to talk you out of believing what your mom says. Of course you're going to listen to her. Just think of it this way: I wanted the same chance to teach the things that I believe to my own child, and your mom took that away from me."

"She didn't kill your child—your child didn't exist."

His face remains neutral, the position that Sybil would begin with when she'd teach me to interpret, and also a face she would sometimes maintain when demonstrating someone feeling an extreme emotion, like this boy might be, intentionally hiding all the extremity that had just been (literally) pouring out of him, just as Sybil would sometimes unexpectedly start to cry, and then do what she would call biting back tears, and I would marvel at her access. Neutrality can sometimes mean that someone is feeling more than they're able or willing to express.

"She took away my chance of having a child—the child I was going to have. Do you not see the cruelty in that?"

"The same rules apply to everyone," I say. "We have to keep the population from getting too big."

"Says her second child." He shuts his eyes then and closes a fist in the air in front of his head. "I just said I wasn't going to argue with you." When he looks at me again now, it's like he's trying to read very small text written on my face. "You're obviously a smart kid. How old are you?"

"Twelve."

"Still a future—and yet, I'm not much older than you." His forehead relaxes and smooths out, and he sighs. "Who's your favorite teacher at school?"

"Helm Roctern."

"Helm. I liked Helm. He was strange, didn't think like the others."

"He asks good questions and listens to my answers."

"Does he ever ask you how you decide who gets a chance?"

"I don't know."

"If he doesn't, then he's not asking the question that matters."

I shrug, not sure what this guy is talking about. I don't even know who he is, just a man at the end of a brick hallway who seemed to be on his way through this metal door.

"Can I explain it to you, the way I see it?" he asks.

"If you want."

His eyes search the air above his head for what he'll say next. "If, through science, we could have saved that boy who was trampled in the stampede, should we have?"

"I don't know. Maybe nature intended for him to die."

He doesn't answer right away; his nostrils flare, his chin wrinkles, and he stays quiet for so long that I wonder if it's my turn to speak, but I don't because I have nothing to say.

Finally his pursed lips open again. "That condition you have—analgesia—it means you need some help living. Which is fine. But does it mean nature intends for you to die?"

"Well, maybe human interference is part of nature," I say.

"Yes. Good. OK. To save lives, though, right? To give life a chance—all lives."

"But your baby was never alive."

"Stop—" he says, suddenly louder, but then takes a slow breath. "You have to see that this is so much bigger than a question of which unborn baby should live. I shouldn't have been so emotional. Unfortunately, what we choose to research is decided by emotional questions. But this is a question of what science should be allowed to do. Should we let humans interfere, as you said, at the cost of what might have been nature's plan? Because, soon, the question might pertain to living people, like that boy who was trampled."

"Sol."

"Sol. We're already researching ways that deaths like his can be prevented in the future. Because, really, what matters more than the life of a child? I wonder what your mother would say to that."

I think he means because I'm a child, and my mother saves me every day. This guy is pretty smart with how he wields logic.

"Are you a WORLD researcher?" I ask.

"Maybe one day. For now, I'm a student here."

"Oh. Well," I say, "to answer your question, doesn't it depend on what the research is? Some research is OK and worth it, but some isn't."

"It's funny you should ask. Your condition's neurological, right?"

"Yes."

"Try to stay with me. We're breeding mammals so we can control their aggression impulses, using an old technique called optogenetics. We've bred rats so their brains respond to a laser being switched on inside a fiberoptic window installed in their skulls. The laser ablates the amygdala so they temporarily lose their stress response, kind of like you. Do you know what the amygdala is?"

"Yes."

"What's your specialization?" He knocks on the metal door behind him. "You want to be a researcher?"

I won't answer. I don't need him knowing anything more about me.

"All those students," he says, "who protested the things your mother stands for—they're all through this door, beneath our feet, coming up with the answers to the questions that matter. They're figuring out how to save lives."

"By manipulating animals' brains?"

"Who knows? One day, we might be turning off the aggression centers in the brains of wolves who wander into Canland before we send them back out into the mountains. Or we'll eliminate fear in cows. Then there won't be any more stampedes. No one will die the way Sol did. It'll be the final step in animal husbandry."

"I don't agree with that."

"You don't see it. Maybe you're too young. Maybe you don't have a researcher's mind, but we're making the world a safer place for all life."

"You're disrupting nature."

"You think so? And what about taking away a baby's chance at life?" One of his sloping eyes starts to tear up again. He digs his thumb knuckle into his inner tear duct. "What's it cost?" he whispers.

A memory accosts me like an unseen wall I bump into: Michael, sitting at the table, his face in his hands. Helena sitting beside him, rubbing his shoulder, supporting her chin with her fist and looking away. I'm watching from the mouth of the hallway. Dylan, unseen, wraps a hand around my chest from behind. "We don't talk about The Spill," Helena said to me once, and conditioned me once for mentioning, even only to her. "Your father's seeking redemption for The Spill," she'd say. The deconstruction of a Texas nuclear power plant, which he ordered, which went awry, and the millions exposed to radiation—we don't talk about it. "Nothing was the same after that," Helena would say. It's why he left. And at the table, she turns to him and says, "It isn't your fault." When he lowers his hands from his face, he looks like someone else, not my father—his eyes too big and his mouth too small, like his lips have fallen off. I used to know Michael's face. Helena says to him, "Hey, come back, don't go there." She grabs his hand and says, "Hey, look at me, we have everything we need right here." Then Michael turns to look at Helena, and I can only see the back of his head, but what slowly happens to Helena's face is something I only see right when I have done something for which she is going to condition me—like a wiping-out of all her features. With a light pressure on my chest, Dylan pulls me back into the hallway, into our room, which we shared then, and he lies on his bed, and I lie on mine because I've been given no directive. After a while, Dylan says, "I guess when you try to save the world you run the risk of destroying it." "Yeah," I say, "I guess."

A month later, Michael left.

The young man is staring at me.

"I have to go back," I say.

"I'm inviting you to come look in on this experiment," he says. "Maybe it'll change your mind."

Beside the door, affixed to the wall, there's a small gray pad. He holds his thumb up to it. A red light comes on, then the light turns green, and the door slides open. There's a long staircase going down. I've never seen a staircase so big. There are very few stairs in Canland, and even less familiar to me is all the electricity I realize must be running the lab beneath my feet—our home is the only one I know of that has electricity, and even Dylan's consumption through his Sensorium is minimal, compared to what I suspect the Canland College Research Center uses.

"I think what you're doing in the lab is awful," I say. "I hope you never touch the brain of a wolf." And while Michael might scoff at that declaration—reminding me of all the good science has done for me, that, yes, I would be dead without it (no, Michael, I do not think science is bad; it is the reason Canland exists, of course, but you're not here, and this is my life, and I won't live it according to what people who have left it think might be best for me)—I'm choosing to defend the people here. I am a Purist.

The boy nods. "Sorry you feel that way. See you around, Tristan."

"What's your name?"

"Byron."

"What's your girlfriend's name?"

"Yuna."

"Well, Byron. I hope one day you and Yuna can have a child," I say. "When you're allowed to."

Byron turns through the open doors, which immediately shut, and the light turns red again.

I hear a man calling my name from down the hall. I round the corner and walk back toward the auditorium. The COHO, his face shield still drawn and his features obscured by the daylight reflected through the windows, lowers his whistler and waves me toward him.

"Your mother asked me to look for you," he says. "Did you see where the boy went?"

"Did he do anything wrong?" I ask.

"Not exactly."

"Oh. Well, I didn't."

The COHO opens the door to the auditorium for me, but he doesn't enter.

I make my way down the aisle, toward the stage, where Helena sits at the edge with her feet dangling off as, below her, people walk past one by one and reach up, and she hands each of them an unlit candle, wearing the sort of smile she gives me in our very best moments together. After each person takes their candle, they go back up to the seats, where there are now only a couple dozen people, all their arms linked together, swaying and humming a wordless melody that is simple but makes me think of a day like today, clear and blue. So I go down the aisle toward the stage, and Helena shakes her head at me, though still smiling, and lifts herself off the stage onto the floor, takes my hand, and links my arm through hers. Beside her, I become the end of the line of people humming, and I try to learn the melody. I raise my voice louder with theirs, and I almost learn the song, and then our voices become softer, and our arms break apart, and people start embracing. Helena turns to the woman next to her, while a man comes toward me with open arms and then, even though I don't know him, we are hugging.

.

The day's blazing blue. With their head on Sasha's belly, AB's shivering like the air over the desert floor.

6

Nov 5, 2088

Helena was making eggs fried in butter for breakfast, which is usually my favorite, but the grill fire got too high and she had to douse it with water, and she screamed that it was the water she was going to use to wash our clothes later, and why couldn't I do anything for myself—she was always distracted by the thought that I'd be off somewhere poking myself with a cactus pin. The house got all smoky, so I had to eat nuts and raisins outside, and sitting on the step, I stared into the garden, hoping to see some life moving, but there was nothing. Helena snapped her fingers at me and said, Eat, while she stood on the walkway and watched the smoke pour out the windows, and Dylan, who'd unchained his chrome bike and was waiting in the street for me to finish eating so he could take me to school, kept rubbing his eyes and yawning, and Helena yawned too, and dragged her hand across her forehead to the edge of her eye so the skin pulled and showed the pink inside her lid. I said, I'm going to school now, and she said curtly, Have a good day, and like an adult I said, Thanks, Helena, I will, and you too.

During the ride to school, there were two small birds overhead threading flight paths over and under one another, disappearing into trees behind us and reappearing in the air ahead of us. I don't know how birds do it.

Where there are trees, there are birds, and where there are birds, there are bugs, and where there are bugs, there is life in places we can't see. It's the first thing they teach in school—interconnectedness, the dependency of all things on all other things, companions and adversaries alike.

The road to school was bumpy and in need of grooming.

We began today in Practical Math with Gwen Horn leading us through the WORLD Sunrise. She said, Let's all make sure we do our part today. Then we all laid our right arms over left, made our top hands into a C, and in unison lifted our top arms up from the elbow at a forty-five degree angle, like the woodblock print of Arturo Eagles.

Leo sat behind me in Practical Math. At the end of class, I went to stroke my ponytail, but I grabbed air. When I stood up, I saw it lying on the floor like a piece of rope too frayed to use. Leo had already left the room well ahead of me. I picked it up and put it in my knapsack, but decided not to say anything—if Sybil had been here, Leo wouldn't have done that, and knowing that was enough. But then, after Creative Thought and Expression—in which Helm had us converse in gibberish (which was difficult for me), and Leo and Lilly argued in diphthongs until they ended up hugging each other, apparently reconciling whatever they were going through—Helm, in the hallway, said to me, New haircut, there, T-Bird?

Leo did it, I replied casually, not intending to get Leo in trouble.

Without your permission, I assume?

It's OK, I said.

Helm replied, It is definitely not OK.

Then, in front of everyone, Helm scolded Leo so loudly that Lilly pressed her hands to her ears and her whole face turned red as her sunburnt nose, and so severely that on the floor around Leo's shaking legs, a puddle formed. There were practically ripples in the puddle from the echo of Helm's voice. Helm issued Leo no further punishment, I suppose feeling that a pee-inducing reproach was worse than an hour in energy manufacturing.

While everyone else then headed to Practice of Agriculture, Helm came up to me and said, Sorry, T-Bird, I didn't mean to embarrass you. I told him he hadn't. Well, he said, I know you can defend yourself, so I'm sorry I didn't give you the chance, I just . . . Then he trailed off and asked if I needed him to accompany me to my exemption period. I accepted because I like Helm's company, but I also wanted to ask him his thoughts about the experiment Byron had told me about.

Doesn't surprise me, he said. WORLD, on a large scale, and even Canland, on a smaller scale, does all sorts of shit—stuff—we don't know about. It doesn't really affect you, if you don't let it. Besides, nothing like that would ever be practically implemented. It's like the Purists' teenage vasectomy proposal. It's not going to happen, but people need to stake their claim in something, to show they're on a side. It's what helps tribes to form and ideas to grow and make people feel like they belong.

Whose side are you on? I asked.

I'm trying to think of a diplomatic answer, he said. Words escape me. Both and neither, I guess. It depends. I suppose I'm on my students' side—the side of creative thought and expression. Then he smiled, showing his yellowish teeth from inside his beard.

We were nearly at the library. I feel like I can ask Helm anything, and I'm not exactly sure why I asked him what I then did, but as I think about it now, I suppose it had something to do with wanting to know if my recent decisiveness was going to lead me in the right direction.

So I said, Do you have many friends?

Which made Helm laugh as if at a joke that was smart, rather than silly. I've got my people. But you don't need to worry about me, T, he said.

I'm not, I said as we arrived at the library and he waved goodbye to me. But then I remembered his wife, from whom he was separating, he'd told me on that day we discussed the history of Canland, and also of his brother, whom we discussed that same day, who died before Helm's eyes during the war. So I wondered if he had other people with whom he was close, or if he was lying.

A few minutes into my exemption period, Roshana walked into the library. She sat on the opposite side of the room with three books open on the table before her. I was at my usual table, reading the first story in Helm's book. It's about a soldier who wants to be a father and has been trying to get his wife pregnant before his redeployment. Then one day he gets to base and is told he's been reassigned for three months in another state. Without much discussion, he and his wife decide she should stay put while he goes on assignment. While the soldier is away he gets deployed to take out a DOTEC militia. After tracking the militia for weeks to a small northern lakeside town, the soldier throws a flash grenade into a trapdoor, and when his squad goes down to investigate, they find a woman holding a baby who is bleeding from the head. The mom's clearly alive and the squad commandant calls CASEVAC to send her and the baby to the hospital. In the ensuing days, the squad captures some of the militia, but others escape, so it's like a half-success. The last two weeks on the soldier's assignment are spent at base, passing the time with gardening and baseball and banter about each other's significant others. One night, he finds a picture of his wife under his CO's pillow with some dried stuff flaking at the edge (I'm not sure what the implication is, maybe a booger or drool. Actually, now that I write it, it's probably semen). The soldier wants to kill his CO, but he can't even bring himself to confront him, adding to his feelings of unmanliness. When the soldier goes back home at the end of the three months, he is sexually impotent. He never tells his wife about the baby in the cellar. That, plus the shame of his failing manhood, becomes too much to bear. He feels so angry that he becomes terrified he'll scare his wife, or worse, so he files for redeployment again without telling her. On the night before he ships back out, he says a prayer that his wife gets pregnant, but he doesn't specify how or by whom, but just that he comes back to a child-bearing wife. They will never have to talk about how or why, and he will be a father.

Once I finished reading the story I put the book down and asked Roshana why she wasn't at Practice of Agriculture. She said, Because I requested it. I asked why and she said, It's none of your business. And I said, But we're friends, you can tell me. And she said, I don't want to be friends with you anymore, you care more about spiders than being nice to people. I said, I'm nice to people. She said, No, you're not. You're not nice to Malakai. You're not nice to me. Just because you don't hit me or pull my hair like Leo doesn't mean you're nice. I asked her what I'd done wrong. She said, Your brother is a bad person and I hate it here, I don't have any friends, people think I'm ugly and weird and they're right. I should be outside planting and harvesting right now, but instead I'm inside talking to you, and you don't even know why you aren't nice, you just watch me like you're doing now. I said to her, People do those things to me too; they call me weird and ugly. And she said, But you don't care, and then she started crying. I sat next to her and put my arm around her shoulders and started humming, but she said, Can you please stop that? So I stopped. I just sat there with her, hoping I was doing it right. When the bell finally rang, she said, Thank you, sorry I said you were a bad person, I don't think you are, it's just hard when your only friend doesn't understand at all what you're going through. And I said, You can tell me whenever you want. Roshana sat for a while as if contemplating whether or not she should talk to me about what was bothering her. She then said she had to go to the bathroom and left, taking all her things, except for a book about dinosaurs she'd been reading, and a picture she'd drawn. The picture was of a dinosaur with too many teeth to tell if it was smiling or angry, sitting in a field, staring up at a sun that took up basically the entire sky. She left the picture on the desk, which made me think she wanted me to have it, so I folded it up and put it in my pocket, and put the book back on the shelf for her.

I've lately been wondering if friendship is even worth the fight. I don't mean to sound haughty, but I've been more curious about the ethics of ablating Roshana's stress centers than about the root of her suffering. Maybe Sybil was right to abandon her friends. Michael provided me tools that might go to waste if I concern myself too much with Roshana's trifles. Even Dylan and Helena both put their work and their causes before me sometimes. What will my work be? Entomology? Piano? My condition presents endless obstacles . . .

At the end of the day, while I waited for Dylan to show up, and it was hot and the sky was practically candescent with sunlit overcast, I saw Malakai and Helm sitting together in the dirt against the fence. Malakai had his elbows on his knees and his fingers all gripping one another, and he was looking at the ground between his feet. Helm turned his head to face Malakai and spoke quietly, scratched his beard, turned his head away to cough, and spoke to Malakai some more. Then Malakai nodded with a hard blink, Helm held out his hand, and they slapped palms and punched fists and snapped their fingers. Helm's snap was like a tree branch cracking. Then Helm got up and went back inside.

I stood there watching Malakai for what felt like a long time. He was sweeping a foot back and forth in the dirt, taking deep breaths now and then, and looking up into the trees that shaded him. An uncommon thought entered my head, which was that, if Canland experienced some life-threatening natural disaster, Malakai was less deserving of aid than me, because he's DOTEC and my parents are founders. I recalled things I'd heard other presents say to him this week, and wondered if it was because of my coevals that I felt this way about Malakai. Hey, Malakai, based on your personal experience, which of us would be the most delicious, and what part do you eat first? Hey, Malakai, do you and your random dad still snuggle up real tight like you're sleeping under a highway? Is there, like, a DOTEC network where you burrow underground and communicate with people in other Parts on how to wreck the planet again? I know it's in your blood to cut power lines, but if you sabotage the Sensatarium, we're all gonna be so bored that we'll all show up at your house and make you tell us stories about what you saw as a DOTEC. Aw, Malakai, you know we're only kidding, please don't kill us all, we know you probably have practice.

I get a lot of WORLD benefits because of my parents, like eggs and a Sensorium and a vegetable garden, and he probably doesn't get any. It seemed obvious as I considered all this that my fortunes are much greater than his. Which might be fine, but considering our personal history—he rejected the guava I offered him, and he also got angry at me because I eavesdropped on him praying to his dead parents, and there was the obvious incident between Dylan and Asher, when Dylan kicked their beloved pomegranate tree in two—I reasoned that Malakai wouldn't want to talk to me. So I stood there, and he sat there, far apart, waiting.

Dylan's glinting bike came whizzing up the path. I put my pollution mask on and climbed onto the back seat. As my hand grazed the frame I received a static shock. I asked Dylan if I was OK, and he said, You're fine, let's go. But then the grooves of my brain parted, and to the front of my mind slid the memory of when Michael went too long without changing my diaper, and my infection went undetected, and Cole had to save my life. I thought, Neglect is another way of being unkind. So then I called out, Hey, Malakai, are you waiting for something? Do you need a ride? I can ride on the handlebars.

Dylan looked over his shoulder back at me.

No, thanks, Malakai said. I've got training.

What training? Dylan said.

Malakai looked up at the sentry tower and the COHO garrisoned there.

Marksmanship, said Malakai.

Dylan stared at him, silent. Then he laughed. All right, Malakai, Dylan said. Just don't use it on us. Then Dylan laughed again and rode on down the path. It was a clear, still day with strong sunlight, and the mountain range ahead to the west held a painted quality, like all the world was contained in Canland before me. Even the multistory adobe stacks, the trees, the carts, the kiosks, and the fields and the people in them, all appeared on one plane, depthless,

implied, and unreal. So I craned my neck back toward the mountains to the east. They held shadow. In the evening, they'd turn
red. I pictured Malakai walking across the desert to get here, not
knowing if he'd find a home. I never had to find Canland. I'm deciding now not to be his friend, but to admire him.

I took care of your boyfriend, Dylan said to me.

Who?

The kid on the hill.

AB's not a boy.

Girlfriend, then.

Nor a girl.

Well, whichever way, I got them a tube with a pretty thick core,
so it'll last them a bit.

OK.

No thank-you?

Thank you, I said, though I was not thrilled by this, and I can't
say quite why.

I'm just playing with you, Beautiful. I'm in a good mood, like
a little bird.

When I said nothing, Dylan said, Don't you wanna know why?

Sure, I said.

Because I'm the smartest person alive.

Yes, I already knew that, I said.

As we passed the coast live oak tree—which, despite so many
changes around Canland, has not changed at all, is still robust and
healthy and kingly and benevolent, providing shade and reaching
down its limbs, and if not providing any fruit, per se, then at least
being a constant source of life and shade and support for those
who rest beneath it, which to me is a hopeful thing, that here in
Canland, life from before the settling, before the war, before the
Evanescence, can thrive, and that even as things change, not everything old dies—AB was rolling down the hillock with the two
children to whom Sybil had given her rations, all laughing, the
children's mother and Sasha the mother-to-be watching together
from beneath the tree. The air smelled like crops and fresh manure.

Want to know why? Dylan said.

Why what? I'd said, already knowing this would frustrate him.

You're impossible sometimes, Beautiful.

I paused, thought, then said, Why are you the smartest person in the world, Dylan?

Attitude! he exclaimed.

Tell me why, I said.

Take a guess, he replied.

We took the bend around the copse of tall leaning blue gums that shade Asher and Malakai's communal housing street, same as we do every day.

I don't know, I said. You finally found Michael.

Oh! he yelled again. Psychic. You ruined the fun. Yes, I obtained 2D video of him from 2300 hours to 0200 hours Central Time, October fourth to fifth, 2088.

So, from a month ago, I said.

Dylan said, Shit, Beautiful, what's the world come to that I can't even impress you? I'm on the scent is what matters, he was some-where in the vicinity of Lake Superior, as I suspected. Found him through the same computer that ordered the satellite to track the plane that dropped the methane bomb. Did I not tell you? It was a plane that dropped a methane bomb that caused the algae bloom. Manmade disaster after all. A former U.S. Military aircraft spray-painted with the Purist mosquito on it. Some stupid fuck who thinks all humans should die dropped a methane bomb into the biggest freshwater lake on the whole face of our celestial orb. Our source of life—dropped a motherfucking methane bomb into it. Beautiful?

Helena said it was because the air got too hot, I said.

Well, then Helena is either misinformed or a liar, Dylan said.

Do you know where Michael is now? I said.

Don't worry about it, Beautiful, you know I'm gonna find him again.

Well, congratulations, Dylan—you did it, I said and patted his back.

You want to see his face? he said.

We turned onto our street. The sound of bike gears was smooth and crunchy at once, like a saw through bone. I was feeling indifferent.

Helena was at her gear contribution. Dylan's room smelled stronger than usual—even stronger than the Actualization of the swamp after the hurricane. All the life in the terrarium was consumed by the bloom, bugs and plants all dead, dead, dead, and the algae so alive.

Dylan turned on his monitor and Michael's face appeared. Dylan pressed a button and the face started to move.

It didn't seem like Michael was doing anything at first—just typing and chewing sunflower seeds and spitting shells into a cup—but I know from spending time with Dylan that doing something difficult often looks the same as doing nothing. Having Michael's face there gave me the sense that I was sitting in a room with him, since when I used to sit in rooms with Michael, he was usually busy with something more important than entertaining me (unless I was the subject of his work, of course).

Dylan whispered, He left his camera on, can you believe it? I mean I would've found him anyway, but now we get to see him. What a dolt. If I ever made a mistake like that, I don't think even he would come to my defense. Why are the smartest people the most oblivious, and why do they get away with it?

When Dylan said that, it separated the screen from reality, and it suddenly felt as if someone had shown me a picture of the Grand Canyon and said, Here, now you've seen the Grand Canyon. But no, I've only seen a picture of it. (Which I guess is why Sensoriums are so coveted and useful—we really do see what's in the Actualization.) So many features of Michael's face had escaped my memory. I was surprised to see that his hair looked more like a shadow, and that his brow and cheekbones and nose and chin were all very pronounced, but squeezed onto a narrow head, like his features had risen from bone and cartilage pushing up against each other. His eyes were close together and he had a scar on his left cheek.

I saw a general resemblance to Dylan, especially how Dylan's jaw hangs when he's concentrating, but it was hard for me to picture Dylan bald since his hair is always hanging in front of his cheeks, even though it's thin hair, and will probably all fall out someday (the evidence was before me). Dylan pushed his face close to the screen and shook his head very subtly as if he were looking into a microscope and was fascinated with what he saw. I even said to Dylan, I thought Michael looked different. But Dylan only said, Well, he doesn't, he looks like that.

I stared at Michael's cheek scar. I felt a bond with him since I have so many scars. I asked Dylan, How did he get his scar? Dylan didn't answer right away.

The only thing that really happened was that at one point a woman came into the room—the room was bare and had another desk and computer in the background, but nobody sat there—and the woman was holding a cup with a white, glossy mound in it, and a spoon sticking out. At first, I thought it was butter, but then Dylan said, That's ice cream. She gave the cup to Michael and he spooned some into his mouth and laughed while looking at her. Maybe she'd said something funny; there was no sound in the video. And her head was above the top of the frame, so I couldn't see what she looked like. She left, and Michael finished his ice cream while smiling down into the cup. After he finished, it took a long time for his smile to fade as he went back to typing.

Dylan asked me if I wanted to watch the rest. It's basically more of this, he said. So I said, No, that's OK. And he said, OK, but you gotta see this. Dylan skipped to the end of the video and played the last few seconds. The skin around Michael's eyes had turned purplish. He yawned and rubbed his eye. Then he glanced straight up into the camera. He mouthed Fuck, then the frame was suddenly black.

Dylan laughed with only his breath and said, Chalk it up to an overworked mind.

I said, Why isn't he here?

Then Dylan turned around in his chair and looked at me in a way he usually doesn't. He said, Because what he's doing is way more important.

To which I shrugged.

You understand that, right? he said. There's no point in him being here. He's done everything he can here, so he's off doing better things.

OK, I said.

Be grateful, Dylan said. He gave you your mind.

I know, I said.

One day I'm going to leave Canland to do the type of work Michael does, and people are going to try to hunt me down, but they're not going to be able to find me, Dylan said.

Don't leave, I said.

Dylan turned back to the computer. I thought he was ignoring me, but then he said, in a voice that sounded dried out, I'm not. And by the way, that scar's from the war. Helena told me Michael committed a crime against humanity, and he deserved much worse than that scar, but she was just trying to slander him. I searched the satellites for evidence of where she said he'd burned up all this land and this family with it, and I'm certain that she's lying. Dylan paused then before he turned around to face me again and said, Don't tell Helena I told you.

OK, I said. Also, do you know who that woman was?

No, he said.

Is he in love with her? I asked.

I don't know, he said. Maybe she makes him happy. Helena didn't.

I spent a moment wondering if I'd made Michael unhappy too, until Dylan said, All right, that's it. I need to get back to work.

He'd been in a happy mood earlier, but now he wasn't anymore. I stood up, and as I opened his door, he looked at me. His face was reddish in the grow lights. He narrowed his eyes at me and said, What happened to your hair?

Leo cut it off, I said, but Helm screamed at him until he peed himself.

Dylan stared at me awhile. Then a small smile cracked his face. He shook his head and looked back at his computer. I let myself out of his room.

I wanted to try to make some eggs, but Helena had failed at that task just this morning, so I thought better of it, and I ate some butter and bread instead as I waited for Helena to come home, and thought about Michael, trying to come up with happy memories of him, but for some reason, I was unable to think of anything but him crying about The Spill, and also the day he failed to change my diaper. The only good memory was of when he hiked with me on his back up to the top of the Notch, but the memory was so obvious that it seemed more like an axiom than an experience from my life, and failed to give me happiness.

When Helena came in the door, she was accompanied by a woman whose hair was pulled back so tightly I could see the veins of her scalp, and her mouth was all wrinkled, but I don't think she was as old as she looked. Her eyes behind her glasses were like two big glass balls in her skull. I don't remember her name. Helena said, Tristan, this is my friend So-and-So. Go do your homework in your room, and I'll be in shortly. Then Helena twitched her nose and said, Still stinks in here, sorry, So-and-So, we had a grill fire this morning. The woman nodded and her mouth strained. I don't smell it, she said.

I went to my room and did some Mammalian Biology home-work and wrote most of this journal entry. Then I checked myself and did all my pre-bedtime stuff and went out into the hall again to spy on Helena. She was talking softly to the woman, who was crying and nodding.

Later, while I was pretending to sleep, I had allowed my imagi-nation to wander into a world where Sybil and Michael both came back, and she and I and my parents and brother were all sitting be-neath the oak on a perfect ninety-degree day watching the work-ers in the fields, and AB was walking by alongside the pregnant woman, Sasha, and they waved up at us, and AB ran up the hillock to join us, right when Helena opened my door and said, I know you're awake, let me check you.

I said, I already did it.

She said, Let me do it anyway.

So we went into the bathroom and she checked my lymphangioma scars and looked over the rest of me quickly and said, Good. How was your day?

It was fine, I said. I'm tired.

She said, Fine, then go to bed.

At one point I heard her swatting the walls, the tables, whatever other surfaces, and cursing at a fly. When I heard her door close, I got up and finished writing this.

There goes Dylan for his contribution, with all his memories, secrets, and wishes.

.

November 6, 2088

I had a dream last night. I picked up an apple that looked good, but when I lifted it to my mouth, I saw it was covered in soft oozing brown spots. It was a big apple. I bit into it anyway and it was tasteless. I spat it out—even in my dreams I know how to identify rotten food, like Helena taught me. Then I was holding a knife and I cut the apple in half. The halves fell apart with a dusty crack. The inside was hollow, and in one half was a small tangle of dried worms. There were also four spiders, two picking at the worms and two spinning webs. In the other half of the apple there was

.

Nov 7, 2088

I had another dream last night. I don't usually remember my dreams or even if I dreamt during the night, but I remember this one too. I was sitting in the desert night by a fire with a fox or a dog—I couldn't tell exactly which—roasting on a spit. The animal still had its eyes, but they were lifeless. Also around the fire were three other people: Leo, a nameless older man who was big and in charge, and AB, who had wings. AB didn't speak, even though I was trying to talk to them, they just blinked at me, or not quite at me, but at the space around my head. They had on a happy expression. In the distance, a figure was walking toward us. Leo tore a leg off the roasting fox with his bare hands and started eating it, but the flesh was still raw. The big man in charge grabbed Leo and held him near but not quite over the fire. As the figure in the distance came into the firelight, we saw it was Sybil. AB started crying because they knew I was going to leave. Sybil said, Let's go. Then she and I started running and the big man tossed Leo on the fire and started chasing us. AB was flying overhead. I could see Sybil's face perfectly in the dream, but I can't remember it now. We ran into the woods and when I looked at Sybil, she wore a crown of flowers. She stopped running, so I stopped too. Just before the big man got us, we were in light. She was standing on a stage. I was in the audience, surrounded by people I didn't know, and I was the only one clapping. The light was pouring down from AB, hovering up there like Remedios the Beauty. I woke up with an erection before it was dawn and couldn't go back to sleep.

When dreaming, your brain operates without the interference of consciousness, or maybe I should say awareness, never asking itself what it is doing. In my dreams, my brain produces an illusion of living that is sometimes stronger than real life. It's a phenomenon that, when awake, I think can only be approached in Sensoriums and when I'm playing piano—alone, when no one is listening, and I play anything I want, and the music makes my hands move, and it's like I am the instrument. Without interference, things appear from within you that you never knew you knew.

I didn't finish my entry from November 6 because I heard Helena coming toward my door. It's not that I think she'd be angry if she found my journal; it's just that there are some thoughts and feelings I want to keep to myself.

I no longer remember how the apple dream ended.

Time for breakfast.

·

Nov 8, 2088

No dream tonight, but a fight. This hasn't happened in a long time. I was woken up by the sound of a porcelain cup shattering and then Helena screaming, Don't you ever again, do you hear me? On my life, I'll have you sent away if you ever, *ever* speak to me like that again, I swear to you! And then I heard Dylan yell over and over, 8! 8! 8! 8! 8, 8, 8, 8! One per day, plus one! I carried them out! One of them was his classmate! I see her when I pick him up! I hope there is a god, and I hope they are fair and cruel to you. And Helena said, I'll have you taken away. I'll have them take all your computers and your plants and your Sensorium and everything and you! You'll never see him again!

Then it was quiet and a moment later, my door opened and Helena came in and held me, and she was crying and saying, I love you, I love you so much. I'll protect you, I'll protect you from all the bad things.

She had bandages on her fingers. I asked why. She said she'd had trouble concentrating at her contribution lately and nicked herself with a needle, but she told me not to worry about that, to just know she loves me and she needs me and she'll protect me, and everything is going to be OK, and do I love her . . .? Yes, yes, I love you, Helena . . .

I asked who it was that had died.

She said she didn't know yet, but who knows if that was the truth.

Then at school the next day, we found out it was Roshana.

She rode her bike across the desert to the trailhead.

I don't want to write about it.

I STICK MY journal under my mattress, evenly spread to prevent lumping, and lie down with my head on my pillow. I hope one day I write a song that makes people happy. Your body knows when music sounds right or wrong. I want to write a song that sounds right and makes anyone who hears it feel like they're cared for. Like they're surrounded. Like they're growing, surrounded by other healthy, growing things.

7

November 10, 2088

Helm read a poem he wrote at Roshana's funeral today, then sat back down beside his maybe-ex-wife, and she put her hand on the back of his neck, then took it away, and I saw him turn to her in profile, his shoulders hunched. Then a friend of Roshana's parents spoke of all the ways and how much, ever since she was a baby, Roshana loved life. And then a present named Marlon told the story of when Roshana was skipping through the courtyard and splattered a fallen guava, and he and his friends thought it was the funniest thing they'd ever seen, and some people laughed at the story in a quiet way. I stared at Mr. and Mrs. Medley, sitting up at the front of the room, Roshana's father wiping his forehead and cheeks with a handkerchief, and her mother just completely still. The Secular Observation House was at capacity. People even gathered outside to mourn. Dylan stayed home. Tobias sat next to Helena and me, and at one point, he was sobbing, muttering, Oh Sweet Pea . . . Like he had at the mortuary when he found out Sybil had left. Was Sweet Pea Sybil or Polly? I thought of Polly's funeral, and thought how maybe this was what Sybil was afraid of Canland becoming, that she would be glad to know this was something she would never know.

People were casting Helena looks that made her tell me to just look down between my feet, which I did, mostly. What I did see was when Roshana's father stood up to speak, and all he said was, Roshana, I—and then he couldn't speak anymore and stumbled out the back door, ululating so contagiously that all who had been stoic then broke into tears. I pretended to sniffle and wipe my cheeks. Mrs. Medley sat staring motionless and blank. She said that if anyone had any kind words to say to please stand up and feel free, but was still motionless as she spoke, so it seemed like the voice was coming from someone else. I began to stand up, but Helena grabbed my thigh and kept me in my seat. I had Roshana's dinosaur drawing in my pocket. I wanted to give it to her parents, but I wanted to keep it for myself too, and I might have given it to her parents if I'd been able to see them after the funeral, but Helena rushed us home. However, I did see Helm and his wife hugging, and then she walked away, and he stood there, looking up at the sun, bearing his teeth like the dinosaur in the drawing.

The drawing's right here next to me now. I wish I could've known. It's just a dinosaur, its face close to the sun, a mouth full of teeth.

Would someone else have known? Or should someone else have known?

Did someone fail to help her?

We never got to become best friends. Did she have one?

I'd never kill myself. I'm not even sure what would make Roshana want to. If she could've known how much everyone today would cry, she might not have. It's an hour-long, seven-mile bike ride to the trailhead. And then there's the hike—three more hours, they say.

All that time to change her mind.

Helena's talking with Tobias at the dining table over mortuary ledgers, discussing Purist strategies. I don't think child suicide is the Purist intention.

If AB killed themself, there wouldn't be a funeral.

I think I just want to sit and think awhile.

·

I LOVE WHEN a convoy of solar powered vehicles delivers a ship-ment of something we don't produce in Canland, like rice or corn or sugar, because then a day later, there are sweet treats at the kiosks, and because it's fun to see fast things on our roads.

I love when an invasive species is discovered in the foothills or fields, because WEDA conduct research, and sometimes allow spectators as long as we stand behind the barriers. Once, Helena took me to see an overgrowth of vine wrapped around the base of the mountain pines. It reminded me of an Actualization Michael once put me in, of a Chinese forest overgrown with kudzu. The Sensorium has taught me what vine can become if you let it run wild. When I saw the Canland vine I thought, even if we all left Canland, green would still grow.

I love Part Center events too. Theater events (plays loosely based on Norse mythology and the collapse of the United States), sporting events (mostly baseball, but sometimes capture the flag—I enjoy the ovations we give the athletes who compete in the organized fashion for the last time before they turn eighteen and become contributors or college students or apply for other Parts), poetry readings (which are sparsely attended, but it's fun to hear the combinations of words people invent), and Canland's annual Founding Celebration (the one day a year Viceroy Hugo makes a public appearance and gives an encouraging address, and people eat and drink the rarities driven in on SPVs, courtesy of Arturo Eagles in recognition of Canland's contribution to WORLD).

Another thing I love is when the Sensatarium announces ob-tainment of a major world event. I've never been to the Sensatar-ium, though I've been eligible for almost a full year, but hearing what's happening elsewhere on Earth is reassurance that there are people out there working together as we do in Canland. I don't regard solipsism with any seriousness (when Michael taught me what solipsism is, he said something along the lines of, No one's imagination is potent enough to invent everything; don't engage with it, it's not serious philosophy), but since Sybil left, I've realized that some people in Canland must believe it, maybe because their routines feel boring, repetitive, lonely, pointless. So I think people use their benefits on Sensatarium time because, after a visit there, they feel reinvigorated with reminders that people all around the Earth feel the same ways as they do. Sometimes they rejoice (like when cancer was cured in all forms, the Sensatarium was so crowded that some people missed the address from Berlin and had to cheer from outside). Or sometimes they feel collectively sad when tragedy strikes (a few years ago, the last ruins of New York City broke off and sank into the Atlantic, taking thousands of stubborn DOTEC with them; and not long after that, the Delhi cholera outbreak reduced the largest extant city in the world by eighty percent). Or they are reminded of their own emotional complexity, like when they feel both hope and loss at once (last year, the Unified Reorganization of Traditionalists–which was stationed on the western coast of Africa, and from my understanding was the most determined Traditionalist attempt remaining–was attacked and overthrown by DOTEC militia, and although blood was spilled, Purists and Practicalists alike were relieved by the defeat of the attempt to return to how things were before the Evanescence).

I love it when the mountains up north get snow and give us more water. I never see the snow, but maybe someday Dylan will take me for a long bike ride.

And everyone loves it when Cole announces from the Safe Haven another year gone by with zero deaths from treatable afflictions. It's been four years in a row. Another two months and it'll be five. (I guess suicide doesn't count as treatable.)

These are the reasons why I'd never kill myself. Because I love these and so many other things. I know Roshana loved guavas. What else did she love?

I hear our front door open and shut—must be Tobias leaving. He goes to an empty home to think about vanished people. I've been lying very still, watching the candle's flame tremble the tiniest bit. Having just spent all day with Tobias, sad Tobias, I wouldn't be surprised if Helena's feeling a certain way that makes her think I need conditioning, to learn my lesson.

Now there's a knock at my door. Usually Helena lets herself in, but this time she waits. I rise from my bed and pull the door open. She's standing there looking the way she sometimes does after a long talk with me, her eyebrows high, her eyelids half shut.

After a moment's pause, she says, "Are you doing OK?"

"Yes," I reply. She'd want me to be honest, to talk about my feelings, and she might be relieved to know her conditioning has worked—that I'm not the same boy who made jokes at Sybil's mom's funeral. "I'm a bit sad," I say. "I was just thinking about Roshana."

She nods; I can see something heavy sliding off her mind. "Do you want to come play piano?"

I haven't played piano for Helena since the summer, before she started spending so much time at her writing table, drafting proposals to the viceroy and rebuttals to the Practicalists and college students. We'd talk about the great things in Canland, sitting on the front steps to the garden and drinking lemonade. At the end of the day, with my legs in shorts cooling in the shade after some sun, Helena would ask if I wanted to play for her. I'd perform the songs she'd let me, and she always told me I played very nicely. Once when I was playing, I hit a wrong note, and she did something unexpected and reached over me to play the same few notes, but so they sounded right. I asked, "Can you show me again?" But she refused and said, "No, no, you do it—it's good."

She used to teach me some things, like how to sit, how to play scales, how to know what constitutes a chord so I can discover more on my own. Michael taught me how to read music, but I've memorized all the songs I know so I never need to sight-read, and besides, I've fallen out of practice since he left. I've never really heard Helena play freely, and certainly not since the beginning of the summer, when the world—our Part, our home—more often sang the happy songs, and she would listen with a small smile to the birds and contributors and my playing, and she never interfered or criticized, which made that one time when she played those pretty notes so special.

I sit on the piano bench with my hands in my lap until she tells me I can play. She pats my thigh and I scoot rightward to make room for her beside me. When she sits, the bench groans. She puts her right hand on the yellowed keys, lightly, like a harvestman perched on a leaf. She presses her thumb into the D next to middle C, then her pinky up to the A above it, then in time lets her middle finger fall straight to F, pulling the key down into minor. Her fingers don't move as the D minor hangs there for beat four. Then with her hand in the same formation she moves leftward one key to C major and holds the chord—one, two—strikes again—three, four—arpeggiates D—minor—then C—two, three, four . . .

"That's very pretty," I say.

She reaches her left hand over right to take my left hand out of my lap and place it under her right one—my hand the inverse of hers, my pinky her thumb, my thumb her pinky, our middle fingers aligned—and she presses my fingers into the keys. I like the pressure of her fingers. After a few measures she lifts her hand off of mine, and I keep playing.

"What song is this?" I ask. Talking while playing messes me up, and I fall out of time.

She nods her head like a metronome and moves my hand again. I play it for many measures, the same thing over and over, but difficult to get right, harder than it sounds. It calls to mind the image of a man walking with his head hanging, like Tobias today as we left the funeral.

"It's not a song. It's just a melody," she says. "I made it up."

"A song is made of melodies." My fingers stumble again and I keep going. The trick to getting good at piano is letting your fingers stumble a lot, then continuing to play anyway. But as I keep hitting wrongs notes, Helena grabs my elbow and pulls my arm away from the keys, so I stop.

"Sometimes just one melody," Helena says, "and sometimes more than just melodies." She puts both her hands on the keys now and plays a song that calls to mind a pastoral scene—people sitting in the breeze-brushed green, passing the time, talking, I don't know what about, maybe not talking, just enjoying one another through their subtle signs that say, *there's nowhere else I want to be*. But then she takes her hands away. "You try again," she says. "You can slow the tempo if you need to."

I play her melody for a few measures, slowly, and now she places her hand under mine, like I am guiding her this time. Soon I don't have to think, my hand is just doing it. I can add it to the list of songs I know.

"I think," I say, lacing my fingers together in my lap, "that every time a song gets played, Sybil hears it. Not literally—but I mean that I think it's good for . . ." My eyes slide to the sides and up; I don't know what to say. "For the world. But it's more of a feeling."

"It's OK to have feelings you can't describe," she says. "Just remember, Sybil endangered you and then abandoned you and everyone who loves her. Tobias will never be OK."

"Yeah," I say. "You're right." I don't want to talk about Sybil, and I don't want to have to confront the fact that I might have a flimsy argument for still missing Sybil. Ignoring the feelings I can't describe, and wanting to keep Helena engaged and impressed with how solicitous I've become, I ask, "How did you learn music?"

"My sisters were good at it. They learned from each other. Like two people learning to play tennis by playing each other—eventually they'll get good, but only ever so good."

I nod, thinking how lucky I am to have had good teachers—Michael, my first; Helena, the best; Helm, my favorite. Cole was perhaps my most unlikely teacher. His lessons are faraway but everlasting, as he taught me while I was in the Safe Haven recovering from surgery that I am no more lacking than anyone else, that even the strongest among us have their weaknesses, the happiest their sorrows, and the shrewdest among us are plagued by constant misinterpretation of others. Sometimes I wish I could spend time with Cole again, but that would also mean I'm in need of medical attention. His contribution is too important to make time for me, and yet my survival has several times in the past been the primary subject of his contribution.

"There's tennis in one of the books Michael read me. The boys and the girls in the book are amazing at tennis because they devote their lives to it."

She nods and smiles, her lips together, and her eyes blink slowly, as if voluntarily.

"I want to devote my life to something." I wipe my fingers back and forth on the piano and they are tickled pleasantly by the hard edges of the keys. "Maybe music."

She touches the hair on the back of my head. She lets her eyes move all over my face. It feels like it's been a while since she's done this. My guess is that right now she's in touch with the fact that our presences in each other's lives are impermanent, and it's making her sad in the wake of Roshana's funeral today.

"I won't kill myself," I say.

Her frown lines deepen suddenly, the creases red and warm in our home's early-evening mixture of waning sun and candle-light. She lifts her chin and lowers it and takes a deep, long breath. "Were you thinking of it?"

"No. But was Roshana?"

"I don't know," she says.

She swipes a finger along the top of the upright piano, sprin-kles light dust to the floor. She glances to the end of the hall, toward Dylan's room, where he's probably sleeping before his waste run—or commandeering satellites, tubing, Actualizing in the Sensorium, and whatever else he does, not sleeping. Her eyes move up to the clay shelf that protrudes helpfully from the wall above the piano, to the candle burning in its silver stick, the blank wall lit a butter color.

"It's terrible," she says.

"Yeah," I say. I rub the top of the piano too, feeling the smooth, dark, finished wood. It came from a tree that grew and lived and then became something else, just like Roshana, who might briefly power our irrigation system, or Canland's refrigerator, or the next Actualization at the Sensatarium. She could be anywhere. "Why did she do it?"

Helena's face relaxes like an unclenched fist. "I don't know," she says. "You can never know exactly what someone else is going through. It's a normal thought to have, to picture your own death, what people will say about you, that they'll wish they'd been nicer to you, especially when you're imagining your suicide—to be spiteful or be rid of all the dread and pain that comes with life. There are good suicides, and there are bad ones. This one—because Roshana was a child, because we don't know why she did it, because maybe even she didn't know why she did it—this is a bad one."

"Do you blame her parents?"

"Why do you think that?"

"Well, a lot of the reasons I do things is you. You are my main influence, I mean."

"There's no one to blame for something like this. But yes, her parents will blame themselves for the rest of their lives. That said, every child's outlook is primarily determined by their parents' outlook. And while this is a special Part, most of the adults in Canland went through something awful to get here."

"I understand," I say. "Well, don't worry about me. I just wonder what could have been so bad for her." I pause, remembering the day Leo shoved me over, and Roshana wrested my parasol from his grasp and handed it to me. "Roshana and I were friends, you know."

"I know." Helena takes my hand in hers and kisses my fingers on the second knuckle, one by one.

"Helm once told me that the Evanescence made everyone stop believing in god."

"I wish he would stop talking about god in school." She lets go of my hand. "And I wish you wouldn't take him so seriously.

Whatever the Evanescence made everyone stop or start believing, they've forgotten it pretty quickly. Everyone had a near-death experience, but children make everyone the same again. Life no longer has an end. People will always have children. It's the only salve for wounds caused by grief. Grief for oneself, even."

"Imagine the grief of losing a child, then," I say.

Helena nods, staring at me.

"I'd like to have a child," I say. It comes out of my mouth quiet for some reason.

"Why would you like to have a child?"

"Well," I say. "I want to take care of someone the way you take care of me."

"That's a good reason. That's a long time away, though. I think, for now, you just devote yourself to respecting all the life that lives."

"OK." I scratch the corner of my nose, gently, to show her I know how to do it right; it didn't actually itch. "I wonder if she was afraid to die. It's almost better if she was, right? Because that meant her life was actually good?"

Helena's biting the inside of her bottom lip, her mouth pursed to one side.

"I've had near-death experiences," I say. "But I wasn't afraid."

"Let's not talk about it anymore."

"Have you?" I ask.

Her eyes flit to me for a split second. Abruptly, she rises from bench, making the wood creak. She walks to the kitchen. I don't turn around and watch her because she sometimes conditions me when I stare at her. It's a tricky balance, seeming solicitous, but not like an alien. I put my hands on the keys, then stop myself from playing because I don't want to interrupt her. I'm doing very well.

I hear the top come off the grappa bottle, a wide gulping sound like pulling the stopper from the drain. Grappa's made from the leftovers of pressed grapes after wine's been made. Helena drinks it so nothing goes to waste, and also because it's good for her stomach.

She sits beside me on the bench again, but this time with her back to the keys, so our feet are on opposite sides. Her breath smells like the polish that crafts contributors use on pottery fresh out of the kiln.

"Yes," she says. "I've had a near-death experience." She sips and smiles. "One or two."

"What's one?"

"Well, there's the one where I save your father's life. There's a few of those, actually." She shakes her head, but the smile is still there. "You don't need to hear."

"I want to."

Helena sighs, finishes her grappa, pours herself another glass, then leans forward to the dining table to place the bottle down. "No. Because, to be honest, those are just stories. Like how I met your father. I was sitting on the big beach rocks in Maine—it was a gray day, my sisters were in school, my parents had already died, we had already left the farm—and I saw a team of researchers on the beach, pulling something from the ocean. The head researcher was this knobby, wiry kid, the only one not operating a crank. There was a huge black rubbery wave, getting closer and closer to the shore, with this sickening smell. When they pulled the dead whale onto the sand, the boy turned away with his face in his hands. I started—well . . ." She trails off.

"That was Michael?"

"I thought there was something interesting about a researcher who couldn't stomach a dead animal."

I blink and look down and then back up at her like she's taught me to while listening. She's biting a callus off her finger, turning her eyes down the hall again.

"That's just how I remember it," she says. "Two scared young people who had no one else."

"But you had your sisters."

She looks at me with a closed smile that I know isn't happy. "For a little while. My sisters died in the Evanescence. We were all in a Purist militia together. Cassie died in a firefight. Amy shot herself a few weeks later." Helena clears her throat and drinks more. "They would've loved you!" she says loudly, grinning.

I smile too.

"They were too good for this Earth, just like you."

Her smile turns more into a wince, and she brushes my bangs up off my forehead. She corrected my lopsided haircut, but left the front long. It looks good, but I liked it better all long. I used to want my hair and Helena's to be the same, but mine's straight and hers is wavy. She always has it pinned up and back with streams falling down her temples, all its freeness sculpted into a crown.

"You know, Tristan," she says, and I look up at her again. "Some people find their families when they feel like they have no one, but some people really do have no one."

"I'm very grateful for everyone I have," I say.

She takes my chin between her fingers. She makes her hand flat against my cheek. "Good," she says. "You're going to be a force of good."

"OK."

Her hand is rough and callused and warm. She rubs my nose lightly with her thumb and sighs. "It was devotion, Tristan. Devotion brought the world down. Misguided, unrelenting devotion. Devotion disguised as religion, duty, vocation, advancement. People forgot about other people. Don't become obsessed with anything; it reduces you."

"I understand."

"Play me something." She rises from the bench and stands behind me.

"Do you want it to be—"

"Anything."

I shift to the middle of the bench. I hold my chin level and keep my wrists straight with a soft curl to my fingers. I don't want her to condition me for playing something I make up, and she's probably sad after telling me all that. She needs a good, happy song. So, even though there are songs that reach deeper into the heart, I play "Twinkle, Twinkle, Little Star." I add decorations, I expand it with variations, but I keep it simple, never veering far from the lullaby's sweet melody.

When I'm done, we're silent. I'm not sure Helena's still behind me, or if she's waiting for more. I start to play the song she just taught me, but she stops me with a hand on my neck.

"That's good," she says. She kisses the top of my head. "That's enough."

I smile to myself. As I turn around, she's sitting down at her writing table, taking her metal nib out of its inkwell. She lights a new candle in the heaviest, most beautiful candlestick we own, which has leaves worked into the metal and winding like vine up the candlestick, and never moves from its place on the writing table. She's always had that candlestick; she's never been without it. It was the only thing she took with her when she and her sisters left the farm they grew up on in former Pennsylvania. That candlestick was the only material object that made it from her first home to this one. She pauses, puts the metal nib to the page, and starts to write.

Not wanting to bother her to make me dinner, I go into the kitchen and cut a big square of cheese off the block and eat it like Dylan. From the corner of my eye, I watch Helena. Her devotion is generous and expansive, and I am not the sole object of it. She has a whole personal history I'm not aware of, which made her a person who was equipped for a certain kind of life. And then, somewhere within that personal history, I arrived. Maybe I was perfectly suited for that life; nights like tonight make me think so.

I wish I could have been perfect for AB's life, and that they could have been perfect for mine. In all my quiet moments, I can only think about their wet-looking curly black hair, those yellow-veined dark-blue black-containing eyes, and that smile of crowded teeth with the red tongue poking through. If I could have spent this very same night with Helena, or off somewhere with AB, hidden in a copse of trees, telling each other our secrets, with only the Earth to hear us, making new secrets, seeing each other close, touching each other's hair and skin, holding hands, hiding and finding each other, like the only two people on Earth, to set aside for just one night all the people in my life who I feel I must constantly solve–if I could, I'm not sure I wouldn't choose to wave goodbye to Helena as she tends the garden and shouts out to me, "Have fun, be safe, see you soon!" and I start walking up the road, around the copse of trees, into a purpling desert, with every intention to come back, but I don't know when . . .

I taste iron. I hide my face and touch my tongue–glossy, bright blood appears on my fingertip, sticky as I rub my fingers together to make the color go away. I swallow the last bite of cheese whole and wash it down with a glass of water.

"I'll check myself before bed," I say to Helena, who's switching the metal nib from her right to left hand. She's sweating along her hairline, the flyaway hairs separating and glowing. I walk slowly to the hall, waiting for her to answer me, but all I hear is the scratch of the nib growing more furious against the wooden desk.

I go into my room and sit on my bed, waiting for this unfamiliar feeling to identify itself, or for it to subside.

·

November 10, 2088 (Cont.)

I remember a day a long time ago—years, I was eight or nine, maybe—when Helena had stepped out of the bath and gone to towel off in her room. I opened the door and watched her. She was rubbing her face with the towel and her breasts and stomach hung in front, and when she lowered the towel, she saw me, and she covered herself and slammed the door. A moment later, she came out of her room wearing a damp linen shirt and shorts, and she conditioned me—first on my butt cheek where I don't have scars, then on my face. I think Michael was away on a research assignment. She said if I was curious about bodies, I should ask her, not spy on her. I'm reminded of this because, tonight, while I heard her running a bath for herself, I snuck out of my room and glimpsed her writings on the table, which likened the compartmentalization of space as an evolutionary necessity to a parent's duty to know when she must distance the child from herself, i.e., to no longer let the child sleep in the conjugal bed. By conditioning me, Helena had at once taught me to give people privacy, and also discourage perversion.

Which is why sometimes I find it hard to think about AB, who I was thinking of tonight before I had to get up to pee again, because they are so beautiful to me that just the thought of them made me turn myself over on my sheets and start to rub, but then I stopped, and I got up to write the memory of when Helena conditioned me with the towel.

I miss AB—miss talking to them, miss looking at them. I want them to know that they aren't alone. That they don't have no one. That even though I haven't seen them in a while, they still have me. Tomorrow I'll ask Dylan if we can see them on the way home from school.

Also, I guess it's possible for memories to unexpectedly come back to you. In this way, the past has a life of its own. I am a container for the past, and like a microbiome, it is a whole universe inside you.

· · ·

SINCE MY LAST name begins with W, I was one of the last kids at school today brought into Gwen Horn's office to talk with the counselor, who said that if I had any thoughts of suicide or if I heard anyone else express similarly concerning thoughts or if I had any concerning thoughts myself whatsoever that exceeded a human's natural innocent curiosity, or even not exceeded but just had thoughts about death of any kind, to feel free to come talk with her before the thoughts become concerning. Helena said it's normal to picture your own death, so I resolved not to waste the counselor's time. This was just before my last class of the day, which was Helm's Creative Thought and Expression, so I arrived to class late, during the open discussion in which students shared their own ideas for what might happen after we die, and the point seemed to be that we could imagine anything we liked as happening, from riding on a unicorn, to eating only your favorite food for the rest of eternity, to becoming a star or even a starfish, whatever brought us comfort. For the other half of class, we expressed with pencil on blank paper our feelings about death, which we were not required to share, but could after class, if we felt compelled. There was not this much talk of death after Sol died.

But it was before that, during my walk from Gwen Horn's office to Helm's classroom that I heard the first rumble of thunder, which sounded like a titan had dropped a heavy object on top of the sky, and it was while the class was expressing opinions on heaven and reincarnation and abyssal nothingness that the drizzle began. Plinking ringing through the steel ceiling. By the end of class, the drizzle let up so there was no discussion about keeping us at school until the showers stopped. I waited for Dylan to arrive on his chrome bike, which would have been dulled by the sunless sky, but even after I was the last one standing outside the school and the drizzle had started up again, he still hadn't come. So I started walking . . .

And now I'm stepping out of the tree-lined path leading away from school and toward the clearing from which I can see basically all of Canland, and the tarps are all out and waiting but not yet unfurled. Somewhere, the chemists have tested the rain's pH and are giving the thumbs-up or -down to the tarp-rollers. If the water is good, which right now it seems to be, given the tarplessness, then this will be one of those events in the history of Canland that will momentarily convince even the most despondent contributors that what we are doing matters and will be rewarded.

The drizzle stops. The sky gains a deep yellow glow, the clouds ripple like messy blankets, and the yellow turns whiter and dimmer and then back to lightless gray. People are looking up. A sky-gazing man walks into the opposite lane of the road. A bicycle swerves to avoid him, the tires grind in the Earth, slip out, and crash into a mess of shrubs.

Another boom of thunder, and another. People start running off the paths and toward the vine tents and kiosk awnings. In the distance, agriculture contributors sprint through rows of bushy alfalfa toward the Part Center, darkening under the sky. A drop of rain hits the back of my hand.

This morning, Dylan handed me a small paper card crammed with as much writing as he could fit, stuck inside a waxed canvas fold, and said, *If you ever need to leave, go here.* Later, when I looked closer at it, I saw he'd written coordinates and directions, but I could make no sense of them. I wouldn't even know why I'd have to leave, and if I ever did, why he wouldn't come with me—unless he was planning to leave without me, like he said he wouldn't. I have the card in the side pouch of my knapsack, but when I get home, I'll say to him, *I don't know about you, but I will never lose hope for Canland. I am part of it, and it is part of me.*

I squint up, but the humidity has made my goggles too foggy to see through. The cloud that has become the whole sky has made all of Canland like a room with its windows covered. Since the last clap of thunder, a thick silence has taken hold—until someone breaks the stillness with his loudest cry: "Run!"

Arms over heads, legs churning fast in the search for cover. But I feel stuck, turning left and right, looking for Dylan.

And then, the rain is here.

Like every insect stridulating all their legs and wings at once, like thunder rising from the desert floor, there are billions of tiny explosions in the sand. Rain, rain, rain. All there is, rain. Cattle run for cover beneath the roofed paddock, but there are no children in the pasture to be trampled. The wall of water becomes too thick to see through. I wipe my goggles, but the beads turn to streaks. I rely on the feeling of my feet in fresh mud sucking greedily as I make my way along the road.

Why didn't Dylan pick me up? Or Helena? Maybe he had a tube and passed out. Maybe he's toppled over on his bike somewhere and Helena's worried about us both. Is she coming to get me? Is she running for cover?

I recall the poem I wrote in Helm's class:

Dear Friend
Do not hate me
When I'm dead
(Wishes from a memory.)

I don't understand poetry.

I'm sideways against the ground and half my body's muddy, but then I'm pulled up by someone I can't see, and the mud's washed off as I'm hurried off the road. The rain's cold. My clothes cling to me. Into a copse of eucalyptus trees where the rain punches through in patches, but the waxy narrow leaves diminish the force. I wipe my goggles and hear a man shout over the deafening miracle happening in our desert greening project.

"You're Helena's boy! We met when she spoke at the college. Hey, I hope these houses don't slide away. You need help getting somewhere?"

Is this the Purist man who hugged me after we all linked arms and hummed together? Did he even know Roshana? Would he care if this rainstorm killed yet more people? Or would he rejoice, say it was nature's plan, and sing another song?

"No," I say to him.

"You've got an umbrella there," he tells me.

My parasol is sticking up out of my knapsack, which means all my things have gotten wet through the open pouch, and I'll probably be conditioned for that, but I have limitations like everyone else, and when I'm not perfect, I start to think I should never have tried; should have stayed inside the school; not gone up the hillock with Sybil; done nothing, remained safely alive, a second child requiring more than everyone else in Canland, contributing less, teetering on the edge of vestigiality. If I only resolved myself to become nothing, would I be free? Does it take great strength to become nothing, no one? Is that what it means to walk up the Notch—to be free? No, no, no, no, no.

I check my heart rate on my watch: 84, aka permissible, barely. I open my parasol and step out of the vine tent, but the pink cloth is soaked, permeable and useless. I'm slashed sideways with rain. The wind nearly takes me off my feet, spraying rain upward off the ground, and buckling the armature of the parasol up into itself. I drop it. The storm relaxes in the next moment, like a screaming baby pausing to draw a breath.

I run—though I'm not supposed to; I don't know the last time I ran—to the road north of market. My legs struggle in the mud. I can see the oak through the rain from here; I'm getting closer. The rain speeds up again. This must be the loudest Canland has ever been, except maybe the stampede, though I couldn't hear that from my house, and I'd be able to hear this storm from anywhere. What does the edge of a storm look like? Will we see it? Or will it lift first, then drift past?

I see some of my classmates far up ahead running onto the residential side streets off the road east of the hillock. There are WEDAS and COHOS directing people under the trees, even as a limb snaps off and hits the ground audibly. I hear someone behind me yell, "Off the road!" I turn to see contributors rolling a tarpaulin along the path to protect the road from ruin. Then the tarps start getting rolled over the fields to prevent flooding. Will our house be safe in this, or will we all become part of the Diaspora of the Environmental Collapse?

I step off the road, into the sodden pasture. The water rises up into my shoes. They get stuck in the muddy sand. The right one comes off. If AB dies in the storm, then they'll think they died without me. I should have been a better friend.

Wild hair rising above their head, sliding down the hillock on their backside, hopping to their feet as the Earth flattens out, running toward me—no, to the right, to the COHO who's always there on the hillock, right up to the COHO, who puts his hand on AB's chest and backs them up toward the hillock.

"AB! AB!" I shout and shout. "AB!"

Everything is too blurry, fractured and refracted in the water on my goggles, but I carry on across the flattened grass toward the hillock. My left shoe keeps getting stuck, so I stop and take it off. AB's running toward me now. They're smiling and waving, and their hair is soaked and curling past their eyes, their tank top hanging off them like molting skin.

"Tristan! You cut your hair!"

"Hi, AB."

"Hi." They smile and put their hands on my shoulders. "We need you to help. Sasha thinks she's going into labor—she's in so much pain. She can't tube because of the baby. We need to get her to the Safe Haven."

"Get off the pasture!" the COHO shouts, coming closer to us.

AB glances at the COHO, then back to me. "That guy says it's not safe for them to send a carriage."

A gust of wind blows. AB keeps me anchored. I reach up and hold their hands.

"What does AB stand for?" I say.

"It's just what people call me. It doesn't matter. Please, just listen—Sasha's going into labor. It's three months early. We need a doctor."

"DOTEC! Step away from the boy!" the COHO says.

"I'm sorry I didn't help you, AB," I say. "I really wanted to."

"It's OK, Tristan, it's OK! You can help now! Ask him to send a carriage for Sasha."

Under the oak tree there's a huddle of DOTEC.

"Tristan." AB turns to the COHO and shouts, "Please!"

"AB, I want you to know you're not alone," I say. I turn around and unzip the side pocket of my knapsack and point inside. AB takes the card out. I turn to face them again.

"If you ever need to leave, go here," I tell them. "But I'll always be your friend."

"I know, Tristan. But right now you have to help us." AB looks over my shoulder. "Remember our deal?"

The rain gets lighter, then heavier. I nod vigorously, with all my heart.

"You'll tell the COHO to send a carriage?" they say.

"I will," I say. "I'll help."

AB's face is close enough that I can see them through the rain, but doing none of the things I remembered their face doing, just looking straight into my eyes, as if waiting—holding my shoulders, me holding their hands. They push their face into mine. Our mouths are against each other's, closed then opening. They shut their eyes, so I shut mine. And with our faces together, I feel a swelling in my chest, which is what happens when you kiss a person you love. My heart skips, one-two. I take my hands off theirs and roll up my sleeves to feel every drop of rain on my skin, both cool and warm. All of AB's tongue germs are becoming mine. When they pull away, they're smiling with all their teeth again, nodding. I want another kiss—to kiss forever—but I have to help first. With AB's hands still up near my neck, I now face the COHO, getting nearer in the rain. He raises his whistler, and I feel AB take off running behind me. I turn, and a sound like a needle through glass

PART TWO

1

March 8, 2090

I'm home.

My head felt foggy on the ride. Out the windows, I saw morning desert, an absurd orange. The mountain ranges receded as we
neared. Birds circled up high, and then were gone. I closed my
eyes.

The driver hadn't tried to make conversation, but if he had, I'd
have been too tired to engage. I tried to work backward in my
mind, but I could only go as far as when I last woke up, a couple
hours before I got in the SPV—a couple hours spent sitting at the
edge of an exam table, being debriefed on my time there. A young
man, whose muscles strained the seams of his scrubs, read aloud a
brief summary of the tests conducted over the past sixteen months.
The language seemed designed to confuse me, but I might have just
been processing slowly. What I understood before I stopped listening (after I realized that he'd led with the most important information) was that I'd been admitted to a WORLD Neurological Research
Center for long-term monitoring and convalescence after suffering
severe brain trauma from a whistler perforation. He also noted that

I spent most of the past sixteen months in Actualizations because without the complete sensorial stimulation of a Sensorium, my brain might not have made a full recovery. The main side effect, however, was near-total memory loss of my time in there.

The man put down the report and said, I'm going to give you a brief cognitive exam. I had to repeat sets of words like *Carpet, Bubble, Baby, Saddle, Summer* in order, then recite several separate series of numbers in reverse. Then he had me follow his finger with my eyes, tested my balance, had me describe morning and nighttime as an abstract thinking exercise, and asked me what I would do if I was drowning, to which I said, Swim. Apparently, it was an acceptable answer. Then he asked me to tell him his name, which was etched into a name tag on his left pectoral—it was either a trick question or a joke, but when I pointed to the name tag and said aloud, WNRCA Julius Broch—I pronounced it *Broke* and thought of Helm Roctern's name, *Rock-turn*—Julius plainly nodded and said, Good, and yours? I told him my name. Then he said there was a communal SPV waiting outside, and I was free to go. On my way out of the Research Center, I walked through a tunnel with walls that were an intensity of whiteness I've known only in sunlit clouds—I couldn't even name the material. The hallway was lined with windowless metal doors, each with a keypad similar to the one Byron used to enter the Canland College Research Center. Two men, each at least as old as Helena, in hushed conversation, approached and walked past, their footfalls like soft clapping.

It was warm outside, and the sun had only been up for an hour. There was a breeze.

The communal SPV was like other SPVs I'd seen, only larger—sleek and symmetrical down the center, resembling an arced porpoise, or perhaps something less elegant, like a slug that somehow manages to slide along. I boarded the four-row SPV and waited for an hour in my soft seat, staring out the window at the Research Center. At first, I only noticed the building I'd just exited—an unremarkable few stories with long, thin windows. But then my eyes wandered up and found, almost blended with the sky, a building behind it—a structure that looked more like a sculpture of a wave freezing into a glacier, with stone cutting through massive glass windows in curving chaos. And not only were there trees all around the Research Center, but there was grass—green, cut grass, as if stretches of Canland's desert floor had been poured with paint. I stared so long I forgot to blink, marveling, wondering just how far I was from home. I closed my eyes and gently massaged them, making bright phosphenes dash through my vision like a map of the electricity in my brain. I bowed my head and waited.

Finally, a man and two young girls boarded the SPV and sat in the front two rows. Their eyes were wide and blank, and I assumed mine looked similar. We were driven to an unloading point, where we transferred to smaller SPVs. The girls shared one, while the man and I each got into our own. Over the next several hours, I was driven back to Canland.

To keep myself awake—not knowing if I'd forget everything prior to the next time I woke up—I fished for memories of Canland from before I was taken to the WORLD Neurological Research Center. I uncovered a crucible of acrimony between Purists and Practicalists, a slew of suicides, the abandonment of Sybil, the absence of Michael, the reclusion of Dylan, and playing piano with Helena. And I remembered rain.

We were still hours from Canland. The mountain ranges hypnotized me as they came and went on the endless road. The sky was too blue, the cotton clouds too white. I had to shut my eyes again.

When I opened them hours later, the roadsides were risen and bucolic. Coast live oak trees festooned the smooth hills—same as the one atop Canland's hillock—casting hard shadows that lifted them up to float. The sun turned the green gold. I was convinced that this was the richest, healthiest land I'd ever seen, and it was spreading.

After my nap, looking at those smooth hills, I was relieved to remember my conversation with WNRCA Julius Broch. I searched my person for traces of what I might have undergone in the last sixteen months—turned my hands over, rolled up my sleeves, wiggled my toes. I dug a fingernail deep into my cuticle until it left a dent. I felt a pressure and a tingle, but nothing that made me want to stop. I touched my head and felt my hair was as short as the bristles of a toothbrush. I rubbed it back and forth, pleasantly stiff, but I was sure it looked childish. It's infantilizing to have no say in the style of your hair. I was able to see my faded reflection in the window, tilted in the glass from the high sun. I noticed that my hands had gotten bigger. I popped my dentures out and back in, and ran my hands over my face. I felt the hearing aids. I recalled that, first thing this morning, WNRCA Julius Broch had shown me how to adjust the volume. I turned them up and a high sound, like the instant a welder's hammer strikes, stretched through infinity, filled my head. Then I turned them off, and it became so vacuously quiet, it was like I was in outer space. I left them off for a while, soothed by the recess for my senses. It made me less tired. I touched the scars running along both sides of my head, like the seams of a baseball, though asymmetric. I still didn't know what the scars were from, specifically. Surgery to save my life, I could only assume.

But of all the times I've eluded death, and despite whatever else I've lost, this felt like the first time something had been taken away from me.

The SPV stopped at an outpost outside Canland, and the driver directed me to exit the vehicle and transfer to a waiting carriage. My only possessions were a water bottle and my watch. The man didn't say goodbye, so I said nothing to him. By contrast, the Canland transportation contributor in the carriage greeted me effusively, saying how exciting it was for all of Canland that I was returning healthy. It was impossible to reciprocate his enthusiasm. As we entered Canland, though, I became reinvigorated, enraptured by a beauty greater than any in my memory, despite the love I've always felt for the Part. The streets were smooth, terra-cotta red; walking paths of rich packed soil inlaid with stones connected the main roads and the fields, like the rungs of a spiderweb; the mountains' pine forests had thickened, and within just a few steps of the horse-drawn carriage, sky-scraping bunches of fluffy blue gum trees with their lizard tongue leaves and curling peeling bark, revealing trunks smooth like skin or soap, shaded patches of bright-green moss; rows upon rows of fruits and vegetables were stitched into the land like the circulatory system of the planet's sleeping titans; the pasture's cows and sheep and horses roamed freely, and strong dogs sidled up beside the hoofed animals, then loped away in small packs; a jackrabbit bolted through the pasture, chased by something no one else saw; hummingbirds sniped the hearts of flowers with their needly beaks; a spiderweb slung between two trees caught a glint of sunlight and the orb weaver in its center resembled a precious jewel; the arroyo, filled with water, clear and quick, fed the fields; the verdant hillock was absent people, and the people who moved about the Part did so with a happy languor, content to be dependent on and deferential to the Earth they walk; their baskets were full, their muslin clothes were clean, their arms were suntanned and sculpted; a breeze cooled the Part as the registered squinted with smiles at the sky; the oak had gotten somehow even bigger and its limbs glowed in the lingering sun.

I looked forward to reading my journal, to remembering, and to writing all this down.

But my journal was not where I'd left it.

When we pulled up to the house, I saw there were no longer parsleys growing in the garden, but untidy heaps of poppy, forsythia, and hyacinth. I didn't know at first what to make of the fact that what now grows in our garden is inedible (if perhaps a chromatic improvement), but I'd soon learn it was a consequence of a separation, an amputation of sorts. Like the removal of a kidney—unseen, but restrictive. A new set of rules.

The door was unlocked and the interior of the house looked much the same, aside from a novel crispness to the light, as if not a single particle were out of place, and my motion would shatter the crystalline fragility, darkening everything. I stepped in—and lo, the properties of photons appeared unchanged.

Dylan's top half sprang upright from the couch as if waking from a nightmare. The roundness of his cheeks had been scooped out. His eyes were bruised with exhaustion.

They said you'd be back this week, he said. Haven't moved from the couch.

He laughed and coughed, rubbed both his eyes simultaneously with the fingers of one hand, stood up, and came to hug me. He'd gotten taller and much thinner, though his arms looked strong—I could see his bicep tendon bulge in the crook of his elbow. When he hugged me, my feet came off the floor. My nose was in his armpit. I smelled him without having to inhale deeply—he smelled somewhat less rotten than I'd remembered, but still odoriferously like himself. His hairline looked as if it had been raked back off his forehead, and his cheeks were colonized by whiteheads. He smiled at me so hard that all his narrow teeth showed, and his Adam's apple slid up and down like a pulley. His breath was a wheeze. He rubbed his eyes again.

My first guess, that he was going through withdrawal symptoms, contained also my second, third, and fourth guesses: that he'd been taken hostage by psychosis and a symptomatic trichotillomania, explaining the patchy hair loss; that he'd lost his appetite or unwillingly changed his diet; and that he'd been stricken with illness. Alas, I know my brother well.

Are you OK? I asked.

Better than ever, Dylan said, not sounding it. I got off tubes. Gonna live a long, long time. Sensorium was actually pretty therapeutic. But now I can hardly function without that. Better than drugs, I guess. Not sure I'll ever sleep again, though. At least I still make all my waste runs. He paused, then said, Do you remember anything?

I said, No, but I do sense a passage of time.

Do you remember getting perforated? he asked.

It's hard to know if I remember it or can just imagine it, I said.

Story of my life, he said. Getting off tubes is an exercise in telling yourself you're a terrible person when you don't even remember what you'd done in the first place.

What don't you remember? I asked.

He said, Well, I don't remember, then laughed thinly. Days, he said. Conversations. Parts of my life.

I nodded. I wanted to tell Dylan I didn't think he was a bad person, but I didn't want to undermine his process. So I changed the subject and asked, Where's Helena?

Dylan sighed and turned away, implying I should follow him. Inside my bedroom, the light was murkier. There were boxes of candles, thin volumes about Purism called *Here and Everywhere*, pieces of shale carved into a point at the bottom to drive easily into the ground, coffins the size of a child's shoe, and small surgical scissors (symbolic, I assume)—all of which were stacked on my floor and desk. My bed was shoved into the corner and made with a sheet and a pillow and a note from Helena that said: *Welcome home, Tristan. Love, Helena.*

I moved some boxes, cleared a path, and lifted up the mattress. My journal—the stack of papers that comprised it—was gone.

Have you seen my journal? I said.

Didn't know you kept a journal, Dylan said.

I wedged myself between a stack of boxes and my desk, pulled out a drawer to find a few stray sheets of paper, a pencil, a set of instructions for nighttime checks, and Sybil's ring. I put it on my left ring finger. I couldn't find Roshana's drawing. I might've had it on my person when I was perforated, in which case, it's gone forever. A unique creation of hers, gone. All I have is my description of the drawing by my old friend Roshana Medley.

When I turned to squeeze out from behind the boxes, I knocked one over, causing a rockslide of shale. Dylan kicked the small headstones toward the fallen box, and we left them there.

Back in the hallway, I asked to see his room again. Where once was a wall of boundless foliage and a miniature planet in which invertebrates suffered Dylan's self-appointed role as creator, there was now a windowless slab of adobe. Monitors rested on his desk like lenses through which the universe could be seen, and the Sensorium was still plugged into them as if no time had passed, and he was about to offer to show me everything everywhere else. For an instant—a hope that feels like an event that's already happened—I thought he was going to show me an Actualization of Sybil, wherever she was.

Helena took all the life out of my hands, he said, gesturing to the bare wall. Unilaterally.

It was like he walking me through a house that wasn't mine.

Did Sybil come back? I asked.

He left his room first. With his back facing me, he said, No.

Back in the hall, I glanced at Helena's closed bedroom door curiously. Dylan went into the living room and wiped a cloth along the shelf above the piano, folded the dusty side of the cloth inward, wiped the shelf again, folded it again. He lifted a pewter candlestick and wiped the spot under it, then placed it back down. Routinely, he wiped the top of the piano and then the keys, lightly enough so they made no sound. I think I had a brief urge to play, but it was snuffed out by a lack of inspiration, no song in my head, like trying to start a fire in a room with no oxygen.

I asked what had been going on in Canland.

Well, no more DOTEC, he said. They registered everyone who'd been here, plus an influx that kept moving west after the Lake Superior algae bloom. Built some housing in the southeast. They call it the Hovels, as if to remind them their homes are shit. So Canland has closed itself to newcomers. There are more contributions: infrastructure, transportation, scrapping. They mine resources from old cities. But to keep the ecological detriment low, Viceroy Hugo has publicly endorsed Helena's obsessive morbidity.

What does that mean? I asked.

Well, I haven't personally gotten my vasectomy, he said. Yet.

When I didn't react, he reminded me about Helena's teenage vasectomy proposal, which became a bill, which passed: registered males between the ages of fifteen and nineteen have randomly been mandated vasectomies, and will be given WORLD benefits, such as extra Sensatarium hours, and anyone who wants to volunteer to have a vasectomy will be given benefits too. Registered with certain disciplinary records have been automatically assigned vasectomies with reduced benefits. Dylan said, So, being eighteen myself, and having gotten kicked out of school for an act of violence . . .

He knelt to inspect the molding, scrubbed it with the cloth.

Doesn't personally make a difference to me, he said, then mumbled, If it couldn't be with Sybil, why would I want a kid?

The questions in my mind were starting to build up and I didn't know which to ask.

Dylan kept on talking as he scrubbed the floor. He said, Arturo Eagles wants more satellites coming over Canland too, and wants to Actualize Canland for other Parts. He wants people to see the success of Restoration, that people are smart enough to undo what's been done. He's awarded Canland travel permits, but only to the scrappers so they can get metal and piping and all that in order to bolster the irrigation systems.

Stop, I said. I closed my eyes to see my thoughts, and keeping them closed, I asked, What about our immunity?

Minor issue there, said Dylan. He stood up. Our family's had some benefits revoked, he said. You might've noticed our garden's full of things we can't eat. And Michael told me if I break another person's spine, it's off to Long Term for me.

What do you mean Michael told you? I said.

He came back, Dylan said and put the cloth down on the arm of the couch. He sniffed and said, Shook my hand, sat me down, gave me a tutorial on some new declassified WORLD technology. It was all very fun and exciting. He was impressed with the work I've done. He seemed to have no idea I'd found him that one time. Remember? I thought of telling him, but I didn't want to set myself up for him to not be impressed. Then he took me outside and asked if I'd been keeping up with my tai chi, and before I could answer, he spun around and kicked me in the side of the head. Well, he slowed down just before he made contact—a bit. Then we sparred for a while; he threw all his kung fu energy at me, and I threw it all back at him. We had a laugh. Then he told me to stop interloping on satellites because we would no longer have the privilege of his protection—he and Helena were making their separation official in the eyes of the law, and he would never be coming back to Canland because Arturo Eagles offered him a position in his personal, elite circle of researchers, and he wouldn't be able to live with himself if he turned it down. He said his conscience would never be free if he completely abandoned his sons—so we are now no longer his sons.

I asked what that meant.

We've been disowned, said Dylan. Divorce and disownership in one afternoon. He didn't even stay for dinner. He took most of the books, as you can see, except for a few reference books and a dictionary—I guess those are for you. He didn't say a word to Helena the whole time he was here. And before he departed, he gave me a bit of encouragement to snack on, if you'd like a taste.

I looked to the bookshelves in the corner by the hallway and, sure enough, they were nearly empty—perhaps Michael didn't want me getting caught with illicit literature. I said to Dylan, Go ahead.

Dylan replied, He said no one ever did anything to help him. And that we—you and I—were smart enough to figure out life on our own. So, first thing I've decided to do, on my own, is keep interloping, because what else is there to do?

I nodded. So Michael's gone forever, I said.

Effectively dead, Dylan said, and swiped a finger along the top of the piano—a sudden, strange, spitting image of Helena, except he had already wiped off all the dust.

I stood there, doing the math of Michael's power. I said, So you have to get a vasectomy because of Helena's law and Michael's absence.

Yeah, Dylan said. Basically.

Even though Michael wasn't here until he came back just to tell you he wasn't going to be here.

Dylan said, When you think about it, it's worse that we ever had immunity in the first place. So I'm scheduled to go under the knife two weeks from today. My first-ever surgery. Any advice? he said, and smiled.

I ignored that and said, What about when I turn fifteen?

I don't know, said Dylan. Maybe you'll get exempt because of the contribution to WORLD research you made over the past sixteen months.

I felt then like I was not a person. Like this was all somehow not real. And yet, I was in my house, talking Canland politics with my brother, waiting for my mother to come home. How familiar.

Dylan tucked the folded cloth into his pocket and I asked, trying to change the subject, if he now liked cleaning. He looked at me with one eyebrow up. No, he said. Helena gives me tasks to keep me sane. For all her—he said, but then stopped himself. Well, he continued, she's been a help to me.

His eyelids seemed heavy and his mouth was pulling down at the corners. I took Sybil's ring off my finger and handed it to him. He thanked me, put it in his pocket and said, Well, I'd offer to make you something to eat, but my stomach isn't really up for the scent of ingestibles.

Are you OK? I asked him again.

I'm getting used to it, he said. It's sort of a constant state.

I asked if something had happened that made him stop doing tubes.

He shrugged and frowned more and shook his head.

Then he said he had to go lie down. He gave me a hug and said, Sorry if I smell like a grundle. I told him it didn't mean a thing to me. The truth is, I missed Dylan's smell—his uniquely foul stench that's never bothered me one bit.

Before he went into his room, he looked me up and down, and said, I'm pretty sure everything's about to change again, Beautiful. I asked what he meant, and he said, Well, you know how people in Canland are always angry and skeptical, bickering about nature? I've been in Actualizations of Parts with less foliage than our desert-cum-farmland, and you know what the people there do? They just stand in front of the few trees they have, all staring up and holding hands. Then, at the end of every day, everyone goes into the Part's Sensatarium. Dylan swallowed some saliva and continued, And here, you know, eighty people have launched themselves from the Notch since you were taken away, and now they're talking about extending Sensatarium hours. I can't help but think it's all related.

I think Canland looks prettier than ever, I said.

And you just spent a year-and-a-half in a Research Center, he replied.

Then we were both silent for a moment. I weighed whether I had the brainpower to follow another one of Dylan's theories, then finally asked, Do you know why I was in there for so long? What contribution did I make?

He sucked in his hollow cheeks, twitched his eyes, and huffed. He slowly said, I think they were probably researching your condition, to see if they could somehow use it for advancement or Dominion or something. They might've also been using you as a test subject for this stuff I'm talking about with the hypnotized wackos. All we were told about you was that they didn't want to release you until you'd regained all your faculties. But hey, maybe they were telling us the truth. Maybe Canland really does look prettier than ever, and they didn't fuck with your brain, and it's just my tubelessness talking—or the fact that I'm in control of the Actualizations I'm in.

I consciously took a deep breath, then another, and shrugged. I decided I didn't have the energy to press Dylan on whether or not he was being facetious.

Anyway, he said, nice to have you back. You look older.

I am older, I said.

Yes, he said. Yes, you are.

I made myself a cheesy toast on the stove and read *Fearsome Allies* while I ate. I bit my cheeks a couple times. The book didn't hold my attention the way it used to—it felt paltry, like a failed attempt to convey the collective intelligence of arachnids; it felt like a book for children. I closed it and focused on chewing so I wouldn't cut my mouth up. That made me feel for a moment like nothing had changed. But then, when I put my plate in the washbasin, I noticed I didn't have to reach up and over the rim of the basin. So I went to the bathroom to examine my body for more changes. I can see the outlines of my stomach muscles. My Adam's apple, I can feel, is pressing through my skin. My penis is still only about as big as my pinky (though my hands have gotten bigger) and I have a few blond hairs around it, and on my shins too, but none in my armpits yet. I would've liked to look at my face to see if my jaw's thickened or anything like that, but we don't have mirrors, aside from Helena's small vanity, and I didn't bother trying to find it. I know well enough what I look like. I sat back at the dining table and waited for Helena to get home. Her writing table was messier than I remembered it.

The twilight was lingering when Helena walked in the door. She gasped like she'd just come up out of water, dropped her sewing kit, and came to hug me. At first, it was like any other hug, with me seated and her standing over me, but then she started crying, cradled my head against her chest, and dropped to her knees. She said, I'm so, so sorry, I'll never hit you again, Tristan, I love you so much, I'm so grateful you're alive. I'll never hurt you ever, ever, ever again, I promise, OK, I promise. Oh, my sweet boy, I love you, I love you, I love you.

The scar on the right side of my head is from when the COHO perforated me, though he was aiming for a young DOTEC, who I'm told was assaulting me. Helena said the COHO couldn't aim his whistler through the torrential downpour. Yes, I remember rain.

The scar on the left side is from a hemorrhage in my inner ear that had clotted. It could have killed me had I not gone to the hospital. The hemorrhage was from one or all of the times Helena conditioned me. I never noticed it.

She produced a piece of padded cloth and tied it under my chin. I made you a new helmet, she said. I want you to wear it wherever you go. But you don't have to wear your pollution mask anymore.

When I asked her if that meant I had to wear it to school, she said, You're not going to school. You're going to contribute. You won't be allowed back at school until the fall, she said. Then she paused for a while and said, Our family's not—

And paused again to think of how to say it.

So I said, Dylan told me.

She just nodded, looking at her lap, dabbing tears with a handkerchief while sitting in the chair across from me. Then she said, The Board of Advancement decided that because you spent the year in a Research Center, they want to hold off on making you a present to see the effects of your time away. Your case was referred to the Contribution Council. Tomorrow I'll take you to the Safe Haven. Cole said he may have a contribution for you.

I said, I thought you just aged in to being a present. I didn't realize you had to be awarded the status of present. Then I paused to consider what it meant that I wouldn't be returning to school—that I wouldn't see get to see Leo or Lilly or Malakai or Helm, nor choose a specialization, go to Creative Thought or Practical Math, see the guava tree fruit—but also that I wouldn't have to live a constant comparison to my previous life with Sybil and Roshana. Then I asked, Do they suspect I'm ahead, or behind?

Helena took a while to answer, during which time I suspected the answer was behind, but then she said, Your brain's development is just lopsided. They tried to see if they could improve your intuition, or give you a fight-or-flight response. They ran nonstop tests in a Sensorium, Actualizing situations that should have been exhilarating and terrifying.

I wonder now why Dylan wasn't made aware of this. I suspect Helena thinks he might do something rebellious and dangerous if he knew the truth—a truth she only knows because she was allowed to visit me. Anyway, it didn't occur to me in the moment to compare this information to Dylan's theory, perhaps because he wasn't too far off. This isn't the first time one of Dylan's theories has been right; he had once claimed to be the smartest person alive. I just never thought I'd feel protective of him, as I do now, deciding that I won't tell him the information Helena told me.

Back to my conversation with her: They tried to make me feel pain? I inferred, and Helena nodded. She couldn't look me in the eye. I asked then, Did Cole save my life after I was perforated?

Yes, she said. A WEDA rolling tarpaulin over the paths saw it happen and put you on her rickshaw and cycled you to the Safe Haven. Cole induced a coma to reduce the blood pressure in your brain so you wouldn't sustain more permanent damage.

Aside from the deafness, I said.

Then Helena cried for thirty seconds or so. I waited for her to stop. She drew breath like she was about to speak, but then turned away and looked down the hall. Dylan hadn't made a sound in his room.

On that day, she then said, when no one came to get you at school, I was at my contribution. Dylan had a contribution review. But he didn't tell me. He swore he did. But he didn't.

If he had, I might be dead, I said.

Helena stared at me. If she was angry, her anger was subsumed into the greater sadness of facing my proximity to death.

Do you have any questions about your father and me? she said.

I shook my head without thinking about it.

After a pause, she said, It's better this way. I told Michael he's either here or he's gone. I feel so sorry for you.

It's OK, I said. Nothing's changed.

Helena put a hand on my shoulder, reached up and touched my head, my padded helmet, then took her hand away. She said, When you were taken to the hospital, I nearly resorted to prayer. I was in so much pain, imagining my life without you, thinking of everything I'd done wrong. I never wanted you to be blank. I wanted you to understand. But now I know that it isn't my job to make you understand. You're going to learn your own way. Michael exploited your painlessness. He reduced your individu-ality. He took your purity and turned it into an experiment. You were never going to be a kid like any other, running around and falling down. Maybe you could have seen the world like a child, thought and spoken like a child, had friends. But Michael put your developing brain in a Sensorium, flooded you with stimuli, tried to make you feel something, tried to lower your sensitivity threshold so your daily life would make you feel something more, but you just walked around so unaffected, seeing the world as one big logic problem.

Helena's voice got loud and strained as she said, He's the reason you're not a child.

Then she cried again. She grabbed my hand and said, I'm sorry . . . I'm so sorry.

I wonder where Helena was, all that time, when Michael was doing that to me, and why she never stopped him. She only cares so much now because she almost killed me.

She collected herself and looked right at me. I saw you in the Center, she said. I went back and forth on whether or not to tell you this, but I know I have to. I read your journals, and they broke my heart. I've only ever wanted you to feel normal and loved. I wanted you to love your life. When I visited you, they had me participate in one of your Actualizations. I went into a Sensorium Dome, like a small Sensatarium, and there you were, playing a real piano, on a promontory overlooking the sea—diamonds on the water, the sky such a soft blue that it eased my eyes. There was a breeze bending the grass. When I walked in, your back was to me. I went up behind you and put my hand on your shoulder, and you stopped playing. I could hear the waves washing up against the rocks at the bottom of the cliff. There were people around, sitting, walking, talking, laughing—it was idyllic. But you had electrodes strapped to your head and your head was shaved and you had tubes in your arms and pads on your fingers. The sight of you broke me down. When I said hello, you stood up from the bench and took my hand. You led me through the field to the edge of the bluff. You waved to people on the way and they waved back. I tried to talk to you, but you were speaking words that made no sense together, as if you were just reciting random vocabulary. You don't know the pain of seeing your child in pain. Suddenly, we were looking down the sheer drop into the sea with the wind blowing up at us. The Sensorium was so real that the height made me nauseous, and I had to sit. I remembered then that I was in a manifestation of your imagination. I asked if you could please just sit with me. Then you let go of my hand, and I asked you not to do this. You said the word Purest, or Purist, I don't know. Then you stepped off the edge, and the whole Sensorium flipped, and we were both falling. The sea rose up fast, and we hit the rocks. It was so loud. I fell forward, it was so real. Then everything was silent. It was so cold, I could hardly breathe. But in the darkness, you stood back up straight and went to the piano, and you played like I'd never heard you play before. It was so beautiful. Then a researcher came in and said, Go to him. So I did, I kissed you on the cheek and rubbed your back and spoke to you. You didn't move, you just kept on playing in the darkness, and they told me you would play for hours, so they had me leave the Sensorium. Your brain had no secondary functioning at that point. It was like you truly believed you'd been disembodied. If they'd cut off the synapses that were firing as you played, there would have been nothing left. You were just a nerve of creation. There was no reaching you. I had to say goodbye through the wall. That was a year ago; the last time I saw you.

I'm not sure what Helena wanted me to gain from this, but I said to her, That wasn't real.

But you thought it was, she said. Why did you want to kill yourself?

I don't know, I said. I didn't. It wasn't real, I repeated.

But it was your own imagination, she said.

I was growing tired, and tired with Helena, so I said to her, Where are my journals now?

I have them, she said. I didn't want to put them back where I'd found them, so I wouldn't be tempted to lie to you, but I read them all. Then she said, There's a character in your journals, AB. This was the DOTEC they say was assaulting you when you were perforated. The COHO was aiming for them, not you. Do you remember that?

No, I said. Why did the COHO try to perforate AB? Why couldn't he have just tackled them?

Some people just need an excuse to eliminate another DOTEC, she said. The COHO was expelled.

What happened to AB?

Expelled too, Helena said.

I asked for my journals back. She went down the hall to her room and brought me the papers and then apologized for the mess in my room, said she would clear some space. After she did—not removing anything, just making a path from the door to my bed, picking up the spilled headstones—I asked her for some time alone. It's worth it all to have you back home, she said, then shut the door.

I don't believe that AB's been expelled—maybe they're in the Hovels—nor that they were trying to assault me. But who knows, they might have been tubing—for that and for all the good days, too. After all, my first journal entry was about the day Sybil was assaulted by a DOTEC. So now I'm faced with the question of whom to trust: my new self, my record of my old friends, or Helena.

If I hadn't read my journal, would I even know to miss AB?

It's time to go to bed before I start writing things that make no sense. I'm glad I've kept a record of everything I once believed.

2

March 10, 2090

My first memory of Cole:

When I regained consciousness after going into shock because Michael hadn't changed my diaper in too long, and my lymphangioma scars became infected, and feces contaminated my anemic blood, Cole's head, round and bare as an icy planet, orbited the limits of my vision as I lay on my side, my arm held straight by a turquoise splint, an IV in the crook of my elbow, taped to my skin. There was a voice, not Cole's, but as if coming from a soothing Earth titan in an echoey ravine between two folds of my brain, saying, Earth is a pinpoint to Jupiter is a pinpoint to Sirius is a pinpoint to Aldebaran is a pinpoint to Betelgeuse . . . . Cole tilted his head sideways so that when his eyes found mine, the world corrected. His eyes smiled at the corners. He wore a surgical mask. I smelled the plastic of the mask I wore, inhaling what it exhaled. In a count of one, two, I was asleep; three, four, I was awake again. Lying on my side in a bed with sutures freshly bandaged, my eyes opened to find my mother lying on her side in bed with me. After a few minutes, she had to go, but said she'd be back later. After she left, Cole sat in a chair—his mask had been hiding a shapely cupid's bow, long lips, and a straight, square chin—and talked to me. Did you know, Tristan, that I have been all around the world? I've seen reassembled dinosaur skeletons, bathed with elephants, met ostriches so large and scary that I ran, not to mention people of every sort, and of all the creatures I've ever met, I think none have been so indifferent to me as you. It makes me feel like I can do nothing wrong. I like this feeling. He grinned hugely, lit a bundle of dried herbs, and waved it throughout the room. He had let me keep the turquoise splint, but one day, it mysteriously vanished from my desk drawer.

There was one more time he'd have to excise the lesions impairing my lymphatic system, and it was after that time, a year later, that he noticed a shift in me—that I'd become so piercing in my rational analyses that he no longer felt like he could do no wrong, but that he wanted only to do right. This, he said today—my first day contributing in the Safe Haven's maternity ward—was something he still, at seventy-one years old, needed to be reminded to do.

I change the sheets and pillowcases, sanitize forceps, speculums, amniotic hooks, etc. In the nursery I feed, hold, and play with the babies, plus change their blankets, diapers, etc. As needed, I help administer oxygen to delivering mothers.

Two boys were born today. The mother of the first—a twenty-year-old with reddish hair who didn't look pregnant anywhere other than her belly—delivered with a complication: the baby had swum a knot through the umbilical cord. I held an oxygen mask to the mother's face. She was screaming and crying, as Cole told me she would, not from the pain but the terror (the brush with death). Cole turned the baby in the uterus and guided him out headfirst to avoid an oxygen deficiency and permanent brain damage; those first few breaths are vital. The baby announced his arrival louder than I could've thought possible. The mother went limp, her face blanched and her eyelids fluttered shut. Cole instructed me to hold the oxygen right where I had it. Cole showed the ostensible father his new son and offered words of assurance. The man, who was older than the new mother by maybe ten or fifteen years, stood in the corner, and did not come toward his new son—he merely nodded with understanding. Cole explained that they were going to take the baby to the nursery to clean him up and run some basic tests, and that soon we would have to move Mom to a different bed, but she could rest for now. Even though she looked unconscious, she repeated the word Mom, and she started to cry. After Cole left with the baby, the man asked me how old I was. Fourteen, I informed him. He said, You've done this before? I ignored him while a nurse supported the woman's head and I changed out her sweaty pillow. The mother said, Thank you. Her eyes were still shut, as if she were being visited by a helpful phantasm. The man, frowning, asked me why I wear a helmet. Again, I didn't answer, just sterilized the oxygen mask and the tools. Then Cole reentered, and in his slow-speaking manner said they were going to have to keep the baby overnight to monitor him, but that Mom could also spend the night. The man started asking Cole leading questions, like where he'd learned medicine, if he believed in Purism, if a child ever died on his watch. Cole's voice was relaxed yet firm as he said to the man, If I engage with you, I won't be able to give my full attention to your child and his mother, who need me most. Then the man left the room. Cole excused me so he could speak with the mother. The father was in the hallway, pacing the floor in front of the nursery window. I passed by him and entered the other side of the glass to help change diapers. I noticed the man watching me, shaking his head and wiping his hand over his mouth.

A few hours later, a young couple came in asking for Cameron, who runs the nursery. She has short hair that's a layer of blond over a layer of brown, and so many freckles that her white skin looks tan. She helped the couple through the process of adopting one of the ten babies.

It was a busier day than most, Cameron told me gladly. An adoption and a delivery in one morning. Cameron's probably around forty, which means she was young at the beginning of the war, about my age. I didn't ask her about it, and I probably won't. I've heard enough war stories—everyone has war stories. But she's delighted by the babies.

Apparently, I enjoy taking care of them too. I spent most of my afternoon with a baby in a crib labeled #105. The baby had the number stitched onto her shirt too. The number referred to the order of orphaned newborns, abandoned newborns, and newborns put up for adoption since the founding of Canland. #105 has darker skin, like Helm's, curly black hair, spherical green eyes, and cheeks that overlap the corners of her mouth. She's the oldest baby in the nursery, sixteen months, and born on the day I was perforated.

In my journals, I'd written about a woman named Sasha with whom AB used to play games beneath the oak tree. A DOTEC woman—AB's friend and true savior. She found them, and together they made it to the ocean, then to Canland. But now Sasha's nowhere—gone forever in the realest way, Cameron told me. They couldn't get her to the Safe Haven in time through the rain. #105 made it, though.

I asked Cameron what happens to the babies who go unclaimed. She said, There are Parts for orphans. They'll stay here for two years, and if no one adopts them, we send them there. They have a good life—they go to school, they contribute, they grow up like anyone else. It's rumored there's a lot of crime in those Parts, but that's because there aren't family units the way there are here. The older orphans raise the younger ones. It's like a limbo before they go on to new Parts—when they're ready—but some people just stay there, raising the younger ones, she said. In all my time here, we've only sent three babies away. They almost all get adopted. But we've also never had ten at the same time. Well, nine now, she said, smiling as she cleared out the crib of the baby adopted today, #111.

But the number soon became ten again. At the end of the day, a malnourished woman came in to deliver. Her oxygen levels were low. Quickly, her liver shut down, then her lungs. Cole diagnosed her with peripartum cardiomyopathy. Her heart couldn't get enough blood to her organs. I held an oxygen mask to her face, uselessly. Everything was fast and loud, until it was quiet and still, like her heart. Cameron took the baby to the nursery.

After the mother's body was moved to the morgue, Cole pulled up two chairs, and we sat. He said, Are you OK? I said I was. He said, Sometimes having a patient die is not a failure on our part. Everyone dies, and sometimes there's nothing we can do to delay that. You'll open up space in yourself for that possibility, every time you take on the responsibility of helping a new life enter the world. You accept that your hands might be the last on someone before they die, your face the last they see. When you do this work, you become a servant to life.

Keeping in mind Helena's philosophy, and the needs of the Earth, and my own suicide—which I decided to keep to myself, though I considered telling Cole—I asked, If someone's death is unpreventable, should you expend resources trying to save it?

Cole didn't really provide an answer to that question, but rather said, Dying with dignity is the gift we get as humans, to know when and how. Bringing someone in is always much scarier to me than helping someone leave.

I said, What about helping them stay?

Are you asking me about yourself? he said.

I felt like Cole had extracted and examined the cells of which my question was comprised, but which I could not see. I know he noticed the realization on my face, but he still waited for me to say yes.

He replied, I'll do everything I can to help a child live. You know, I lost a son. That was fifty years ago. I've lived a lot of life, but I still only know what works for me. Canland is a better place than some I've seen, and worse than others. Here, I get to help people in a way that makes me feel fulfilled. I suppose it makes sense that, for all the times I've helped you, now you help me. But as far as the axioms of life and death to which humans should ad-here—I don't know any more than you. Over most things in my life, I have no control. Medicine gives me some. I try not to live as a reaction to the past. Then he drew a long, head-wrinkling sigh, as if he were not completely satisfied with the clarity of his answer.

Recognizing that, in a way, Cole was just about the most important person in my life, I asked if he could tell me about his own, and he said yes, but not now, that we would talk more later, he had some things to take care of, and that, really, today was an anomaly, much busier than most—perhaps a perfect first day. He stood up, thanked me for my work, and asked me to change the bedsheets in the delivery room, which were still wet with blood.

·

March 12, 2090

Quiet morning. We sent the young redhead mom home with her son, both healthy, but the father wasn't here. Hopefully he's waiting at home.

When Dylan and I passed Asher and Malakai's street on the way here, I asked him how they were doing. Dylan said, About a year ago, Asher bit a guy who allegedly said to him, Thirty DOTEC I killed in the war and I'd've killed you too, if I saw you. The guy had the bite treated at the Safe Haven. Asher was expelled and sent to Long Term Rehabilitation. But Malakai's actually a COHO now. So maybe it's like a one step backward, one step forward thing.

So, not really progress, I said.

Everything's an experiment to discover what can go unnoticed, Dylan said.

Canland was radiant in the morning sun. I could see light reflecting off the wings of insects, like flying sparks. So many cows were in the pasture, still as wooden toys. The grass on the hillock looked hand-laid. The scene was like something out of an Actualization.

What's the use in healing the Earth if the people on it still suffer? I said.

Dylan said, Utilitarian suffering. Unfortunately, everything is dependent on the suffering of something else. We are all instruments. Then, after a long pause, he said, But at least in a Rogue Part, I wouldn't be WORLD's.

Why would you want to live in a Rogue Part? I said.

Because it's where smart people live, unnoticed—maybe even Sybil.

So why don't you, then?

He was silent. We pulled up to the Safe Haven. I got off the bike, but I lingered.

Finally, without looking at me, Dylan said, Why do you think? Then he rode off.

.

March 13, 2090

Today Cameron explained the water situation in Canland. The water economy's been thriving over the past year because of improvements made to the desalination plant WORLD built in the years after the war, after the former city of Los Angeles became uninhabitable due to earthquake liquefaction and the coast moved twenty miles inland. The plant was completed ten years ago, but WORLD stalled to determine which proximal Parts would receive water until the Parts demonstrated cooperation with WORLD regulations and proved sustainable and beneficent. Because of Canland's positive environmental impact, low rate of population growth, and adherence to WORLD's Transitional Phase Social Regulations (such as limited cultural exposure and stringent education and advancement policies, aka why I'm not allowed at school right now), Canland was granted permission to use resources to build infrastructure to connect its reservoir to the desalination plant two hundred miles southwest. Cameron said Canland's access to coastal waters was a poetic reversal of early twentieth-century water privatization malpractices and proletariat exploitation. Then she appended, Although it's not like we're stealing water from anyone now, since everyone who thought they could wait it out down there is decomposing along the new continental slope. Then she laughed to herself, as she does, and went back to talking to the babies in their cribs, describing objects, telling clever stories about numbers who wander off the number line.

However, since Canland water contributors built so much of the infrastructure with the help of contributors from other Parts (which were also granted access to desalinated ocean water), legions of DOTEC have attempted to reroute sections of the canals and aqueducts, and siphon off water for their Rogue Parts. In reaction, WORLD rovers and ecological defense agents have uprooted these factions of DOTEC, offering passage to nearby xenodochia or other Parts accepting DOTEC applications—or, as Cameron says, Probably taking them to Long Term Rehabilitation Parts to do the work they would have volunteered to do in Parts like Canland, if only they were allowed in.

Basically, Canland is under siege, in a sort of nagging, not-immediately-threatening way. But the water-siphoning—though exterior to our Part—has given the registered even more reason to distrust DOTEC, perpetuating the cycle: the registered in the Hovels are sometimes shunned when they go to market for their rations; a small band of DOTEC were turned away from Canland yesterday by a COHO, sent back into the desert, while standing fifty feet or so behind the COHO was a gathering of registered men holding rocks. I can only imagine what the DOTEC students are going through at school.

My best friend ever has been DOTEC for a long time now. I wonder if she's suffering from thirst. If she's been taken by a rover. If she's in Long Term Rehabilitation. I hope she's still alive. I wonder what Canland, and my life, would be like if Sybil had never left. The same, I suppose, somehow or other. Like Cole said, we're mostly powerless.

I sat for a long time beside #105's crib today. She played a game where she'd hold a blanket up in front of her face and let it fall. Whenever she revealed herself, she babbled happily, showing her pink gums and nascent little teeth. When I got home, I checked my loyal dictionary to see if babble and Babel are cognates, but I found nothing. I do however know that babies babble with slight variances depending on the language they're raised to speak.

What keeps us all alive is water, but what keeps us living is the language between us. And yet, its consistent tendency to fail in its purpose of giving people a means of expression has caused endless disputes. The differences between us all begin immediately, because of how we speak.

Afraid of dying misunderstood and limited, people make decisions on how they want to spend their lives. I can reason myself to be afraid of death, but really it's just that I don't want to die—maybe a distinction without a difference. And yet, I committed suicide in the Sensorium (at least once). Whatever it is that the mind must override, the thing in our bodies that takes hold a moment too late—when the jumpers are somewhere between the edge of the Notch and the ravine below—is something I don't have. But suicide never seriously crosses my mind—my real mind, that is. I only did it to eliminate my human interruptions; to make me into music.

I did not speak. I played piano.

Today I said to #105, Your mother was loved. She was DOTEC, and she was brave, and she cared for a person whom I loved. You're going to be taken care of, and you're going to have a home, and you're going to live a good life. She held the blanket up in front of my face and let it fall. She laughed.

On the ride home, I caught a whiff of the fields being watered, the sweet smell of petrichor. That's when I saw rain, a gray world, and AB's face so close to mine that all the details I've written down were right in front of me, almost touching me. When I tried to hold them, they went away. I shut my eyes to let something fill the darkness.

I saw a person alone in a room welding golden fish, like each one could come to life. A fish for everyone, made by a person who wants to love even more than to be loved.

"THIS IS MY younger son, Tristan."

Dylan stands bent over the kitchen washbasin. He slowly drinks a cup of water, keeping the cup to his lips. When he's done, he's out of breath. The way he holds himself, it's like he's trying to blend in, or disappear, like a lizard on the side of the house.

"He has a congenital insensitivity to pain."

He eats one peanut and almost a second, but can't stomach it, and wipes it off his tongue and into the compost chute.

"He spent the first three years of his life in hospitals and Research Centers."

Dylan pours another cup of water from the pitcher and tries to sip again, but it dribbles down his chin and wets his shirt.

"Doctors said it was unlikely he'd live past a year, but if he did, they could monitor a brain that had for all intents and purposes never been in danger."

Dylan wipes the water from his chin all over his face and shivers, straightening up.

"I'm Kelly. It's nice to meet you," says the woman with a peeling sunburn, hooked nose, wide-apart eyes, and narrow chin.

"You too." I smile down at her on the couch.

"And here he is, thirteen years later." Helena smiles at her and then at me.

Dylan—vanished against the paleness of our adobe walls in late-afternoon window light—slips out the door. I can hear him right his felled bike, can feel him taking off up the road, around the bend—but then I lose him.

"Fourteen," I say.

Kelly could be twenty or forty—it's hard to tell with the sunburn, like you could maybe scrape it off to find younger skin beneath.

"Oh my god, fourteen, you're right." Helena puts a hand to her forehead. "That was weird. We lost the past year and a half together, plus the three at the beginning," she tells Kelly. Helena glances back at me and purses her mouth. New lines have developed since I went away. She rarely got sentimental before that, but now her eyes are quick to mist. "Kelly was approved for reproduction," she says, smiling again.

"Four months along now—just starting to show." Kelly rubs her stomach. I can't see the bump because of her posture and the sweater she's wearing, but her breasts are ineluctable. I feel sorry for her that she has to lug them and a growing baby around all the time. I hadn't ever considered that sort of thing before my contribution.

"Congratulations," I say. "I contribute in the Safe Haven, so I'll see you there."

Kelly nods with her head and shoulders, making a pleasant face, then looks at Helena.

"Give us some time," Helena says to me.

I go down the hall to my room and open and close the door, but don't step inside. I slide down the wall and sit on the floor, and then untie my helmet and turn up my hearing aids.

"Sweet," Kelly says.

"You have no idea," Helena replies.

"What's it like?"

Helena sighs. "Hardest thing I've ever done in my life. Every day, I think 'This is it, this is the day he doesn't know he has an infection.' But that's my own problem—his limitations don't bother him. I don't think he'll ever have the dignity of total independence, though."

"Did you ever think of aborting?" I hear Kelly ask.

A long pause. I turn my hearing aids up all the way. In the fuzzy quiet, I think of how Helena used to show Dylan techniques for tending the garden, pruning the bushes, planting the seeds WEDA administered, encouraging his love for nature—even before Dylan ever said he wanted to specialize in botany, and before Michael ever showed him how to use a Sensorium—and I think of how, when I'd go in the garden, she'd condition me. I think of how my disembodied consciousness brought her to the edge of a promontory with me, reminiscent of the day she sat on the jagged Maine beach rocks and smelled the dead whale as it washed ashore, and she felt the first notes of love for my father.

"Sometimes I still wonder," Helena with the bottom of her voice.

Suddenly my sixteen months in the Sensorium feel purposeful. The center of my feelings has expanded ever so slightly, just close enough to the nearest edges of the extremes, to know, without having to reason, that Helena hates me—I've brought more pain than love to her life. If I still haven't proven to her that I was worth keeping, then I never will.

"I worry she'd feel it," Kelly says.

"She can't feel anything," Helena replies.

"But she'd be dying."

"That depends on what you believe makes something alive," Helena says.

One of them sniffles. It sounds like dry leaves in my technologized ear canals.

"I take care of my mother," Kelly says. "She's sixty-five. She has severe respiratory problems."

"Many of us do," says Helena.

"Hers is bad. She lived in a city that was destroyed in the Evanescence. All that debris sliced up her lungs. She grew up on the ocean—an athlete, a surfer. When I was a kid, she'd always tell me stories about it. She raised me in a Part that had a small lake. We'd sit by the water and she'd promise to take me to the Pacific one day. But there was infighting in our Part and we had to leave. We've been in Canland for ten years now, and we're lucky, but she hasn't mentioned the ocean once since we got here."

"From the ocean to the desert," Helena says.

"She can't go anywhere. She can't take more than twenty steps at a time. She contributes for the census department from home. The boredom is too much sometimes. She becomes cruel. Sometimes I think a baby would fix that. But then I ask myself, what stories would I tell this kid? Who am I? It's like I only know how to ignore myself. We left my old Part when I was your son's age, and then we were out there for three years before we arrived here. I'm twenty-seven. I think my body wants the baby, but my brain asks, is it better to make something you'll have to protect, or to not make something that will be in constant danger?"

"We all need love, we all need protection," Helena says.

"Sometimes I doubt I have any left to give," Kelly says. She pauses. "When my mom's dreams died, mine died. For a long time, those dreams were all I had."

She starts crying. Helena hushes her. It's like it's all happening right next to my head.

"You need to give it to yourself first," Helena tells her, "no matter what you decide to do with this baby or with yourself. Not everyone who goes up the Notch is miserable, and not everyone who is miserable goes up. I've known fulfilled people who go up and not come down, but I've also known people to find hope up there. A couple weeks ago, a friend of mine came to me, miserable. His boyfriend was abusing him. He said he was a willing participant, and was filled with such self-hate that he decided to hike up. We even said goodbye. When he was up there, he said it was that self-hate that kept him alive; he couldn't ignore it. He went home and collected his things and moved into a new communal house. He said to me, 'I realized I don't hate myself. I hate that someone else hated me.' Up there, he was able to consider if it was worth pursuing a new life. He decided it was."

"But he's only himself. Who would I be taking a chance away from?" Kelly asks.

"Someone who was never anyone," says Helena. "Your own imagination."

They wait in silence for more thoughts to form. I find myself anxious to return to the nursery.

"Does the father know?" says Helena.

"No."

"So you want to decide soon."

"Only for myself. I don't ever want to be part of DOTEC again.

And," Kelly's voice was suddenly lower, more even, "I couldn't live with myself if my child ever . . ."

Part of DOTEC—the words alight in my head feathered in fear, but glimmering with an edge of pride for this union of survivors. Sometimes I forget that Helena spent years out there without a home.

"Canland is safe," Helena says.

Why did she always try to make me afraid? Why didn't she ever tell me I was finally safe? She wanted me to be afraid of everyone. Could it be that she's afraid of me?

"Look," says Helena, "the population of Canland has stabilized. You were approved. But I'll just ask you to remember that, if you abort, it will help our Part. It will help the Earth. Don't take too much responsibility on yourself. You'll always be trying to make up for it, and you'll always fall short."

"You're right, yes. I'm only me," says Kelly.

"You're so fortunate that you know that so young." Helena sighs. "I hiked up the Notch maybe twenty times after Tristan went to the hospital. I found it gave me a sense of place. This is all there is. We're not living in scarcity anymore. I have everything I need. If you decide to hike, my hope is you gain clarity about your own life, so you'll be able to decide about your baby's."

Even with the changes to our family's status, Helena's influence has remained. On the other hand, Michael's gone from Canland forever, but in that way, he has positioned himself in my memory so he can do no further harm. I won't ever overhear him saying something so incriminating as *I still wonder if I should have aborted my child.* Michael's job is done.

"I'll grab you a candle," Helena says.

I stand and open the door to my room. As Helena appears in the mouth of the hallway, I walk toward her, past her, ignoring her, though I can tell her eyes are on me. Kelly's on the couch, looking down at her belly. In the kitchen, I eat a peanut, waiting for Helena to come back. Immediately she does, holding a candle in one hand and a small coffin in the other. Kelly makes a soft sound.

"Just for you to know, to see," Helena says. She hands Kelly the candle, and Kelly accepts it, but when Helena holds out the tiny coffin, Kelly waves her hand and looks away. I see her eyes land on the piano.

"Who plays?" she asks.

"I do," I say, though I haven't touched it since I've been home.

Helena looks at me, but I keep my eyes on Kelly. She smiles and says, "I'd love to hear."

While watching me, Helena rounds the couch so she's standing behind and to the side of Kelly, leaning with her hand on the back of the couch. "Go ahead," she says.

I put the peanuts back in the cupboard, then go sit at the piano. My hands span nearly an octave now. I close my eyes. I see sparkling water . . . no, I don't, I want to, but instead I see violent waves, rising fast, darkness, and then calm. Alone at this piano, my fingers sink into the song Helena played for me the day of Roshana's funeral. I see a man walking above me, on the other side of the water, his head hanging, looking down through the surface. What he's looking for, but can't find, is visible to me, along the bottom, beneath a layer of sunken matter: the strung-together hearts of kids my age, bobbing in elastic time. I take them in my hands and dredge them up. I'm down here to save them. My fingers slip between them, feeling the beats and the rests, playing the score of forever sleep. One note at a time, I make the melody a song for them, down here where only we can hear me.

When it's over, I rise from the bench. I turn around and bow. I lift my head and see Kelly softly applauding.

Helena's frown lines are deep, but she says, "Wonderful."

"Thank you, Tristan," Kelly says. "That was beautiful."

"Why don't you do some reading in your room and I'll be in shortly," says Helena.

I bow my head to Kelly again. She smiles, wide but incomplete. Cole taught me how to tell a fake smile: the eyes don't move.

I hope Kelly doesn't come to the maternity ward for another five months.

In my room, I wedge myself between the boxes, sit at my desk, and light a candle. I turn my hearing aids low and open one of Helena's pamphlets, *Here and Everywhere*. After reading only a few words, I close it. I don't want to think about Purism, or Practicalism, or how fragile our existence is. I want to spend time with what feels familiar and permanent, like a friend. I open *Fearsome Allies* to "Opiliones."

There are three pictures on the page. In one, a harvestman perches weightlessly on the tip of a leaf; the next is a close-up of two eyes atop a spiny, wrinkly body segment, like an old man; the third is of a cluster, a smoky black mass of too many legs to count. It reads:

> According to legend, the harvestman is the deadliest spider on Earth. Other myths say it's bad luck to kill a harvestman. More still believe that the sight of a harvestman indicates rain is coming. So what makes these creatures so full of fantastical mystery?
>
> The order *Opiliones*, or harvestmen, or Daddy Longlegs, are a myth in themselves—they aren't spiders at all! The harvestman doesn't have silk glands or venom glands, meaning they can't spin webs or poison their prey. Can you spot some more differences between this arachnid and spiders?[*]
>
> What else is so interesting about this strange creature is its gregariousness. As a defense mechanism, harvestmen cluster in groups of hundreds and even thousands![†] When a predator gets close, the cluster will scatter, scaring the predator away. But if a stray happens to find itself in danger, it can detach its leg and make its escape while the leg continues to move in the predator's mouth, fooling it with this "decoy limb." Also, harvestmen can emit a foul scent to ward off threats.
>
> Harvestmen are thought by some to be the oldest known arachnid, and one of the longest-extant arthropods, arriving on Earth over 400 million years ago. Early fossils reveal that they looked the same as today, meaning they have

reached the pinnacle of their evolution! They live in most climates, so no matter where you are, be kind to this gentle, ancient creature.

*See answers in appendix, page 60.
†See Fig. 74.

I've read this passage a thousand times. When Dylan gave me this book on my birthday—my first birthday without Michael here—I spent the day reading it, cover to cover, over and over. I'd always loved arachnids—their patience, their fear function. I think AB reminded me of a harvestman—afraid and harmless and strong.

"T–st–" I hear.

I turn my hearing aid up.

"Tristan. Tristan."

I turn around. By a trick of the light—the candle burning in my room, the hall dark behind her—Helena appears to take up the whole doorway.

"Sorry," I say. "I had my hearing aids on low."

"Don't do that. Don't ever do that. What if there was an emergency?"

"Sorry," I say again.

"Listen. You're listening? If you ever eavesdrop on me when I'm with a patient again, I swear to you, I'll break my promise. Promises go two ways. Understand?"

"Got it."

"Number two," Helena says. "If someone asks you to play, I don't care where you are, if you're in our own home or in the amphitheater in front of all of Canland and the viceroy, you play a lullaby. Play "Twinkle, Twinkle." Play a Chopin nocturne if you're feeling immodest. But don't ever play anything your mind has made up."

"You showed me that song."

Helena pushes her fingers into her eyes and screams. Then she shakes her head. Her hair is down by her shoulders, and it moves.

"I don't want you writing songs! Why is that so hard? I don't want you thinking you're any good."

As I say it, I'm considering it seriously for the first time: "What if I want to go to an Arts Part?"

"People go there if they have nothing in their lives. They don't do anything meaningful, their art circulates the Part, and people from Idealist Parts come to gawk at it, like Traditionalist snobs, and then the art gets buried, and their lives end up a useless heap of trash."

"Helm is an artist."

"No, he's not. He wrote a bad book. And guess what? He doesn't live in an Arts Part. If you want to be creative, take up pottery, or basket-weaving, or even smithery."

"Or stitching clothes?"

Her lips curl in. She takes a step into my room. The rosacea at the corners of her flaring nostrils wasn't so noticeable before I went away.

"No one else is going to take care of you," she says.

I nod. Part of me knows she's right. But part of me knows, too, that when I find someone new who will take care of me, my life will begin.

"I don't get to be hurt," she says. "I have that conversation with a young woman who just wants to do the right thing, and then I come in here and give you a simple command, and you question me and insult my contribution. That's disgusting, Tristan. And I can't get an apology from you or your brother that would mean a thing, because you don't know what you've done wrong. Do you know how many apologies I'm owed? Yet still, where am I? Every day. The least you could do is what I tell you to do. Don't play your own songs for people."

She turns away and leaves. I go to the door and close it.

Surrounded by boxes of death material, I start my nightly check, not knowing whether Helena will come in to do it again for me. She still has, every night, since I've been home.

When I'm finished and changed into pajamas, I turn my hearing aids up until I hear the faintest scratch of her metal nib against her writing table. Then I turn the volume back to normal, and sit on my bed and wait, and wait—just wait.

.

It's sunny, the sky's vibrating like it can't wait, and AB's face is split with laughter. Then the clouds move in and AB's laughter turns to shaking worry. The yellow light turns white and AB starts to cry. Their tears become rain. The light dies. I put my face to theirs so they're all I see. Their face is pressed against mine, and they're calm like a baby. I try to speak, to apologize, but I have no voice. They start to pull away, their face happy, then unhappy. So I wake up. It's like something has slipped from my grasp, a word I can't recall.

I get up. I put on two pairs of socks and two wool sweaters and pop my teeth in and then without thinking walk through the near-total darkness to my door, somehow not knocking anything over. I have no idea what time it is. The whole house is dark, but the path from the hall to the front door is easy because there's nothing in the way. It's strange—walking through our house, without entering his room, you'd never know that Dylan lived here. There are no shoes by the door, no book on the couch, no uncleared plate on the table. We once shared my room, when Michael used Dylan's current room exclusively as his office. Dylan and I slept in separate beds against opposite walls, and he'd talk to me until I fell asleep, asking me what I liked and thought and wanted, and telling me that one day he would invent a new species of plant through cross-pollination and genetic modification that needs no water and grows quickly and is edible to humans and poisonous to vermin, and makes Canland's ecosystem utterly incorruptible. When he got kicked out of school, and Michael started teaching him, Dylan spent all his time in what's now his room, and he never slept in mine again.

It's cold out, as usual, in the desert night. I sit on the front step. I rarely go outside after dark. The sky's full of stars that make visible silhouettes of everything–the tall, tall eucalyptus trees across the road, showing night between their leaves, soughing in a light wind that, before the trees were here to cut it up, howled tempestuously; the jagged sierras, sculptures made by ice and heat and unthinkable pressure, like stacked bones of beasts buried in the Earth; and above those peaks, a full huge pale stony moon hangs like a clock, in perpetual motion relative to us so it only ever shows one face to the Earth, a likelihood so infinitesimal that I wonder for a moment, as Michael might, who placed it there just so. Maybe scientific singularity is an argument for god, and that's why ancient civilizations worshipped the cosmos.

His lopping footsteps near, arms flailing like tentacles, slowing his run in the middle of our street. He puts his hands on his hips and looks up, spits into the dirt, grabs his knees, and spits again. His hair hangs by the sides of his face. Dylan. He turns around and takes off sprinting up the street again, his footsteps no softer, just getting farther away. The insects make music. He disappears at the bend. He must be spitting and bending and looking up at the stars again before he comes running back down the street, with dust clouding around his skidding feet as he stops, groans, spits, and sits, leaning back on his hands, his elbows locked, wheezing.

"Hi, Dylan."

His head turns over his right shoulder toward me. The darkness erases his face.

"Beautif–" His breathlessness eats the last syllable. "Whatcha doing?"

He's facing east, down the section of street we rarely use, where Canland peters out into mostly undeveloped desert. Where night-creatures lurk and leave behind turds as evidence, but never show themselves.

"Had a dream that woke me up," I say. "What are you doing?"

"Running." He pinches his waist and jiggles a wheel of unexpected flesh. "Lose this weight." He clears his throat. "Plus the air. Cold"–he strokes the air beside his head–"keeps me clear."

"You got thin, though," I say.

"Yeah . . . well"–he spits–"thanks."

"Did you have your contribution tonight?" I call across our night-purpled yard.

He shakes his head and spits again. "Off." He leans his head back, trying to breathe deeper. "Some moon."

"Yeah, it's amazing."

"Yeah? You like it?"

"Yeah." I look up at with just my eyes, not my whole head like him. "Is running better for weight loss than biking?"

"Why? You trying to tell me something?" He flashes a quick smile; I see the teeth. "Just kidding." He spits, then breaths deeply and coughs once. "I don't know. Something about . . . fast and slow twitch muscles. Who cares. Keeps me sane. I can't sleep, and this"–he swallows–"feels like . . . something."

I get up and walk down our path and sit in the road beside him. "I don't want to shout and wake Helena," I say.

"You won't." He lies back in the road with his knuckles on his forehead. "Once she's out, she's out."

"Not always. She used to come into my room in the middle of the night to talk to me."

"You could smell the grapes, eh?" He rounds his lips into an O and breathes out. "What'd she say to you?"

I don't know if Dylan knows the way Helena used to condition me. He's so protective of me that, if I told him, he might become so enraged that he'll do something stupid and violent–matricidal.

"She'd just tell me she was afraid for my safety," I say.

"That's not a good reason to–whatever." Dylan's hands slide down over his eyes. "She lost it when you were gone–always drunk, telling everyone to jump." He shakes his head. "She's never had the power to make anybody do anything. They're all so bored and miserable, they just need permission, and then they feel like they're not alone, and that it's better than actually living alone, dying together." He puts one hand on his stomach. "It got bad with me and her." He removes the other hand from his eyes, slides it up to his forehead. His eyes in the night are gray, the same color as the rest of him. "You want to hear a fucked up story?" he asks.

Even if Dylan has changed, he'll never surprise me. "Sure."

He chuckles and puts his forearm back over his eyes. "I brought a body back." His cheeks suck in, then he turns his head away and spits. "I did a tube before I left for a waste run, and at the bottom of the Notch there was a girl–young girl, pretty face. Her limbs were all bent and tangled and her spine was broken in half and the back of her head was open, but her face was still all perfect, like she was asleep. Instead of taking her out to the Waste Reallocation Center like I'm supposed to, I put her in the wagon and biked her back here and carried her through the door." His voice just dropped. He bends a knee up so his foot's flat on the ground. "Helena was writing at her table. I didn't say anything. She got up and started shouting at me, how dare you this, you sick whatever that. She smacked me in the face, but I didn't even feel it–from the adrenaline, from the tube. She threatened to have me expelled; empty threats. She didn't even look at the girl. I carried her back out to the wagon and finished my waste run. What else could I do?" He bends up his other knee, makes a lot of small fidgety movements. "A couple days later, all the plants in my room were gone. I didn't give a fuck about Helena, but I felt so guilty that I'd used this dead girl to make a point. I don't know. She wasn't right in the mind, is just what it was, like all of them. But that guilt, the whole situation we're all in, it became so vivid. It scared the fuck out of me so bad, it made me want to stop tubing."

I'm trying to find fault with Dylan, to feel for him what he feels for himself, but with the girl dead and Dylan on tubes, defining his transgression feels a bit like dividing by zero. Still, I can trust his feeling without knowing it for myself. I wait for him to say more.

"When she got back from visiting you," he says, "she was different." He takes his hand off his face. His eyes stay fixed on the sky. "That's when she helped me stay off tubes, and gave me things to do. We went for walks together. I even left the door open to my room when I was in the Sensorium so she'd hear it if something went wrong." He sighs halfway and clears his throat. "Then today she said I was eternally indebted to her for not turning me loose. It's better when we just ignore each other."

I asked Dylan this morning why he doesn't go live in a Rogue Part. He answered my question with another question. Now I'm certain of the answer: me.

"So how you doing?" He lets his head roll toward me. "What was your dream about?"

I put my sweater sleeves over my fists to keep them warm. "AB, my friend on the hillock."

"The DOTEC."

"I think they live in the Hovels now."

"Based on what?"

I shrug. "Hope, I guess–hope that they're still in Canland."

Dylan sits up, grunting. "You sound like you're in love."

"I only knew them for a little bit."

His elbows rest on his knees, and his hair falls to the sides of his face. "I was in love with Sybil from the moment I met her."

"You've known her for her whole life," I say.

"Minus the past year and a half." He rakes his hair back and sheds loose strands from between his fingers into the dirt. "Isn't that strange? Knowing someone up until a certain point, and then you don't anymore."

"Imagine missing a year of your own life," I say.

"Imagine needing a Sensorium on your head just to feel alive," he says.

"Imagine never feeling pain."

"All right, all right." Dylan smiles. He lets his head hang. His breath is visible. He shivers.

"Do you want one of my sweaters?" I ask.

He shakes his head. "The cold is good. I'll get to warm up inside." He flexes his jaw.

In all the time I've known Dylan, he's always been chasing after something.

"Can you try to find Sybil on the satellites?" I ask.

"Bit of an ethical gray area there, Beautiful. She chose to leave." He blows into his cupped hands. "I did try once, though, but I got bounced. Turns out for every skilled interloper there's an equally skilled bouncer."

"Did she ever tell you why she left?"

He shakes his head. "She wasn't talking to me a whole lot at the end there—I hadn't been too nice to her. But I think it was because she needed to pursue a certain type of, I don't know, experience, that most people here are content not to." He shifts his weight and winces. He draws a breath and makes a noise like he wants to say more, but then closes his lips and exhales nasally.

"Well," I say, "if we can't find Sybil, can you help me find AB?"

He looks at me with his close-together eyes half-closed. "I don't want you going to the Hovels," he says. "It's not safe down there—full of disease and shit. They call it housing, but it's just human storage."

Sometimes I think Dylan exaggerates. He's a romantic, and his heart hinders his capacity for reason and makes him inconsistent. Though, I suppose, given Canland's attitude toward DOTEC, I have no reason not to believe him; I just don't want to. I need to know if AB's OK, and if they're not here, only a DOTEC would know where they went.

"I kissed them," I say, fairly certain and full of hope that it's what happened on the hillock.

"Who?" His lip turns into a snarl and his forehead wrinkles. "Sybil?"

"AB," I say.

"Oh." He puts his hand over his heart. "When?"

"Right before I was perforated, I'm pretty sure. I can't remember it, but I have a feeling."

"I thought the report said they were attacking you."

I shake my head. For some reason, the boredom of Canland now truly dawns on me. People invent stories, make villains, craft a narrative of Canland that our work here will save the

Earth. But Canland is just made up of DOTEC who tell themselves they're a Part.

I place a hand on Dylan's shoulder. "I'm going to make a deal with you."

He laughs, then blinks. "OK."

"We leave Canland."

His face relaxes, his eyes open fully. He looks at me, from my mouth to my close-cut hairline, as if to determine whether I'm the same child he remembers, or if I'm new, and if I know what I'm saying.

"But before that," I continue, "I want you to take me to the Hovels to look for AB, just once."

"You want to leave," he says. "Why?"

I think—but don't say—that it's because I want him to be free. What do I have here that's worth keeping him arrested to Canland? Cole, the orphans, the cycle of reward and punishment from Helena? I don't despair, but Dylan does. So I tell him half the truth. "I'll never be complete here."

"You might not be complete anywhere," he says, and puts his head into his elbow. His voice muffled, he adds, "You sound like Sybil."

I shrug at what I take as a compliment. Dylan's teeth begin to chatter. I used to think he could do anything, that he was a higher form of being. But now it's clear—we're brothers.

"Give me a week," he says. "Just to get some stuff together and arrange a route. I'll take you to the Hovels on our way out."

"OK," I say.

Dylan lifts his head and stares at me, resting his ear on his bent knees. He doesn't say anything, just stares. When people stare at me, I know that it's because they're pitying me, taking note of my disadvantages, and then suddenly pretending they weren't staring at me in the first place. Sybil taught me that, and it bothered her. But Dylan has never once stared at me like that.

"Where did you go earlier?" I ask. "When Helena was with that lady."

"Oh, just . . ." He turns away and wipes his forehead with his sleeve, then pinches the neckline of his shirt and flaps it out. "There are these trees by the arroyo I like. I used to go there when Helena and Michael would fight. They were just saplings then, but they've grown fast. I just went to think about some stuff today."

I nod. I scoot closer to Dylan and lay my head on his shoulder. The moon has lowered, turning yellow and plump. It must be getting early. "What did they used to fight about?" I ask.

"Everything," Dylan said. "Where to put the chairs. What they wanted Canland to be. What it meant to have lived through the war. What to do with me."

"And me?"

Dylan's quiet. I close my eyes, feeling tired again.

"Never," he says.

I let my head slide down the front of his shoulder. There's still meat on it, but I can feel the bone too, against my cheek. I put my nose in his armpit and smell him. It's the same as he's always smelled—all his toil, his departures, his violence, his shame at failing with his talents to convince Michael to stay, his sorrow over Sybil and whatever else, and all the anger he hates to have, the things he wants to change, things he's never told me and doesn't need to, but could and I'd love him anyway, everything exhaled by him and inhaled by me through his sour scent.

"Hey, Dylan."

"Yeah, Beautiful."

"Do you know that I'm good at piano?"

"I haven't heard you play in years."

"I'm good."

"I bet you are."

"I am."

He sighs, then very softly says, "Sorry if I wasn't there."

"It's OK."

"Is it?"

"Yes."

"Thanks, Beautiful."

3

March 14, 2090

Today, in idle conversation while I was making my rounds through the nursery, Cole said to me, Some technologies are nonnegotiable—after all, we're doing this so we can live on Earth, and if that weren't the goal, we'd all just willfully perish in a hedonistic inferno, take it from me. (Then I took some notes on Cole's life.) The waste and water contributors go unseen, even though they're the most important, but the farmers and the masons and the vendors and even us, we all get thanked and chatted with. People, for some reason, want to know what we think about how the Part is doing, but I want to know what the guy riding his bike across the desert at night with a tank of shit hitched to the back of it thinks . . . Then he told me a bit about the harsh jobs of his childhood, e.g. skinning and gutting animals, heating frozen pipes with splintery wood, scrubbing boats in the Yakutat Bay marina for cash. He said, We all have time to ponder, it's just that, for some people, it's a luxury they have to pay for with sleep. But you and I get to talk about things like this while making a contribution people love us for; not really fair, is it? Well, what I was trying to say, before you let me distract myself (Cole winked at me) is that, in the absence of some technologies, we resort to grim solutions. I'm not sure there's ever been a civilization that's required men to take anatomical measures against procreation; it's always been the women saddled with that unfortunate position. Coincidence that there's never been a civilization that hasn't collapsed? Cole shrugged. He said, I'm trying to be funny, to see the light, because I really do not want to do this. I could protest and lose my contribution. I could leave, and leave behind all the people I'm also helping. In principle, I don't disagree with controlling our population. I suppose the boys don't feel much pain. Recovery is only a week. Then they can pursue sex to their heart's desire. Perhaps it's not such an unenviable position I'm putting them in. He sighed and said, They can always adopt.

Then he left the nursery to perform a vasectomy.

When Cole returned from the surgery, he was no longer talkative. I thought of telling him the plan with Dylan, but decided not to—not today.

Cole vaccinated one of the orphans that was brought into the Safe Haven just weeks before I'd returned to Canland, and had me administer the baby's last shot. Cole left the nursery to tend to other patients while I held and calmed the crying baby. When Cole came back in, he said it was time for #105 to receive her last dose of vaccines. He had me administer all of them. Her flesh was so soft when the needle went in. Her eyes were big and filled with tears, and her lip quivered, but she barely made a sound.

Cole left the nursery again, and she and I sat on the floor and played with blocks. I built a tower as high as I could without it wobbling. She swept a hand through the middle and laughed shyly. The bottom half was still intact. Then she watched as I built the tower up again, even higher. She stared at it awhile, as if waiting for it to fall on its own, before pulling a block out from near the bottom. The whole tower fell and only the very bottom blocks stayed in place. She frowned at the destruction. She looked at the block in her hand as if she'd just learned something important, then threw the block a few feet away. Cameron came over and explained that we don't throw things. Then #105 picked up another block and just held it, looking back and forth at Cameron and me, her bottom lip puffed out. Finally, she jerked her elbow and let go of the block in a clumsy motion similar to—but not quite—a throw.

.

March 15, 2090

Dylan told Helena he had to be at his contribution early tonight and couldn't pick me up from the Safe Haven, so Helena agreed to get me, and on the ride back, she told me about a Canland College student named Penny Foy who painted a triptych inspired by an experience she had in a Sensorium: a bizarre representation of confusion and displacement painted by a practiced hand that depicted tranquil, fecund gardens, violent, barren wastelands, and technological apparatuses buried in graveyards, animating and pushing up through the layers of the Earth beneath the emaciated people hard at work. Penny's triptych, which she titled My Grandmother, underwent review by the Board of Advancement. They determined that if Penny wished to continue painting, she must do so in an Arts Part. She accepted the terms. She will embark, without her parents, on the Green Line this weekend. It happens, Helena said to me from the front of her red bicycle. You can have a poet's heart and a philosopher's mind and you can love the land like bees love nectar, and you can express it as creatively and as skillfully as you want, and there are places to foster those talents, but Canland is not one of them. When we forget what we are, we become something else.

.

March 16, 2090

Dylan went to his contribution early yesterday to arrange transportation from the Waste Reallocation Center to the Green Line with the help of the waste contributors, or the beetles, as in dung beetles. I said, That's funny, in the maternity ward we call ourselves the storks.

He said, Is that true?

I didn't respond, which amused him.

I asked if he knew where we were going, and he said that he was on it. I said that we should go where Sybil was, and he said, We'll see.

I said, Remember when I used to find you facedown on the floor of your room after you'd get home from your walks with Sybil?

He said, No, I don't remember that.

I asked if there was anything I should be doing and he said, Start saying goodbye to people—just don't make it obvious you're saying goodbye.

And remember—you, whoever you are, if you're reading this, just remember—I can see you, and I will haunt you if you tell a soul.

.

March 17, 2090

Today Cole asked me to go to the lobby of the Safe Haven to pick up a delivery of antibiotics. I find it careless that the Safe Haven and Canland's lab, situated in the basement of Canland College, are on opposite ends of the Part. Sure, it's only a ten or fifteen minute ride, but still, I'm starting to wonder if ostensible design flaws are actually intended inhibitors of Canland's efficiency.

The medicine was delivered by a girl with pink hair and deep tan skin. I took the bag from her. Then her brown, almost black eyes went over my shoulder. Byron, she said.

I turned around and saw, sitting in the waiting area, the boy who threatened Helena with a fake whistler at her Purist address, before I went away.

He said, Yuna. Hi.

What are you doing here?

He shook his head. His eyes were wide. Nothing, he finally said.

Yuna said, You just weren't going to tell me? Then she let out a whimper and closed her mouth, but kept looking right at Byron. So what? she said. That's it?

Quietly Byron said, It's my life.

Yuna left in a hurry, and Byron and I were the only people in the waiting area. I sat next to him. He leaned forward on his hand, covering his mouth while he talked. He said, That was my ex. We had a mandatory abortion a long time ago. I don't know if you remember what I was going through when I said that stuff to your mother—not my proudest moment. But I'm getting this vasectomy voluntarily. The benefits are too good. And I can't . . . He trailed off and sat up straight and sighed with a soft smile. He said, Plus, I'm going to try to become a researcher. That experiment I told you about—do you remember, with the ablation of the stress response in mammals—they're actually in real-world trials now. So, you might see some optogenetic animals around Canland with cranial fiberoptic windows. You probably already have and you just don't know it, unless you see a light on in their head, but then they're gonna think it's feeding time, so run. He smiled brightly then. Maybe one day I'll get to work at a WORLD Research Center. That's what I'm devoting my life to. The world doesn't need any little Byrons running around. Anyway, how've you been? You're contributing here?

I told him that I was in the maternity ward, and his face changed shape—projecting anger onto me, maybe. I don't care. As a courtesy, I kept it to myself that I thought he should focus more on Restoration, since we live in a Restoration Part, and less on Dominion. Besides, once I leave Canland, the animals won't be mine. They never were, and never will be.

I figured that by sparing him my opinion, I was saying goodbye in a way. I wished him luck with his research and with his vasectomy. He said, All right, see you around, Tristan.

You need a permit from Viceroy Hugo to leave the Part. If your expulsion is reported as autonomous, you can't come back in.

Mine and Dylan's will be autonomous.

And seriously, it's not very nice to read someone else's private journal. How can you even live with yourself?

·

March 18, 2090

I have my contribution tonight, so I slept until 1600h today. When I woke up, Helena was out, so I played piano for a while, as well as I could. I started with the songs I knew and tried to let them evolve at my fingertips, like weather in its cycle. But the notes evaporated and never fell, and all I could do was sit and wonder if I'd ever get to play piano again.

As a goodbye to Canland—stop reading and dispose of this paper now, before your moral fiber deteriorates beyond salvation—I opened up The WORLD Official History of Canland: a Restoration Part, which is on a high shelf I never could have reached until now. The volume's only about an inch thick, and most of what's in there is technical information about Canland's infrastructure, where the materials came from, etc. There are some dates and names, including Helena's and Michael's, and a few pages about Viceroy Hugo's indomitable work ethic and indispensable leadership; some brief mentions of the Evanescence, the severest natural disasters of the American West; and an exposé of the Parts System and how Canland serves as a massive brick in the bottom of the WORLD pyramid, sustaining Research Centers and Idealist Parts, contributing to Arturo Eagles' vision for Restoration, Longevity, and Dominion. But mostly, the book is a physical description of Canland, the flora and fauna of the fields, flatlands, and mountains. It also includes a chronology dating back to the 1800s of what this land once was. It was in reading this obvious and ubiquitous document, that I learned that the land on which Canland is built was once a concentration camp for Japanese-Americans during the second World War. The American president at the time ordered police and military personnel to arrest American citizens of Japanese descent and imprison them here, in a place once called Manzanar, where they worked for virtually no benefits and lived in flimsy, squalid barracks (nothing like our sturdy adobe communal houses). After two years, the prisoners were released to find that none of their homes or places of business had been protected in their absence— all because Japan's military attacked an American military base.

I want to live in a place where I don't eat the food grown on graves.

Helena came home with a patient, and didn't say a word to me. I went to my room. I'm just waiting for the hour to turn so I can knock on Dylan's door and he'll take me to the Safe Haven.

I've started looking for things to bring. Aside from *Fearsome Allies*, I'm not sure if anything holds a meaning greater than its weight.

·

March 19, 2090

Helena ended up taking me to the Safe Haven last night, and picked me up again this morning. I didn't ask where Dylan was. I didn't want to upset her. I want these days to be good ones—but then I heard him moaning and shouting through his closed door when we got home. I don't know who he was yelling at, since there was no else in the house, so maybe it was a vision or memory or himself. Maybe he was just having a nightmare.

But before that, Helena and I went to market on the way back from the Safe Haven. While Helena traded vouchers, I saw Helm by chance. I hadn't seen him since getting back to Canland. Both his hands were spoken for, a bag full of rations in one and a bouquet

of dried flowers in the other, so he proffered me his elbow, and
I bumped it with my own. I asked who the flowers were for. He
stuttered and bumbled, Oh, uh, no one. Hey, I'm sorry I haven't
come by to see you. It's not easy for me to admit, but I felt a great
responsibility for you getting shot by that COHO that day. I took it
real hard. In fact, I still feel responsible. I'm sorry, Tristan.

I told Helm that I wasn't shot, I was perforated—maybe I was
trying to be funny, I don't know.

Call it what you will, he said, you were nearly killed, and it's
my fault. I should have been there to take you home in the storm.
Then I said, You actually saved my life, in that case. What do you
mean? he asked. I told him that I'd had a blood clot in my head
that they wouldn't have found otherwise. And he said, Oh, does
that explain the helmet? Then he smiled and said, Looks good. You
look ready. He narrowed his eyes and sort of growled. I told him
about my contribution and he said it sounds like the job's a perfect
fit. I told him I wished I could still go to his class. But then he said,
Well, funny story, I've actually been reassigned as an agriculture
contributor. The Board of Advancement determined I was delaying
students' advancement, so I'm on hiatus from teaching. He said this
all with a smile inside his beard, which had more gray hairs in it
than I remembered. His eyes looked smaller and yellower than I
remembered. I told him I learned more from him than any other
teacher. That, in fact, I was writing a creative something I thought
he'd like. He said, Oh yeah? What's it all about? I said, A life. I didn't
tell him it was about Cole's life—I want to finish it first, with Cole's
continued help, and also ask Cole's permission to disseminate his
life story, which I'm honored to write, as it feels like a small gesture
of gratitude toward the man who has so many times saved my life.
Helm said, Well, all right, I can't wait to read it.

That made me smile.

Helena interrupted my conversation with Helm and said we had
to get going because I had to get some sleep, and she had to get to
her contribution. Helm said, Maybe I could come by some time and
hang with you guys? And Helena said, Sure, Helm, whatever you like.

Then she put the provisions in her basket and turned her back to Helm to sit on the bike seat. I proffered my elbow to Helm, and he bumped it with his own. He didn't pretend it hurt.

As she pedaled us back home, Helena said, Did Helm just invite himself to our house?

I don't know if she was expecting an answer, but I said nothing.

Don't end up alone, Tristan, she said.

OK, I said, then added, Good thing they're lining up for me.

She didn't laugh at my joke. Helena's alone and at least halfway to death, but I suppose that's enough life left to find someone.

She jerked the bicycle to avoid something. I glanced back at the path. It looked only smooth to me. All the people in the Part Center shrank as we got farther away, but I could still see them just before we came up and over the slight grade before the last turn to our house.

·

March 20, 2090

Last night Dylan told me that Helena was absolutely shmookied [sic] while I was at my contribution and they got into their first fight in a while—he had ignored some request of hers and she said to him, You're afraid of living and it's turned you into a shell of a person. He seemed proud that he responded by saying, All your solutions to all your traumas are futile, you live a futile life. Dylan said they went back and forth calmly, eruditely, and insultingly— but the good news was that he was close to finding a route for us.

Helena drank a lot of grappa tonight. She and I were eating together and on her way to the kitchen, she bumped her writing table with her hip and knocked over a bottle of ink and started swearing, and I went to get some rags to help clean up and she said to me, Just get out of the way, out of the way, out of the way.

So I went to lie on my bed, and I closed my eyes and thought about AB. My imagination formed a picture of AB without any clothes on. Curious about the point where their legs meet, I ended up turning onto my stomach and pressing myself against the mattress and sliding back and forth.

Helena pushed open my door without knocking, and when she saw me she said, Jesus Christ, and shut the door. I stopped and got up and wrote some of Cole's story, still surrounded by all of Helena's Purist bric-a-brac. I have to finish writing it before Dylan and I go so I can leave it with Helm. I wish I had a copy of his book. The last time I saw him did not feel like a goodbye.

I saw Kelly in the Safe Haven today through the window of the nursery. She went into an exam room. Cole went in shortly after. A couple hours later, Kelly left. She didn't see me, which I'm glad for. Personally, I had no feelings about Kelly's decision, but I asked Cole if he hated performing abortions. He said it wasn't for him to have feelings about; he's a servant to life, to living life. That made me feel similar to him, which made me feel capable.

I would have liked to spend this evening doing something fun, like going for a walk, learning to ride a bike, playing piano with Helena. But knowing I would've liked to do these things is almost as good as having gotten to do them.

And you, nosy reader: I know where you live.

• • •

DYLAN TAPS ME on the shoulder in the late predawn and whispers in my ear, "Two days."

•

I wake up after what feels like one second of sleep, smiling. I follow the smell of char down the hall to find Helena in the process of burning the oatmeal, scraping out what's stuck to the bottom of the pot. She serves that to me with some salt flakes and a dollop of preserves.

"Do we have any eggs?" I ask.

"We don't get eggs anymore."

"Tastes like mud," I say.

Helena's eyes are red and puffy, and the veins in her hands are like blue worms. She sits across from me with a mug of tea. She lifts it halfway to her mouth before she puts it back down. She leans an elbow on the table and lets her head fall into her hand.

"Tristan," she says, "in the kitchen, there's a bottle on the—"

"I know where it is."

I bring her the sleek glass bottle and a porcelain cup, which I know is not the cup she usually drinks from, but I'm curious what she'll say. "Can you pour?" is all she says. Her head's still resting on her hand. I pour a slow pulsing ribbon. She drinks it all with her eyes closed, looking like a newborn when you put a bottle to their lips. Then she pours herself a second cup, bigger than the first, and takes a small sip that makes a bright echo inside the porcelain. She clears her throat and drinks some tea.

"Finish up, and then Dylan will take you," she says. "Viceroy Hugo asked me to give a talk today in the Part Center about the people breaking into homes and rearranging things."

I can feel my brow twist up. "What?"

"How have you not heard about this?" Helena says.

"I spend most of my days talking to babies."

"Don't be snide. Just come straight home. People are breaking into houses. They're not taking anything or hurting anyone, they're just moving objects around. Or maybe no one is breaking in. Maybe there's a coalition of people rearranging their own belongings and pretending that thieves, or non-thieves, are doing it. Which is worse, in a way."

"What are you going to say in your speech?"

"It's just a talk." She lifts her tea to her mouth and blows on it. Her left eye starts to water. She doesn't seem to notice. "We're going to discuss measures we can take to protect ourselves. No one's being physically harmed, but it's creepy."

I take another bite of mostly preserves. I like the sweetness. I foresee lots of dried fruit on the journey with Dylan.

"Helena, when you settled in Canland, did you know it had once been a prison?"

"The school was once a prison, yes." She blows on her tea again, then swaps it for the grappa and takes another small sip that sounds like water over pebbles. It briefly reminds me of an Actualization. Soon, maybe, Dylan and I will sit together by a real brook.

"The land," I say.

She puts the cup down and holds a finger beneath her watery eye. "I see. Manzanar—yes, we knew. Why?"

"Why did you settle here then?"

"You'd have a hard time finding land in America that isn't the site of an historical atrocity." She takes her hand away from her eye. "There was already infrastructure here from the military base. We wanted to prove we could inhabit and restore a piece of Earth that resembled the fate of once-fertile lands." The eye keeps producing tears. She closes it and wipes it. Sometimes Helena sounds like she's practicing a speech. "Why are you asking me this?"

"I just learned it the other day."

"Tristan, it's one of the first things they teach you in school. I wrote it into the curriculum. It's in the *Official History*." I can tell she's frustrated, in an old, familiar way. When I first learned about it, though, it must not have meant anything to me. I didn't know to feel bad for those people, so I had no reason to remember it. It makes me wonder what else I've missed. I put the spoon down.

"Eat, Tristan. You have to eat."

"Why are these people rearranging other people's belongings?"

"Psychological terrorism—to give people the illusion that they aren't safe; to make them paranoid."

"Why?"

"Power," Helena says. She turns her face away and holds the heel of her hand to her eye.

I don't know anything about power. It never occurs to me that I have any, despite all the thousand little ways I must, both sinister and propitious. Helena has called Michael a *slave to reason*, yet he's the most powerful person I know. He's so powerful that he can leave his family for a life in which he helps Arturo Eagles heal the planet. "Why power?" I ask.

"Because," she says, getting up and going to the kitchen, "power makes people feel safe."

Dylan comes striding down the hall. He grabs me by the elbow and tugs me out of my chair and back to his room. He shuts the door. The computer monitors are slate gray and dim. He sits on the edge of his bed and then stands up, like he can't stop moving. He pulls at his hair, tearing strands out. His eyes are red and wide like a furious animal's. His breath is fast like he's been running. I sit on the edge of his bed. He looks at me.

"Beautiful."

"Yes, Dylan?"

He throws his arms around me and starts to sob. His whole body convulses, like a thing out of control. He falls to his knees. "I'm sorry," he says. "I'm so sorry."

"Why?"

"I fucked up. I fucked up forever. They're coming for me."

"Who?" I say, not fully comprehending, not wanting to comprehend.

"They caught me. I got bounced from a satellite. I wasn't thinking—I just . . ." He pulls back. He does not look like himself. He does not look like Dylan. Something else has taken hold. He shuts his eyes tight so his face crumples up inhumanly and he slowly, deeply wails. Strings of saliva materialize between his widely parted lips. Then the deep wail is gone and he's silently open-faced. Tears bead in the inner corners of his eyes, and then drop like rain.

"What's happening? I thought you said you could never get caught."

"They're gonna take me to Long Term."

"Michael can save you."

"No, he can't, no, he can't," he says. Snot bubbles at the end of his nose. "He doesn't care about us, he doesn't want to be our dad anymore, he said he wouldn't help me if I was stupid, and I'm so stupid!" He buries his face into the bed and bellows, punches the bed, punches himself in the back of the head, one, two, three times. He straightens up and faces me again. He wipes his face—tears, snot, saliva smear the back of his hand, caught in fine black hairs. I never realized Dylan had hair on his arms.

"Get away," I tell him.

"There was a message from Arturo Eagles on the screen," he whines. "Espionage! Data theft! Interloping! Treason!"

"We can leave right now," I say.

"On my fucking bike . . ." He coughs, his eyes closing. "They have cars."

"Tristan!" I hear Helena's voice from down the hall. "Finish your breakfast!"

On his knees, Dylan turns and fishes a folded piece of paper out of his desk drawer and hands it to me. "Anywhere here—go anywhere. Don't show anyone this. The last place is where I told Sybil—it's where we were going to—" He stops talking and turns and holds still, staring at where the wall meets the floor, like he's thinking of a way to escape, and seeing the plan play out. His spine rolls like a lurching snake. He vomits onto the floor, foamy, white, and loud. "Fuck," he says, "fuck you, you fucking nothing." He throws his fist down into the floor, knuckles first, so hard, he screams—must have broken his hand.

Tires crunch in the dirt outside. We never hear tires like that. I stuff the paper in my pocket and slide off the bed to my knees and throw my body against him, squeezing him as tightly as I can.

"It's OK," I say.

"It's not OK," he says, high-pitched and watery. "It's not OK."

There's a bang at our front door.

"I love you, Dylan."

"I'm sorry, Beautiful, I'm sorry."

"I'll see you again. It will be OK."

"If you find Sybil, just talk about the good things, OK? OK, Beautiful?"

From down the hall, we hear Helena's voice, husky and definite. "Stop! What are you doing?"

"You will see us again," I whisper into his ear.

My door across the hall slams open. We have one second. I hold him tighter than could ever be separated. I breathe him in. I shut my eyes tight, dark, just me and Dylan. I would give the rest of my life to stay like this forever. But could I live forever without caring?

So easily, I'm peeled away by hands around my chest.

"Get out of my house!" Helena yells. "We paid for this! I'll show you the papers!"

"What he did is not included, Helena," a COHO says.

I open my eyes. I'm no longer being held. I look up. Two COHOS march Dylan out of his room, his hair hanging, hiding his face. He doesn't even struggle, he makes no unexpected athletic maneuver—because his wrists are cuffed.

A COHO stands at the desk, dismantling the computers and putting the pieces in a box—everything, including the Sensorium.

"Please!" Helena screams.

When the COHO at the desk turns around, I see, in the muted light, the face that used to wait outside the school—watchful eyes in cave-like sockets, angry and patient and calm and quiet. A marksman's eyes. He's an overseer of human order; a DOTEC who now arrests data thieves; a boy with no parents, but a friend of Helm; a good person who hates me and my family, who now I must hate—Malakai. He looks away from me and leaves my brother's room with my brother's most precious things. I follow him into the bright hall, full of morning light.

"What did you do, Dylan?" Helena cries. "What are you doing to us?" She sounds like I have never heard her—impossibly uncontrolled, as if being choked. "What was the use, Dylan?"

They carry him out the door, a COHO on each side, with his feet dangling like he's floating. Malakai follows them outside. A fourth COHO backpedals in front of Helena to block her from the SPV as she stumbles down our walkway to the edge of our lawn, and Dylan is forced in, and the SPV door shuts.

"Please, Dylan, please!" Helena's voice breaks. "I'm sorry!" She turns around to look at me, her face all red, her hair flying off in every direction, golden in the sunlight. She looks like she'll never blink again. I take one step outside. She turns around and crumbles, holding her head against the ground in the street where Dylan and I sat, watching the moon, hatching a plan that's ruined everything.

Our neighbors, Rod and Rosemarie, are watching from the edge of their lawn.

Out beyond them, the trees catch a breeze and shake. The grass is pale and light. The desert's red, the mountains gray, the sky blue. My watch says my heart rate is 78.

I go back inside to Dylan's room, and lie on his bed. When I was in the Research Center, he could have left any day and he didn't. I am certain this is my fault, and I can't even see how. I condition myself, but my helmet cushions the blow. Why is my heart so calm?

He was using tubes again; he must have been. I grope under his pillow, but find only hairs and flecks of his scalp. I flap out every last black T-shirt in his dresser. Sybil's ring falls out, a tinkling against the floor. In his desk, I find papers and pencils and notes written about Actualizations, but no tubes, not even empty ones. He got off tubes. He did it.

He just slipped up on the satellites.

I have to go to my contribution. I go back outside and see Helena biking east, her elbows flared, practically running on the pedals, following the trail of dust. I put on my sun goggles and start the hour-long walk. One day, maybe, I can live in the Safe Haven like Cole.

4

March 29, 2090

Helena bikes me to and from the Safe Haven every day. Today she hit a rock and we went flying. Cole treated us for scrapes and bruises. He popped my dislocated shoulder back into place. Helena stayed and rested awhile.

Helena doesn't have patients anymore. Every night, Tobias comes over and they go into her room and I hear them crying. So now I put on a jacket and wait on the front step for him to leave. Most nights it's clear, but last night was overcast. One giant cloud blacked out everything, even the mountains.

A letter arrived.

March 27, 2090

Dear Aggrieved Family Member of Arrested Delinquent,

I write to express my deep sympathy for your difficult situation. I know you are probably saddened, angered, and confused by the recent events in your personal life. It is with overflowing condolences that I extend to you an invitation

They only took him because he let himself get caught, Helena
said, but they always knew. She tossed the letter on the table
and started biting the calluses off her fingers. She hasn't eaten
all week.

Today a woman came into the nursery and adopted a baby. Her
hair was gray at the roots, and despite some wrinkling, she had
an otherwise youthful face, and an unusual accent (you hear a lot
of accents in Canland, but not like hers). She spoke to the child,
who was less than three weeks old, as if she were speaking to an
old friend who'd been reincarnated. It was the baby boy whose
mother died in childbirth from heart complications on the first
day of my contribution.

Oh, those green eyes, just like yer mam's, she said. She told
Cameron that she knew the boy's mother from working in the
fields with her, until the mother had sunstroke twice in one year
and was reassigned to the storage centers to peel, dry, and bag the
harvest. She'd have made a wonderful mammy, the woman said
while looking at the baby in her arms. Just as I'll be.

I sat on the floor with #105, who built a small village out of
blocks as I told her stories I'd heard about brave DOTEC—some of
which I made up, but might as well be true—and how it must be
no coincidence that, since Canland's registered the DOTEC, the Part
looks more beautiful than ever.

Cameron and I call the babies by terms of endearment—Sweetheart, Honey, Perfect. But today I told Cameron I was going to start calling #105 by her mother's name: Sasha. She said to talk to Cole about it because the number system is his.

So I said to Cole, One day Sasha's going to grow up and people will be unkind to her because of things she can't control, things that happened before she was born, and every day she's going to have to make a decision about whether or not to be kind back to a world that will be unkind to her. Her mother chose to be kind to the world. Sasha deserves to remain a piece of her mother—no matter who raises her, where she goes, or what she chooses.

Cole said that was fine—for some reason, he just never felt compelled to name them.

I think I might know why: he's only ever named one person before.

Now I have too.

• • •

THE SAFE HAVEN Administrator informs me that Helena arranged a rickshaw to take me home this evening. The cyclist is a few years older than me, Dylan's age, and has the physique to transport several pre-weight-loss Dylans at once. Dylan rode his bike every night through the desert to deposit human waste and dead bodies at the Waste Reallocation Center to make the energy on which our Part runs, hauling a heavy, putrid tank forty miles round trip, to come back home and slip through satellites just to feel alive until it was time to get on his bike again and ride another forty miles round trip. It never made a difference in his weight—he was always so oddly shaped, as if bagged up, once bursting, then spilled.

I climb up into the rickshaw carriage. The cyclist turns halfway over his shoulder to shoot me with a finger gun. He says, "Where to, Partner?"

If Helena sent a rickshaw, she's either not going to be home for a while, or she's planned to drink so much grappa that she can't ride a bike. Or maybe she'll just be home writing, using contribution benefits to arrange transportation so she doesn't have to deal with me.

"They didn't give you directions?" I ask.

"Must'a slipped out one ear or the other. Don't believe they expected a great mind to come with the lungs and legs they hired." He lifts his foot off the ground and we roll forward. "Oh, you're a light one. Take y'all around the Part, if you like."

Why not? The plan to leave with Dylan was thwarted the moment he was arrested, or the moment he slipped up on the satellites. The paper he gave me before he was taken is still in my pocket. I haven't taken it off my person since then; I even sleep with it under my pillow, just in case I need to leave at a moment's notice. But how could I leave the orphans now? We've come to need each other.

"You all right back there?" he says.

I need to know what happened to AB. I want to talk to them again. I want to get close to them. I want them to tell me we kissed, and I want to do it again.

"I live in the Hovels," I say.

"Neighbors, then! We know each other?"

"I don't think so."

"Yeah, it's a busy world down there. Name's Shane."

"I'm Tristan."

"Tristan. They got you contributing up here already? You must be precious cargo. Just holler if you need anything."

"Actually, Shane?"

"Yeah, Partner."

"Do you know anyone named AB?"

"Not unless I forgot."

Shane lets the wheels turn down the small slope where Dylan always used to downshift so he could speed up and zip through the other bikes on the road. Shane stays a safe distance behind the bike ahead of us that turns right at the apple orchard. We turn left, and he starts pedaling steadily now, his upper body like a shield in case we go tumbling.

I untie my helmet and put it in my lap. My hair's growing in. Now I can grab it between two flat fingers. It's nice to no longer have to wear a pollution mask. I can taste the air, and people can see me, if they look.

Rarely have I been on this southbound road. The Safe Haven is north; the school is east; west is the Part Center; further west is Canland College; and south of that is my home. But in the southeast of Canland, there's a tract of three acres enclosed by eucalyptus trees bending toward one another a hundred feet up in the air. The trees serve as a windbreak to keep the flatland sands out of the Canland air and the crops safe from heavy gusts, but the acres inside have served many purposes. At one time, it was a COHO training ground, then an experimental permaculture, and most recently, a knacker's yard where scavengers could swoop down or crawl up and feed on the offal of slaughtered animals. Though it kept the vultures and lizards and flies happy, every gust and breeze carried the miasma of decomposing organic matter into the olfaction of Canland's eastern residents. So when it came time to build DOTEC housing, the Part Planners decided it was a good time to move the knacker's yard into the desert north, and repurpose the acres inside the blue gums, yet again, as the Hovels.

Lanterns line the streets; flames housed in glass like harnessed stars. Agriculture contributors pass us on the road back toward the storage centers, pedaling wagons filled with harvest up the hill. It was hot today, so they probably didn't start until the sun had nearly dipped behind the mountains. It's the time of year again when, even after the sun's gone, there's still an hour left of light.

"Where'd you come here from?" I ask.

"Texas, originally—one of the Parts chased out by the nuclear spill. Spent a few years on the road, hitched myself to an outfit of Matthews. Surviving came to fighting when we crossed paths with a Purist militia seeking to destroy. But my mom always taught me that fighting didn't do no good. Her first husband died in the war. It was her next man who was my pop, but he was about as gentle a pickaxe. My mom was too good a soul; never did stop mourning."

Shane steers the rickshaw around a turn, past the austere stone Registered Affairs Hall, alone on its lot. Dylan's being held there right now. I can't picture the scene because I've never been inside. Is he chained? starving? begging? Or has the torture of waiting until a determination is made regarding his expulsion finally put him to sleep? Data theft, satellite interference, espionage—will they bring up old charges of violence? A world in which he's set free wouldn't be a safe world. I turn my head away and forget it. Yes, I could spend forever not caring.

"Yeah," Shane says. "My mom, she got cancer from The Spill. It spread pretty quick. Just a couple months, and it took her." He slows to let some children cross the road. "But now things are settled for me. We all been through something hard; I'm sure you got your stories. I'm just looking for a little life now. A pretty lady, some kids—that's all happiness is. But all this WORLD garbaggio—telling us we can and can't procreate, can only eat what they tell us we can grow, and only when they say so, can't travel to see nobody or nowhere else—power's a drug."

Shane looks both ways, then starts pedaling again. "Just waiting and hoping now that they don't make me choose between extra rations and shootin' blanks the rest of my life," he says. "It could scare the mane off a lion. But the world does correct itself. Like the Book of Matthew says: the meek shall inherit the Earth. This land is ours, and we are God's creation."

So he believes in the goodness of an all-powerful being. But it was Michael's mistake that killed his mother and splintered his Part. How long is Shane planning to wait for his god to reward him? And if he knew he was transporting Michael's son—who never should have been born, never should have survived—would he feel the same?

Since I've been back in Canland, I sometimes feel like I'm wandering around a room in which my old life is playing out—like a

Sensorium Actualization of Tristan Weekes' life—and I now and then wish my life were still that way, and I now and then wish I could change the way things were. But that life is locked inside an impenetrable glass house, and I'm looking in on it, deciding not to go banging on the walls.

I tie my helmet back on. We pass a well covered with a grate to keep children and animals out; a locked cage of rickshaws and carriages; a stable full of quiet horses; and a lumberyard of pallets, mostly empty. There's one street lantern in view, and the evening's finally getting darker. Shane slows to a halt, even though there's no one else on this road. Ahead, in the fuzzy fire-light, there's a snake halfway in the path. Keeping his eye trained on the snake, Shane dismounts the bike and picks a rock up from the dirt. I was born in Canland, but Shane knows it much better than I do. Crouched behind the bike, he throws the rock at the snake. The rock skips in the dirt, and the snake darts out into the black desert.

"Just a rattler," he says, and wipes some sweat off his temple. Then our eyes meet squarely for the first time. He's strong-jawed and heavy-browed. His face betrays his surprise and pity for me. I'm used to this. He quickly looks away.

"All right, then." Shane mounts the bike again. "Just another hundred yards. Ready, big man?" he says, being kind.

"Ready."

Shane keeps a slower pace than before, and we stay quiet as we approach the walls of eucalyptus trees.

Before we reach the entrance, which is just a low archway through the branches, the slaughterhouse smell greets me, but as we ride on into the Hovels, there are other ingredients too, de-tected by my fearless nose—roasting vegetables, blunt fires fed with fast-burning material, clay ovens, waste tanks, sweet euca-lyptus, of course, and a certain sourness that would sometimes fill the school classrooms on hot days, mixed with the tang of heated metal ceiling beams, I recognize, as we arrive at the first intersection.

"Which way?" Shane turns halfway around.

These homes, made from corrugated metals and recycled industrial material, synthetics, and fiberglass, are barely taller than any person, and look like they might collapse in a strong wind. Small alleys divide the land untidily into plots sprouting dandelions, firethorn, purslane, and more weeds I can't identify. A gaunt woman picks up a few strips of shed curling eucalyptus bark from the ground and throws them into the fiery mouth of her chiminea. The flames flare and the flue coughs smoke. She tears a handful of purslane from the ground and sits in a chair beside her fire. She eats a handful of the raw vegetation, staring at us.

"Left," I tell Shane—aka away from the woman.

People glance up from their meals, games, and drawings with knotted faces and slouching spines. Two smooth-skinned women thread their fingers through a taut hexagram-like maze of string, together making new layers and angles. A teenaged boy loops a chain around his bike's crankset and screws in a new chainring bolt, then mounts the bike and passes us. There's a guy wearing what looks like a rabbit skin for a hat, taking a girl with long flat hair by the hand, and leading her into an alley. Two middle-aged men sitting on the stoops of adjacent Hovels speak philosophically, while outside the next domicile, a young woman teaches a child to read. An older, sinewy guy is sawing a pipe in half, and out from the Hovel behind him steps a same-aged woman, holding a pot with both hands, and she walks it down a road lined with barbed wire toward what looks like a waste tank.

"Shane," I holler. We're at an intersection with crisscrossing clotheslines hanging overhead between Hovels, garments flapping like the body parts inside have vanished.

Shane gently but suddenly stops the rickshaw. He flips the kickstand and gets off the bike to help me down. He holds out his hand. I put my knapsack on and let him take my forearm.

"Thank you," I say.

"Sure thing, Partner."

I try to walk away, but he's still got a hold on me. I look up at him. He wears a look of concern like a simple sketch.

"Your parents alive?" he says. After all the time shouting back to me on the ride, his voice now sounds like a whisper from the base of his throat.

I shake my head. He nods, and lets go of my arm, but then extends his hand for me to shake. I grab it as hard as I can. "We may be orphans," he says, "but we're God's children. He looks after us."

I nod. Shane pumps and then releases my hand and points over my head. "I live down that way, near all the noise. Sometimes I even make some of it." He laughs. "All right, well, I gotta make some rides, but I'll see you 'round. Nice talking with you, Tristan."

"Thank you for the ride, Shane."

I watch him pedal away. I've made a new friend. I turn my hearing aids up to listen for the noise he was pointing to, but all I hear is shouting, sawing, fires breathing, and pots clanging. I look up into the walls of trees swallowing the sounds.

A woman in a headscarf steps out of a Hovel. She gets up on a stepladder and hangs some long worn socks from the clothesline.

"Excuse me," I say. "Have you seen someone named AB?"

"AB? No, dear." She pulls the clothesline and it advances. She pins up more socks.

A scrawny dog trots up to her and sniffs her feet. She kicks it lightly in the snout, and the dog turns to me and sniffs between my legs. Then it jumps up and puts its paws on my chest. I can see fleas on its coat.

"Oh, no, dear, don't let that animal do that to you." The woman gets down from the stepladder and kicks the dog in the ribs. It slinks away with its tail between its legs. She looks at me and says, "Are you all right?"

"Did you know someone named Sasha?" I ask.

"I'm so sorry, I don't know a Sasha either."

"It's OK," I say. "I'm just looking for my friend." I wave to her and walk away. When I'm several paces gone, I start to shout, "AB! AB!" Then I worry about a hernia and take a breath.

The air down here is practically brown. A curly-haired child drops an apple slice into the dirt, picks it up, brushes the dirt off, and eats it with their nose scrunched up, chewing with their tongue out. A man passes by me, swinging above his head a chain of rocks tied together by a rope. He lunges at an imaginary enemy. Three men sitting together at a table laugh at him. The man keeps walking. The men keep laughing.

"Has anyone seen AB?" Someone here must have been on the hillock with them.

A man pokes his face out the front door of his home and says, "Hey, kid, need a correctomy?" I shake my head and walk past.

I come to the intersection where Shane had turned left, and cross into the other half of the Hovels. Some of the homes are adorned with wreaths or decorative sheets and blankets painted with sunflowers. A woman pulls a rack out of a chiminea and curses at the food she burned.

"AB." My voice is getting weak from shouting. "AB."

"Tristan?"

I turn my head in search of the voice. I see the mangy dog following me at a distance. It looks away and sits, pretending not to see me.

"Tristan?" says the voice I don't recognize. The hair, find the hair, the wild and curly wet jungle vine; look for the berry-red tongue poking out between rows of crowded teeth; the springy step, the bare feet that walk on clouds.

"Tristan," I hear once more. There's a woman waving to me, sitting at a table with two children in front of a home built from synthetic material painted with green three-eyed martians in purple suits. I wave and approach the table, despite not recognizing the people.

"Do you remember us?" the woman says. She's sharp-nosed, with small alert eyes and braided brown hair. "I'm Gale. You and your friend once gave us your rations, a couple years ago now, probably. This is Conrad and Valerie. Say hi, guys."

Conrad, who's just a bit younger than me, eyes me with his head turned half away. He looks well sculpted, like his mother. Valerie, who's younger than Conrad, looks smooth and unfinished, as if fashioned from dough.

"Hello," Valerie says, chewing on an oven-browned medley of nightshades.

"I remember," I say, my mouth involuntarily spreading into a smile as I recall my very first journal entry.

The shadows on their faces are soft and everywhere, lit by the weak fires from the chimineas yawning outside every other Hovel. If they have to provide material for burning every night, how long will it be until the Hovels are deemed unsustainable, and the DOTEC are cast out again? *Human storage*, Dylan called it.

"Well, how are you?" Gale says, glancing at my helmet on my head.

"I'm good," I say. "How are you?"

"Oh, we're fine, thanks. But I meant—well, the last time we saw you, it was the rainstorm. I'm sorry to bring it up. We were so concerned. You had been so kind to us."

"Oh." I touch the sides of my helmet with both hands. "I'm healthy now."

"Yeah," says Valerie, "we saw you." She taps her finger against her temple and goes, "Pew!" and slowly tips her body sideways.

"Valerie." Gale puts a hand on her daughter's arm. Valerie shrugs and eats another spoonful of nightshades. Conrad hasn't taken his eyes away from me.

"How's your friend?" Gale says. "The one who gave us rations."

"Sybil," I say. "She left Canland."

"Oh, that's terrible. I hope it was for a good reason. It's so hard to get registered in a new Part."

"Are you happy to be registered here?" I ask.

"Happy enough." Gale crosses her forearms on the table. "Aren't we, guys?"

"It smells," Valerie says. "But I'm happy enough."

Conrad has an overbite and a missing cuspid. He shakes his head.

"They've started at school," Gale says, turning to Conrad. "Tell Tristan how you like it."

Valerie sucks tomato juice out of her spoon. "Boring," she says.

"Do you guys ever see each other?" Gale asks Conrad.

When he still doesn't answer, I say, "I actually don't go to school anymore. I have a contribution in the Safe Haven."

Gale looks at me and nods. "That's excellent."

"Do you have a contribution?" I ask, trying to ingratiate myself before I ask about AB.

"Scrapping," Gale replies. "I just got back from a mission the other night. I was away from Con and Val for two weeks." She puts a hand on the back of Valerie's head. Valerie leans her head back and touches her nose with her tongue. Gale taps the bridge of Valerie's nose, making her tongue retreat.

"Did you die?" Conrad says to me.

"No," I say.

"Hey." Gale pinches Conrad's ear. "Eat."

"Yeah, Conrad," Valerie says, making a face at her plate. "Eat."

Conrad's bottom lip is trembling.

"Do you remember AB?" I say to them all. "My friend on the hillock? They had curly hair."

"Of course," Gale says. "They talked about you all the time."

"What happened to them?" I ask.

"You were face-facing," Valerie says, kissing her spoon, making sounds. "I saw it."

"Valerie, stop," Gale says. She looks at Conrad, who's got one tear running down his cheek. Gale squeezes his shoulder. "Finish eating, guys," she says.

"I'm not done." Valerie says. She puts a hand on her stomach, closes her eyes, tips her head back. "I'm just resting."

"You were bleeding from the head," Conrad says quietly to me.

"Conrad, why don't we go inside? Tristan." Gale smiles at me. "It was great to see you."

"What happened to AB?" I say.

"Let's go, Val." Gale puts her hand over Valerie's and shakes her belly. Valerie groans.

"They were perforated in the stomach," Conrad says to me.

"Conrad," Gale says.

"I thought you were dead," Conrad says.

"Enough." Gale turns to face me. The skin beneath her eyes is tired. The look she had when she was first happy to see me is gone. She says to me, "They were sick. They'd been doing a lot of tubes. And they had you—" She puts her hand on her neck for an instant, then lowers it. "The COHO raised his whistler—"

"I saw you die," Conrad says.

"I didn't," I say.

"But I saw," he whispers.

Suddenly, Valerie screams. The dog's head is on the table, lapping up the rest of her dinner with its gray tongue. Gale shoots up out of her chair and brings her fists down hard on the table, shaking the plates, scaring the dog away. Valerie starts crying. She reaches for a tomato and brings it to her mouth, but Gale slaps her wrist and the tomato rolls under the table.

"What are you thinking?" Gale shouts. "What is wrong with you?"

Through tears, Valerie says, "Don't waste food."

"Go inside," Gale says. "Now!"

Valerie gets up and slides the steel door open and sits on the bed inside their Hovel. I think it's only one room. She takes a frame down from a shelf and, still crying, brings it to her chest.

Conrad says, "Is there a heaven?"

"Conrad—go inside." Gale lifts her son out of his seat by the underarm. "I'm sorry, Tristan. Your friend was attacking you and then got perforated in the stomach and was left there while you were taken to the Safe Haven, and then after a while, an SPV came for them, and I don't know what happened next."

"OK." I don't know what else to say. "I hope I didn't disturb your dinner."

Conrad's staring at me. His overbite is digging into his lip. Gale puts her arm around him. "It's OK," she whispers in his ear, kisses him on the side of the head. "He's alive."

Conrad nods. I nod to him too, and he smiles a little. I think he knows I meant it as an answer to his question. Or maybe I nodded because Shane believes in god, and he seems so optimistic. What could be the harm in telling a child there's a heaven?

"We're a bit tired," Gale says. "Have a good night, Tristan."

"Good night," I say.

"Bye," says Conrad.

They go inside and the door closes. I can still hear Valerie crying. I picture Conrad comforting his little sister with promises of heaven.

After a few paces, I glance back at the Hovel and see the dog trotting off into an alley and the man with the rock rope picking at the remains of Conrad's dinner.

Somewhere, someone screams.

AB's gone; perforated. Taken out of Canland—dead at worst, but I don't know what at best. And who could know, who would want to know, why would anyone care to hear the end of the story about another orphaned DOTEC?

At the end of everything, who will I be left with? It must be Helena. I see it as clearly as if my fate's written in the stars. I'm in the Hovels by myself, and Michael and Dylan and Sybil and AB and Roshana are all gone, but she's still with me. I can either keep looking for ways to escape her, or accept that I need her.

Up ahead, there's a semicircle of people playing music to a stuffed teddy bear that's facing them all. Some of them are singing, one is tapping drums of canvas stretched over wooden rings, one keeps rhythm with a shaker filled with pebbles or dried beans, and another blows into a wooden flute. This must be the noise Shane mentioned, in which he sometimes participates. The song they sing asks someone called Mother questions about government, war, and dreams. I've never heard anything like it. I didn't know music with a melody like a lullaby and confessional lyrics like my journal entries could exist. Whether it's happy or sad, I can't tell; for once, I hear music that isn't innate. I want more of it—but it would never be allowed in the Canland outside these walls of trees.

Across the street, a young man sits on the stoop of a hovel reading a book. I approach him and ask, "What are you reading?"

He shows me the cover of the book: *This Blood Is Not My Own*, by Helm Roctern. One of three handwritten copies. Or, who knows, maybe Helm's made more.

"Found it on the back of a wagon," he says, flipping to the inside of the cover. He takes a graphite nub out of his pocket and writes something on the page. Then he looks up at me and asks, "You've read it?"

I nod, and he hands it to me with the graphite. At the bottom of the list of names—Josephine, Yuna, Renata, Will, Malakai, Antonine, Helior—I write my own.

"You're Helior?" I ask, handing the book back.

He bows his head to me.

The band sings on, asking questions to Mother.

"Nice to meet you," I say.

"You too." He looks at the inside cover. "Tristan."

I smile and then ask, "Do you like it?"

"It's OK," he says. "Pretty good. Sad. Makes me glad I didn't have to fight."

"Yeah."

I feel someone brush up against my back. I glance over my shoulder and see the man with the rock rope walking past, snickering to himself and muttering, "Sorry, sorry."

"Did you like it?" Helior asks me.

I stick my hand in my pocket, distracted by the absence of the paper Dylan had given me with all the places I could go written on it.

"It's my favorite book," I tell Helior, though I've only read a couple stories. I'm distracted—I want to talk more with him, become friends, play along with the band, maybe even stay in the Hovels or become part of DOTEC and learn what they've all learned, but I need that paper. I can't remember the details of the Rogue Part Dylan had told Sybil about, and if I can't remember it, how will I ever find her, and will I have to stay in Canland forever? "OK, well, bye," I say and turn away before I can know if he's looked at me to remember my face.

I try to picture Dylan's tiny scrawl.

> *42.3732° N, 72.5199° W: W. MA accessed 8/14/2089 remote Part [unspecified]. valley. good land. current publications. Purist. no Suicidalists. pop ~7k. nearest Part 12 m. E. access via Green Line to [signs] Philadelphia; Albany; Hartford; <u>Amherst</u>.*

> *43.1436° N, 93.3788° W: N. IA accessed 10/5/2089 nearest Part to Lake Michigan. Technocratic Part. small metropolis w/ education + other institutions. Suicidalists. violence. WORLD rover presence. seek application to Arts Part once there. access via Green Line to [signs] Kansas City. Waste reallocation rides north-south. take major highways NE to <u>Clear Lake</u> (blockade around Part; prep for holding period).*

Everyone in sight swivels their heads in the same direction, but the band keeps playing. A COHO cuffs together the ankles of a prostrate man, then helps him to the side of the road so he can sit against a fencepost. The rock rope is lying in the dirt like a shed snakeskin. The COHO comes jogging toward me, and for the second time in a week, I'm face to face with Malakai. He hands me back the folded piece of paper. I'm too overcome to speak—to even utter a thanks. This has never happened to me before.

"Are you OK?" Malakai says.

I nod. Helm has helped us all more than he will ever know.

"You should go home. You could get hurt here."

I pocket the paper. "How far is it to the Part Center?"

"Two miles, that way." He points west, through the trees.

I want to ask if he'd send a rickshaw for me, but I've been given my ride tonight, and I chose to take it here—fair is fair, and I have two legs. Malakai seems to know it too. He jogs back to the man he's detained and kneels beside him. I want to apologize for our history, but maybe another time. He's as strong as Helm: he was a DOTEC, and now he makes Canland a safer place. Asher will never know that. What might Dylan never know about me?

I pick up the rock rope and head west through the Hovels.

A boy in an elf costume holding a guitar sits with the band. They start up a new song.

I focus on my stride, and when I get to the edge of the trees, I drink some water and check my pulse on my watch: 70. I peel a bit of bark off a tree to reveal the yellow, bone-smooth trunk. Then I slip between the trees, out of the Hovels and into dark quiet Canland.

If there is a god—a presiding incorporeal entity with generative powers and influence over future events—and it is taking requests, then I ask that it please see to it that AB is safe and not in pain, and that Sybil, wherever she is, is acting happily and finally feeling connected to her mother's memory, and that Dylan isn't sent away forever so he can one day come back and continue to make himself a better person, and that I see them all again in my lifetime.

I don't know if that's how you do a prayer. But I have a hunch that prayer is like a vocation—a giving-over of oneself. For example, just as I pull the sheets perfectly tight to each corner of every mattress I dress; and the trained pianist sits with back straight and tempo sure; and the batter places his feet in the same spot in the box, every time; and Helm agonizes over commas and modifiers; and Helena darns every sock and glove absent a single superfluous thread; and Dylan never slipped his bike into a gear that might've made it harder to pedal or loosed the chains; when we do these things right, no one ever knows we'd done them, just as, with prayer, you do it in deference, without sloppiness, so that, maybe, one day, talking to your dead parents becomes enough to fill the hole of never hearing from them again.

Without color, Canland's fields appear as a giant body of water at night. Does it move? How deep is it? Am I near, on the shore?

I wonder, is love like a vocation in the same way as prayer? Is it what Dylan felt for Sybil? Is it what Sybil couldn't feel for Dylan? Or is the giving-over of oneself the job of a caretaker like me? Is my love consigned to the orphans of Canland, or is there hope of recovering it for a person who will be in my life until its end? Is love the guise worn by fear of death? If I don't fear death, can I truly love?

The road splits. I still can't see the Part Center. I close my eyes and visualize Canland in the daytime. I'm somewhere in the eastern fields, maybe south of the food storage centers, north, I think, of the Part's newest solar panels, and it's sunny, bright, and vivid. Canland College, with its three strange buildings, is straight ahead, but not for a mile west along the arroyo past my sun-smacked pink-orange adobe home, which is south of the bustling Part Center. I haven't passed the school, which means the Part Center is to my right. The leftward road most likely leads to the undeveloped edge of Canland–the cracked desert road that SPVs take so they can go as fast as they want without hitting anyone. I take the road to the right, toward the imagined people.

Is Helena worried about me? Everyone is afraid of something. Finding out what that is seems to me to be the clearest path to discovering a person's motivations for doing what they do, and what a person does makes a person who they are. Michael left us, so he's a leaver, and he researches, so he's a researcher. Dylan snuck around, so he's a sneaker, and he kept the Part clean, so he's a cleaner; he broke that boy's spine, so he's an injurer; and he worried for my safety, so he's a worrier, but also a carer. Helena hit me, so she's a hitter, and she's saved me a thousand times, so she's a saver. I help at the Safe Haven, so I'm a helper. And I neglected to help AB, so I'm a neglecter. If I never acted out of fear, and so never compensated with love, then was I just a mindless . . .

The thought gets too heavy to lift the folds; too tangled to untie.

A boy with a waste tank hitched to the back of his bicycle rides past me without taking notice. The kiosk tents reflect a bit of starlight. I'm nearly at the Part Center. Home is three quarters of a mile southwest of that. I've been walking for forty minutes. My watch says my pulse is 118–too high. I stop, take a beta blocker, and dab some water on the back of my neck, substituting the sweat my body won't make.

Maybe I've never had any agency at all. But I'm not nothing. I'm here–I can move my hands, I can make music, I have a pulse, and right now it's too fast, but soon it will slow down. I'm a pianist. I'm an arachnophile. I love my brother and my mother and my teacher and my friends. I'm a lover.

I turn up my hearing aids. The hot breath of nature floods my head–the enchantments of new mates, the territorial debates, the ululations of triumph over another day survived, the long songs of lonely creatures calling out for company. In my imagination, I turn to Sybil. *Sounds like people,* I say, and throw my head back, and together we laugh.

We don't know the end of our advancement. But those who believe that the Evanescence was a necessary step toward an apotheosis of human genius had better first recognize the common genius in the evolutionary design of an arachnid. Everyone is bored, but Arturo Eagles wants us to be bored because maybe then, we'll learn to appreciate what is boring.

Yet I can't help think that what keeps me rooted to Canland is not a devotion to the Earth, but to people here. Helena. Helm. Cole. Sasha. Malakai. The list changes, but the reason remains the same.

I come upon a road once spattered with Dylan's bile. The pomegranate tree is gone–not even a stump left on which to rest. I sit in the road and look all around at the small forest. It's denser than I remembered from the day of the effigy burning. The adobe stacks are like Earth rising to invite dwellers. I suppose one day I should live in communal housing. I'll look forward to it.

I lie down and make up constellations in the milky tea sky. Alas, I don't see my fate, or anyone else's, written up there. Maybe I just don't know how to read it.

I hear a rustle in the woods, patterned like footsteps, that makes me think I haven't stopped walking–a Sensorium-like sensation of being in two places at once. But then reason moves me to act. I unwind the rock rope from around my forearm and rise up to my knees. Stepping out from the trees: a yellow-eyed gray wolf. It moves slowly. In the darkness, I can't tell how close it is. I moan to let it hear my voice. It comes toward me, clarifying, so close now that its ribs are visible through its tight skin and stiff coat, and I can smell the hot breath off its white tongue. I take off my knapsack and get out the jerky I bring with me every day, but usually forget to eat. The wolf eats it out of my hand and licks my fingers. I touch its dry nose.

I think of Gale and her children. They remembered me and they hoped I was OK.

I slip my hand under the wolf's chin and scratch. The rock rope falls from my arm. The wolf thinks nothing of it. It lowers its head to me. I pet between its ears–and touch something cold and hard in the top of its head; look and see, with fur growing over the edges, the glint of a fiberoptic plate.

I put my thumb on it, and remember Byron's words about how when the light goes on, it's feeding time. The light inside is off.

I lie down on my side. The wolf lies next to me with its back pressed to my front. I lay my arm over its wasted flank. We stay like that. It's cold out, but the wolf is warm, breathing fast. It sighs, still hungry, and it will stay hungry until nature corrects, or the light in its head turns on.

.

Helena's asleep on the couch. Thin white bones drip from a pool of liquid wax to the base of the candlestick on her writing table. A flame struggles but perseveres. She's pale. Her mouth is slack like when she's too angry for words, mystified. One foot is on the floor and her pant leg has ridden up, showing varicose veins that glow purple in the sepia light like desert sun through eyelids.

I go to the kitchen. I draw a knife from the drawer and come back to Helena. I hold it over her with the tip pointed so if I drove it down it would pin her to the couch. But I feel no invasion of unfamiliar emotion. Her eyes open, red and glassy, empty and without claim. They roll back and close again.

I bring the knife to the bathroom. I bandage the fresh blisters on my feet. I place a wet cloth on the back of my neck. There are cuts on my wrist from the rock rope; I clean them. When I'm finished with my body check, I return the knife to the drawer.

In bed, I turn myself against the mattress so my body is touching itself without intention, as if a stranger's touch, my brain fooled. AB's head tilts back, their throat exposed. It's soft to the touch. When their head levels out again, their eyes are red and glassy—Helena's eyes. *Bad, Tristan, you don't ever look in while I'm changing!* She sweeps a hand through the side of my head, like I'm hitting the surface of the sea after a great fall.

I open my eyes and stare at the ceiling.

I did it. I made it.

It used to be that when Canland was asleep, and I was still awake, I'd think of all the people I would see tomorrow.

5

March 30, 2090

I walk home from the Safe Haven now. I stop at the coast live oak each day like a man returning to a loved one's grave. Sometimes I sit beneath it, lean my head back on its trunk, pet its roots, listen to the wind through the leaves, and watch the sunlight turn the unrevised desert beyond the long chaff-colored grasses of Canland terra-cotta, gold, periwinkle, blue.

Today, several WEDA took soil samples from around the base of the tree, shaved its bark, clipped leaves and acorns from its many huge bent gnarled limbs, and stood back to monitor the sun. I asked one WEDA what he was doing and he said it was Viceroy Hugo's intention to plant many more oak trees throughout the valley, so they were studying this one to learn why it has thrived.

I asked the researcher why they wanted to plant more.

He gave me a funny look and said, Step away from the research site.

I said to him, An ecosystem that can't sustain itself without human intervention isn't a viable ecosystem.

He almost smiled, and said, Who told you that?

I said it was just something I knew to be true.

He stepped to me, leaving a ladder leaning against the tree while other researchers fondled it like the test subject it was. He said, Listen, you seem like a smart kid, but what you just said is a Purist way of thinking. Humans are part of the ecosystem. Without them, Canland would shrivel up like a worm in the sun.

Humans are here because the Earth allows them to be, I replied.

He shook his head, annoyed. If one day you become a botanist, he said, You'll learn for yourself that all plants and ecosystems have sentimental value, and that's never worth sacrificing the science they provide. And if you don't become a botanist, then that's all the more reason to believe me.

I then started to levitate, propelled upward by fury, and my voice resounded throughout the valley, That tree thrives because it was home to dozens of people without homes. Its coverage provided safe passage into the world for a girl who no one yet knows or cares about, but she's grown and thrived already, like that tree, because of an innate love for being alive. It thrives because it doesn't make sense to thrive here as it does, and no one knows where it came from or how it got here, but even as the American West burned up and the Atlantic Coast washed away under a melted Greenland and the Midwest shook and cracked and spun, and the frightened people killed each other to make homes, this tree remained and grew and thrived. Use me for good, it says, bending its crown as a favor to you as you pluck its fruit, offering itself up to your scrutiny, older than you and I and anyone we know will ever be.

Then I returned to the ground, not speaking. I turned and wound my way back down the hillock.

A planet was visible in the early-morning sky—I don't know which one—winking yellow-red. Over the eastern mountains the sky was a stripe of icy blue, and above that a swathe of lavender, and then the whole dome arced overhead in fused and darkening shades. Though it wasn't bright, the shadows were severe, and the people who stopped to gaze at the oak were reduced to anonymous silhouettes.

As I walked back home, I relived yesterday in my mind. Helm was sitting at the table with Helena when I came in after a day of no births and no adoptions. Helm held a cup of lukewarm tea that looked tiny in his hands, staring into it. Helena pointed me to my room. I lay on my bed with *Fearsome Allies* on my chest, not reading it, just holding it until Helena called me out. She and Helm were standing at the front door—Helm facing me, Helena facing Helm. Her arms were crossed and she was looking down, maybe at his shoes or at the dirt he'd tracked in, which I hadn't swept outside yet. Helm glanced at her, then turned to me again and said, T-Bird, I brought you something. From his shoulder bag he handed me a copy of his book. Had a spare lying around, he said. So that's yours, I hope you like it. His whole face was lined with smile. I took the book and thanked him. No, no, he said, thank *you*. I squashed an impulse to ask what he was thanking me for. I smiled back instead, and he held out his fist, and I punched it, and he shook it out like I'd hurt him—his favorite joke. Helena stared at the floor the whole time. Helm looked at her and then let himself out. But in my relived version, I am following him out the door and walking him wherever he's going, promising that I'd have my story finished and ready for him soon, that I just have to write the ending.

After Helm left, Helena poured his tea into the washbasin and drank some grappa. She was watching me from the kitchen. What? she said.

I shook my head innocently. I was expecting Helena to take the book away, so I tucked it into the back of my pants.

Helena pressed her fingers into her forehead and dragged them outward.

Why was Helm here? I asked.

Advice, she said.

On what?

She looked at me and blinked slowly. Her face sagged. Marriage, she said.

Why didn't he stay longer?

I don't know, Tristan. He had things to do.

I went to my room and read halfway through Helm's book. At times, it felt like he was here with me, and other times, I could not imagine where the voice on the page had come from.

That was a day ago.

Tonight when I got home Helena was with Tobias, so I sat outside. On the wall of our house was perched a crepuscular Opilione. Its leg span was the size of my palm. I wanted to hold it, but I didn't want to hurt it. I wanted to see it move to know it was alive. I tapped the wall, but it didn't move. I poked it and it twitched, but it didn't crawl away. I thought of capturing it in a glass with some dirt and leaves. Then this morning, it was gone.

On today's walk home, after speaking with the WEDA under the oak, some failures of my perception crystallized in my mind, as if the spectrum of what can be seen and heard had shifted, and ghosts were everywhere.

Some possibilities occurred to me: I'm not a very good or even decent musician, and everyone who has heard me play has only pretended to be impressed; I am pitiable, and Helena was never afraid of my talent, but afraid I would discover my absence of it; all her proposals, laws, and stances are symptoms of some craving in her that I can never understand, will never succeed in explaining away, but never for lack of trying; the Restoration is Arturo Eagles' way of subjugating everything and everyone; harvestmen will die off sooner than humans, and humans will be around until everything is gone because we are able to decide when we don't want to live anymore. We have evolved to our maximal capacity—the mutant that defines the Anthropocene.

Last night, while Malakai was patrolling the Hovels, women hung clothes to dry and stoked fires under cooking veggies, children fiddled with bikes and invented new games, men watched bats zigzag tree to tree and told themselves that sitting and thinking was time well spent. A band etched their signatures in time . . . And three men craving power decided to obtain it through torture. When Malakai heard the cries of pain and terror from a dark, distant corner of that other world in Canland, he ran and threw himself between the force of the three men and the defenseless young woman. But with three of them, one of Malakai, and now less than one of her, they pounded him into the Earth, as if to pin him there forever.

Cameron was assigned to attend to the woman today. Cole said to me, We won't go in there.

When I went into Malakai's room, he was cradled by braces, unable to move or even notice me. His face was misshapen, the bones hidden, eyes swollen shut. I hoped those men would die.

I thought of the boy, the painter, whose spine was broken by Dylan.

And I thought it was possible that Dylan had only made my life harder.

I thought Sybil was right not to be in love with him.

And I wondered whether continuing to love him made me a bad person.

Tonight, Tobias ignored me as he stepped past me sitting on the front step, waiting for him to leave. I went inside, where Helena was writing at her table by candlelight. She said, Hi, sweetie, I'm sorry, but I'm going to be working all night.

I said, I'm not wearing my helmet anymore.

Without looking up from her writing, she said, It's your head.

I shut myself in my room and finished Helm's book. I imagined being in the war with all the people I've ever known split and fighting for different things. I was willing to remain blind to everything that would unravel my certainty that, if I had to depend on one person, it would be impossible for me to choose AB or Sybil or Dylan or Michael or Malakai or even Helm or Cole. It would be impossible to choose anyone but Helena.

6

Completed March 31, 2090
(with assistance from the subject)

Cole was born in Yakutat, Alaska, in the Tlingit tribe, the Raven moiety. His father was a skilled carpenter, his mother was the painter and seller of her husband's works. After his father fell ill, a shaman declared his mother a witch, and exiled her from their tribe. His father died soon after from cirrhosis of the liver. As a child, Cole learned to predict the patterns of animal movement, to disguise his breathing, to leave no scent, no tracks in snow, to make them feel safe, and to leave them utterly exposed. This connection, as such, remained after each animal was skinned, eaten, and forgotten, as if their souls clung to his, or his to theirs. With his heart ensconced in the deepest cave of his chest, hibernating to protect itself from the cold unknowing eyes of each nearly dead face, he drew the arrow on its bow, and collected his game over and over again.

Tradition married him to a Tlingit Eagle with eyes like emeralds. Her warmth made his hiding heart sweat and redden; he wanted to keep her away, and found himself the same petulant young man he was in boyhood, fearful and moody, before he'd learned to survive as an expert in camouflage. But she persisted with curiosity and patience, and in nature's time, they had a baby, a son who shared his mother's verve. Fear of being unkind to and unloved by his new family reawakened Cole's heart entirely, yanked it forth from its cave and up against the underside of his skin. Exposed now, he feared as animals fear. Fear your son, his wife told him, And let him see that when you are afraid, you will love him, because you need him. I need you both, Cole replied. And in the depths of that cave within him, stones fell loose from the wall and glowed with every color, and it was as though he had a thousand uncontainable hearts.

Cole apostatized; he rejected Christianity's warning of inhuman realms as reward and punishment for being human, and believed instead that when he died he would return to Earth an elk, an eagle, a salmon, a spider. He already was what he had been and would be.

Before the dawn on his twentieth birthday, he slipped out of bed to listen to the lapping bay. He faced the mountainside above the village, that proven terrestrial authority, the lights of buildings hanging on its face like tiny fires. He climbed the road up through the sturdy, unromantic structures littering the winding path, offices and houses that ran light and heat all day and night. With the phosphorescence of the sea and its reflections far below, he wondered if a deference to the oil-driven status quo could suit his spartan spirit if it meant protection for his family. He wondered who his wife was and who their child would be. He feared he hardly knew them, and that he was hardly known. When his hike was complete, he sat at the edge of a promontory. The moonlight turned the sea a rumpled quilt of silver. Fishing rigs sat unmoving on the surface like a garrisoned fleet. The only sounds he heard were the ones he made. The yellow moon set, the morning turned blue, and fog rose off the sea.

Then, an unthinkably potent light spread through those thin clouds below, as if a sun had exploded, turning the village bright for an instant, then thick with smoke. If there were screams, they went unheard; if there was blood in him, it froze; if there was life before or after this, he didn't want to know it. In the moment it took for the sound of the explosion to roll up the mountain to his ears—in that momentary silence—the hearts inside him burned too hot, too red, and came to rest as coal. A blast fishing accident—the illicit transportation of dynamite—erased his village, his family, his life.

Who was there to tell?

He left, sailed the Pacific and the Arctic, and disembarked in Russia at glassy Lake Baikal. When it froze, he walked it, and when the sun again turned the top to water he swam among the flashing fish that waited through the winter at the bottom, as if in outer space. He gaped as gulls nosedived, massaged the blubbery seals, and hunted with wolves. Every day for one year, he bathed in the lake, whether the shore was slashed with icy shards, or a solar runway glittered out to the horizon as the summer winds pushed the water this way and that. In Earth's clearest lake, he shed every element in him that once bloomed awesome color, froze them, and flung them into the abyss.

He motored through the tundra, sailed the Sea of Japan, and brought to the island at the mercy of volcanoes and tsunamis his obsession with the waters and those seemingly soulless things that dwell where humans can't, studying the eternal motion of the lightless depths of Earth's most precious and unknowable ecosystem. His peripateticism sent him back across the sea and into Asia's mainland, where he sought the history of human spiritualism through Taoism, Buddhism, Hinduism in what he would years later blink away as a puerile straw-grasp for the meaning of his family's incineration. One of unfathomable tragedy's cures is the mirage of fatalism, but with too much of this antidote comes the side-effect of atrophied morality . . .

He learned ancient commerce along the eastern shores of the Mediterranean, convinced that good conversation was the closest that a god would come to revealing itself. At the end of his

time there, friends sent him on his way with gifts—spices, textiles, sculptures, music, recipes, and languages—which he carried
across that salty sea, and through Europe.

Between the bucolic hillsides and the burnt cities along the trail
of endless struggle for a fair and self-scrutinizing government, he
snuck into museums with paintbrushes, and with a natural skill
inherited from his mother, he twice corrected Western art's grand
folly, the erasure of history's most recognized visage, the anthro-
pologically obvious error: the whiteness of Christ. He celebrated
his pigmentary corrections in breweries and brothels, which gave
way to ruinous roaming. He drank to blindness, screamed silently
with loneliness, and pilfered those weaker than himself. He sired
children he'd never meet. He wanted to tear his eyes out to remove
the mechanism from the memory. He wished to die.

We are born with magnets in our hearts, Cole said to me. His
took him through the Germanic lands and across the North Sea into
Norway, where for ten years, he sat beneath a sky that bloomed
pink and green auroras, speaking and singing and apologizing to
his wife and child and children. He used to watch the northern
lights alone, then with his wife, then with his son. Every day, he
chose to live because at least he could call upon visions of the three
of them gazing up at the brilliance, his son cooing with awe before
he'd ever spoken a word, his wife's tranquil green eyes coming
down from the sky to meet his, and maybe he would dream of
them, the illusion torn from him each morning when he woke.

Days dragged and years flew by. He worked in a tannery, handling the hides of dead things; assisted alchemists in their quest to
create from nothing the material to save everything; apprenticed
with an innovator in aeronautics; patrolled the mountains for injured, lost, and dying skiers, sledders, and snowshoers; mapped
the land and the stars; studied human anatomy; and saved his first
two lives.

One night, waiting for voices, he fell asleep by a fire, blanketed
in snow. The fire dwindled. He heard their voices. She said his
name.

Then, with hot urine running down his leg—his body's final attempt to wake him from a deadly sleep—he heard the cry of a woman that could only mean a brush with death so near that escape would bring new life. Guided by the echoes through the blue-white meadows, he came to an abandoned village. He found a woman who'd dishonored her family so gravely that they left her as soon as the child, who they said would be no child of theirs, had begun to announce his entrance into the world—the living reminder of an adulterous betrayal. (What was the nameless father's punishment?) Cole climbed into the shelter of a wooden steeple and there, beneath the bell, delivered the mother a son. He remained with them for days, building fires, roasting the meat of animals who had slipped out of the white-brown winter for one last careless instant. When the snow subsided, they hiked across a sheet of white so blinding, it was as if it had contained the very sun it reflected. At a village beneath Preikestolen, Cole backed away as the mother and son went forth. They weren't his, and he wasn't theirs. You are brave and strong, Cole said. So are you, the mother said. Out of earshot of all judgmental beings, he turned and looked up at the sheer cliff jutting out above the fjord, too high to climb, and wept so desperately that one stone in him was heated, it glowed with the faintest red, as an ember burning back to life.

Thenceforth, he devoted himself to the intersection of heart and matter; to the stones in us that bloom color under heat. South through the English Channel, he sailed, transferring vessels at a shipping port under the pretense of seeking work, willing to help load unassembled machinery that the UK sold at cost to underdeveloped nations inundated with fearful capitalists seeking refuge from the unraveling of everything as they'd known it since long before they and their fathers and their fathers were born, betting on places in which everything would begin again. They accepted all hands. The ship unloaded in Côte d'Ivoire, where he learned, from sleepless doctors, modern medicine at once beyond and necessitated by his new intentions: more life, always more.

He brought his knowledge inland to the poorest people who ever lived, where he healed the sick, and likewise failed. Most of them had nothing besides the love and tradition in everything they did, and in that way, he was reminded of his childhood. He could have spent the remainder of his life there as an ascetic, an observer of humility and selflessness, a giver, and might have if not for the ineffable atrocities that slayed those least deserving, those with the most generous hearts. The violence he witnessed had broken his hope that a world run by humans could ever subsist on a commitment to goodness.

That there was nothing he could do to change the persistent patterns of history felt like permission to do something he enjoyed. A new obsession took hold, and he immersed himself in the study of what he believed was the purest form of human tribalism—the thing that made children smile whether they played or watched; made men scream with strangers in protest and exhortation and celebration and agony, gape with awe, cry in defeat; form and function cooperating autonomously to write the rules, as minds and bodies aspired to an ability that could not be contained by rules; all the aphorisms of good and evil distilled into a refuge dressed as a battlefield: sports.

In South Africa, he aided the world's most masochistically devoted athletes, taught them that the body is not an obstacle nor a limitation nor an awaiting injury, but the soundest instrument ever created, a self-healing one if its mind is right. For what was one of the last international sporting events to ever take place, he accompanied South Africa's rugby team to Melbourne, boarding a plane for the first and final time in his life. Several players collapsed in the heat. The teams met at the halfway line and agreed it would not be worth losing a teammate to finish the match. The crowd was gravely silent, but there was no protest.

Cole stayed in Australia and lived in the outback with environmentalists who promulgated the simple and replicable key to preventing our total destruction of the planet—stop polluting, pull carbon out, cool it down, of course, but do so not by vilifying multinational corporations building factories in underdeveloped nations to circumvent manufacturing sanctions; do it instead purely through conservation efforts, by preserving every species, saving every single savable animal, not just two of every species—nothing Biblical about this, nothing parabolic, nothing techno-logical. Yes, let's foster self-sustaining ecosystems, grow trees, clean rivers, stop dumping into the ocean, but not for us, because humans don't need saving. Don't you know that the one thing that every human with the money to actually make a difference will deny is the fact of his own mortality? Don't bother saving humans. Save birds—nature's song, the last remaining dinosaur—by spik-ing the loggers' trees; save whales, the colossal unconquerable; el-ephants, the kind majestic; and octopuses, the brilliant lock-pickers and shape-shifters by hunting those who hunt them. Yes, a war against those who war against the environment. Save the thickest, hairiest spider your brave imagination can muster—like the one about to crawl onto your neck, Cole!—because without it, we'll neglect others like it on precedent, and without the others, an ill-ness carried by a mosquito will get the best of us before the next generation can carry on this heavenly crusade.

But then the island continent was engulfed in flames.

He was rescued by a crew of photojournalists documenting what they believed was the last glimpse of a recognizable Earth. The group doctor's emphysema had been exacerbated so extremely by the smoke that they accepted Cole on their ship's journey to Antarctica. In Earth's largest desert, the ghoulish crash of calving glaciers, the long gaps between penguins as they lay down to cool themselves instead of huddling for warmth, and the temperatures he read in the forever-sun eroded moulins in his spirit, down which the glowing stones inside him fell into a lightless ocean with the faintest plink. Nightmares of the flare on the base of the mountain kept him awake, no longer softened by happy memories of a family marveling at the aurora borealis. But somehow, for the first time, he was entirely glad that he hadn't been swallowed up by the explosion too. He missed his family, but without guilt or anger. He saved the emphysemic doctor's life—the only consolation to the boundless horrors of the South Pole.

While in the civilized world above them, war raged like a captive beast.

When the crew arrived in Argentina to photograph the Evanescence, Cole departed from them on the basis of his concession that hedonism was the only worthwhile answer to the downward spiral, and that there was nothing to be gained from documenting the misery.

Militaries rounded up the poor and desperate to rape the mineral mines, smuggle firearms, defend the nation's power plants against deconstruction. Cities along Argentina's eastern shore were throttled by shipping embargoes in the early stages of WORLD's first international siege. People launched themselves from cliffs, and swam out into the rising sea. The living revolted with stolen weapons in what resulted in martyrdom—a more glorious suicide. The saturnalia in the city streets augured the end of a world made from invented rules. It would take an abundance of arrogance that he did not possess to claim that human laws are unnatural because the most basic among them are employed by inhuman beings. Instead, he ventured a more equivocal stance: people had lost all sense of scope, and the rules can't apply to the scales we've achieved, the distances we cover, and the awareness of ourselves to which we aspire. It is easy to believe that a lot of information is enough, but one simply cannot comprehensively investigate the mechanism by which one investigates. We can learn only through doing. For all its false starts and failures, the heuristic experience is the only true one. And here everyone was, learning.

With society breaking down to adhere only to the most basic laws of corporeality, he joined the revelry with Dionysic zeal. As he wondered if he was really transcending, painted with sweat, his heart thrumming, the room and everyone around him spinning, he accepted that he would be one of the ones to see the end of it all. He shut his eyes, and a hand fell on his shoulder. When he opened his eyes, he saw hers, green as emeralds. He shut them again and opened them again, and they were still there. But she was someone else.

As the world flipped rapidly toward the chapter's close, love blossomed between her and Cole, a love like a candle flame that needs a hand to guard it. Any day, they could be rounded up and shipped away, consigned to fates decided by more powerful men. In fact, he wondered why they hadn't. They danced in large crowds and retired to remote rooms. When they were apart, he hid in attics and basements, clutching a gun to his heart. Winter temperatures crossed over one hundred degrees in the subtropical climate; the boiling blood of unchecked men ruled.

But they found each other, again and again. She was like a state of being in which he existed. She was everything between now and the end.

Until one day she failed to meet him beneath the stage of the Teatro del Libertador as they'd agreed. Cole, shaken and crumbling, wished he wasn't here for the end of everything, to see Arturo Eagles take apart the planet, looking for answers deep within.

Another week passed without her—another week without his death.

When she finally returned, she spoke tersely, did not even kiss him. I have protection if I leave, she said. I must go. I can't tell you where, but take this train ticket, and go north, before they close the borders.

Whose protection do you have? he said.

She withheld the answer, but it was obvious: she was never his. Whoever protected her was more powerful than any love Cole could give. He accepted the ticket and told her he'd wish for her happiness.

He rode north, wishing for her misery.

Waterfalls crashed from the tops of mountains and ran rivers through rainforests. There was still beauty, but he could hardly look. The offshore pollution of the Caribbean made him consider the urchins sucking up scum from the seafloor—a vague metaphor, but his mind was tired, he couldn't clarify its contours. Besides, did it matter? The metaphors were so obvious, they didn't suffer without exactness. He counted the stones inside him, felt them for heat, turned them for color. He was alive; there was certainty in that. When one abandons their inclination toward the metaphysical, questions without answers are no longer roadblocks. One simply has to proceed without answering.

He gave indiscriminate first-aid to the wounded in the war—treated burns in the charred ruins of mosques, and amputated the infected limbs of men and women who prayed to Christ on the table.

When the war ended with WORLD's ascension and the introduction of the Parts System, he was offered contributions in Idealist Parts and Spectral Parts, Arts Parts and Athletics Parts, on Waste Rakes and at Research Centers. There were still people on this fundamentally changed planet. They had to live somewhere.

With a band of DOTEC seeking some say in the new way of doing things, he came to a Restoration Part in a desert valley where life sprang. On the first sunrise of a new year, he delivered a baby who cooed as if at the wonder of his own birth. But when the boy barely blinked at the touch of a needle and received everything as if it were nothing, the news of his diagnosis traveled as if the Part had just received a shipment of ice. After a tireless two weeks, Cole had stabilized the baby—just as soon as WORLD researchers arrived to take the boy. They wanted to know what kind of person a child who feared nothing would become.

What else is there to fear? Cole asked himself, safe now in this place where he could atone for everything through the simple, repeated act of delivering more life.

7

IT'S BARE ALL the way out here, soaked in red sun. The viceroy's house is an hour's carriage ride north of the Sensatarium, which is the northernmost point officially in Canland. Between that and the viceroy's house, there's nothing. The Sensatarium once served as an indoor sports and recreation center for the United States Military base. Every WORLD satellite Dylan ever commandeered was accessed through Sensatarium network conduits. The trick was that he'd always appeared to the Sensatarium technicians as normal network activity—more like a chameleon than a ghost. The gist of the report, which arrived at our home just a couple hours ago while Helena was getting ready for dinner at Viceroy Hugo's house, was that during an Actualization of a thousand-square-mile Israeli desert-greening project opening ten thousand carbon-free single-family homes after thirty years of self-sustainability and isolation, the Canland Sensatarium conductor detected a brief interruption in satellite communication. On a risky hunch that could have made her lose her contribution on the grounds of network tampering, the conductor suspended the satellite's feed by reversing the channels, simultaneously blocking any new signals from entering the pathway, and essentially changing the figurative color of the code. Thus, exposed was the invader: a sleep-deprived seventeen-year-old data thief in the room across the hall from mine, who lapsed ever so briefly in the upkeep of his technophilic disguise. At the bottom of the report was Dylan's sentence: waste reallocation in a Long Term Rehabilitation Part.

They'd already taken him out of Canland by the time the notice arrived because, the notice said, of the prolonged, severe, and incontrovertible nature of his rebellion against WORLD law and principles.

Every day for the next decade or more, Dylan will don a hazmat suit, dredge up the contents of centuries-old landfills, pump tanks of human feces into fertilizing machines and bag up the fresh mulch, and unearth graves to use the bodies as an energy alternative for Earth's natural resources. He'll eat food that's nearly necrotic to salvage the labor of WORLD contributors. He won't have plants or terrariums or a Sensorium, and he'll be perforated if he tries to escape.

I hope he has access to tubes.

I see him staring dead-eyed into an empty field, at a blank wall, at the sky, waiting for a satellite to drift overhead, picturing the view of Canland, looking for me.

Before the carriage came for us, Helena sat me down and said, "He sent us Dylan's sentence today on purpose. The timing is intentional. This isn't going to be a pleasant visit. Viceroy Hugo's technically a friend, but we've always despised each other. We have a prosperous professional relationship, but only because he's too proud to meddle in the work of his inferiors. He's made a capable leader because he assumed he was in charge since before we even founded Canland, and he never once wanted to abdicate, no matter how bleak things looked. Any leader who steps down when things get hard is no leader." Helena shifted in her seat and drank some grappa. "Hugo knows no one could possibly work harder than him, but he resents everyone for it anyway. When we settled, he slept thirty minutes every three hours so he'd never lose a train of thought to a night's sleep. He'd be in the middle of telling you that a hundred and fifty miles from Canland there was a steel yard, and for the canals, he needed you to scrap for—and then it was nap time, so you had to busy yourself for the next half hour so that when he saw you again he wouldn't tear you apart for being a lazy DOTEC, and do you even want to contribute, or would you rather go back to how things were, et cetera." She bit a callus off her left middle finger and spat it out. "What made him a reliable leader was that he'd admit when he didn't know something. He'd always ask Michael, and Michael loved having a friend." She finished her vial and filled it again. "He only cared about being a good advisor to Hugo. The advisor's supposed to know everything, since he can propose action without worrying about public opinion. But it almost didn't matter if they were right or liked, because together they were so good at making you feel like an idiot. Even when they were praising you, Hugo would say something like, 'Whoa, you're a natural at digging holes!' It was like a way of making fun of themselves for even bothering to make fun of you." She adjusted the bobby pins in her bun. "I think it pleased Michael that I never liked Hugo. Hugo was impressive, commanding, charismatic, but also loathsome in too many ways, and impossible to have a relaxed conversation with. Your father thought it made him superior to me—being capable of befriending a person like that. If I ever challenged your father, he would just look down his nose, convinced he was smarter, funnier, whatever. I don't think your father had friends as a child. So he always held status in higher esteem than his relationships. You were never just a son to him." She glanced at the door as we heard Tobias' bicycle fall in the road. "You were an opportunity." She finished her drink and poured again. "Hugo encouraged your father's aspirations and introduced him to Arturo Eagles. And now, who knows where Michael is? Don't mention that tonight. Don't ask where Michael is. Don't ask the same question twice. Smile and answer the questions he asks you. If he asks a hard question, don't just sit there and stare." She sipped again and poured again and bit another callus off. "If you don't know, tell him you don't know, but that you want to find out, and you wonder if he has any insight. He'll probably say something like, 'How should I know?' He just wants us there so he can show us he doesn't want us there. The only thing that could be different at the end of tonight is that Viceroy Hugo might promise to consider letting us have a Green Line pass to visit Dylan. And don't mention Dylan. OK?"

"OK."

Tobias came through the door an hour before the carriage arrived. He said my name, tersely, as if double-checking it was in fact Tristan, then sat at the table facing Helena and asked if I should be there to hear what he was about to say.

Helena said, "It's fine, he's going to hear it all anyway."

Tobias glimpsed me from the corner of his eye and cleared his throat. "Ten this week—an elderly couple who wanted to go together, a livestock farmer in her sixties whose friends say she checked out a long time ago, a panel technician in his forties, a college student who left a note behind blaming his ex-girlfriend, and five teenagers, all in school, four of them recently registered former DOTEC."

Helena said nothing. She examined a callus and then looked up at Tobias with bored eyes.

Tobias glanced at me and then said to Helena, "Are you sure you don't—"

"I'm sure."

Tobias lowered his chin. He turned his body to block me off. "What are we doing?" he whispered.

Helena's frown lines got so deep—as they are now, as she looks out the carriage at the purpling desert—that I thought she was going to slap him. She said to Tobias, "You came here to tell me to get the viceroy to put some measure in place to stop this. Is that right?"

"I'm just not sure we need it anymore," he said.

Helena said Tobias' name, but then was silent for a while. She stared at him, and the frown lines stayed deep, but I think something besides anger was happening, like she was remembering instead of judging. Or maybe I'm only recognizing that in retrospect, because when she spoke again she said, "My son's just been taken. Eighteen years he's lived here. Long Term in waste is his sentence. I might never see him again." She took a deep breath. Her chin was shaking. She quickly finished her vial of grappa. Then, ostensibly soothed, she said, "You don't need my blessing to do what you think is right."

I couldn't see Tobias' face. All I heard him say was, "Just . . . overwhelmed . . ."

Helena said, "Yes, I understand."

Tobias turned to me and stood up. "I'm sorry about your brother. I know how terrible it is."

"Thanks," I said, knowing he meant it, having felt it, as I have too, with Sybil.

Then Tobias smoothed his thin hair over his baldness and left the house. Helena looked at me, and I was already looking at her, and for some reason she started laughing. "There are some things you should be glad you'll never understand."

She was right—I hardly understood what they'd been talking about. But, for once, I wasn't eager to find out.

Soon after that, the carriage came. We haven't said a word on the hour-long ride.

The horse pulling us shits mid-stride. A buzzard draws circles in the creamy red sky, and never seems to rise or fall, like it's on a string. Three wiry doglike creatures in the distance trot out toward the brush in the foothills.

"Where did the wolves come from?" I ask.

Helena doesn't reply. I'd once heard—whether from her or Michael or someone else, it doesn't matter—that the United States government once released wolves into the National Parks to curb overgrazing, aka to eat the deer ravaging the vegetation. For how long did it salvage the land?

On a hill in the distance, the viceroy's house appears—a crenelated adobe rotunda, like a rook, with two corridors branching off to the sides. Beyond, the shadows lain by the cuestas on the sierras are hard and moonlike.

Helena grunts—awed, I think. She's always recognized beauty.

The horse draws up the driveway flanked by aloe, jade, echeveria, and tall long-needled cacti. The high arched wooden front door opens. Standing in the brightness from inside is a woman with a ropy braid of black hair down to her waist, almond-brown skin, and a lilting accent when she calls out, "Hello, Helena and Tristan! Thank you for coming to our home."

We disembark. Helena leads the way up the stone steps to the door.

"Hi, Maria," she says, taking our hostess' smooth, small hand.

"It's a pleasure to meet you. And you too, Tristan," she says, bending to me and offering her hand to shake. I think she's closer to my age than Helena's. "I hear you've been doing some wonderful things in our Safe Haven. Thank you for your contribution."

"I feel privileged to contribute to Canland."

She grins so hard, the cords in her neck bulge. "Come in, please. We're so excited to have you. I know Hugo is."

We step inside. The candles in the wrought-iron chandelier, in the three-pronged candlesticks, and in all the sconces curling from the walls like tendrils, lit and melting onto brims, might total more than two hundred, lighting every surface, every decoration, and every column of air.

"You can leave your shoes by the door," Maria says.

I undo my shoes and place them near a dog that's sitting completely still, not moving at all, not even breathing, but whose eyes are open, too shiny, and cold to the touch.

"And of course," I hear Maria say to Helena, "thank you for everything you've done."

I squeeze the tight-haired hound's leg—stiff and stuffed.

Helena steps out of her shoes and sniffs the air.

"That's the goat." Maria's lips press together in a tight smile. "It's been braising for hours."

"Of course we're having goat," says Helena, looking at the floor.

"It's his favorite," Maria replies, flashing a grin.

A door slams overhead. There's a spiral staircase winding tightly to a landing halfway up the cylindrical tower. Viceroy Hugo descends on the balls of his bare feet, smiling at us through his thick fire-and-smoke beard, which blends seamlessly into an impressive shock of hair. His cheeks are ruddy to match. He wears a short-sleeved white T-shirt and has tattoos of faded color spreading up from his knuckles to under his sleeves. He claps three times, then strides up to me with his hand outstretched, and in a loaded, crackling voice says, "Tristan Weekes, what a fucking pleasure to finally meet you, man."

I shake his hand. "Thank you. It's a pleasure to meet you too, Viceroy Hugo."

He holds his arms wide and says, "Helena—my god." Then he hugs her and kisses her cheek. Holding her around the waist like they're dancing, he says, "I'm so fucking sorry about Dylan. Jesus Christ, what a tragedy." He hugs her again and then steps back and wipes his face, shaking his head. "Awful. Hopefully he can get well now. He's obviously a sick kid. And fuck Michael for not being there for him, right?" His voice is deeper even than Helm's.

Helena smiles at him in a way I'm not used to seeing her smile, with her hands overlapped in front of her waist, her chin sort of tucked, her eyes looking up through her brow.

Viceroy Hugo does a whole body grunt-shake, like he's shedding an unpleasant feeling. He looks at me then and claps a hand on a fist—it makes a pop—and he snaps and points at me, and appraises me from my feet up to my face. He smiles. His teeth are flat and broad inside his neat orange beard, like the teeth of an herbivore.

"I remember when you were a baby." He starts nodding. "I'm really happy you're here."

I give him a thumbs-up. "Me too."

He keeps nodding and grinning at me, then finally looks at Helena and says, "He turned out all right. You must be proud.

What was Michael thinking, leaving you to work alongside the big man? Always the god complex."

"Yes," Helena says, "he's missed a lot."

Viceroy Hugo raises an eyebrow at me and says, "Your dad's a very smart guy, but he's very stupid not to be here with you. Even if he is getting to research with Arturo Eagles." He sighs. "But I think you're the real marvel. Alive and healthy after everything you've been through. Do you feel that?"

"I don't know," I say.

He waves a hand back and forth in front of his face. "I bet you see things in ways other people don't. I don't know, maybe not. Michael had expectations for you. He said he was going to make you the most unself-conscious being there ever was. He said music played itself through you." Then he makes a face like he's asking me if Michael was right.

"Truthfully, Viceroy Hugo, I'm not sure how good I am."

"Let's find out. We don't hear much music these days. There's a grand piano in the other room. I've stopped trying to make sense of it, but I'd love to hear you play."

Maria squeals, bringing her fists up to the sides of her face. When I don't reply to him, Viceroy Hugo looks at Helena and points at me.

Helena says, "It's OK, Tristan. You can play."

"We're not gonna send you to an Arts Part." He winks at me. "Don't worry."

"OK," I say, trying to sound very happy and honored, even though I am thinking that an Arts Part is the only thing that could take me out of Canland; maybe Helena would even come with me.

"Nick," Viceroy Hugo says, to someone not in this room. His voice is on a frequency that doesn't need volume to be heard from a distance. "Helena, clear as usual?" he asks.

"Thanks," Helena says.

"Tristan, how does apple juice sound?" Viceroy Hugo asks.

The man who determines who gets to be registered, who gets

expelled, who contributes, who lives in a single-story adobe, who lives in communal housing, and who lives in the Hovels; the viceroy who reports Canland's ecological detriment to Arturo Eagles and decides what benefits we need (sugar, solar panels, new flora, optogenetic fauna, current Actualizations); Canland's embodiment of WORLD law, Arturo Eagles' appendage, has just offered me apple juice.

A moment later, a person who must be Nick comes out with a tray and four glasses. Nick's face is young and clean, sharp and serious.

"Apple juice, Tristan?" Helena says. She makes a brief angry face.

"Oh. Yes," I say. "Thank you."

Maria hands me my glass and takes her own mug of steaming tea. Viceroy Hugo hands Helena hers and takes his own glass of brown liquid. He raises it and says, "Hey, I wish it were under better circumstances, but it's great to have old friends here."

We all tap glasses and drink. The juice is thick and slightly brown, and deliciously tart.

"All right, Tristan," Viceroy Hugo says. "Let's hear it." He places his hand on the nape of my neck and guides me around the back of the spiral staircase into the main room where there's another chandelier, more candles, and a stately black piano. The top is open. The wood and the strings and the hammers all shine. It's like peering into a maw. Or a mind.

I sit down at the bench and place my fingers on the keys. I look up at Helena for some sort of signal as to what I should play. Her face is inscrutably slack around her mouth and pinched at the outsides of her eyes, watching me. I could play the song from the Hovels. The song from the day of Roshana's funeral. A lullaby . . . Could I turn my self-assessment mechanism off, like Michael wanted me to, play some classical piece I first heard in a New England snowstorm, as he flooded me with hormones and I shivered, sitting at his—Dylan's, now no one's—desk? Could I play what I played in the Actualization of my death?

My fingers start and stumble, I don't know what I'm playing, and so I strap them to the simple, incorruptible, one-finger melody, and feeling like a small child–waiting to be instructed, praised, or conditioned–I sing along in my head: *Twin-kle, twin-kle, lit-tle star / How I won-der what you are / Up a-bove the world so high / Like a dia-mond in the sky / Twin-kle, twin-kle, lit-tle star / How I won-der what you are.*

I am not as unself-conscious as Michael wanted me to be. I'd never considered my education in those terms. Eliminate the self; become what enters. Not so different from Helena's philosophy.

"Hey," Viceroy Hugo says. "It's better to try to do the hard thing, and to do it wrong, than to do the easy thing perfectly."

"You can play, Tristan," Helena says. "It's OK." She blinks at the piano, and her face slowly empties of all expression. She finishes her drink.

I set my fingers on the keys again. I close my eyes and picture myself falling, plunging into the darkest depths of the ocean, where for a moment, I lie still. But the Earth is alive. A rumble, so deep it's almost silent, as if from inside me, shakes me awake. Louder and louder, the quaking grows, as if trying to swallow me into a new trench. But a high note lifts me up, then another, higher and brighter, rising like bubbles, lifting me nearer to the surface until I'm bursting through the water, and though I expect to see lightness, all I can see is storm–harsh cadences crashing like waves, the panicked and the shipwrecked gasping for breath. But like all storms, it rages to exhaustion. The steady rotation of the Earth takes over, and we drift along the surface with our eyes on the parting clouds, the loyal sun laying a gleaming runway on the water. In one heavy instant, we remember everything we were taught and told, everything we thought up on our own, all of our friends and all of our days, spinning together toward the shore, a pearly white beach where we can rest, and nothing bad can get us, and we can all be safe because, there, we all have the power to play whatever we want.

When my song is over, I stand. They're all clapping for me, even Nick, whose eyes flit to my hands at my sides. I bow my head.

"All right," Viceroy Hugo says. "Thanks, Tristan. You clearly have some imagination." He finishes his drink. "Your food's up next, Maria. And then, Helena, maybe we can get you to darn some socks." He turns and leaves the room without waiting for anyone to answer.

Maria bends to me like when we came in, says, "Bravo, Tristan," and then follows her husband. I sip my apple juice, holding in a smile because it feels so good to play freely for other people.

Turning to Helena for some approval and to share my good feeling, I find a pair of eyes looking at me the way they'd stare at Dylan when he ranted and screamed at her, and she'd sit there waiting for him to stop, already knowing the words she could utter that would reduce him to a small boy–like in my very first journal entry, when she whispered something in his ear and he just stood there, wide-eyed, biting his lip, and pulling at his hair. A look she gave me one night this week, a few days after Dylan was taken, when she came into my room while I was sleeping and lifted me out of bed to bring me into the main room to sit at the table while she went through all our possessions, asking, "Do you think we could do without this, Tristan? What if we lived in a house without books? How about our chairs? What if we just stood to eat? What if we went without light–could we do it? This candlestick was my mother's–she died of boredom–I'm not even sure why I have it anymore. How would you feel if we got rid of it? How about all of your things, the things important to you? Your bandages, your ointments, your pills, your helmet, your sun goggles, your watch–do you need those things?" I said yes, we need it all. And with that mystifying look in her eyes, she stared at me for who knows how long–I was so tired–before she finally permitted me to go back to bed.

It dawns on me that I might be missing something so obvious that it kills her to see me unable to notice it, and she needs to cauterize the two-way channels in her that permit both suffering and bliss if she's going to live sanely with me in her life.

I proceed ahead of her to the east wing of the house. A glass chandelier sprays shards of rainbow light in patterned layers onto the flame-yellowed walls and ceiling. I sit at the table, set with four places with porcelain bowls of hot stew and metalware, and a goat's curved horn serving as the centerpiece.

"I hope you all enjoy it," Maria says. She does a small dance with her fists.

Viceroy Hugo lowers his nose into his bowl and sniffs for so long, he must have either a lacking or exceptional nose. Maybe the scent for him is like Dylan's shirts for me (I've put one over my pillow to sleep on). When Viceroy Hugo takes a bite, he tips his head back and stares at the ceiling. "Perfect," he says.

I blow on it before I taste it. It's stringy and has many flavors that touch parts of my mouth I'm not used to.

"Do you like it, Tristan?" Maria asks.

I'd prefer eggs, but don't say so. I hum affirmatively, which makes Maria happy.

"The goat's from Canland," Viceroy Hugo says. "Still a kid. When goats get older, their meat gets this sour taste." He stabs another cube of meat and eats it. "I slaughtered this one a week ago. If you're gonna eat something that blinks, you should look it in the eye first. Eating meat was never the problem," he says, sipping his drink. "Producing it was. You tell people they can get it whenever, wherever, however much they want, can even have someone else do the killing for them, everyone's going to want steak for the whole family. Helena, you remember the meat plants?"

Her head bobs languorously. She's resigned, quiet, as if too focused on her interior to interact with her exterior—something she used to condition me for doing.

Viceroy Hugo takes another bite and chews loudly. "You could smell it a hundred miles away. Tristan, in war, when you're starving, and you smell an exploded meat plant, that's the stuff that makes you want to die."

I blink and nod and eat a softened coin of carrot.

Then, almost laughing, he says, "Helena, do you remember outside the data center, all those people trying to get on the fucking internet for one last email, when the maritime renegades were bombing the undersea cables, and people were getting shot for hacking down power lines, and the power lines were starting forest fires, and when we finally got out of there, do you remember what you said? Tristan, your mom goes, 'If I could just have a fucking beer and a burger right now, I'd be all right to die.' It's that simple stuff we missed."

Helena pushes her bowl slightly away from herself. Her thumb is on her lips and she's looking off into the main tower. Viceroy Hugo smiles at her, then goes back to eating.

"Is the food OK, Helena?" Maria asks.

"It's fine," Helena says. "I'm just feeling sick from the ride."

"Oh, no," Maria says. "Would you like something to settle your stomach?"

Helena takes a small sip of grappa, and then another quick one.

"Tristan, your dad got you into insects, is that right?" says the viceroy.

Knowing Helena would want me to stay engaged, I say, "Well, partly." I'm inclined to credit Dylan, but instead I add, "I just think they're interesting. Maybe it's because of my analgesia."

"Hell yeah—that's badass. They teach you about fear and instincts, right? I tell you, I learned more about human nature from insects than from any person. Insects can get organized. Thousands of people fighting one another outside that data center while a thundercloud of flies descended on a meat plant, eating and breeding. Seems pretty smart to me." Viceroy Hugo laughs, so I laugh too. "We all have to choose what we want, and it's our responsibility to keep the next generation in mind, right? Your dad chose to help write the rules, but he doesn't get to do this with you. He made a sacrifice. And I don't blame him for it because we all make our own choices, but look what happened to Dylan. Your mom chose to be here with you. Don't forget that. She has made you her purpose." He eats a fast few bites, nearly finishing, barely chewing before he swallows. "Everyone has theirs. Me, I knew I was in the right place when I was killing people who valued the steak above the cow." He lays his fork down and looks up at me.

"I hope you don't judge me. We've all got war in our biology, just like insects. They're twisted. Do you know what a parasitoid is?"

"It's a type of wasp that uses a living organism as a host for its eggs," I say.

He rolls up his sleeve to reveal a freckled shoulder and a tattoo of a wasp injecting a cockroach with eggs via its tail. "I love them," he says.

"I'm partial to arachnids," I say.

"Bastards, those spiders—they're too good at what they do." He lets his sleeve fall. "We had to reduce the spider populations in the fields because they were eating up all the pests. Too many weeds then, and too much competition for our crops."

Among the many tattoos, there's one on the inside of his forearm that says: 2-21-48 E.V. I think it must be a date and initials. In 2048, he probably would've been around fifteen, eighteen, twenty years old.

"See, Tristan, by making use of insects, we respect their abilities. Everything we use them for is within their code anyway. We just use them for our own ends—that's Dominion."

I nod and eat some goat, but it's all gristle. I don't know what to do with it, so I chew and chew until it's broken up enough that I can swallow it.

"Do you like it, Tristan?" Maria says.

"Why do you keep asking if they like it?" Viceroy Hugo says, eating more. "They like it."

"I was just asking, honey," Maria says, scratching the back of Viceroy Hugo's head.

"Every time a kid visits us up here, she gets all googly-eyed," Viceroy Hugo says, chewing and bunching up his cheeks like a smile, but not quite.

"I do get excited," Maria says. "Children are so refreshing. I spend most of my time working on recipes, or doing Aztec ceramics. We have a kiln out back by the stables. My grandparents taught me. The three of us came here from a Part in former New Mexico about twelve years ago. They built some of the adobe houses in Canland–helped to build. I met Hugo when he reviewed my request to transfer to an Arts Part."

"Those places are the end of everything," Viceroy Hugo says. "Higher suicide rates than Canland. Speaking of which–Helena, you see this stopping some time in the near future?"

"It will stop when it needs to," Helena says.

"My nightmare," Viceroy Hugo says quickly, "is building a Part of a certain size, and then too many people expel or kill themselves, and suddenly we can't sustain the Part. Then this is all for nothing."

"There are DOTEC waiting to be registered all throughout the continent," Helena says. "We'll take them before it comes to that."

"Why, so they can kill themselves here?" Viceroy Hugo's leaning forward over the table, his bowl of stew not only empty, but clean. He has a small smirk on, and a restless leg beneath the table is jostling his head on his neck. I think he's about to say something more, but he just keeps his eyes on Helena, who's taking a sip from her glass.

"Need the opposing force," Helena says. "Otherwise it moves too fast one way."

"This is no longer the opposing force." Viceroy Hugo raises his eyebrows and scratches his beard. He doesn't take his eyes off Helena. I eat some goat to appear as Helena wants me to. Helena sighs through her nose and fingers something out of the inside of her eye.

"I'd love to have children," Maria says, looking at Helena. "Some day." She eats goat off the fork, metal hitting her teeth.

Viceroy Hugo slowly turns to face Maria. His eyelids are half closed, yet his mouth is active, tongue probing for remnant flavors. "How do you do it?" He sighs in a higher pitch. "This dish, every time–it makes me forget the things I loathe about you." He leans his chin on his fist. "Tell me again how you make it."

There are blurry little rainbows on Maria's face reflected from the chandelier. She drapes her braid over her shoulder, then puts it down her back again.

"Well," she says, her eyes getting heavy and glossy. "There's garlic, onion . . . carrots . . . goat, of course." Her jawbone flexes through her skin and she swallows. "I braise it."

"Wow." Viceroy Hugo starts clapping. "Chef Maria!" He raises his full-again glass and then shoots it back. Holding on to his forearms, he rubs his thumb against the tattoo of the numbers and letters. "Twice now you've mentioned having children in front of guests. Do it again, I'll reach up inside you and tie your tubes myself." He clears his throat. "Everyone thinks they're so fucking deserving. Nick, bring us dessert, please."

Maria's cheeks become craters. She glances up at me and smiles with the outside corners of her eyes, making deep crow's feet. I think her eyebrows are painted on.

Nick clears our plates and returns to serve us each a bowl of berries and cream—a dessert Leo once bragged about receiving as a gift from Viceroy Hugo for his parents' invaluable contribution, making all his fellow futures slobber with envy. It's funny how I could be, should be, an object of envy.

Viceroy Hugo dips his finger into the cream and dabs it on the center of his lips. He leans over, kisses Maria's earlobe, then licks the cream off her. She shrugs, tickled, then flits her eyes to Helena and me, and erases her smile.

Viceroy Hugo leans back in his chair, looking at his wife. "I'm sorry, baby," he says. "That wasn't very nice of me."

"It's OK," Maria says, casting her eyes back down into her own dessert. Her neck blushes.

Helena puts a spoon in my hand. "Eat."

The raspberries and blueberries make my mouth tingle everywhere. I mash them against my palate, let the cream melt and turn filmy on my tongue. Without question, it's the most delicious thing I've ever eaten. If only I could eat them with the right people.

"So, Tristan," says the viceroy, "Canland's sacrificed an awful lot to keep you alive. You like your life?"

"Yes," I say.

"Good. You know how many times your parents nearly died, to make a life for you? With all the times they saved mine, I sometimes think I still owe them a debt." He sniffs brassily. "But you're their child, so you don't owe them anything. And one day, you're gonna be telling the next generation how you made it through this time—and guess what? Those children aren't gonna owe you a fucking thing. Because it's your duty to make it through." He leans back, his white T-shirt tight against his muscly stomach and dotted with sweat, and looks up into the rainbow chandelier. "I almost wish I never knew what it was like before the Evanescence. My foster parents died at the beginning and never saw the worst of it." His face lowers toward Maria, who is smiling at him. Viceroy Hugo looks at me again. "When I was ten, they were on vacation, driving on a suspension bridge, and an earthquake brought it down. That was even before what people called the beginning, before deniers like my foster parents ever would've admitted that we were in the middle. But forget the politics. If those two had missed a traffic light, or gotten out of bed a minute later, who knows? What forces conspired to put them on that bridge at that time? It shows you," he says, leaning forward again, elbows on the table, intertwining his tattooed fingers, "the only force that gives a shit about you is other people."

He looks at Helena then. She's staring down at her hand, turning it over in the refracted shards of rainbow. She has a bit of cream at the corner of her mouth, but her dessert is mostly untouched. She had too much grappa before we left.

"We all made choices we didn't want to," says Viceroy Hugo. "And yeah, now we all serve Arturo Eagles' vision for the fate of the planet, but it's sort of the only way of availing yourself of the fact that you were once trying to kill the parents of the children you meet today. That's something we always carry with us. But I look at you, and I think, maybe we did it the only way we could've."

Maria curls her hand around Viceroy Hugo's bicep. He shrugs her away. "You don't know what it was like either," he says to her.

She holds an eye-smile at him. "No," she says, "you're right. Just remember, baby, you get emotional about it."

"We were in the highlands," he says to me, ignoring her. "I don't know—Wyoming, Montana, Idaho. It was November, sixty-five degrees. Goddamn," he says, turning his head away so his chin touches his interlocked fingers, "I think about these people all the time. We were starving." He faces me again. "Food storage facilities were all being raided, everyone was DOTEC, no one was too proud anymore. There were maybe six of us in our company at this point. We'd buried your mom's sisters just a couple months before. We followed a river, pretty shallow, and the forest was struggling, but it was something. One day, right as the sun got low, we found a farm. Nothing lacking about it. Like a magical land from another time. A mother, father, three kids—two teenage boys, and a girl, maybe ten years old—met us at the perimeter, each one of them armed and looking like they had practice handling visitors. Michael talked them into letting us stay for a night. The mother went and got us some stew. The father said to us, 'You can pitch your tents right here as long as you hand over your weapons.' Michael said, 'No way, we'll eat and then be on our way.' But your mother, always so perceptive, she was looking around, and said, 'Hey, you seem to be having trouble with your well. What's all that groundwater doing in your grass, all turbid and shit, want me to take a look at your pressure tank?' So we struck a deal that she fixed it and we got to sleep with our weapons. Well, not sleep—we were too tired to sleep. Our brains were on fire." He takes a sip of whiskey. "What did they have that we didn't? It was like they were spared for refusing to participate in the thing the rest of us seemed to have no choice in. I wondered when was the last time any of them had spoken to a human being outside their family. And then—has he heard this, Helena?"

"I don't know," she croaks, like her vocal cords are going to ossify.

"Well," Viceroy Hugo says, "we got this bright idea that one of their goats was worth more to us than it was to them. So in the middle of the night, your dad, this guy Fenwick, and I snuck out of our tents to the goat pen. We wrangled one up, muzzled and tied it, figuring we could use it for milk for a while, or companionship, and eventually for food. Or maybe we'd start a new civilization with this one goat. Like I said, we'd gone crazy." Viceroy Hugo glances at the same spot on the table where Helena's looking, beside the goat horn, then back at me. "On our way back to the tents, we see a pair of waist-high eyes staring at us from down the barrel of a shotgun. We three idiots have our hands all occupied by this strung-up goat, but all I thought of was how the recoil of a shotgun would send this little girl flying. I didn't even think about how we'd be dead. She tells us to drop the goat. So we set it down slowly, but then Fenwick makes a sudden move to her, and she blasts him in the gut. The recoil sent her back a few steps, but she was still standing. And then, before we could process what just happened, she's reloaded." He takes a deep breath in and out through his nose. "Fuck." He brushes his hair back. "Moon presiding like a judge, wind blowing hard—and then everything started happening at once. Helena, I don't know where she came from, but she jumped on top of the girl, held her down in the grass. Sod started exploding at our feet. Michael and I took off running toward the barn, away from the house." His eyes have drifted over my shoulder.

I've seen Helm look this way before—the tight frown and blank stare, as if watching the event, or reliving it in a Sensorium. Why didn't Helena ever talk about the war like this? If she was the only person I ever spoke to, I'd hardly know how we got here.

"We shut the door, but the wood was exploding as shots came through. I'm sure you know the scar on Michael's cheek," he says.

The scar I noticed when Dylan showed me the video of Michael, and I asked how he'd gotten it. Dylan said Helena once told him Michael had incurred it as insufficient punishment for a crime against humanity, but she wouldn't tell the story. Dylan had searched through satellites for evidence, and found nothing.

"Yes," I say, listening for what atrocity that scar reminds my father of daily; reminded Helena of every time she saw his face.

"Your father looked at me, and I fucking wish I could remember what he said, but my head was like a balloon. Real death is just pure fear. There's no clarity—only an acknowledgement of every stupid thing you ever did." He coughs into his shoulder. There are tattoos of flames on his arm, a cross-section of the Earth with an eyeball in the core, the moon in all its stages, symmetrical doves, twisting flowers with thorny stems, the face of a smiling fat man with big earlobes, and a goat standing on top of a mountain with rays of sunshine behind it. "Michael pulled the pin on some homemade explosive for just such occasions, and then went somersaulting out the barn doors, wheeling the grenade at the house. On contact, it swallowed the near facade of the house. The wind was so strong, the fire spread so fast through the field that we barely outran it. We lost our tents and most of the shit inside. The goats, the fields, the house, the family—it looked like daytime." He clears his throat. "We got into the SPV in the driveway and peeled out. I can't fathom our luck that the vehicle started for us. After about ten minutes of sitting in blank shock, I turned around. In the back seat, Helena still had her hand clamped over that little girl's mouth. Saved her life."

Nick refills all the drinks but mine, his face impassive, as if he's already heard this and worse.

"Thanks, Nick," Viceroy Hugo says, and drinks maybe his sixth whiskey of the night in one go. "We dropped her off at the nearest xenodochium we could find, with maybe a dozen other DOTEC, a few hours' drive from the farm. Then we were on our way again." He looks across the table to Helena. "You ever wonder where that girl is?"

She shakes her head. "I don't want to talk about it," she says.

"You're not talking about it," Viceroy Hugo says. "You never talked about it. It's like all your Suicidalism justifies that some folks don't get a say in when they go."

"I wasn't in that barn with you," Helena says. "And I didn't steal that goat." She hiccups.

Viceroy Hugo licks his teeth, pushing his mustache forward. "We were starving," he says in a light voice, "and in danger. Even if we were stealing from them first, they had what we didn't. And you saw what we drove through. There wasn't anything else. Maybe we didn't have to kill them, but we also didn't know we didn't. And we're here now. Think of everyone we've given a home in Canland."

Sasha: dead. Her child: orphaned. Sybil: DOTEC. Dylan: expelled. AB: disappeared.

"Tristan." Viceroy Hugo is looking at me. "I hope you don't think we're evil. We've built a good Part. We're doing a good thing for the Earth and for one another. At a certain point in everyone's life, everything they do is an act of atonement."

"I know about forgotten people," I say. "They're easy to forget." I stand, and everyone looks up at me. "I have to go to the bathroom," I say, truthfully. And, just as truthfully, I don't want to be at this table with these people anymore.

"I'll show you to it," says Maria.

"Insensate, not insensitive," Viceroy Hugo says. I tilt my head, and he smiles, but his eyes look sad. "That's how Michael described you."

Maria gets up out of her chair. "Come, sweetie."

Viceroy Hugo puts the heel of his hand on his forehead. With his other hand, he runs a finger in circles on the rim of his empty glass. Helena watches him. I notice a tug at the corner of her mouth. The start of an expression I don't get to see the end of.

Maria leads me through the house, past the piano, and into the darker wing. She opens the bathroom door for me and lets me pass. It's a cavernous space, and smells like stagnant water. When I'm finished peeing, I see myself in the circular mirror on the wall, flanked by candles in sconces. At home, we have a handheld mirror for my checks, and at night, I now and then see my reflection in a dark window. But I can't remember the last time I've seen my whole face so clearly as in this mirror. I move my mouth like I'm talking. I pretend to laugh. I tilt my chin and part my lips until I'm happy with the way I look. I brush the hair off my forehead, but it falls back down, still too short. I'm different—the reasons I'm here are plain to see, written on my face, reducing what it takes for someone to know me. *Beautiful*, Dylan always called me. I wonder how he meant it.

Maria's waiting outside the door. She bends to me and lowers her voice to a whisper, "I'm sorry. You've done great. It won't be much longer."

"OK."

She puts a hand on my cheek. "I'd love to have a child like you."

"I'm very difficult," I say.

"I'm sure that's not true."

"Have you ever had anyone run away from you?"

She nods. Her big lips curl inward, as if smothering a voice that wants to escape.

"Do you know where they went?" I ask.

She shakes her head. "No." She swallows, then sighs, releasing tears down her cheeks. She wipes them quickly. "Please don't go up that mountain," she says even softer. "I don't know if you'd planned on it. But please—life is . . ." She shakes her head once, then smiles.

"I won't," I tell her. But how could I say that I never would? It seems like such a near fate for so many people, and I've stepped off a cliff who knows how many times before . . .

Maria grabs my arm, squeezes twice quickly, and walks me back into the main tower. Helena's stepping into her shoes, smoothing the pleats of her long linen skirt, and Hugo is watching her with his arms crossed, his shirt discolored by a diamond of sweat centered on his solar plexus, with more sweat beneath his arms. The almost babyish liveliness in him at the beginning of the evening is now gone. His lips are dry from all the talking. He steps to me and holds out his hand. I take it, briefly, then let go. I notice that he holds a bottle of clear liquid in the other.

"Really, it was an experience to meet you, Tristan," he says, his voice broken apart. "Thanks for your contribution. Keep it up."

I nod. He laughs, then wipes his mouth, but the smile remains.

"Man," he says, "I remember when they took you–fourteen years ago–before anyone knew what was going to happen to you. If I ever see Michael again, I'll tell him everything worked out. His work was worth it." He smiles. "Little genius."

"OK," Helena says. "Thanks, Hugo. Thanks, Maria."

"Hey," Viceroy Hugo says, still looking at me. "You like it here? In Canland?"

"Yes," I say. I make sure my face stays completely still. I don't want him to think he knows me. "But I've never been anywhere else."

"That you remember," he says.

"That's all that matters," I say.

"Yeah," he says. Then he hands the bottle he's holding to Helena. "We'll let it go on a little longer," he says to her. "But it's not going to be the air we breathe."

She takes the bottle. In her tired voice, she says, "I don't make anybody do anything." Then she nods and turns away.

Maria opens the door. I kneel to put on my shoes, and come face to face with the taxidermy hound. I notice it has on its neck two small holes, like a snakebite.

In Viceroy Hugo's world, nothing leaves and nothing enters, not dogs, not children–only guests.

As we leave the viceroy's house, I look back. Maria's waving with one hand and combing her braid with the other. Viceroy Hugo bends to the dog, kisses its snout, and lays his cheek on its head.

The desert floor is black, but the sky is bright. The carriage horse's lantern lights our path home. The transportation contributor doesn't say a word.

"We didn't get a Green Line pass," I say.

Helena hums with her eyes shut. She swallows saliva. "Your song," she says, and adjusts herself to get comfortable. In spite of myself, I'm desperate to know what she thought. But she says nothing more.

Eventually she falls asleep. After a while, she starts shivering. I almost rub her back, but when I start to think of everyone who didn't choose to be here, everyone who came here without a choice, and how that's all we're made up of, individually, as a Part, and as a world, I start bouncing my legs up and down to make warmth for myself.

.

As soon as the horse pulls the carriage away from the front of our house, Helena pukes in the street. I take her by the elbow, but she jerks her arm and says she's fine and walks up the path ahead of me by herself. She can't get the key to fit in the doorknob, so I do it for her. When we walk in, she reaches up onto the shelf where there's usually a candle she can easily light to illuminate the space, but her hand knocks a different object to the floor and it shatters. Her hand's like a blind rodent up on the shelf, knocking other objects to the floor, none of them a candle. Cursing, she steps inside and her shin collides with something that's not where it's supposed to be. "Fuck. Fuck. Don't move." Slowly she makes her way to the kitchen. She climbs over something–the couch. I hear her slump to the floor on the other side of it. Finally, in the washbasin, she finds a candle that takes several tries to light. Holding the candlestick and the weak pulsating light, she climbs back over the couch, clumsy but careful in her state. The candlestick is the one that once belonged to her mother, the one that's always on her writing table, which is not where it should be, but is wherever the home-rearrangers put it. She waves the flame over a shattered porcelain bowl beneath the mudroom shelf. She sniffs and spits into the corner by the door and then screeches, her voice ripping through her voice box, like the instant of a welder's hammer-strike bleeding through the seconds. She kicks a chair and it tumbles over. "Don't move," she says again. She feels her way through the house, discovering cosmetics and first-aid supplies and medication on the shelf, Dylan's desk where the couch used to be, a mattress beneath it. I close the front door and feel my way through the darkness to my room. There's a candle and a match atop a displaced dresser. There are books in the drawers and clothes on the bookshelf. My bed is against the wrong wall. I take the candle down the hall to Helena's room, where her writing table is, and the boxes of headstones, pamphlets, surgical scissors, and small coffins have had their contents spilled everywhere. Something in the other room shatters and Helena screams again. I go back into my room and lift my mattress to look for my journal. It's there, but on top of it there's a document I've never seen before, signed by Helena Damon-Weekes on January 10, 2089, two months after the day I was perforated on the hillock.

The document's header reads, WORLD NEUROLOGICAL RE-SEARCH CENTER: TERMS OF AGREEMENT FOR NEUROLOGICAL EVALUATION VIA LONG-TERM SENSORIUM ACTUALIZATION. I hold my candle close to it, and read a list of transactional benefits in exchange for possession of research Subject: expungement of Dylan's prior offenses, reduced contribution hours for Helena, priority relocation in the event of a natural disaster. There's an amendment that says, *Pursuant to the divorce of Helena Damon-Weekes and Michael Weekes, the California Inland Valley Desert Greening Project-registered Weekes family shall retain certain benefits including single-family housing and personal-use Sensorium (stored Actualizations only) in exchange for twelve additional months of research on aforementioned Subject.* A disclaimer that WORLD assumes no responsibility in the case of my death or permanent neurological damage or changes resulting from the evaluation. A conditional clause that says, *Pending Subject's classification of spectrality, Subject shall be transferred to a Spectral Part for further neurological research. Transfer to Spectral Part will be decided by the undersigned, following aforementioned research, and rewarded with further transactional benefits.* Finally, a stipulation that public disclosure of this agreement is punishable by expulsion from current Part.

"What are you doing?" Her voice is behind me.

I turn around, kneeling, holding the paper. She sees it. She tears it out of my hands. With eyes wide, she remains motionless. She doesn't look like Helena.

The paper is too close to the flame.

"You let them do all that to me?" I say.

Fire blooms. She jerks her hand away from the paper, and it falls and curls up in a slow flash of brightness.

"Where are you?" she says. "Are you in a Spectral Part?"

"No," I say.

"Then don't be so ungrateful!"

"You used me for benefits," I say. "So you could live in this house. So Dylan could keep his Sensorium."

"He would've died without it! Do you know what it was like living with him, always fucked up out of his mind unless he had that thing to keep him sane? And it still wasn't enough!"

"Why are you mad at me?" I ask.

"Do you know how much pain you cause me, Tristan? How hard I try, and still you look at me like that. Where's Dylan? Where's Michael? Why do you love them more than me? What did I not do for you?"

"You're a bad person."

She brandishes the candlestick. It comes close to my face. Then she holds it close to her chest and she starts crying. "Don't say that." Her mouth pulls taut and her nostrils flare. "I'm sorry," she says.

I stand straight, close enough to her height now that we don't tilt our chins. "I hate you," I say as I walk past her. She pushes me in the back. My face hits the wall, but it breaks my fall. I run out of my room, past all our rearranged possessions. I hear her trip and fall behind me. The candlestick clatters against the clay floor. She grunts, sobbing sporadically. There's a weak light coming from my bedroom.

I run out of the house.

There's a story in Helm's book that's not the most poetic, and it's repetitive, and there are typos, and it's by turns too slow, too fast, vague, and then gratuitous, but I still like it, and it goes like this: A kid gets kicked out of his house by his parents, and with no place to go, he joins the military. Every night in basic training, while trying to fall asleep, he cries. He thinks he's crying quietly, because none of the other cadets ever mention it. But they're all crying too—softly, they all think, because no one ever mentions it, because they're all crying. When they all finally graduate from basic, and it's time to go to war, and they're out there fighting, they all make good soldiers, and they're not afraid of anything, and none of them are crying. In the end, the main character's best friend is killed in action. But after the first shock of horror, the kid tells himself that none of this is real—that it's just a simulation—and he doesn't cry. He swears he hardly even knew the guy. And he goes back out to the battlefield the next day, like a good soldier, ready to kill.

Dylan's chrome bicycle is still leaning against the side of the house. It's coated in dust and windblown sand, but the headlight works. I get on it, and in spite of every warning I've ever received against running, biking, playing in the garden, farming in the fields, standing in front of a fastball, doing anything I don't know how to do but have always wanted to, I start the seven-mile ride east to find out if the lesson I overheard Helena tell Kelly was true—about finding who you are when you're standing at the top of the Notch, looking out over Canland, and then looking down.

8

April 2, 2090

Have to write quick w. Helena asleep. Early a.m. Found paper, Helena's nib in oven. Everything out of place.

Reached trailhead, left bike against tree, detached headlight, wrapped it around my arm via cord, armed self w. rock, ran up trail. Fell off bike x20. Took three hours. Fell more on hike, four hours. Bloody.

After climbing Notch, can reason Michael's abandonment & see him clearly as thief & murderer who knew his passage into this land & land itself were stained & took me up Notch to believe by passing it on to me, his son, that he was good > bad. Then left to absolve self further.

He should be punished.

Had to stop freq. on way up, let pulse settle. Signs were posted: Turn Back. You Are Worth More Than Your Absence. Listing names & families of jumpers.

But also signs pointing to Notch.

Crawled up escarpment. Failed to find purchase over scree. Broke hand. Scraped legs. Very cold, fingers blue. Pines tall but far apart. Saw thousands-year-old bristlecone pine leafless twisted trunk artifact. So much mountain still above me, unscalable, but saw footprints too.

When land leveled into lookout over canyon, large rocks spelled:

U r LovED

Whole hike, had view of clear sky full of stars no moon. When I got to clearing at dawn, sliver of waxing crescent so thin looked not like moon, but rip in sky.

Then for first time ever saw bright object slide across sky from one horizon to other. Took minutes. Must've been satellite. Watched it go.

Vista beautiful, blue, smooth.

Then saw Helm. Huge, sitting slumped forward at edge of cliff. Has bald patch in back of head.

Tried to call his name but voice was too hoarse. Got closer. When he saw me he shot up & nearly fell but kept balance, said, Look at you, your hand, have to get you to Safe Haven.

Were you going to kill yourself? I said.

No, he said. Why are you here?

The view, I said.

We stared at land. Light was like liquid metal pouring over mountains.

Stepped to edge. Peered down. Saw body. Facedown, crooked, broken. Shorter drop than imagined. Helm grabbed back of my shirt, led me to bivouac in small outcrop. Tore tarp off ground inside & fastened into harness, strapped to his back.

Meanwhile saw names etched in walls of outcrop.

Found Roshana. Put my hand over it.

Helm helped me climb into harness. He ran down. A few times I had to get out & walk.

Asked again b.c. I knew he was lying, Were you going to kill yourself?

I don't know, he said.

Why were you?

Shame.

What are you ashamed of?

Everything.

Say one.

No.

Told him M. once carried me up & down mountain on his back. Then I told him DOTEC farm story. Told him my shame for not helping AB, Sybil, Dylan, Malakai, Helena.

I spent my whole life thinking bad things are good. Maybe myself, I said.

You're still young, he said.

What do you have shame about? I said.

Tried my best to guide and be good, but world is cruel, and I'm tired, he said.

Then quiet awhile.

I'm bringing you to Safe Haven.

Take me home, I said.

You need medical attention.

Helena can take me. I need her to take me. (Need to know if she'll take me.)

Can't do that, T. Infection, internal bleeding.

Cole knows what to do, I said.

After a moment he said, And you really feel no pain?

No.

If it's what you want.

Then I said, There's a DOTEC orphan in Safe Haven. If she's not adopted she might have to go to—

Don't call her DOTEC. She's a child, not vagabond, not militia-woman. And I don't want to be anyone's father.

When we got to trailhead, bike was still there. Helm got on front, me on back. Morning was so bright. Something flared inside me like heated stone dislodged and fallen. Empty cave became beautiful colored light & I said to Helm, Helm I

PART THREE

1

June 2090

One week after I came home from the Safe Haven, the animals started dying. First, a calf. Then for two days, her mother keened until she, too, lay down to die. A day after that, two dozen chickens they said you could smell a mile downwind from the coop. Then the wild animals all fled the desert floor for the nighttime chill of the highlands, more animals than most people knew existed in the unchanged land surrounding Canland—cottontails, foxes, coyotes, ringtails, tiny nocturnal and half-blind things, fossorial and arboreal mammals, butterflies, dragonflies, skinks, and big spiders—baking into the sand on their exodus. Even the wolves with chips in their heads tried to escape. Viceroy Hugo declared a natural disaster and ordered energy and water contributors to remain at their contributions for extended hours while the rest of the Part lent their services where applicable and transferable. Carpenters erected more lean-tos in the shade of trees, horticulturalists strung vine up massive trellises to absorb some heat before it melted homes, entomologists contrived insect activity in the arable soil to abate fungal growth, agriculturalists kept the fields covered with tarpaulins, and the Sensatarium sheltered the elderly and the children whose homes were uninhabitable. Three straight days of 130° F. It had happened before, but never with Canland's population so high. They had to pump half a year's supply of water to keep people alive for a week, so the ecological detriment hit an unprecedented high, mocking the core principles of all Restoration Parts, and people became blameful and angry as they questioned why there had been a Part established here in the middle of the desert in the first place, what hubris it required to turn a desert into a pasture and think you'd outsmarted nature when, on day six, it hit 134° and the Safe Haven was overcrowded with victims of heat stroke, dehydration, and respiratory difficulties. Ten people died there, and another twenty by jumping off or trying to reach the Notch. Meanwhile, Helena came and went without a word to me, and I spent most of every day in bed surrounded by light snacks and jars of water and had my bedpan dumped, my wound cleaned, my bandage changed, and all my usual checks done once a day by a contributor from the Hovels named Gale, mother to Conrad and Valerie, who were living in the well-insulated Sensatarium during the days, taking classes from Gwen Horn and Helm Roctern, and fighting for physical space and also for the respect of their coevals who never were DOTEC, until their mother returned to them at the end of the day with modified rations—Squash, she'd say to me, So much squash—and promises that god was watching over them and they would make it through this trial of the lord's, as she once said to me too, and told me a story about two sets of footprints in the sand becoming one, and I just wanted her to leave, and whenever she did leave I would wait for her to come back the next day while I listened to Helena talk to herself from the other side of my door with no hope or expectation that she'd knock for permission to come into my room to make sure I was all right, but acceptant that she would instead continue to wait for me to become so desperate that I admitted I needed her help and called out begging for it, while she wrote new proposals to cull Canland's population as the heat seeped into our homes and

made the very air so cumbersome to breathe that, in the middle
of the eighth night of the heatwave, a furious and delirious trio
stole a SPV that was traced two hundred miles north to Lake Tahoe,
but not returned from there before it was stripped by Purist extremists residing in the mountainside outside the WORLD Research
Center—the same Center to which I was admitted after I was perforated—and who knows what happened to them, who cares, and
who could even blame them when, in Canland, there was one
overworked water contributor who started accosting registered at
knifepoint, demanding more for doing more, and he was arrested,
but then other water and energy contributors took a more organized approach to appealing for more benefits for their contribution once the heatwave breaks, since they are the ones maintaining
the reservoirs, keeping the drinking supply clean, running and
digging wells in the oppressive heat, and are in communication
with WORLD to ask for resources even though, according to WORLD's
philosophy, a Part that requires extensive outside assistance isn't a
viable Part and relies on a fundamentally different philosophy
from WORLD, and if we're not getting assistance from WORLD because our ecological detriment gets too high, then why are we
living under WORLD's jurisdiction at all? Hugo came to the Part
Center to address anyone who could bear the heat, and those
people then relayed his message to the rest of Canland: that Arturo
Eagles sees the life we live here, admires it, and rewards it; we're
in a transitional period between the end of the world and the beginning; never in history has there been a more a determined,
unified group of people; the planet will snap at us and try to expel
us, but that is the burden our fathers left us; it's normal now, and
that's almost too sad to stop and think about, but we must, because
it's happening everywhere; we just chose to live in a place where
it will happen more extremely, and that is our greatest contribution, that we are choosing to try to change it. Helena wrote his
speech. She came into my room in the middle of the night one
night and read it to me, woke me from a dream in which AB had
appeared to me in the form of a wolf, carrying my testicles in their

mouth. I'd reached out to take them back, but then I woke up, my hand was where my balls used to be, and AB's face was there for a flash in the darkness, and Helena was reading her own thoughts to me about what it means to die knowing you left the world a better place. Even if Helm had taken me to the Safe Haven right away, Cole said he wouldn't have been able to save them—A double testicular torsion this severe, no chance, and good thing you came in when you did, if you came in earlier, then we might've missed it entirely and an infection could've spread. Lucky again and again and again. After I came home from the Safe Haven Helena said to me, We always told you not to run or bike. But then she just sighed and said, I'm glad you're OK. And after she read me the speech in the middle of the night, she stared at me, eyes half-lidded, and said, So you're all grown up now, huh? Impulsively I just said, Yeah. She looked down at her speech and mumbled, We are all friends because we need each other to get through this. Then she wrote on the page, presumably that. Still, people became increasingly desperate, and two days after Viceroy Hugo's address (the Founding Celebration canceled), with the temperature at 136°, an energy contributor was caught in the middle of the night filching crops straight from the fields, and he was perforated not by a COHO nor a WEDA, but by a vigilante, and the next night, after a band of young men were caught trying to steal water from the arroyo in the hundred-degree night, Hugo garrisoned COHOs and WEDAS all along the canals and the arroyo, all the way up to the reservoir, resulting in a shortage of officers in Canland, which invited more thieves into the fields, and more vigilantes. The heat-related death toll by the middle of the second week was at sixty-five as the temperature hit 138°, and packs of people left Canland in the middle of the nights with their bikes and what they could carry on their backs, never to be heard from again. All applications for approved leave were denied, no DOTEC were admitted, and all expulsions were final, including that of a sixteen-year-old present who, when permitted access to the underground Canland College WORLD Research Center (as presents specializing in sciences were, as refuge from the heat), was caught tampering with ongoing research, and was put on the Green Line to a Short Term Rehabilitation Part—and though he wouldn't be allowed back, he'd escaped Canland's heat, and so, in the wake of his expulsion there followed a slew of petty crimes, but instead of producing more Green Line passes, these resulted in the perpetrators' detainment by COHOs in livestock pens where space had opened up since so many sheep, cattle, and pigs had succumbed to the heatwave, ending the trend of pilfering, battery, and fraud, which was being inflicted especially on the people in the Hovels whose unguarded homes, unmaintained, out-of-sight, and considerably cooler (because of the eucalyptus walls), had become easy targets, as Gale expressed to me near tears one day after her home had been ransacked. Gale pleaded with me that after I'd convalesced, I would promise to be a source of love and goodness for the Part, a person that her children could look up to and learn from. A few days later, when she came to dab my body with a cold compress and change the bandage on my groin, she said there'd been a real shift in the commitment to spiritual togetherness among all people in the Part, registered, DOTEC, orphaned, energy or gear contributor; man/woman/other, Black/white/other; people were starting to share, spread positivity to one another, look after each other's kids, teach each other special skills, make up games, sing songs, paint with whatever materials they could a mural in defiance of the artistic limitations that have been enforced since Canland's founding. We're like a blaze of phoenixes, she said. And while I was glad for that, I wished right then that I had left Canland so much sooner, though I also knew that there were reasons I'd stayed, things I had to learn, and I thought of that night I went to the Hovels, when I learned so much and met so many people, and I realized there would always be friends to make, here or anywhere else I'd go. The next day, Helm stopped by the house and brought a big salad with a bunch of vegetables harvested before they died in the heat, plus some spicy stew he said vaguely resembled an Indian dish called curry. He said, The spice is good, makes you sweat and cools you down.

And I said, Thank you, but actually anhidrosis is part of my analgesia, meaning I can't sweat. And he said, Oh, right, shit . . . sorry.
I laughed and said it was OK, and we shared a delicious meal and
chatted for a while. He apologized for going up the Notch, but that
between Malakai in his condition and his wife, or ex-wife, leaving
Canland to contribute on a Waste Rake in the Great Pacific Gyre,
some old traumas had painfully returned, including from before
he'd even joined the military, some injury his mother had incurred that sent his father into a psychological tailspin and their
family into financial ruin, and Helm became homeless for a time
before he joined the military, and that when he went up the Notch,
he was more focused on the people who wouldn't remember him
fondly than the people who would. Then he apologized for not
bringing me right to the Safe Haven, and I told him what Cole had
told me, about how the timing was what saved my life. Well that
makes twice, Helm said, and smoothed his very short hair and
smiled, but not with any humor. He said, I'm sorry I haven't come
to visit more. I told him it was OK, as long as he visited me again.
He nodded with a serious look on his face. I gave him my piece
about Cole, and he said he was honored to be chosen to read it. He
apologized one final time and said, Growing up, I never learned
how to handle my emotions, but I think you're doing an excellent
job, T. Thank you, Helm, I said. In the two weeks I spent conva-
lescing, I read his book three times through. It's become my favorite book of all time, better than *Fearsome Allies* or *One Hundred Years of
Solitude*. But I never heard back about what Helm thought of my
writing. The next day, with the temperature 140°, Helena came
into my room wearing a muslin poncho and said it was time for
me to start moving. She helped me bathe and showed me how to
clean the stitches of my double orchiectomy, and we had a nice
conversation about all the things I'm still capable of doing, and I
asked her if now not being able to procreate made me vestigial in
the grand scheme of nature, and she just continued to pour water
over my head until she said, Why don't we go for a walk? So, when
the sun went down and the evening temperature dipped to 115°, I

put on shorts and a white T-shirt and filled a water bottle, and as we ambled across Canland to see the oak tree, she broke the news to me that Helm had gone missing, though no suicide had been reported. We arrived at the tree, the real reason for the walk, despite the risk of overheating, to see the WEDA cutting down the coast live oak because its roots had been infected with a fungus brought on by the heat, and they had to make use of the wood before it rotted and became weak, diseased, and unusable. I gripped my pink parasol tightly, as if hoping that, if a gust blew through, it would catch on the parasol and carry me away. I wondered if Helm had left because he was inspired by what I'd written about Cole. I would understand. I returned to my Safe Haven contribution to treat people suffering from the heat, filling IV bags, sterilizing needles, washing sheets, and scrubbing everything. I wanted to talk to Cole about it all, but he was so busy that days went by with us speaking to each other about nothing other than medical matters, if we even spoke at all. My waking hours were mostly spent sitting at patients' bedsides while they slowly sipped water and lamented their own lives, which they'd spent worrying about the wrong things, and should have spent more time with their children, who were now cramped in the Sensatarium with no certain future. What the hell was going to happen when they got out of the Safe Haven? Who's even looking out for them? Many of them said they felt so alone. I just listened. One woman cried to me, not out of sadness, but from what she called *a return to human form.* I asked what she meant by that, and she said that it seemed like she'd spent so much time worrying about practical matters that she didn't feel like a person who was blessed with all the faculties that differentiated her and all of us from animals. Survival is just miserable, she said, laughing, all teary. She said, And everyone's working with WORLD to try to save the planet, but I just want to talk with my kid again, make up words, laugh with him. Hell, I can't wait to yell at him again, just so I can tell him I'm sorry. Then she cried without laughing. After a few days of nursing people back to health, and after watching one man go into cardiac arrest and

seeing the nurses save him, I finally told Cole I wanted to go back
to the nursery. He said I could the next day if there weren't any
new patients. So the next day, I went back to the nursery. There
were eight babies, seven I knew, including Sasha. She was pushing
an empty stroller from one end of the room to the other, knocking
on other babies' cribs and saying, Come? But she was the oldest
child in the nursery by at least a year and none of the others understood what she was asking. She pulled her shirt over her head
and balled it up and put it in the stroller. It had only been a few
weeks since I'd seen her, but it seemed like she'd aged months. I
asked her if she wanted to build blocks with me. She frowned at
the balled-up shirt in the stroller and said, OK. We built a whole
town on the floor. While we were building, she pointed at the cast
on my broken hand and said, Ow? I nodded and repeated, Ow. The
town we built had spread into the walkway, and Cameron accidentally kicked some of it over. Sasha looked at the destruction as if
her own home had been obliterated, then she palmed her forehead
and dragged her hand down her face, sighed and said, OK, started
nodding again, and reached for another block. She directed me to
help rebuild the city lengthwise along the walkway. That night,
Cole offered me a bed in the Safe Haven, as a contributor. I accepted, happy to not have to make the journey back to my house
through the heat, and to not have to deal with Helena, but it also
meant that, in the middle of the night, when Leo Laughton was
brought in to the Safe Haven having seizures, I had to stay awake
all night at his bedside to hold the tongue depressor down every
time he convulsed. What I initially assumed was heat-related was
actually tube-induced. I thought of not saving him, and although
I never seriously considered it, I did rely on my promise to uphold
Cole's commitment—more life, always more—every time I had to
wedge that life-saving wooden stick into my classmate's caustic
mouth. After a few days of sleeping in the Safe Haven, three weeks
into the heatwave, the temperature dropped to 130°. There was
one new baby born in that time by a young woman who so excit-
edly came in, saying her application to have a baby had been

accepted, and here she was, nine months later, ready, like she always knew she'd be. She had brassy hair, freckles, and big blue eyes. She reminded me a bit of Helena. She called me by my name, and when I asked her how she knew me, she asked if I didn't remember her from Halloween a couple years ago—Lydia. I said that I was sorry, but I didn't. She shrugged and didn't say much else, except that she couldn't wait to introduce her child to the world and all its little wonders. A few days later, another woman, about the same age, with similarly light hair, but a very different sort of expression on her face came in and said, in a timid voice, that she was told this was where she could get an abortion, but didn't know where to go or whom to see, and I told her I could set her up in an exam room. After I gave her a gown and fresh sheets and told her to just relax and that someone would be in there soon to help and I'd be back to check on her in a bit, I returned to the nursery to find that Cameron was handing Sasha over to a person sitting in a wheelchair, their neck in a brace. I rounded the scene and saw Malakai gently taking Sasha in his arms. His face was stoic and dutiful, and I saw his throat move as he swallowed, and sweat gathering along his hairline. The child tried to scramble out of his arms, and he let her, and she went to Cameron and clutched her pants, and Cameron explained to Sasha that Malakai was her daddy. Malakai waved at her, then smiled as if remembering to. Her eyes narrowed as she leaned her head toward him. Then she looked at me. I nodded and she looked back at Malakai. Then she waddled across the room to push her stroller out of the walkway—her shirt from the other day still serving as the baby in it—and went back to Malakai and reached up to try to grab the handles of his wheelchair. I picked her up and we pushed Malakai back and forth down the walkway. After a minute of this, I set her on the floor, and she told Malakai all about her blocks, Wide and Sturdy and High and Wobbly. Malakai struggled to lean forward to place a blue one on top of a tower, and when he did the whole thing came crashing down. Sasha threw her hands up and ran around the room until she tired herself out. Malakai looked at me and asked how I had been. I said I was fine, and that I was grateful Sasha was going to have a good home. I added, You don't have to call her that, but it was her mother's name. He just nodded and said, Thanks, yeah, I'll need some help caring for her because I might never fully recover from the nerve damage, but they moved a family from the Hovels next door to me into the communal house since so many people have left Canland—two kids and a mother, who's a caretaker named Gale. I said, Gale's wonderful. A moment passed before I asked if he had heard anything about Helm. He left, Malakai said. Told me he was gonna try to find a xenodochium where he could help traveling DOTEC. Then Sasha came running back to Malakai and tugged at his hand. He explained to her that he couldn't get up. She looked confused, and then started playing with the blocks again, looking up at Malakai after every placement, through her top eyelids, as if to pretend she didn't care that he was watching. I asked Malakai if he was upset that Helm left. He said, Yeah, but it's good, it's what he needed to do. I nodded and told Malakai I had to go check on a patient. Malakai said, See you around, Tristan. I went and checked on the waiting young woman. She was biting the skin off of her cuticles, and I asked if she wanted me to talk to distract her and help the time pass. She said sure, so I told her that Cole had saved my life many times and she had nothing to fear. I told her Helena Damon-Weekes was my mother, and that I had no allegiances to her, but what I'd learned in the Safe Haven is that having a baby is as much a choice as having an abortion, and that whatever her reasons were for whatever choice she made, they were good reasons. She didn't give much reply, and I wondered if my words were useless or even harmful. I busied myself by sterilizing instruments until I was sure that Malakai and Sasha would be gone. I supposed there was a world in which I'd one day see her and Malakai out and about the Part, and I'd tell her that I used to take care of her. But that wouldn't really even be true, because I am in part the reason she doesn't have a mother, because Canland did not give her mother access to the Safe Haven, while I've had my life saved countless times by the Safe Haven because of the

status of my parents, who founded a Part in which her mother
Sasha had not been safe, so it must be that my duty is to help
people who are afraid and disadvantaged and altogether worse off
than a boy whose main obstacle to a happy life is that he can't feel
pain. I'm not sure we could ever be friends. Then Cole came into
the room to attend to the young woman. I stepped out into the
hallway and slid down the wall and sat and thought with an unusual degree of straightforwardness and clarity. I hadn't heard
from Helena at all since I'd been in the Safe Haven; she must have
been up to her neck in contributions. The temperature dropped to
110°, and most people had returned to their normal contributions,
no longer building odd emergency structures or manning the
fields on the lookout for camouflaged nocturnal looters. When
Cole came out of the young woman's room after her abortion and
found me sitting on the floor in the hall, he held out both his
hands to help me up. I lifted my face and held his gaze. It's OK, he
said. There's nothing for me here, I said. That isn't true, he replied,
then added, But it doesn't matter whether that's true or not. You've
been everywhere, I said. Believe it or not, I haven't, Cole smiled.
But again, that doesn't really matter. I took his hands and let him
help me up, and I said, Did you ever know Sybil? I'm not sure I did,
he replied. She was my best friend, I said, and she left just a couple
months before I was taken to the Research Center. If she had stayed,
that might never have happened, and everything might be different. Maybe, Cole said, and maybe not, but it doesn't really matter.
No, I guess it doesn't, I said. He put his hands up by my shoulders
and said, If you're going to leave, just let me know first—I'll give
you everything you'll need to take with you. When I said nothing,
he lowered his head so he could meet my downcast eyes, and he
said, Everyone here is better for having known you. Thank you,
Cole, I said. I always remember him somewhat impersonally,
which is not to say he didn't love me, or that I didn't love him, but
only that he helped me, not because I was Tristan, but because I
was just another human being. I remember him often. I even
thought, that sleepless night before I left, of studying with Cole,

absorbing his wisdom as a substitute for a life of my own, and one day becoming him. But that was just a what-if—really, I'd already made up my mind. When I left the Safe Haven that evening, not yet knowing I had only two more nights in Canland, the sky was thick and gray like the belly of a whale, and people were standing outside their homes staring up at it as if praying, or not having to pray anymore but watching their prayers as they were answered. I had my head tilted up as I walked home, the clouds darkening like wet stone. The sun set colorlessly. Then, so distantly that I swore at first that it was my imagination, I heard a clap of thunder. Everything and everyone was still, waiting, listening for another, and when a second, louder thunderclap quickly came, the animals that remained started bleating, barking, and chittering, and a whole new set of contributors were deployed to manage what was coming. I walked slowly home, the long way, past the brown treeless hillock, and as the light faded, the rain came, soft at first, and then in fast needles, steady and strong but never angry, and I let it soak me as I stood outside my front door before I went inside. Helena was sitting at the table. She looked at me and, with a steady hand, held up an envelope. She said, The viceroy thanks you for your contribution. Inside the envelope was a Green Line pass. There was a world in which she could have kept it from me, but she didn't, which I took to mean that she didn't want know if I was using it, if using it meant that I wouldn't be coming back—if, in two dawns, I was going to board a carriage I arranged with transportation without saying goodbye. That evening, I made us both some tea and sat with her at the table, staring down into our cups while we listened to the rain.

2

HISTORY IS WRITTEN in footprints: the wolf and the deer. In this story, one's padded paw prints, thick and methodical like simple drawings, swirl around the other's airy two-toed hooves, tripping over themselves in a dance of defeat. A record of survival and failed escape. Two readings—one walks on, and one remains.

Tree-cut sunlight lands amber on the deer's wiry fur—glossy and matted with fresh blood, his opened insides sparkling. His antlers are mid-molt with velvet hanging as flesh does from his vermilion ribs. A marbly eye, wide open, captures nothing.

I sit on a rock facing the deer and take many deep breaths of this clean air. I remove my shoes to check my bandages, change the one over the blister that's been bloody for a couple days now, not getting better. I switch out the insole with the last spare Cole gave me. I've used everything he said I would, and seen everything he predicted, plus some. It could be any day or moment now that I arrive where Dylan told me to go.

I lick the mucus running over my lip, take my goggles off and wipe them, tip my head back into the light. My legs don't have much energy in them yet. I haven't eaten anything today, and haven't seen anyone in five full days—this the sixth—since I saw the mother holding her son, looking asleep in a parched arroyo, but not asleep, as I determined after shaking her shoulder. So this is the seventh day since I've seen a living someone. That was a band of twenty or thirty, walking westward across the plains at dawn. I'd woken up in the shade of a mesa and called no attention to myself. I haven't spoken to anyone since two days before that, when a WORLD rover splintered the camp I'd made with DOTEC outside an Athletics Part where you could hear cheering from inside the walls. Someone had written IDAHO in the dirt where we slept. The rover transported anyone who accepted a ride to a WORLD xenodochium, where my blisters were treated–rudimen-tarily–and I acquired some iodine capsules, dry goods, salt, and sugar, in exchange for being an audience member to a lecture by a WORLD officer, who warned of the dangers of being part of DOTEC, and promised that a rover would come the next day to take us to a Part accepting applications. Mistrustful, I left the xenodochium before dusk set in. I've seen one rover since then, but not the people inside it. So, nine days since the xenodochium–my longest stretch without conversation since the Green Line dropped me in Lake Tahoe in May, two months ago.

It's noon now, and I've been walking since sunrise through the woods with the aid of my compass, keeping the road buried in the mountains on my left, the flatlands on my right, heading east. Three days ago, I found a creek and I tracked it for two days until I found the river, which I've been following since last night when the mosquitoes were out. Near the water, they hum crazily.

Everything is close and contained here in this old-growth forest. Chickadees sing in the tree above me, a whole chorus, hop-ping along the limbs. I turn the volume down on my left hearing aid and the song vanishes. I toggle the right, but it's still dead. I turn the left up again and the song returns. There's a snap in the air. An eagle floats between branches and alights, statuesque. A ripple runs through its mottled brown and gold feathers. The song rises like the little birds are singing to announce the eagle. Its neck is long and springy as it surveys its land, water, and sky.

It waits, maybe listening, but only for a minute, and when it decides to take flight again, the forest quiets, as if in reverence. The chickadees are still. The eagle flies upstream. Everything but the water is silent. When the eagle is out of sight, and after one moment more, the chickadees start up again.

The compass needle hovers around seven o'clock. I turn on my bottom to advance it three hours, so I'm facing northeast. I consult the paper Dylan handed me the morning COHO came for him. I've memorized it, just in case.

> 44°28'04.0"N 111°56'07.9"W *Rogue Part* DOTEC *encampment good land river in foothills. Green Line Tahoe* E *to Salt Lake* N *to Kilgore go* E *of 15* S *of* ID-MT *border. Road thru mountains. Keep flatlands on right. Stay in green.*

It's all I have left of him, plus a shirt of his I wear, though his scent has been worn away.

He never told me what to look for. People, I assume—Sybil. If I find her, I hope she'll want to see me, that she hasn't outgrown me. But if she isn't at the Rogue Part, I'll have no reason to stay, other than that I've come this far.

I remember her mother's funeral, holding in our laughter. But maybe she wasn't laughing. Maybe that's a false invention of my memory.

I stare at the deer a few yards away, a thousand flies doing their slow-fast cleanup of nature's mess. I try to press it into my memory. Journaling has helped me remember patterns of behavior, the true what-happened of events in my life. Even if the big things sink through the surface of the pond, at least the surface is clear, and with some effort, I can try to dredge up the big things from the bottom. Some things will be buried forever, but that's OK. That's the basin—the container for the water and all that grows in it.

I change my socks, put on my shoes, and take care down the slope to the riverbank. I reach past the still, foamy water and into the clearness, cup my hand, coat my neck and arms, dunk my cloth helmet and tie it on. I fill my bottle and drop an iodine tablet in. I sit, listening to the river, until the iodine has done its job. Then I sip some and start walking again.

Now and then I think about what Helena wanted, if it was for me to be happy, or for her to be rid of me, or for me to understand what she believed, and for me to believe it too, or else for me to discover what I believe on my own. I often wonder what she's doing right now. I picture her writing at her table; proselytizing outside the mortuary; seeing Tobias out the door; pouring herself grappa; sitting in my room and talking to an empty bed. I try to focus on the land as it rumples and lifts and tilts beneath me.

Earth permits me. That's all I know, and I know it because I'm here, because the cold river water feels amazing on my neck and down my throat. It makes my lungs bigger, my vision sharper, and my legs stronger. Maybe it's miraculous that I'm still walking, but maybe I'm just stronger than anyone thought.

The only people who've seen all my scars are the people who've taken care of them. Helena, Michael, Cole, Gale, Dylan at some point, probably, and Sybil. I'd like to show them to someone who likes them and doesn't see them only as threats to my health, but also as marks of strength, not weakness. The good thing about scars is that they don't require my memory of them—I've never willed scar tissue into form. They tell their own story.

I stop and nearly finish the bottle of water. The pass narrows. The river's hastened into a white rush. I have to gain ground on the slick rocks to avoid falling in. I take my time in search of ledges where I can set my hands and feet, ingratiate myself with its facade—like with all the people who helped me on my journey—the Canland waste reallocation contributors who gave me a whistler when I told them I was Dylan's brother; the Green Line conductor who kept me company on the last leg of the trip to Lake Tahoe because she thought I looked scared as we neared the WORLD Neurological Research Center; another woman who disembarked with me in Lake Tahoe, having boarded the Green Line under the pretense that she was visiting her spectral son at the Center, who had in fact once been a test subject there until he died in a vegetative state—I told her I had once been a test subject at that facility too—and said she was going to join one of the companies on the outskirts trying to infiltrate and dismantle the Center, and that she would think of me while she did; the bivouacked men who taught me how to build fires, the children in their camps who sang songs and asked me to join them, and the mothers who eyed me skeptically, concerned first and foremost with their kin, but who offered what little they could; the WEDA who extinguished those giveaway fires and took my whistler and told us all to find any one of the many developing Parts, to which they could take us if we were willing and able to contribute; the gun-toting men scattered deep in the forest, picking off rovers, looting weaker DOTEC or Purists or anyone aligned with a faction or way of life that differed from their own, the same people to whom I'd wave and say in my most casual vocabulary with as little of a lisp as possible that I was trying to get to a Part in Idaho, to find my sister there, and so many of them were looking for family members too, and they were the ones who helped me most.

The gorge has widened and the river's slowed. On my left, the topography has raised me to a sheer drop, thirty, fifty, I don't know how many feet above the water. On my right, the land is too steep and rocky to test. I take my hands out of my climbing gloves; my palms are pink with heat, but uncut. I look down, see the rocks through the water. From upstream I think I hear laughter and shouting echo off the boulders above me. I press myself flat against the outcrop, with my eyes right up against the dazzling minerals welded into the rocks, every irregularity, all the smooth roughness, the bits of lichen. If I turn back, I might slip on the downhill. If I keep on, the path might narrow to a close. I breathe the way Cole taught me, feeling the swell of my belly— just a being who needs air, like everyone else. I get ready to yell.

The Earth slips and falls away. But I'm floating upward, the straps of my knapsack digging into my shoulders, my feet dangling–hoisted up from the precarious wedge between immovable rock and a free fall. The sky turns and I land on my back, higher than I was before, staring up into the clear, safe blue. A metal rod swings between my eyes, an inch from my goggles. From the other end of the foreshortened gun, a pair of mild brown eyes assess me.

"Name?"

"Tristan."

"Purpose?" His voice is reedy and post-pubescent.

"I'm hoping my friend is here."

"Your friend's name?"

"Sybil Chariots."

"How'd you find us?"

"My brother found you on the networks. He was arrested for commandeering satellites."

"State your case."

"I have no one. I have nowhere. Just me and my knapsack."

"Where you from?"

"A Restoration Part called Canland, short for the California Inland Valley Desert-Greening Project."

"Stupid name for a Part."

"I didn't name it."

He hesitates. "Your face. You've been in fights?"

"No. I have a condition called analgesia, meaning I can't feel physical pain."

"You a tuber?"

"No. I don't have a stress response. I don't need drugs. What you see is mostly self-inflicted, from when I was a child."

"Mostly?"

"My mom used to condition me–hit me. She's a Purist suicide advocate and a seamstress and a lawmaker. I ran away from her."

"How'd you get here?"

"Green Line, relocation rovers, my legs."

"No one followed you?"

"No sign of anyone in a week. Some DOTEC wandering the plains, but the opposite way."

"Do you have WORLD affiliations?"

"My father's a researcher. I don't know where he is or what he does."

The young man lowers his gun.

"Sit up."

He's wearing a green-brown tank top; his hair is curly and cut close; a big, thin nose is the centerpiece of his face; his arms are taut with young muscle; ammunition hangs in catenaries on his belt, handgun holstered on his hip, what looks like a grenade, and a knife; he wears a bracelet of stone charms carved into hearts and flowers.

"Do you need medical attention?" he asks. His lips are parted. He appears at ease.

"Probably."

"I'll take you to Ava—she'll decide about you. Give me your backpack."

I do as he says. He helps me to my feet by my elbow.

"Is Sybil here?" I ask.

Instead of telling me, he motions me forward. Once I'm ahead of him, he presses his gun into my back, to the left of my spine. He shepherds me around an outcrop. As I look back, the rocks of the gorge close over the view of the water, as if protecting itself from my eyes—Earth's drabness guarding its beauty, skeptical of me and saying, *Stay away.*

.

The ridge fans out into a meadow with forested hills rising on all sides, giving borders to the utter galaxy of bursting flowers. The young man stands beside me, my knapsack hanging from his shoulder. He lets a hand off his gun and curls his thumb and forefinger between his lips and whistles so loudly it chases birds from trees. I count the impossibly abundant colors. I feel like I'm living in one of Michael's Actualizations of the past.

"Do you mind if I have some water?" I ask.

He shrugs my bag down to his elbow and reaches inside. The gun stays trained on me. "You got a lot of shit in here," he says.

"On the side pouch," I say.

"Not much left." He shakes the bottle and then hands it to me.

My tongue feels rough and clumsy, like a stone in my mouth. I had to give my watch away last month or maybe the month before in a trade for food, so I check my pulse now by counting the beats and the seconds at the same time. It's imprecise, but enough to know my heart rate is too high.

"I have a pill in there I need to take," I say.

He eyes me as though the gun were not sufficiently conveying his mistrust. "Can it wait?" he asks.

"No."

He dumps the contents of my knapsack into the grass: pouches of dried fruit, salt tablets, iron tablets, iodine capsules, one un-burned candle and one melted halfway down, matches, Helm's book, Dylan's T-shirt, sun goggles, climbing gloves, a pair of damp socks, a sweaty insole, metal nib, pencil, compass, gauze, scissors, tape, cloth, bandages, sterilizing gel, antibiotic oint-ment, oral antibiotics, and a nearly empty bottle of beta blockers. I tap a beta blocker out, and it rolls down my palm and touches the band of Sybil's ring, which I haven't once taken off this whole journey. The band's rusted because it's not real gold. I wash the pill down with what water's left. Then I drop the empty water bottle into the pile of my belongings.

Across the meadow, I see a figure walking toward us, head wrapped in a scarf gleaming whiter than the passing clouds cast-ing shadows on the verdant hills. My head's covered in a soiled piece of padded cloth. The man and I don't speak as she nears. She has a gun strapped to her back that mocks the unit being pointed at me. Her cargo pants are rolled halfway up her shins. She's wearing sneakers like I've never seen—they cover her ankles and they're chunky like toys, dyed orange and blue. Her tank top re-veals brown arms and shoulders, muscly like the young man's. Her eyes are sharp and green, and her lids are daubed with a black substance. We're the same height, which makes her short. She regards me with a polite smile.

Through the sunny field, I trace the path she walked back to the woods where I see, protruding from a high shelf of rock, a long-barreled turret. I wonder how many others are presiding over the forest, mountains, and hills.

"I wish I lived in a place like this," I say.

"We're very lucky to," she says. "It's sacred, and we treat it like we were put here for a reason."

I'm certain, by the squint in my upper lip, that I appear less than awestruck, but I am.

"Did you all choose to be here?" I ask.

"To the extent that anyone can choose."

I exhale once, like a laugh. "Are you implying some divine purpose put you here?"

Her smile turns into an incredulous snarl, showing two slightly overlapping front teeth. "Do you know the reason you're here is that Yusuf found you and chose to bring you to me? Yusuf here, he's your god now."

I skip from her eyes to his, and back to hers. "I'm sorry, I didn't mean to correct you. I've had a lot of time to think about free will since I left my old Part, Canland—the reasons I left, how much agency I have, what kind of life I want."

"It's OK. I did not expect to get into a teleological argument with a child today."

I nod. The river whispers distantly; insects dance in crowds above the flowers; we three stand still and comfortable as trees. What happens here when Earth's position changes?

"Are you Ava?"

"I sure am. And you are?"

"Tristan." I scan the meadow again. The colors are so varied and so vibrant that they seem to move, like all the flowers are mingling. "Just so you know, I don't take teleology seriously as a branch of philosophy. I don't believe I have an innate purpose. Maybe I used to believe it, but not now."

"What do you believe now?"

"Well, I liked the way my surgeon put it—he said we have a magnet in our hearts. I play piano. I like music because it doesn't require representation to be understood. It just is. We innately know what's harmonious and what's not."

"And you value that? Precision?"

I shrug, then nod, looking past Ava, and all around.

"What brings you here?" she asks.

"I'm looking for my friend."

"What's your friend's name?"

"Sybil Chariots. That was her name when I knew her."

Ava says nothing, but not with any imploring look. I'd guess she's about Cameron's age—a child during the war—but it's hard to tell with her headscarf and the shadow it bands across her eyes. I glance at her and then away again, to a bee climbing an orange stamen inside a pink-petaled flower.

"Philosophy is a study, not a guide to living," she suddenly says. "Which isn't to say it can't spark an illuminating debate. But practically speaking, everyone here in my Mazra'a serves the purpose of my Mazra'a, because they believe in that purpose, which we have determined ourselves." She squints up at the sky, making a thinking face. "So, you know what, I take it back. I meant what I said, and sometimes it's necessary to state the obvious. We are here for a reason, many reasons, as are you."

I look at her. "Is Sybil here?"

She angles her face slightly away from me toward Yusuf, and it's in this three-quarters profile that I notice her nose bridge is pinched in the middle and quite asymmetrical, in fact. When her face returns to me, I can see, by comparison, that she held a welcome countenance upon meeting me, because now she looks more serious.

"No one knows we're here," she says in a deeper voice. "Our Seers constantly monitor satellites so that we appear to WORLD as a fully functioning Part a hundred miles from here, but invisible where we really are."

"My brother called this place a Rogue Part."

"He wouldn't happen to be the satellite interloper who accessed us about two years ago?"

"Probably."

"No one's accessed us since then. Our Seers protect us in the sky, and people like Yusuf protect us on the ground."

Yusuf is unmoving and impassive, his eyes boring into me.

"Years of theft and reassembly of WORLD equipment have given the Mazra'a electricity, supply access—all the superficial benefits of a real Part," Ava continues. "I turned away three strong young men a few weeks ago, valuable farmhands. I didn't trust them to honor our peace and, frankly, our complacency. We don't live in self-denial. The people here do things they enjoy. But I can't over-state how important this land is to me. It did not always look like this. We'll protect it from WORLD at any cost."

"I come from a Restoration Part."

"I know," she says. She sighs, creating a strange type of smile. "I can't in good conscience keep this from you—there is indeed a girl here named Sybil Chariots, who came from a Part called Can-land."

"Oh," I say. "Oh," I say again. I feel so happy I could die; I could just lie down and rest.

I make saliva in my mouth and swallow. I blink hard and open my eyes wide. The day is getting brighter. "Do you mind if I put on my sun goggles?"

"Of course."

I kneel, rummage through my scattered things, and grab my sun goggles. My attention's interrupted by a sonorous metal creak, like many bicycles in need of lubrication together grinding to a halt. I lift my face to locate the noise. Ava seems unfazed, and doesn't even turn as, fifty yards behind her, a grass-covered hatch yawns open. A person emerges from underground, sporting wild dark hair and knee-length shorts, naked from the waist up. They stretch their limbs, letting their face bake like a roll in the sun. They close the hatch and walk a spiral path for a minute with a gait like a creature whose feet never quite touch the ground. Then they sit, lie back, and disappear among a splash of flowers. Yusuf stares at the person, but his gun never sways.

"You're all right, Yusuf," Ava says.

He lowers the gun and walks off. I take one long last look at all the flowers before I take off my goggles, and everything becomes blurry, and then with my sun goggles, everything is clear again, but gray. Ava's eyebrows go circumflex as she watches me. I stand and give her a thumbs-up to show I'm ready to proceed, and she smiles in a way that seems acceptant.

"I'll bring you to see her in a bit. But listen—we've had zero infiltrations since your brother was bounced by our Seers, and we plan to keep it that way. If rovers come in to splinter us, we've got protection all over." Her hand comes up and makes a loose gesture, indicating the ubiquity of sentries like Yusuf. "But if it comes to it, everyone in my Mazra'a—those who are able to—will have to fight to defend it. This is my home, and I'm careful about who I invite to call it theirs too. As you can see, we treat the land with love, and we treat each other with love too, even when we don't like each other. We want nature to thrive, but I have to say, not at the expense of freedom of thought and physical comfort. I think it's wonderful you're a musician. To me, love between humans requires a reverence for forces more powerful than humanity. Does that make sense to you?"

I want Ava to know that even though I'm here for Sybil, I will do whatever I can to fit in with the way of life here. If Sybil has stayed after all this time, and Dylan sent us both here because it's safe, and they have land like this, then where else would I go?

"It does," I say. "My mother acted like she was the most powerful force on Earth. She was a Purist leader and suicide advocate. On the other hand, my father abandoned his family to do research, to save everyone else, because he accidentally caused a lot of deaths." I do a smile like I'm joking, and say, "So I'm just trying to find a happy medium."

Ava grins, her cheeks making her eyes narrow, though she doesn't laugh. "My father told us that the dead love a good joke, especially ones at their expense, and my mother told him that if he kept saying stuff like that to us, she'd make sure he was laughing soon." Her smile eases. "This land was once my family's farm." Then her smile fades. "They were killed when it was burned down by Purist extremists during the war. I spent years as part of the Diaspora of the Environmental Collapse, before I returned to rebuild my home."

She doesn't have that blank stare that Helm and Helena and Hugo had when they'd talk about the war. No, Ava talks about it without reliving it.

"The militia who burned it down drove me to an outpost and left me there. WORLD provided us nothing. There are few things we can do to rebel against WORLD, but living here, outside their jurisdiction, using their supplies to live within our own society, is one. In short, we do what we want. But everyone here has also lost something that, if not for losing it, they wouldn't be here." She takes a deep breath and presses her hands together in front of her. Her welcoming expression returns, and her hands fall back by her sides. "There are a hundred and ten of us—twelve children under the age of twelve, some of whom were born here, and eleven between thirteen and nineteen, thirty twentysomethings, twenty in their thirties, about a dozen in their forties, twenty or so older that. Not everyone's ideal is the same, but majority rules, and we've never had to kick anybody out."

"You're like Robin H—" I start coughing. My throat's too dry. I suck my cheeks in, trying to make my salivary glands work. Ava unhitches a canteen from her belt and lets me drink from it.

"Thank you." I offer it back to her, but she urges me to drink more. I finish what's left.

How many Seers beneath my feet right now are doing the thing Dylan was arrested for? I look down at my dirty, bursting shoes, then up at Ava again, our faces barely five feet off the ground, trying to ignore the similarities between her story and the one

Viceroy Hugo told me, and the possibility that my parents had once been here, doing the burning she speaks of. If I choose to tell her, I first need her to understand who I am, so she doesn't see her humorous parents' eyes on fire every time she looks at me—if, in fact, this is even the same place; how many identical stories are there?

"WORLD kept me in a Research Center for over a year to study my brain for spectral properties," I say. "My mom traded me away during that time for future benefits."

"That's awful."

"She did the same thing when I was a baby. WORLD took me away, and I didn't come home until I was three."

"We have people here who've been through something similar," she says. "Magda and her daughter Rêve escaped from a rover that was transporting Rêve back to one of the Parts where they cultivate autism in children."

"What do you mean? They were in a Spectral Part?"

"We say autism here. Euphemisms protect evil men. You understand what I mean by that?"

"Yes. You don't have to simplify the language. I have abnormal verbal processing skills."

"All right, then," Ava says. "Under the guise of societal advancement, WORLD has done what they want with children—children like you. Most people don't know this, and we only know it because of our Seers, but Arturo Eagles' long-term intention is to engineer the human trait of hypersensitivity, so people can be satisfied and subdued with less sensory stimulation. His theory is that an overabundance of unnecessary stimuli has caused humans to evolve in the short-term to favor desensitization. Arturo Eagles wants to disseminate treatments to increase sensory sensitivity—through Sensorium, electrotherapy, even fecal transplants in pregnant women, to cultivate the intestinal microbiome that produces the gene for autism."

She pauses, waiting for me to absorb this information. She can't see my eyes because of my sun goggles. Her headscarf's crisp whiteness is like the bedsheets in the Safe Haven. I try to escape to there, in my mind—dressing beds, feeding babies, helping scared sick people get healthy—it was safe there.

She was a child, younger than me, when her family—

I touch my helmet, bow my head, and close my eyes. If I was an early research subject, I'll never know. Does Helena know? Did she and Michael make some decision together? Was his office a makeshift Research Center for Spectrality, and did he engineer in me a trait that would alter my perception of the world, to make me his experiment; his superfluous second child? Isn't one of the axioms of humanity that we surrender posterity to forces more powerful than a parent's ego?

But what the fuck does it matter? I don't care. I don't want to fight this. I just want to see Sybil. I know what I've been given, and I don't want to search anymore. I just want to live.

"Why?" I say. It just comes out. I'm not sure what I'm asking, or whom.

"Well," Ava says, as I try to hush the distractions of what I suspect—who would ever know this place had been a field of ashes?— and her voice is subdued. "Let's say a million people live in a city in the foothills of a forest, and all the human activity in the city starts to kill the forest. But everyone in the city has had the trait of sensory-hypersensitivity engineered in them, so the aesthetic value of the forest remains the same, in their eyes. They hear one birdsong as a thousand in chorus; a trickling stream is a rushing river; a handful of evergreens inspires the same sense of connection with nature as before the forest was cut down. In that case, they'll feel less inclined to rebel against the forces that are killing the forest, because they only know what their senses tell them. So, if a dense population of human beings lives pressed up against what seems to be a thriving natural ecosystem, then WORLD can move at its own pace toward Dominion without the threat of another war over environmental control. In short, give people less, but make them think it's more. The concept of austerity is right, but kidnapping children, manipulating their perception . . ." Her top lip makes a duckbill and she shakes her head, gives a sigh. "I don't know the end of the story."

I don't move my head, but with just my eyes—hidden by my dark lenses—I watch Yusuf walk the edge of the meadow, bending, pulling plants from the Earth.

"Are you OK?" asks Ava, keeper of WORLD secrets.

She wears a sash of ammunition; she spends her day perched in a turret; she's always on guard for the next band of vandals to take what's hers and leave a trail of ashes. Yet, she's talking to me, of all people, like we're friends.

"Yes," I say. "I'm fine. I have a congenital insensitivity to pain. It has caused a hormonal imbalance that results in behavioral abnormalities. So, whatever extreme reaction I should be having, I'm not."

Ava nods slowly, her mouth pinched in a kindly sort of frown. "Sybil talks about you."

"I'm happy to hear that. Keep going, though, please."

"Our Seers," she says, "are the best satellite surfers in the world. They've accessed Arturo Eagles' conferences with his researchers. He tells them the story of his brother, who had autism. Arturo would take his brother into nature to soothe him, but the Evanescence had already begun. So, even before he officially founded WORLD, Arturo and his researchers invented the Sensorium so his brother could always be in nature. He could see polar bears in the snow, monkeys in the rainforest, whales in the ocean—and believe it. In the Sensorium, his brother found tranquility. But, as you might know is possible, his brother became dependent on the technology, and couldn't bear to take the Sensorium off his head. Arturo Eagles moved his brother into a Sensorium Dome where he ate, slept, and lived until he passed away."

"Shouldn't you make this information widely known?"

"The institutions are already in place. This is the result of the war, not the start of a new one."

"The result of one war is always the beginning of the next," I say. I imagine what Helm's response would be: *That's keen of you, T-Bird.*

Yusuf's kneeling with his back to us, far out there, blending in with the woods.

"I don't want to fight," I say. "I just want to see my friend."

"I understand," says Ava. "And there's a good chance you'll never have to. But like I said, there may come a time." She looks at my mouth, which I have made into a short, brave frown. She sighs. "What do you say we go find Sybil?"

I'm here. I've made it. I made it all the way here. I don't have anywhere else to go.

"Ava," I say. "Did you have two brothers?"

Her face changes—narrowed eyes and a smile. "Yes. How did you know that?"

I don't know whether to nod or shake my head. I take off my sun goggles and switch them out for my regular ones. Her hands ball up and flex open and then rest on her hips.

"And you had goats?" I say.

"Yes," she says, in a different tone of voice.

I keep my eyes open and locked onto hers, green and sharp and wise, and I see them staring down the right side of a gun—just a child, shooting an invader in the gut to defend her home.

"I think my parents were the ones who burned your farm—Helena and Michael Weekes. My mother fixed your well, and then my father tried to steal one of your goats. You shot one of their company, and then my mother dove on top of you. My father threw an explosive at your house. They were with the viceroy of my old Part."

She doesn't move. The sun bounces off the high drifting cotton balls, birds cut through the great inverted sea, a leaf drops prematurely, a bee brings loot to the hive, the river runs its own ordered universe beneath the mountains it erodes, and somewhere, someone is being killed. I don't know what else to say, but for all the people who hated me for just staring at them, saying nothing, I have to speak.

"I'm sorry. I wish I was nervous to be saying this to you, but I'm calm, and I'm sorry. My body doesn't tell me when I should be upset and afraid. I'm sorry if I shouldn't have told you, and I'm sorry it happened. I'm sorry I came here. I didn't know. I don't think I knew."

There's now sweat on her forehead beneath the hem of her headscarf. Her mouth is long and straight. Her eyes are wide open; they flutter, then flit to my helmet. She turns her back to me and takes two steps forward, then stops.

I could name what she's feeling, but I'll never feel it. People are complicated, and I'm not—this is what Helena always meant.

"I'll be fine, whatever you do with me," I say to the gun strapped diagonally across her back, the barrel pointing to the ground. "No matter what," I say, "I'll be fine."

Ava holds a hand up. She looks off to Yusuf, who's standing straight, turning around, coming back toward us, holding a big bouquet of flowers—orange, pink, yellow, purple, blue, white.

Why didn't Dylan tell me he found this place while searching for the site of what Helena told him Michael had done? It's like I'm answering for Dylan too, again and again and again.

Ava turns her face halfway to me, then starts shaking her head, unable to look at me—the past coming back to haunt her in physical form. She's gazing off at some space that's meaningless to me, but not to her. She must know what every part of this land used to be—where the house stood, the barn, the goat pen, the driveway with the SPVs, and all the spots where she played and fell and learned and laughed and cried and grew.

"I don't know you," she says. "But you're a helpless child." She pauses, letting that fact sink into me. "Yusuf will take you to get medical attention."

She walks off toward Yusuf, who's kneeling to the Seer, and the Seer's sitting up and taking the bouquet and stuffing the flowers to their nose. Their wild hair is tangled and full of grass. Their skin is the color of heartwood.

Ava stops, says something to Yusuf, who nods once, and then she carries on, getting smaller and smaller, until she disappears into the forest.

The Seer turns around to see me, and waves—wide smile, hair in their eyes.

AB.

No—just a strange trick of the mind. My dreams and my obsessions—the days I yearn for, when I could sit and picture their face, looking forward to the next time I saw them—alive in me and making noise, wanting to be seen. The Seer sniffs the bouquet of flowers again. They lie back in the grass.

Yusuf comes striding toward me. "Good?" he says. A smile breaks across his face. "Welcome to the Mazra'a," he says, walking past. Quickly, I stuff my belongings into my knapsack. Ava's empty canteen is in the pile. I pick it up and run after Yusuf, less concerned with the reasons Ava's let me stay than with the distance we are from the moment in which this coincidence was conceived.

3

I'M SPINNING SYBIL'S ring on my finger like a screw that's holding my luck in me. She's sitting with her waist folded so her elbow's resting on the bench of the laavu, still in her second-act makeup—feline around the eyes, yellowish down her cheeks, heavy scarlet on her lips—and her head is leaned toward me and staring into the low fire. After our first few talks—her journey was similar to mine, landmarks in common, but the details too many to recount—I worried that she might ignore me (the way I ignored AB), seeing how close she was with her friends here, and how they spoke to each other in clips like they could read each other's minds. I thought about how I've always had to spell everything out for everyone and have everyone spell it all out for me. I hope Sybil's not exhausted by me. She'd often cut our conversations short to run to rehearsal, or go off to do things I shouldn't, like swim in the river or climb the boulders. At first, she didn't en-courage me to come along, perhaps not wanting the responsibil-ity of me. But the other day, she invited me to the river with her and some of her friends, and I just sat with my feet in the water, looking up at the cliffs that protect the Mazra'a from intruders. For every time Sybil's told me she's so happy I'm here, there's been a time that I've felt like I shouldn't have come. But then I remember that she was never obligated to be my friend; that my house was an extra mile-and-a-half round trip walk from hers, and yet, she'd walk me home from school every day; that I was the only one, aside from Dylan, to whom she confessed her plan to leave; and that, maybe, she's been carrying a guilt with her this entire time for leaving me behind in Canland, even though she's never said so. Sometimes I worry that she only did all that to fill some hole inside herself that has been so nourished here that I am, in fact, an inharmonious reprise.

She was hypnotizing tonight, onstage, like a glass bottle keeping a storm trapped inside—if the storm shattered her, everything would vanish, and yet, how could she willfully release something as rare and precious as a storm she could hold?

Yusuf—who wrote the play's musical score, and despite our first encounter is actually quite garrulous—says to her across the fire, "You were so good, just like, so full of life, and so, you know, in-the-moment. And yeah, like, we all knew you would be because of rehearsals, but that was like another stratosphere."

Sybil smiles and says, "Thanks. The music's the most important part, though. No one realizes that it's how they know what to feel."

Yusuf laughs, and I'm reminded of the entity that Helm once said is responsible for giving some people great talents and giving other people disease. (I myself am a reason to believe it's all determined by the same entity.)

When I first saw Sybil right after the show, she didn't seem as excited as everyone else seemed for her. She said Nadine always warns her about post-show depression, and she's felt it before, but she doesn't yet have a way of dealing with it. Nadine has a post-show ritual, which she learned in her Arts Part, to combat the addiction of performance, so she's in her A-frame now, meditating, and won't come back out tonight. And even though Nadine fit perfectly into every line and beat as if it were her contribution, Sybil stole the show.

"I loved the music," I say across the fire to Yusuf. "I didn't know music like that existed."

"Hey, thanks, man," he says in an affectedly nice sort of way, like he does whenever someone compliments him. He's still wearing his tuxedo–though the audience could hardly see him in the pit, behind his music stand, surrounded by the other musicians–which he says is how musicians used to dress, and that he'd meant it ironically. "I guess you'd call it like prayer-punk," he says. I don't know what he means. Yusuf knows a lot more about music than I do, but he's teaching me with the CDs and instruments we have here.

He turns to Jolie–who's sitting on the ground next to him, working at a leaf with her thumbnail, trying to separate the top layer to reveal the inside–and starts explaining to her all the ways that Ava, who's of Israeli heritage, married different religions and cultural myths in her writing of the play. Jolie just keeps sliding her thumbnail back and forth against the thinnest edge of the leaf. She's claimed to have succeeded in peeling apart a leaf before, but everyone, myself included, doubts this very much, unless she had the assistance of precision tools, which she brags that she did not.

Sybil and I look at each other, and she smiles. I smile back, and then we both look into the fire. I like sitting, doing nothing, listening to Yusuf talk aimlessly.

On my third day here, as I was leaving the infirmary, I asked Sybil if she'd yet seen or heard from her mom. Suddenly solemn, she nodded, and said, I see her all the time. I couldn't tell if she was happy or sad about that, but then she sort of changed the subject and said that she enjoyed life here so much more than in Canland. "It wasn't that we weren't free there, it was that it was so boring, I thought I was going to die," she said. She then explained to me a theory of hers that everything we do is to combat boredom. "Boredom leads to loneliness, and loneliness makes life meaningless, so the true challenge of life is finding excitement everywhere." I asked her, "Couldn't you have found excitement in

Canland?" She shook her head, and said that, in Canland, she'd stopped seeing. "Couldn't that happen to you here?" I said. "Well," she replied, "it hasn't yet."

Then we stopped talking about Canland, and we walked the quarter-mile main path through the Mazra'a. We began at the mouth of the meadow, where I first entered with Yusuf—though I'd hardly noticed a thing about the Mazra'a then because I was too distracted by my first encounter with Ava. Sybil showed me the thirtyish wood-and-canvas A-frames, arranged like random pieces on a chessboard. They were separated from the adjacent metal generators and storage units by a swath of rubber—fascinating material—used to protect some underground wiring. She waved to the couple of people working in the fenced-in vegetable patches, like miniature Canland fields, before skipping toward the brick and clay studios, which she was excited to show me because of all the music and art made in there as well as more practical creations like textiles and small motors. At the end of the path, where the boulders rise and the forest thickens, we stopped at the modest stone prayer houses, and Sybil said, "Personally, I prefer to pray to the hills and trees and the river and—well, real nature." To which I said nothing, only smiled with my lips together, not wanting to go further. Then we veered off the path, where she introduced me to a couple people her age relaxing on the benches in the laavu—a hexagonal pyramidal structure, with three sides open and three sides walled, supporting a pointed roof pitched forward over the center, where a metal hood hangs above the fire pit for the smoke to rise through—the Finnish equivalent of a lean-to.

I met Magda that day, when Sybil showed me to my A-frame. There were children's books on the floor, a circular jute rug, a writing table that reminded me of Helena's, a kitchenette with a hot plate, wires of twinkle lights strung up in rows to meet at the high central roof beam to look like stars, and two beds pushed to opposite walls of the one-room house. Rêve, who's a year younger than me, and a bit taller, but about as thin, was sitting on her and

Magda's bed with her knees up, sliding her bottom lip back and forth against her top teeth. There was a poster at the foot of the bed with pictures of animals and objects, and cards with words on them: *eating, sleeping, running, laughing, carrot, cold, friends, wind.* Some words were in their proper place next to the illustrations, just a bit askew, and the rest were untouched, as if Rêve had lost interest in the matching game. Magda slid a battery-powered keyboard out from under my bed, and said to me, "Ava says you play." I nodded, and she replied, "Good, Rêve will love to hear." So I played for a bit, and Rêve didn't seem to react one way or the other. But later, as we were going to sleep—Magda and Rêve in bed together, twinkle lights on overhead—Rêve started to scream, but less in fear than just to make noise, something Magda calls *stimming.* Magda said, "You want to play something?" After a moment, I realized she was talking to me. So I picked up the keyboard and played a song I thought was soothing, and soon Rêve was calm and quiet. Magda said, "You like Tristan's songs?" I played some more, and within minutes I heard snoring. I slid the keyboard back under my bed. I was glad to help Rêve fall asleep. I'm not sure Magda ever sleeps.

Right now, at the end of the bench to my left, Magda's seated with her legs crossed into a nest, on which Rêve's cuddled up with her head pressed between her mom's collarbones, staring into the fire and doing the back-and-forth thing with her lip, while Magda's looking off through the open face of the laavu at the visible starry sky. If Magda moves too much, then Rêve might start, and they'll have to go back to our house, but if so, I'll follow them so I can play a song for Rêve. I don't want to get up, though—I want to stay until the fire burns out.

I glance at Sybil again, and I say, "Dylan would've loved that."

She makes a face and says, "Would he?"

We don't talk about Dylan much. Right before he was arrested, he told me to only say good things about him, and while I have plenty of good things to say, Sybil, maybe two weeks ago, in a tired and exasperated moment, said, "He was a bad brother to you, and a bad friend to me, and I don't want to talk about him!" Sybil apologized later for her outburst, and said that if I ever felt the need to talk about Dylan, I could. But I definitely don't bring him up every time I think of him.

Now, I shrug, and say, "Maybe he would've liked to have an opinion of it."

Sybil laughs. I know she knows we wouldn't be here if not for him. I've told Sybil—only Sybil—that Helena and Michael and Viceroy Hugo were once here at the Mazra'a. When I told her, she said to me, "It's not your fault, Tristan, and you did the right thing by saying so, and now, actually, Ava might be able to exorcise some demons." Sybil's prone to this spiritual talk, like many people in the Mazra'a—but she was right about Ava . . .

After I came out of the infirmary—I was so malnourished that I had to stay in there for a few days—I went to Ava's house to return her canteen, and she said to me, "Do you want to tell me what's become of the people who killed my family?" I gave her a quick summary of my family, Canland, and myself. She sat at her desk, face unchanging, perhaps even distracted. She said, "We don't choose our parents, we only choose how we see them." "I don't need to protect them anymore," I replied. She stood up and thanked me for being honest with her, and we shook hands. Then I looked around her A-frame. There was an electric guitar leaning against the wall, and her two dogs, Alpha and Beta, were curled up on pillows on opposite sides of the room. The one-room house smelled like rosemary. Ava sat back down at her desk and picked up her pen, and said, "Tristan, if you don't mind, I have to make some revisions to these pages before rehearsal this afternoon." So I thanked her again for letting me live here, and left.

Six of us are around the fire now, and there's a moment of quiet.

"It's funny," Sybil says in a hushed voice meant only for me, scooting closer on the bench, sitting up, pulling the blanket that's warming me over herself too. "I want to talk and joke around and stuff, but I feel like I've just been talking for two hours, and if I keep talking, I'll seem like an attention-hog."

"Ha," I say. "Probably."

Sybil scrunches up her nose.

"Maybe thinking that means you're assuming that everyone's still seeing you as the center of attention," I say.

"So you're saying I am an attention-hog."

"I don't think I said that."

Yusuf starts talking again, to either Jolie or Magda, whoever will listen. Magda's not-listening face is more obvious than Jolie's, perhaps because Magda's older and doesn't feel like she needs to pretend, so Yusuf ends up turning toward Jolie again, who's just a year or so older than Yusuf, in their early twenties.

Sybil says to me, "Maybe to be an actor you have to be an attention-hog. Maybe it's like my way of showing everyone that I think I have a deep emotional well that I can draw from, and that I think I'm deep enough that I can stir their hearts and illuminate something in themselves."

"Or," I say, "maybe everyone has a deep emotional well, and you're just being generous by doing what most people would be too afraid to do."

"Or maybe I'm being selfish by handling my emotions through Ava's words, while everyone else copes with their shit in a totally normal, healthy, semi-private way."

"Yeah," I say. "If you were bad, maybe. Or maybe it's just a vocation and you don't have a choice."

"What do you know about acting?" she teases.

I think of Byron and the first time I ever feigned hostility, and how we strangely became something like friends. I've never told Sybil about him, though for no particular reason, and yet I also know I won't. I want to keep certain memories, and to not have to explain them. They help me think of Canland fondly, which I want to, despite everything.

"This is the biggest production we've done," Sybil says, "but whenever I perform, even if it's like a vignette at night by the fire, when it's over, I feel like that time is gone forever."

"It is," I say.

"I know," she says, "but I mean in a way that's different from living, or even other arts, like writing. It happens once, and then it's gone."

"Maybe that's what makes it special," I say. "It's more like real life."

"Maybe," Sybil says.

"But you love to do it, right?" I ask, momentarily worried she'll find a reason to want to leave this place too.

"Of course," she says.

I nod and see Makenna and Charlie coming toward the laavu, and I involuntarily look down at my hands and start spinning Sybil's ring again, then turn my head to face Sybil. Her hair's longer now, almost touching her shoulders, and so curly that if you stretched one of her hairs straight it would reach down to the middle of her back.

I catch a snippet of Yusuf's conversation with Jolie. "All the concepts are basically transferrable, the djinn being the dark spirits in Islamic mythology, and the embodiment of spirit in Christianity, and also reincarnation in Buddhism, which is also a Jewish concept, even though they don't call it reincarnation," he says.

Ava wrote themes of the Jewish diaspora into the play, which was set in an unspecified country in 1492, the year of the Alhambra Decree, which exiled Jews from Spain, and the same year a European explorer crash-landed on the American continent—not that the audience necessarily needed to know this to enjoy the play. Obviously, everyone in the Mazra'a can relate on some level to diasporic struggle.

Since I've been here, I haven't heard the word DOTEC spoken by anyone but myself. Religion, however, is a common topic in the discussions of history.

Magda and Rêve stayed home from the play, just in case. They were sitting out here in the laavu by the fire before any of us came to join them. Rêve loves the heat, light, constant movement, and soft sounds the fire makes.

When Makenna steps into the firelight, a couple strides ahead of Charlie, she says, "Hello, everyone," and sits on the bench with some space between Sybil and herself.

"Hey, guys," Charlie says, sitting on the bench next to Makenna, and I realize that, collectively, the people here now in the laavu hang out more with me than with Sybil. I'm not sure where Sybil's close friends are—not that she doesn't get along with Makenna, Charlie, Yusuf, Jolie (who's still working her nail back and forth in the smallest motions against the edge of the leaf), Magda, and Rêve (who has a small obsession with Sybil's curls, maybe because Magda keeps Rêve's hair short, styled with cute swooping bangs). It's just that, when I spend time with these friends, Sybil's usually not there. Sybil's friends are, on the whole, harder for me to converse with. Which isn't to say they're rude or conceited, but just that they don't ask questions so much as posit potential rules of existence, love, and sex, and as much as I'd like to participate, I don't feel I have much to add; I feel invisible to them. But tonight, after the play, when I was expecting Sybil to go off with the rest of the cast or with her friends, she instead asked what I was going to do, and when I said, "Sit in the laavu," she came with me.

"Sybil, you were beautiful tonight," says Charlie, though it's hard for me to hear him, with my hearing aid dead, and him being to my right, at the end of the bench. I put in a request to the Seers for a new battery. They estimated it would take at least a month, and I've been here for a month, so every day now, I hope.

"Thanks," Sybil says. She draws a breath like she's going to say more, but then doesn't.

"Good job, Makenna," I say.

"Oh, you're nice," she says, putting her hair up in a ponytail. "I just had to remember my lines."

The reality is that Makenna's so noticeably beautiful that, to paraphrase Wes and Kamal's assessment of her performance, it almost didn't matter what she did up there on stage. "I could watch her knit for an hour," said Kamal after the play had ended. "Yes," Wes said, "but what about her performance?" And Kamal answered, "That's just the thing—I didn't notice."

I think what he said is unfair, though, considering that Makenna was the main villain, and if her performance failed, the whole thing would've failed. The curtain rose to reveal her sobbing over her father on his deathbed, right at the moment she assumed the throne. For the whole play, she was a bit histrionic, but with Nadine's steadiness as the main hero, and Sybil's storm-in-a-bottle fragility, Makenna's indulgence actually provided some comic relief.

Yusuf has stopped talking to Jolie, and it almost looks as if he's been consumed by the darkness behind him. Jolie, who has Filipino ancestry, looks the very color of the fire itself. I look to Makenna, whose dark skin has turned purple in the firelight. Charlie's, Magda's, Rêve's, and likely my own pale skin have all turned yellow. Sybil's makeup has small streaks of sweat in it. I wonder if she's forgotten it's still on.

The total silence has gone on for longer than I expected. Everyone must be on their own private thought-trains. Jolie looks up from her leaf and around at everyone, keeping her hands very still, raises her eyebrows, sighs, and returns her attention to her leaf. It makes me giggle for some reason. That sends everyone else into a fit of laughter, except for Magda, who just laughs with the corners of her eyes. I suppose I have an unexpected effect on people sometimes.

After everyone settles down, Makenna says, "Hi, Rêve."

Rêve's flicking her top lip back and forth against her bottom teeth now, still staring into the fire with half her face lit up. Magda says into the top of her daughter's head, as if putting it into Rêve's brain, "Hi, Makenna," and then kisses her hair.

I've gotten to know Magda the best. We talk every night before bed, sometimes briefly—*How was your day? Good and yours?*—and other times for so long that it takes us all the way to sleeping. I've been cautious not to superimpose my relationship with Helena on my friendship with Magda, but Magda understands me in a way none of the others quite can because she's a mother, and not only that, but the mother of a girl with autism, and not only that, but a mother who was given benefits to keep the baby, and underwent a procedure she wasn't informed on the details of until after Rêve turned five and still hadn't said her first word, and the two of them were transferred to a Part where they cultivate and study autism in children. She once said to me, "You can either be angry at everyone—and no one would even blame you—or, you could not."

Yusuf says to Jolie, "How long is that going to take?" And when Jolie doesn't answer, he says, "Do you want to do it for any reason other than to do it, or are you curious about the inside? Haven't you ever seen the inside of a leaf? Isn't it boring?"

"No," says Jolie.

"No—no to what?" Yusuf says, and makes himself laugh, deep and loud, the way he does at his own jokes. I've seen other people look away or shake their heads when he laughs, or even overheard them say he's annoying, but I love Yusuf. He's always kind to me—he invites me to his house and shows me music—and for every minute he spends chatting and laughing, he spends an hour perched in the forested mountains defending the Mazra'a. Also, I've deduced that he's in love with that Seer with the wild hair (who I've still not officially met because the Seers hardly ever come out), because he doesn't feel the need to always be talking to, around, or at them. Similarly, when he finds a song he really likes, he stops talking, but when there's no music on, or he doesn't like what's playing, he talks nonstop. And yet, I know just how stolid he can be, from the day he pulled me up from the crag above the river. Maybe I'll tell him that I was in love once, and that it made me only want to listen, and see if he mentions the Seer to whom he brought flowers.

I've since gone back to the place where Yusuf pulled me up, and looked down on the trail I walked and the river beneath. I don't know how I stumbled upon that trail, but it's clear that if I'd taken another few steps, I would have fallen.

I keep spinning Sybil's ring on my finger.

"Where is everyone?" Sybil says. There are only eight of us around the fire.

"A bunch of people are at the observatory," Makenna says. "We came from there. It's really clear. You can see stars all the way down through the pass. The stars are lower than the mountains, and there are two planets out."

Part of me wants to go see, and part of me knows that there will be other cosmological phenomena to look forward to, perhaps even the same arrangement in the sky one year from now. But the fire, the blanket, and Sybil next to me are all warm and cozy, and I like who I'm sitting here with, and this might never happen again. I could probably ask them all, or maybe we'll just start doing it on our own, but I also feel that there's something still lingering in the air from after the show—a tension that doesn't need to snap, but can just rest, like the moon settling into its orbit, a pocket in space, a rare and singular alignment.

"If you could go to the moon, would you?" I say.

"Oh, yeah," says Yusuf, like he's considered the question a thousand times, even visualized himself on the moon.

"No way," says Makenna.

"Why?" I say.

"Because," she says, but then pauses. "Well, would I be guaranteed to live?"

"No," I say.

"Then no way," she says.

Magda has a small smile on, like she's just enjoying listening to us talk.

"I wouldn't," says Sybil. "There'd be nothing to do."

"You could see Earth," I say.

"I don't need to," Sybil says. "I don't need to see the Earth from outer space to know it's small. Or that it's big, but relatively small. It doesn't feel small, and I don't want it to. I find no comfort in thinking about how big the universe is." I can tell she's shaking her head the slightest bit by the way her hair moves. She thumbs the band of one of the rings she wears. I don't know where Polly got those rings, or where the stones came from, but Sybil might— she's never said.

I noticed that in Ava's play, there weren't any existential or philosophical questions. It was all about the ways the characters related to one another. There was one character who devoted his mind to esoteric questions, but we never heard more from him than half a soliloquy, which was interrupted by Nadine sauntering onto the stage to literally and symbolically shut him up.

At the beginning of the performance, the clouds were heavy and indigo as the sun was setting, but the weather held. Makenna was bereaved over the death of her father, who was also the king, though it meant she would assume power. During the king's funeral, when the city should have been quiet and somber, there was great chaos. As men were being robbed, animals disappeared from sight, and a prayer house was vandalized, Nadine—a poor homeless orphan—was crashed into by a street vendor—Sybil—and Nadine's dog was crushed beneath the weight of Sybil's cart. The poor and homeless were taken to trial for this disruption. Their defense was to blame it on the djinn—the dark, shapeshifting spirits—and Makenna exiled all the vagrants from the city. However, Nadine was so bereaved over her dog that she didn't attend the trial, and so was chased out of the city by royal guards. Sybil felt so guilty that she followed Nadine outside the gates. Most but not all of the djinn-seers survived in the desert, wandering first away from, and then back toward the city. Slowly, Sybil and Nadine turned from enemies to friends. Though Nadine could not teach Sybil to see djinn, she taught Sybil to recognize when the djinn were acting up. Now allied, they both disguised themselves in identical feline makeup and snuck back into the city. Then, to gain access to the Royal Palace, Nadine ingratiated herself with Makenna's suitor, the philosopher (perhaps to show how easily metaphysical thinkers can be swayed by physical temptation). With Nadine and Sybil both in disguise, they were able to advance through the palace. But when Makenna discovered their deceit, she ordered Sybil—thinking her to be Nadine, who was in fact in the royal chambers—immediately to death. Then, Nadine's dog—who had really never died, but was always a djinn in disguise—returned to save Sybil's life. (Ava's dog Beta had played the djinn dog, following every command perfectly.) Makenna rushed to the safety of her royal chambers, and found Nadine there, who warned Makenna of what awaited her outside the city gates: retribution for having valued the ceremony of her father's death over the lives of the poor benighted. Weapon in hand, Nadine ordered Makenna out of her own city, and that she must walk the same path the wanderers had trod—for forty days and forty nights—before she could return. As she left the city for the desert, Makenna passed by all the djinn-seers returning home. Sybil said goodbye to Nadine and left the Royal Palace, went out into the street, and sat on the curb beside one of the djinn-seers. The djinn-seer was looking out into the sky; Sybil turned her gaze up, and Nadine smiled over them from the window of her tower, and the curtain fell.

I won't tell Magda all the details of the story, though. I'll tell her about when the second-act stage was lit up in the darkness, and how I hardly have words to describe it.

"Actually," Charlie says in a pensive way that draws all our attentions, touching the bridge of his wire-frame glasses, "my first memory is exactly that, Sybil. It's more of a first-feeling, of being small and held in a huge dark atmosphere, safe but next to fear or danger. Years later, I learned what the memory was. I don't know if it was only once, or many times, but I was a baby, despite whatever science about memory formation says. I grew up in a seaside Part. My dad would go down to the beach at night and swim. My mom and my brother and I went with him. My dad ran into the loud, black ocean. My older brother cried and screamed, thinking he was gone forever. I was in my mom's arms. I didn't cry. I think I was feeling wonder. Then my dad came running back up the beach. If I concentrate really hard, and then let go, I can see the sea and the stars and feel my brother screaming and myself being held. I think my mom took my brother's hand."

We're all quiet for a bit, and then Charlie adds, "Has anyone else here seen the ocean?"

"Desert babies," Sybil says, pointing to herself and me. No one else says anything, signaling the answer's no. We're all looking into the fire.

"Well," Charlie says, "does anyone have a first memory?"

"I do," Magda says.

We all look at her, even Jolie.

Magda says, "It's of me running after my sister in a field. It's sunny, and we're happy."

"I have one," Yusuf says. "I'm standing on a rock, holding my arms out, and a gust of wind blows, and it catches my jacket, and I start to fly away, I swear, but my dad catches me."

That makes Jolie say, "I don't believe you."

Yusuf looks at her. She looks up from her leaf, and they stare at each other for a moment, and then Jolie, eyes back down on her leaf, says, "At one of those xenodochia, my sister gave me half her rations, and I ate them, plus mine, and then I asked her for more, but there wasn't any more, so I started crying and hitting her, and she wrestled me until we fell asleep. I woke up in the morning with her still holding me, and there was a meat plant smoking in the distance—the sky was yellow, and everyone was wearing masks."

"Mine's of a view of my old Part," I say. "My dad put me in a harness on his back and hiked me up a mountain to this cliff where people jump off, but I didn't know that then. To me, it was just a view. But half of the image in my memory is eclipsed by his face, because I was on his back, and he was looking halfway over his shoulder at me."

Sybil puts an arm around me, but we don't move our spots on the bench. She says, "Mine is of my mom. She was an apiarist. She put a bee in a cup against my arm and then shook the cup so the bee would sting me, to see if I was allergic. I wasn't. Then she gave me some honey." Her voice breaks on the O. She clears her throat. "What's funny," she says, "is that I didn't remember that that was my first memory until a few months ago."

I nod, understanding. Of course, what's implied is that the

people in all our first memories are now out of our lives. Sybil clears her throat again, like there's something stuck in it. Recalling a memory of my own, and thinking it would be nice to share with Sybil, I say, "Polly gave me honey once too."

Sybil's eyebrows get angry, but her eyes stay big and round, still looking into the fire. With the heavy black makeup around her eyes, and the light so dim, it's hard to tell what she's feeling. I worry I've said something wrong, but still I scoot closer to her and put both my arms around her. She reaches up and holds my wrist.

Within my first couple days here, I'd told Sybil all about AB, my perforation, my time in the Safe Haven, Dylan, Cole, Malakai, and Sasha, and she was teary-eyed but talkative, gasping at all the dramatic turns. She asked me questions about Canland, vaguely at first, so I gave her vague answers about the oak tree, the heat-wave, and the Hovels. I included the detail about Gale, Conrad, and Valerie. After a few days, she broached the subject she'd been afraid to—she said she'd put in a request to the Seers for an update on Tobias, but after a year, they still hadn't told her anything. I told her he still spends a lot of time at my house with Helena—but then I remembered the conversation they had before Helena and I left for Hugo's house, so I revised what I said. "Actually, your dad hasn't been around in a while. He vowed to act against Suicidalism. He's going to try to make Canland better." It took a few minutes for Sybil to be convinced of this, but as I recalled more details, she believed it, sighed, and asked, "Anyone we know?"

When I told her about Roshana, Sybil's face went blank and then she covered her eyes and cried and cried. I don't remember her crying in Canland. I suppose it's good she cries now.

She sniffles and lets go of my wrist. I let my hands fall into my lap. The fire's low, but the smoke is rising steadily through the chimney of the laavu. Far away, one of Ava's dogs barks.

Besides Rêve, Makenna's the only one who hasn't shared a memory, and I doubt she will. She's pretty private.

Just a couple days ago, I was in Yusuf's house, listening to music, and Yusuf was playing his violin along to the song bursting with guitars and drums, and even though it was unlike anything I'd ever heard, I actually thought I recognized the song as the same one the band in the Hovels played. It happened to be a song called "Mother." I thought about going to get the keyboard in my A-frame, to play along too, but decided against it, opting just to listen. Then Ava came in, exchanged no words with Yusuf, just traded CDs with him—she was wearing headphones around her neck—and left. Yusuf put the new CD in the player. The song was a soft piano and a voice so rich it seemed to belong to neither man nor woman, as if from a chamber I'll never glimpse. The voice sang of a hope to be cared for when they die. Trying to be funny, Yusuf muttered, "Again with Ava's sad shit . . ." But I didn't mind that it was a sad song. The voice held me, and I closed my eyes. First I thought of AB, and how I was sorry that I hadn't spent more time with them. I blamed Helena for that. But then, as if against my will, memories appeared of the many times Helena helped me, or tried to help me, like the nighttime checks, and the small corrections, like not talking while chewing, or her strategies for conversation, and all the conditioning, and for a moment I felt sorry. I'd known all along that Helena was a person capable of feeling torment, and that I was not—this had emerged as the central frustration of hers in our relationship, that I could never understand what she was going through. Still, every time I'd hurt her, it was unintentional. That is, until the night we got home from Hugo's house, when our furniture had all been rearranged. As I was listening to that song, I remembered her face when I'd said the words, *You're a bad person.* Her face showed a different kind of hurt then. She'd pulled the candlestick close to her chest, and her face seemed to lose all the control it always had, as if she'd been afraid and surprised at her own hurt, like a child. I realized, listening to that song, that I was capable of intentionally hurting Helena's feelings, and that I'd never get to apologize.

So then I started telling Yusuf about Helena, and how she would condition me, and how I once held a knife over her, and how I escaped from her, and how it's funny because, in so many ways, she was right. I even told him my testicular torsion and double orchiectomy were my fault because I'd gone biking and running like I was always told not to. That might be the only major detail Sybil doesn't know; I'm not sure why I haven't told her. Yusuf listened intently, not interjecting, which was kind of him. But then, after I'd said the thing about my balls, his eyes flitted past my shoulder. I turned around and saw, lying on her side, propped up on her elbow, like a silent empty chair in the corner, Makenna. She told Yusuf to leave the A-frame. Yusuf said, "But it's my house." Makenna shot him a look, and Yusuf left, so it was just the two of us in there.

She said to me, "Only Charlie knows this, but I want you to know that in terms of familial abuse, you're not alone." She told me in vague terms things her stepbrother had done to her. Her voice was flat and her eyes were blank and open wide as she spoke. The story wasn't very long. When she finished, I got up to hug her, but she flinched and quickly waved her hand in front of herself, and said, "No, thank you." "Sorry," I said. "Don't be," she replied, "you're just being kind. Shame lives right in the gut, it's an impulse." "Perhaps that's why I can't conjure it," I said. Then we chatted for a while as the CD kept playing. She asked me if I liked it here, and I said I loved it. She smiled and said, "You should see it when it snows."

The air smells smokey and like the sweetness of nature on the breeze that makes the fire flap. Magda winces as she tries to shift to get comfortable, but she doesn't move much, so as not to disturb Rêve. Jolie, meanwhile, is doing what she's been doing this whole time.

"I'm bored," Charlie says. "I'm gonna go read."

"Bed?" Makenna says to him.

I believe Charlie and Makenna are platonic, but I'm not entirely certain on the specifics of their friendship. They do everything together, except for when Makenna listens to music with us, and Charlie's off reading novels. They share one of the big A-frames with several other teens and twenties.

Sybil turns her head slightly toward them, and then right away back to the fire. "Boredom here is still better than boredom somewhere else," she says.

"That's true," I say, mostly just for the sake of supporting Sybil.

"Boredom's boredom," Charlie says. "It erases the setting."

"In our old Part," I say, "people got so bored that they broke into other people's homes and rearranged the furniture. They didn't steal anything, they just moved stuff around."

Yusuf looks at me from across the fire. He's heard this—and the rest of the story—before. Sometimes he and I and some of the other musicians here will play together in the studio with the good keyboard and the microphones. When I get good enough, I'll play a concert with them. I smile at him. He nods once, then glances at Jolie, and says, "Have you made any progress?"

Jolie slowly brings her hands up. The very tip of her nail is slipped between the layers of the leaf! We all start clapping. Jolie carefully brings the leaf back down into her lap.

Out of the darkness, Wes calls out, "Hi, everyone." His hand is in Kamal's as they're walking along. They won't sit with us—they don't like to spend idle time around the young people because we remind them of their son (they were just a day's hike away from a xenodochium), but they like to lead us all on expeditions down along the riverbanks and through the woods. They don't mind teaching us— they just don't like sitting around, talking, doing nothing.

"Who's coming tomorrow?" Kamal says. "Show of hands."

Everyone but Magda, Rêve, and Jolie raise their hands. I know, though, that Sybil's flakey regarding expeditions; Yusuf's on patrol tomorrow, so his raised hand is wrong; and Jolie will be there, since she's not scheduled for mountain patrol, and she always comes on expeditions when she's free.

"You were all beautiful tonight," Wes says, humorously, but of course specifically meaning Sybil, Makenna, and Yusuf. Then the two of them pass out of sight.

There's only so much time. I don't know why I have that thought. It's a sudden, untethered thought, but as I watch it float away, I find in its place an image of Dylan sitting beneath the stars, looking for satellites, thinking of me and knowing that I'm looking at the same sky. Past the ceiling of the laavu I watch the stars pulse, and for a moment, I wish I was back in Canland.

Sybil squeezes my hand, as if she knows. I smile at her, my lips together.

Charlie groans and stands up. Makenna stands then too, and waves to everyone. "See you guys tomorrow," she says. Charlie steps out of the laavu, and Makenna grabs his hand behind him, and they walk off together.

Magda looks at me with one of her eyebrows up. I shake my head and close my eyes, in good nature. It makes her laugh.

Sybil lets go of my hand and wipes some caked makeup off her cheeks.

"See, everyone?" Jolie holds the leaf up to the firelight, showing us all the exposed inside, strings of sticky moisture clinging to the separated layers, like a tiny glossy harp. "It is possible." Then she leans forward over her crossed legs and drops the leaf into the fire.

"No!" shouts Yusuf.

"You all saw it," Jolie says. She stretches her arms up high, and without using her hands, she straightens up on her crossed legs. "Goodbye, everyone." Standing, she spins around, and her legs uncross.

As she's walking away, one of Ava's dogs comes loping toward us across the grass. Jolie lets her hand slide over its head, and then the dog circles back to Ava and Beta. (I can only tell Alpha and Beta apart when they're side by side because of their size difference, otherwise, they're identical. It occurs to me that, one day, there will be zero dogs here, because both of the dogs are male.) Jolie disappears into the night.

"Ava," Yusuf says, "the Mazra'a turns restlessly tonight, in awe of your creation."

"Oh, stop," Ava says, coming into the light. Her eyes first go to the fire, as I've noticed is a habit of hers, to make sure it's safely low. "It was better than I imagined, which just shows how little I had to do with it."

Magda smiles and hums like she finds this particularly funny for some reason. Then Yusuf laughs loudly. Sybil moves the blanket off her lap and scoots a few inches away from me.

"What do you mean?" I ask Ava.

Ava comes a bit closer to the fire, still standing behind and to the side of Yusuf. Her headscarf's red tonight. She's not wearing her big gun on her back, but she's probably armed with something beneath her loose cream-colored sweater—always, just in case.

Aside from the time I went into her A-frame to return her canteen, she and I haven't spoken very much at all. I help out in the vegetable patches, and I record things for posterity, not just my own thoughts in my journal, but also species I see, weather patterns, ways in which we at the Mazra'a subvert WORLD. I've also started drawing a bit, tracing the silhouettes of the hills. I often find myself in the mindset that everything I do has to be a contribution, but then I see so many of the other people here in the Mazra'a spending moments not contributing, and I go to practice piano, or walk down to sit with my feet in the river, or pick flowers in the meadow.

"Oh," Ava says, "just that our talent elevated it even more than I already knew they would." She smiles widely at Sybil.

"Our fearless leader," Sybil says.

Ava steps further into the light, so that her face actually becomes darker, because of the lowness of the fire.

Yusuf's looking up at her from the ground. "Yes?" he says.

Ava's eyes flit to his bowtie. "What?" she says.

"Your face," Yusuf says. "What do you mean, what?" Then he laughs, but it's a different kind of laugh. "What's going on?"

There's something I'm missing. Ava tilts her head sideways so she's looking down at Yusuf in a sloping sort of way, then she moves her eyes to the fire again.

Rêve's no longer moving her lip back and forth along her teeth. The skin around her lips, though, is all pink and chapped. Magda has ointment in her nightstand for that. Alpha gets close to Rêve, sniffing, and Yusuf shoves him away by the snout. Alpha stops, his ears go up, and he bolts into the night. Beta follows.

Ava sighs. "I'm going to tell everyone tomorrow." She pauses. "But I guess I'll tell you now. Thanks, Yusuf."

Yusuf turns to face Sybil and me. "You're welcome."

It's funny, but I don't laugh because suddenly, it's serious.

Ava hushes him right away. "I was just with the Seers. There was a plane crash off the coast of Alaska. A WORLD plane was shot down by a Purist militia. Arturo Eagles was on it."

"What?" Yusuf says, his voice loud. He claps a hand over his mouth, his eyebrows high. "Oh my god. What does that mean? He has to have someone ready to take over."

"Well," Ava says, "we don't know yet who else was on the plane with him."

Ava doesn't look at me, but Sybil does—she swings her head all the way to face me straight on. I shake my head and look down into my lap. "Doesn't matter," I say.

"It's OK," Sybil whispers.

"I'm not going anywhere," I whisper too.

"Shot down," Yusuf says.

"We don't know what's going to happen," Ava says. "If the Rehabilitation Parts will be liberated. If satellites are going to be a free-for-all. If Parts will . . ." She trails off. "Seers are keeping an eye on it. And Tristan," she says, so I look at her, "as soon as they find out who was on the plane, we'll let you know."

"OK," I say. "Thank you." Though, if Michael's dead, what changes?

Yusuf bows his head. Ava rubs his shoulder. "Fuck," he says.

"No one's coming," Ava says. "We're safe."

"If rovers come—"

"They could've come at any time," Ava says. "We're safe. We're prepared."

Yusuf looks up to the sky and breathes deeply.

Magda, her chin resting on Rêve's head, has her mouth in a certain shape that's not a smile, but it has elements of a smile in it.

She glances at me. I look at her, then Rêve. I want to believe that, if anyone came to take Rêve, or touched a hair on her head, that I would actually kill them. I tell myself I would.

I spin the ring on my finger.

Tomorrow there's an expedition. I'll go on that, bring my notebook, see birds and spiders, maybe even a deer. I'll put leaves under paper and shade the paper with the side of my pencil. I'll go in the river.

"I don't mean to rush you guys," Ava says, "but is it all right if we put this out? It's getting late."

"I got it," Yusuf says, rising, running to fetch some water.

Sybil and I stand up at the same time. As Magda starts to get up, I bend to help her, but she says, "I'm good." I stay near anyway, just in case. Rêve clings to her like a baby, and doesn't make a sound. Magda gets to her feet and starts to walk ahead of us.

Sybil calls, "Wait, Magda." Then she hugs me sideways with one arm. "Love you."

"Love you too," I say.

Sybil grabs a flashlight off the back of the laavu bench and runs ahead to light the path for Magda.

Yusuf pours a bucket over the embers. The fire dies, and smolders in a hiss, a thick but narrow column of smoke. Ava takes out a flashlight of her own, and whistles, and her dogs come running.

We're quiet for the walk back to our houses. I remember the wolf with the chip in its head, and I think that, if it's dead, then Michael should be dead too. I think of all the little creatures who would've died when he burned up Ava's farm. I think of the DOTEC, I think of the oak. I think of AB, Sasha, and Malakai. I think of Helena, and even miss her—miss her all the time. I think of Dylan, who's waiting for decades to pass in a single second, and I hope for a moment that Michael was on that plane.

As we come to my house—a flashlight on inside, Magda's shadow moving in the covered window—I say, "Ava, can you wait a second? I have something for you."

"Sure," she says, stopping.

Yusuf stops too. He's looking up at the stars, still shaking his head—imagining having to fight, I would guess.

I go inside. Rêve seems wide awake now, using her finger to glide a triangle of cloth in figure-eights on a block of treated wood, which is soothing for her. Magda's making tea.

I reach under my bed. I've read Helm's book a dozen times now, and the thing about it that always makes me want to reread it is how I could swear that he's hidden something of himself in it, and if I just read it again, a little closer, I'll be able to see it. Similar to how Sybil went through an experience tonight onstage; how she felt real feelings. But I read Helm's sentences again and again, hoping to find a new detail of him, only to find that there's nothing more than what there is.

Ava smiles at me when I come back out holding the book. Alpha and Beta come trotting up the path again.

"Here," I say, and proffer Ava the book. "This was written by my teacher. He was a good friend too. It's OK if you don't like it, but you might, if you want to read it."

She takes it. "Thank you, Tristan," she says, and looks at the inside cover, where, on this copy, mine is the only name. "I can't wait to read it."

She holds the book up and gives me a short smile, then turns and walks off toward her A-frame—a quarter mile away, at the end of the road, on the near side of the bend leading to the flowery meadow. Yusuf lingers for a second, and brings his face back down, leaving his stargazing feeling behind. He extends his fist to me. I punch it, and he shakes it out like I've hurt him. Then he winks at me and walks off.

I put a hand to my chest. For a moment I feel breathless.

I look up at the purple-silver sky, and think of how many more times I'll get to look at it, and all the people I know who are looking at it too, and how even after one of those stars dies, it'll shine for thousands of years, and no one on Earth will ever live long enough to know it's gone.

Then I go back inside.

ACKNOWLEDGMENTS

For her patience as I figured out what this novel was going to be, my first editor, Annie Adams. For asking questions I didn't know how to answer, and then giving me the answers, Aja Pollock. For knowing when an em-dash is funnier than a semicolon, Liz Gilbeau. For her guidance in publishing this book, Bethany Brown. For getting the word out, Kellie Rendina and Andrea Kiliany Thatcher at Smith Publicity. For their encouragement, ideas, and occasional praise: Adam Ross, Grant Skidmore, Seth Garben, Derek DeVault, and Ben Steinberg.

Many thanks to the neuroscience, entomology, virology, and agriculture team: Alex Skidmore, Christopher Finch, Lea Pollack, Michael Culshaw-Maurer, and Liberty Galvin. I take full responsibility for any scientific inaccuracies.

For all their love and support, Mom and Tom, Dad and Amanda. For always being there as I've become who I am, David and Jake.

And, last because most, thank you Ashley, for the stability I always thought was incompatible with creativity—but which now I know is necessary. Your influence is everywhere.

www.ingramcontent.com/pod-product-compliance
Lightning Source LLC
Chambersburg PA
CBHW031115160726
47991CB00004B/1395